Sophie Kinsella is a writer and former financial journalist. She is the author of the number one bestseller *Can You Keep a Secret?* as well as the bestselling *The Secret Dreamworld of a Shopaholic*, *Shopaholic Abroad* and *Shopaholic Ties the Knot*, all of which are also published by Black Swan. She has two sisters with whom she loves to go shopping.

D0205038

www.**booksattransworld**.co.uk

SHOPAHOLIC
& SISTER

Sophie Kinsella

BLACK SWAN

SHOPAHOLIC & SISTER
A BLACK SWAN BOOK: 0 552 77111 2

Originally published in Great Britain by Bantam Press,
a division of Transworld Publishers

PRINTING HISTORY
Bantam Press edition published 2004
Black Swan edition published 2004

1 3 5 7 9 10 8 6 4 2

Set in 11/12pt Melior by
Falcon Oast Graphic Art Ltd.

Black Swan Books are published by Transworld Publishers,
61–63 Uxbridge Road, London W5 5SA,
a division of The Random House Group Ltd,
in Australia by Random House Australia (Pty) Ltd,
20 Alfred Street, Milsons Point, Sydney, NSW 2061, Australia,
in New Zealand by Random House New Zealand Ltd,
18 Poland Road, Glenfield, Auckland 10, New Zealand
and in South Africa by Random House (Pty) Ltd,
Endulini, 5a Jubilee Road, Parktown 2193, South Africa.

Printed and bound in Great Britain by
Cox & Wyman Ltd, Reading, Berkshire.

Papers used by Transworld Publishers are natural, recyclable
products made from wood grown in sustainable forests. The
manufacturing processes conform to the environmental
regulations of the country of origin.

To Gemma and Abigail,
in celebration of being sisters.

ACKNOWLEDGEMENTS

Thank you to the endlessly supportive Linda Evans, Patrick Plonkington-Smythe, Larry Finlay, Laura Sherlock and all the wonderful people at Transworld. To the fabulous Araminta Whitley and Nicki Kennedy, Celia Hayley, Lucinda Cook and Sam Edenborough. A special thank-you to Joy Terekiev and Chiara Scaglioni for a wonderfully warm welcome in Milan.

Thanks as always to the members of the Board. To Henry, for everything. To Freddy and Hugo for suggesting I write about pirates instead (maybe next time).

And a big thank-you to my parents for taking me in off the streets so I could finish writing this . . .

DICTIONARY
OF INTERNATIONAL TRIBAL DIALECTS

ADDENDUM

(The following terms were omitted from the main dictionary.)

NAMI-NAMI TRIBE OF NEW GUINEA p. 67

fraa ('frar'): elder tribesman; patriarch

mopi ('mop-i'): a small ladle for serving rice or meal.

shup ('shop'): to exchange goods for money or beads. A concept unknown by the tribe until a visit in 2002 by British visitor Rebecca Brandon (formerly Bloomwood).

ROYAL CAIRO INSTITUTE OF ARCHAEOLOGY
31 EL CHERIFEEN STREET, CAIRO

Mrs Rebecca Brandon
c/o Nile Hilton Hotel
Tahrir Square
Cairo

15 January 2003

Dear Mrs Brandon

I am glad you are enjoying your honeymoon in Egypt. I was
pleased to hear that you feel a bond with the Egyptian people
and agree it is quite possible that you have Egyptian blood in
you.

However, further to your enquiry, no part of Tutenkhamen's tomb
is for sale. Not even 'a really small gold coin that no one
would miss'.

Yours sincerely

Khaled Samir
(Director)

BREITLING SHIPPING COMPANY
TOWER HOUSE
CANARY WHARF
LONDON E14 5HG

Fax for: Mrs Rebecca Brandon
              c/o Four Seasons Hotel
              Sydney
              Australia

From: Denise O'Connor
              Customer Service Coordinator

6 February 2003

Dear Mrs Brandon

We are sorry to inform you that your Bondi Beach 'carved sand mermaid' has disintegrated during shipping.

We would remind you that we made no guarantees as to its safety and advised you against the shipping process.

Yours sincerely

Denise O'Connor
Customer Service Coordinator

ALASKAN TRAILS AND ADVENTURES, INC
PO BOX 80034
CHUGIAK
ALASKA

Fax for: Mrs Rebecca Brandon
c/o White Bear Lodge
Chugiak

From: Dave Crockerdale
Alaskan Trails and Adventures

16 February 2003

Dear Mrs Brandon

Thank your for your enquiry.

We would strongly advise you against attempting to ship to Britain six husky dogs and a sleigh.

I agree that husky dogs are wonderful animals and am interested in your idea that they could be the answer to pollution in cities. However, I think it unlikely the authorities would allow them on the streets of London, even if you did 'customize the sleigh with wheels and add a numberplate'.

I hope you are still enjoying your honeymoon.

Kind regards

Dave Crockerdale
Trail Manager

ONE

OK. I can do this. No problem.

It's simply a matter of letting my higher self take over, achieving enlightenment, and becoming a radiant being of white light.

Easy-peasy.

Surreptitiously I adjust myself on my yoga mat so I'm facing the sun directly, and push down the spaghetti straps of my top. I don't see why you can't reach ultimate bliss consciousness and get an even tan at the same time.

I'm sitting on a hillside in the middle of Sri Lanka at the Blue Hills Resort and Spiritual Retreat, and the view is spectacular. Hills and tea plantations stretch ahead, then merge into a deep-blue sky. I can see the bright colours of tea-pickers in the fields, and, if I swivel my head a little, glimpse a distant elephant padding slowly along between the bushes.

And when I swivel my head even further, I can see Luke. My husband. He's the one on the blue yoga mat, in the cut-off linen trousers and tatty old top, sitting cross-legged with his eyes closed.

I know. It's just unbelievable. After ten months of honeymoon, Luke has turned into a totally different person from the man I married. The old corporate Luke has vanished. The suits have disappeared. He's tanned and lean, his hair is long and sun-bleached and he's still got a few of the little plaits he had put in on Bondi Beach. Round his wrist is a friendship bracelet he bought in the Masai Mara, and in his ear is a tiny silver hoop.

Luke Brandon with an earring! Luke Brandon sitting cross-legged!

As though he can feel my gaze, he opens his eyes and smiles, and I beam back happily. Ten months married. And not a single row.

Well. You know. Only the odd little one.

'*Siddhasana*,' says our yoga teacher, Chandra, and obediently I place my right foot on my left thigh. 'Clear your minds of all extraneous thought.'

OK. Clear my mind. Concentrate.

I don't want to boast, but I find clearing my mind pretty easy. I don't quite get why anyone would find it difficult! I mean, not-thinking has to be a lot easier than thinking, doesn't it?

In fact, the truth is I'm a bit of a natural at yoga. We've only been on this retreat for five days but already I can do the lotus and everything! I was even thinking I might set up as a yoga teacher when we go back home.

Maybe I could set up in partnership with Trudie Styler. God, yes! And we could launch a range of yoga-wear too, all soft greys and whites, with a little logo . . .

'Focus on your breathing,' Chandra is saying.

Oh, right, yes. Breathing.

Breathe in . . . breathe out. Breathe in . . . breathe out. Breathe . . .

God, my nails look fab. I had them done at the spa – little pink butterflies on a white background. And the antennae are little sparkly diamonds. They are so sweet. Except one seems to have fallen off. I must get that fixed—

'Becky.' Chandra's voice makes me jump. He's standing right in front of me, gazing at me with this look he has. Kind of gentle and all-knowing, like he can see right inside your mind.

'You do very well, Becky,' he says. 'You have a beautiful spirit.'

I feel a sparkle of delight all over. I, Rebecca Brandon, née Bloomwood, have a beautiful spirit! I knew it!

'You have an unworldly soul,' he adds in his soft voice, and I stare back, totally mesmerized.

'Material possessions aren't important to me,' I say breathlessly. 'All that matters to me is yoga.'

'You have found your path.' Chandra smiles.

There's an odd kind of snorting sound from Luke's direction, and I look round to see him glancing over at us in amusement.

I *knew* Luke wasn't taking this seriously.

'This is a private conversation between me and my guru, thank you very much,' I say crossly.

Although actually I shouldn't be surprised. We were warned about this on the first day of the yoga course. Apparently when one partner finds higher spiritual enlightenment, the other partner can react with scepticism and even jealousy.

'Soon you will be walking on the hot coals.' Chandra gestures with a smile to the nearby pit of smouldering, ashy coals, and a nervous laugh goes round the group. This evening Chandra and some of his top yoga students are going to demonstrate walking on the coals for the rest of us. This is what we're all supposed to be aiming for. Apparently you attain a state of bliss so great you can't actually feel the coals burning your feet. You're totally pain-free!

What I'm secretly hoping is, it'll work when I wear six-inch stilettos, too.

Chandra adjusts my arms and moves on, and I close

my eyes, letting the sun warm my face. Sitting here on this hillside in the middle of nowhere, I feel so pure and calm. It's not just Luke who's changed over the last ten months. I have, too. I've grown up. My priorities have altered. In fact, I'm a different person. I mean, look at me now, doing yoga at a spiritual retreat. My old friends probably wouldn't even recognize me!

At Chandra's instruction, we all move into the *Vajrasana* pose. From where I am, I can just see an old Sri Lankan man carrying two old carpet bags approaching Chandra. They have a brief conversation, during which Chandra keeps shaking his head, then the old man trudges away again over the scrubby hillside. When he's out of earshot, Chandra turns to face the group, rolling his eyes.

'This man is a merchant. He asks if any of you are interested in gems. Necklaces, cheap bracelets. I tell him your minds are on higher things.'

A few people near me shake their heads as though in disbelief. One woman, with long red hair, looks affronted.

'Couldn't he see we were in the middle of meditation?' she says.

'He has no understanding of your spiritual devotion.' Chandra looks seriously around the group. 'It will be the same with many others in the world. They will not understand that meditation is food for your soul. You have no need for . . . sapphire bracelet!'

A few people nod in appreciation.

'Aquamarine pendant with platinum chain,' Chandra continues dismissively. 'How does this compare to the radiance of inner enlightenment?'

Aquamarine?

Wow. I wonder how much —

I mean, not that I'm interested. Obviously not. It's just that I happened to be looking at aquamarines in a

16

shop window the other day. Just out of academic interest.

My eye drifts towards the retreating figure of the old man.

'Three-carat setting, five-carat setting, he keep saying. All half-price.' Chandra shakes his head. 'I tell him, these people are not interested.'

Half-price? Five-carat aquamarines at half-price?

Stop it. Stop it. Chandra's right. Of course I'm not interested in stupid aquamarines. I'm absorbed in spiritual enlightenment.

Anyway, the old man's nearly gone now. He's just a tiny figure on top of the hill. In a minute he'll have disappeared.

'And now,' Chandra smiles, 'the *Halasana* pose. Becky, will you demonstrate?'

'Absolutely.' I smile back at Chandra and prepare to get into position on my mat.

But something's wrong. I don't feel contentment. I don't feel tranquillity. The oddest feeling is welling up inside me, driving everything else out. It's getting stronger and stronger . . .

And suddenly I can't contain it any more. Before I know what's happening, I'm running in my bare feet as fast as I can up the hill towards the tiny figure. My lungs are burning, my feet are smarting and the sun's beating down on my bare head, but I don't stop until I've reached the crest of the hill. I come to a halt and look around, panting.

I don't believe it. He's gone. Where did he vanish to?

I stand for a few moments, regaining my breath, peering in all directions. But I can't see him anywhere.

At last, feeling a little dejected, I turn and make my way back down the hillside to the group. As I get near I realize they're all shouting and waving at me. Oh God. Am I in trouble?

17

'You did it!' the red-haired woman's yelling. 'You did it!'

'Did what?'

'You ran over the hot coals! You did it, Becky!'

What?

I look down at my feet . . . and I don't believe it. They're covered in grey ash! In a daze, I look at the pit of coals – and there's a set of clear footprints running through it.

Oh my God. Oh my *God*! I ran over the coals! I ran over the burning hot smouldering coals! I did it!

'But . . . but I didn't even notice!' I say, bewildered. 'My feet aren't even burned!'

'How did you do it?' demands the red-haired woman. 'What was in your mind?'

'I can answer.' Chandra comes forward, smiling. 'Becky has achieved the highest form of karmic bliss. She was concentrating on one goal, one pure image, and this has driven her body to achieve a supernatural state.'

Everyone is goggling at me like I'm suddenly the Dalai Lama.

'It was nothing really,' I say with a modest smile. 'Just . . . you know. Spiritual enlightenment.'

'Can you describe the image?' says the red-haired woman in excitement.

'Was it white?' asks someone else.

'Not really white . . .' I say.

'Was it a kind of shiny blue-green?' comes Luke's voice from the back. I look up sharply. He's gazing back, totally straight-faced.

'I don't remember,' I say in dignified tones. 'The colour wasn't important.'

'Did it feel like . . .' Luke appears to think hard. 'Like the links of a chain were pulling you along?'

'That's a very good image, Luke,' chimes in Chandra, pleased.

'No,' I say shortly. 'It didn't. Actually, I think you probably have to have a higher appreciation of spiritual matters to understand.'

'I see.' Luke nods gravely.

'Luke, you must be very proud.' Chandra beams at Luke. 'Is this not the most extraordinary thing you have ever seen your wife do?'

There's a beat of silence. Luke looks from me to the smouldering coals, to the silent group and back to Chandra's beaming face.

'Chandra,' he says. 'Take it from me. This is nothing.'

After the class is finished, everyone heads to the terrace, where cool drinks will be waiting on a tray. But I stay meditating on my mat, to show how dedicated I am to higher things. I'm half-concentrating on the white light of my being, and half-imagining running over hot coals in front of Trudie and Sting while they applaud admiringly, when a shadow falls across my face.

'Greetings, O Spiritual One,' says Luke, and I open my eyes to see him standing in front of me, holding out a glass of juice.

'You're just jealous because you don't have a beautiful spirit,' I retort, and casually smooth back my hair so the red painted dot on my forehead shows.

'Insanely,' agrees Luke. 'Have a drink.'

He sits down beside me on the ground and hands me the glass. I take a sip of delicious, ice-cold passion-fruit juice and we both look out over the hills towards the distant haze.

'You know, I could really live in Sri Lanka,' I say with a sigh. 'It's perfect. The weather . . . the scenery . . . all the people are so friendly . . .'

'You said the same in India,' points out Luke. 'And Australia,' he adds as I open my mouth. 'And Amsterdam.'

God, Amsterdam. I'd completely forgotten we went there. That was after Paris. Or do I mean before?

Oh yes. It was where I ate all those weird cakes and nearly fell in the canal.

I take another sip of juice and let my mind range back over the last ten months. We've visited so many countries, it's kind of difficult to remember everything at once. It's almost like a blur of film, with sharp, bright images here and there. Snorkelling with all those blue fish in the Great Barrier Reef . . . the Pyramids in Egypt . . . the elephant safari in Tanzania . . . buying all that silk in Hong Kong . . . the gold souk in Morocco . . . finding that amazing Ralph Lauren outlet in Utah . . .

God, we've had some experiences. I give a happy sigh, and take another sip of juice.

'I forgot to tell you,' Luke produces a pile of envelopes, 'some post came from England.'

I sit up in excitement and start leafing through the envelopes.

'*Vogue!*' I exclaim as I get to my special subscriber edition in its shiny plastic cover. 'Ooh, look! They've got an Angel bag on the front cover!'

I wait for a reaction – but Luke looks blank. I feel a tiny flicker of frustration. How can he look blank? I read him out that whole piece about Angel bags last month, and showed him the pictures and everything.

I know this is our honeymoon. But just sometimes I wish Luke was a girl.

'You know!' I say. 'Angel bags! The most amazing, hip bags since . . . since . . .'

Oh, I'm not even going to bother explaining. Instead, I gaze lustfully at the photograph of the bag. It's made of soft creamy tan calfskin, with a beautiful winged angel hand-painted on the front, and the name 'Gabriel' underneath in diamante. There are six different angels, and all the celebrities have been fighting over them. Harrods is permanently sold out. 'Holy phenomenon,' says the strapline beside the picture.

I'm so engrossed, I barely hear Luke's voice as he holds out another envelope.

'Ooze,' he seems to be saying.

'Sorry?' I look up in a daze.

'I said here's another letter,' he says patiently. 'From Suze.'

'Suze?' I drop *Vogue* and grab it out of his hand. Suze is my best friend in the world. I have *so* missed her.

The envelope is all thick and creamy white and has a crest on the back with a Latin motto. I always forget how totally grand Suze is. When she sent us a Christmas card, it was a picture of her husband Tarquin's castle in Scotland, with 'From the Cleath-Stuart Estate' printed inside. (Except you could hardly read it because her one-year-old, Ernie, had covered it with red and blue fingerpaints.)

I tear it open and a stiff card falls out.

'It's an invitation!' I exclaim. 'To the christening of the twins.'

I gaze at the formal, swirly writing, feeling a slight pang. Wilfrid and Clementine Cleath-Stuart. Suze has had two more babies and I haven't even seen them. They'll be about two months old by now. I wonder what they look like. I wonder how Suze is doing. So much has been going on without us.

I turn over the card, where Suze has written a scrawled message.

'I know you won't be able to come, but thought you'd like it anyway . . . hope you're still having a wonderful time! All our love, Suze xxx. PS Ernie loves his Chinese outfit, thank you so much!!'

'It's in two weeks,' I say, showing Luke the card. 'Shame, really. We won't be able to go.'

'No,' agrees Luke. 'We won't.'

21

There's a short silence. Then Luke meets my eye. 'I mean . . . you're not ready to go back yet, are you?' he says casually.

'No!' I say at once. 'Of course not!'

We've only been travelling for ten months, and we planned to be away for at least a year. Plus we've got the spirit of the road in our feet now. We've become wandering nomads who gather no moss. Maybe we'll never be able to go back to normal life, like sailors who can't go and live on the land.

I put the invitation back in its envelope and take a sip of my drink. I wonder how Mum and Dad are. I haven't heard much from them recently, either. I wonder how Dad did in the golf tournament.

And little Ernie will be walking by now. I'm his godmother and I've never even seen him walk.

Anyway. Never mind. I'm having amazing world experiences instead.

'We need to decide where to go next,' says Luke, leaning back on his elbows. 'After we finish the yoga course. We were talking about Malaysia.'

'Yes,' I say, after a pause. It must be the heat or something, but I can't actually get up much enthusiasm for Malaysia.

'Or back to Indonesia? Up to the northern bits?'

'Mmm,' I say noncommittally. 'Oh look, a monkey.'

I cannot believe I've got so blasé about the sight of monkeys. The first time I saw those baboons in Kenya I was so excited I took about six rolls of film. Now it's just, 'Oh look, a monkey.'

'Or Nepal . . . or back to Thailand . . .'

'Or we could go back,' I hear myself saying out of nowhere.

There's silence.

How weird. I didn't intend to say that. I mean, *obviously* we're not going to go back yet. It hasn't even been a year!

Luke sits up straight and looks at me.

'Back, back?'

'No!' I say with a little laugh. 'I'm just joking!' I hesitate. 'Although . . .'

There's a still silence between us.

'Maybe . . . we don't *have* to travel for a year,' I say tentatively. 'If we don't want to.'

Luke passes a hand through his hair, and the little beads on his plaits all click together.

'Are we ready to go back?'

'I don't know.' I feel a little thrill of trepidation. 'Are we?'

I can hardly believe we're even talking about going home. I mean, look at us! My hair's all dry and bleached, I've got henna on my feet and I haven't worn a proper pair of shoes for months.

An image comes to my mind of myself walking down a London street in a coat and boots. Shiny high-heeled boots by L K Bennett. And a matching handbag.

Suddenly I feel a wave of longing so strong I almost want to cry.

'I think I've had enough of the world.' I look at Luke. 'I'm ready for real life.'

'Me too.' Luke takes my hand and weaves his fingers between mine. 'I've been ready for a while, actually.'

'You never said!' I stare at him.

'I didn't want to break up the party. But I'm certainly ready.'

'You would have kept travelling . . . just for me?' I say, touched.

'Well, it's not exactly hardship.' Luke looks at me wryly. 'We're hardly roughing it, are we?'

I feel a slight flush come to my cheeks. When we set off on this trip, I told Luke I was determined we were going to be real travellers, like in *The Beach*, and only sleep in little huts.

That was before I'd spent a night in a little hut.

'So when we say "back" –' Luke pauses, 'we are talking London?'

He looks at me questioningly.

Oh God. Finally, it's decision time.

We've been talking for ten months about where we should live after the honeymoon. Before we got married, Luke and I were living in New York. And I loved it. But I kind of missed home, too. And now Luke's UK business is expanding into Europe, and that's where all the excitement is. So he'd like to go back to London, at least for a while.

Which is fine . . . except I won't have a job. My old job was as a personal shopper at Barneys, in New York. And I adored it.

But never mind. I'm bound to find a new job. An even better one!

'London,' I say decisively, and look up. 'So . . . can we be back in time for the christening?'

'If you like.' Luke smiles, and I feel a sudden leap of exhilaration. We're going to the christening! I'm going to see Suze again! And my mum and dad! After nearly a year! They'll all be so excited to see us. We'll have so many stories to tell them!

I have a sudden vision of myself presiding over candlelit supper parties with all my friends gathered round, listening avidly to tales of faraway lands and exotic adventures. I'll be just like Marco Polo or someone! Then I'll open my trunk to reveal rare and precious treasures . . . everyone will gasp in admiration . . .

'We'd better let them know,' says Luke, getting up.

'No, wait,' I say, grabbing his trousers. 'I've had an idea. Let's surprise them! Let's surprise everybody!'

'*Surprise* everybody?' Luke looks doubtful. 'Becky, are you sure that's a good idea?'

'It's a brilliant idea! Everyone loves a surprise!'

'But—'

'Everyone loves a surprise,' I repeat confidently. 'Trust me.'

We walk back through the gardens to the main hotel — and I do feel a slight twinge at the thought of leaving. It's so beautiful here. All teak bungalows and amazing birds everywhere, and if you follow the stream through the grounds, there's a real waterfall! We pass the wood-carving centre, where you can watch craftsmen at work, and I pause for a moment, inhaling the delicious scent of wood.

'Mrs Brandon!' The head craftsman, Vijay, has appeared at the entrance.

Damn. I didn't know he'd be around.

'Sorry, Vijay!' I say quickly. 'I'm in a bit of a hurry. I'll see you later . . . come on, Luke!'

'No problem!' Vijay beams and wipes his hands on his apron. 'I just wanted to tell you that your table is ready.'

Shit.

Slowly Luke turns to look at me.

'Table?' he says.

'Your dining table,' says Vijay in happy tones. 'And ten chairs. I show you! We display the work!' He snaps his fingers and barks some orders and suddenly, to my dismay, about eight men troop out, carrying a huge carved teak table on their shoulders.

Wow. It's a tad bigger than I remembered.

Luke looks absolutely stunned.

'Bring the chairs!' Vijay is bossing. 'Set it up properly!'

'Isn't it lovely?' I say in super-bright tones.

'You ordered a dining table and ten chairs . . . without telling me?' says Luke, goggling as the chairs start arriving.

OK. I don't have many options here.

'It's . . . my wedding present to you!' I say in sudden

inspiration. 'It's a surprise! Happy wedding, darling!' I plant a kiss on his cheek and smile hopefully up at him.

'Becky, you already gave me a wedding present,' says Luke, folding his arms. 'And our wedding was a fairly long time ago now.'

'I've been . . . saving it up!' I lower my voice so Vijay can't hear. 'And honestly, it isn't that expensive—'

'Becky, it's not the money. It's the space! This thing's a monstrosity!'

'It's not *that* big. And anyway,' I quickly add before he can reply, 'we need a good table! Every marriage needs a good table.' I spread my arms widely. 'After all, what is marriage about if not sitting down at the table at the end of the day and sharing all our problems? What is marriage if not sitting together at a solid wooden table and . . . and eating a bowl of hearty stew?'

'Hearty stew?' echoes Luke. 'Who's going to make hearty stew?'

'We can buy it at Waitrose,' I explain.

I come round the table and look up at him earnestly. 'Luke, think about it. We'll never again be in Sri Lanka with authentic wood-carvers right in front of us. This is a unique opportunity. And I've had it personalized!'

I point to the panel of wood running down the side of the table. There, beautifully carved in amongst the flowers, are the words 'Luke and Rebecca, Sri Lanka, 2003.'

Luke runs a hand over the table. He feels the weight of one of the chairs. I can see him relenting. Then suddenly he looks up with a slight frown.

'Becky, is there anything else you've bought that you haven't told me about?'

I feel a tiny lollop inside, which I disguise by pretending to examine one of the carved flowers.

'Of course not!' I say at last. 'Or . . . you know –

maybe just the odd little souvenir along the way. Just here and there.'

'Like what?'

'I can't remember!' I exclaim. 'It's been ten months, for goodness' sake!' I turn to the table again. 'Come on, Luke, you *must* love it. We can have fantastic dinner parties . . . and it'll be an heirloom! We can hand it down to our children . . .'

I break off a bit awkwardly. For a moment, I can't quite look at Luke.

A few months ago we had this huge big discussion, and decided that we'd like to try for a baby. But so far . . . nothing's happened.

I mean, not that it's a big deal or anything. It will happen. Of course it will.

'All right,' says Luke, his voice a little gentler. 'You've won me over.' He gives the table a pat, then looks at his watch. 'I'm going to email the office. Tell them about our change of plan.' He gives me a wry look. 'Presumably you weren't expecting me to burst open the door of the boardroom and yell, "Surprise, I'm back!"?'

'Of course not!' I retort, barely missing a beat.

That is actually kind of what I'd pictured. Except I'd be there too, with a bottle of champagne, and maybe some party poppers.

'I'm not quite that stupid,' I add witheringly.

'Good.' Luke grins at me. 'Why don't you order a drink and I'll be out in a moment?'

As I sit down at a table on the shady terrace, I'm just a tad preoccupied. I'm trying to remember all the things I've bought and had shipped home without telling Luke.

I mean, I'm not worried or anything. It can't be *that* much stuff. Can it?

Oh God. I close my eyes, trying to remember.

There were the wooden giraffes in Malawi. The ones Luke said were too big. Which is just ridiculous. They'll look amazing! Everyone will admire them!

And there was all that gorgeous batik art in Bali. Which I *did* intend to tell him about . . . but then kind of never got round to it.

And there were the twenty Chinese silk dressing gowns.

Which, OK – I know twenty sounds quite a lot. But they were such a bargain! Luke just didn't seem to understand my point that if we bought twenty now, they would last us a lifetime and be a real investment. For someone who works in financial PR, he can be a bit slow off the mark sometimes.

So I sneaked back to the shop and bought them anyway, and had them shipped home.

The thing is, shipping just makes everything so easy. You don't have to lug anything about – you just point and ship. 'I'd like that shipped, please. And that. And that.' And you give them your card and off it goes, and Luke never even sees it . . .

Maybe I should have kept a list.

Anyway, it's fine. I'm sure it's fine.

And I mean, we want a few souvenirs, don't we? What's the point of going round the world and coming back empty-handed? Exactly.

I see Chandra walking past the terrace, and give him a friendly wave.

'You did very well in class today, Becky!' he says, and comes over to the table. 'And now I would like to ask you something. In two weeks' time I am leading an advanced meditation retreat. The others are mainly monks and long-term yoga practitioners . . . but I feel you have the commitment to join us. Would you be interested?'

'I'd love to!' I pull a regretful face. 'But I can't. Luke and I are going home!'

'Home?' Chandra looks shocked. 'But . . . you are doing so well. You are not going to abandon the path of yoga?'

'Oh no,' I say reassuringly. 'Don't worry. I'll buy a video.'

As Chandra walks off, he looks a little shell-shocked. Which actually isn't surprising. He probably didn't even realize you could *get* yoga videos. He certainly didn't seem to have heard of Geri Halliwell.

A waiter appears and I order a mango and papaya cocktail, which in the menu is called Happy Juice. Well, that just about suits me. Here I am in the sun-shine, on my honeymoon, about to have a surprise reunion with all the people I love. Everything's perfect!

I look up to see Luke approaching the table, holding his Palm Pilot in his hand. Is it my imagination, or is he walking faster and looking more animated than he has for months?

'OK,' he says, 'I've spoken to the office.'

'Is everything all right?'

'It certainly is.' He seems full of a suppressed energy. 'It's going very well. In fact, I want to set up a couple of meetings for the end of this week.'

'That was quick!' I say in astonishment.

Blimey. I'd thought it would take about a week just to get ourselves organized.

'But I know how much you're getting out of this yoga retreat,' he adds. 'So what I propose is I go on ahead, and you join me later . . . and then we return to Britain together.'

'So where are your meetings?' I say, confused.

'Italy.'

The waiter appears with my Happy Juice, and Luke orders himself a beer.

'But I don't want to be separated from you!' I say, as the waiter retreats. 'This is our honeymoon!'

'We've had ten solid months together . . .' Luke points out gently.

'I know. But still . . .' I take a disconsolate sip of Happy Juice. 'Where are you going in Italy?'

'Nowhere exciting,' says Luke after a pause. 'Just a . . . northern Italian city. Very dull. I recommend you stay here. Enjoy the sunshine.'

'Well . . .' I look around, feeling torn. It *is* pretty nice here. 'Which city?'

There's silence.

'Milan,' says Luke reluctantly.

'Milan?' I nearly fall off my chair in excitement. 'You're going to Milan? I've never been to Milan! I'd love to go to Milan!'

'No,' says Luke. 'Really?'

'Yes! Definitely! I want to come!'

How could he think I don't want to go to Milan? I have *always* wanted to go to Milan!

'OK.' Luke shakes his head ruefully. 'I must be mad, but OK.'

Elated, I lean back in my chair and take a big slurp of Happy Juice. This honeymoon just gets better and better!

TWO

OK, I cannot believe Luke was planning to come to Milan without me. How could he come here without me? I was *made* for Milan.

No. Not Milan, *Milano*.

I haven't actually seen much of the city yet except a taxi and our hotel room – but for a world traveller like me, that doesn't actually matter. You can pick up the vibe of a place in an instant, like bushmen in the wild. And as soon as I looked round the hotel foyer at all those chic women in Prada and D&G, kissing each other whilst simultaneously downing espressos, lighting cigarettes and flinging their shiny hair about, I just kind of knew, with a kind of natural instinct: this is my kind of city.

I take a gulp of room-service cappuccino and glance across at my reflection in the wardrobe mirror. Honestly, I look Italian! All I need is some capri pants and dark eyeliner. And maybe a Vespa.

'Ciao,' I say casually, and flick my hair back. 'Si. Ciao.'

I could so be Italian. Except I might need to learn a few more words.

'Si,' I nod at myself. 'Si. Milano.'

Maybe I'll practise by reading the paper. I open the free copy of *Corriere della Sera* which arrived with our breakfast, and start perusing the lines of text. And I'm not doing too badly! The first story is all about the president washing his piano. At least . . . I'm pretty sure that's what *presidente* and *lavoro pieno* must mean.

'You know, Luke, I could really live in Italy,' I say as he comes out of the bathroom. 'I mean it's the perfect country. It has everything! Cappuccinos . . . yummy food . . . everyone's so elegant . . . you can get Gucci cheaper than at home . . .'

'And the art,' says Luke, deadpan.

God, he's annoying sometimes.

'Well, obviously the *art*,' I say, rolling my eyes. 'I mean, the art goes without saying.'

I flick over a page of *Corriere della Sera* and briskly skim the headlines. Then my brain suddenly clicks.

I put down the paper and stare at Luke again.

What's happened to him?

I'm looking at the Luke Brandon I used to know back when I was a financial journalist. He's completely clean-shaven, and dressed in an immaculate suit, with a pale-green shirt and darker-green tie. He's wearing proper shoes and proper socks. His earring has gone. His bracelet has gone. The only vestige of our travels is his hair, which is still in tiny plaits.

I can feel a bubble of dismay growing inside. I liked him the way he was, all laid-back and dishevelled.

'You've . . . smartened up a bit!' I say. 'Where's your bracelet?'

'In my suitcase.'

'But the woman in the Masai Mara said we must never take them off!' I say in shock. 'She said that special Masai prayer!'

'Becky . . .' Luke sighs. 'I can't go into a meeting with an old bit of rope round my wrist.'

Old bit of rope? That was a sacred bracelet, and he knows it.

'You've still got your plaits!' I retort. 'If you can have plaits, you can have a bracelet!'

'I'm not keeping my plaits!' Luke gives an incredulous laugh. 'I've got a haircut booked in . . .' he consults his watch, 'ten minutes.'

A haircut?

This is all too fast. I can't bear the idea of Luke's sunbleached hair being snipped off and falling to the floor. Our honeymoon hair, all gone.

'Luke, don't,' I say before I can stop myself. 'You can't.'

'What's wrong?' Luke turns and looks at me more closely. 'Becky, are you OK?'

No. I'm not OK. But I don't know why.

'You can't cut off your hair,' I say desperately. 'Then it will all be over!'

'Sweetheart . . . it *is* over.' Luke comes over and sits down beside me. He takes my hands and looks into my eyes. 'You know that, don't you? It's over. We're going home. We're going back to real life.'

'I know!' I say after a pause. 'It's just . . . I really love your hair long.'

'I can't go into a business meeting like this.' Luke shakes his head so the beads in his hair click together. 'You know that as well as I do.'

'But you don't have to cut it off!' I say in sudden inspiration. 'Plenty of Italian men have long hair. We'll just take the plaits out!'

'Becky . . .'

'I'll do it! I'll take them out! Sit down.'

I push Luke down on to the bed and carefully edge out the first few little beads, then gently start to unbraid his hair. As I lean close, I can smell the businessy smell of Luke's expensive Armani aftershave which he always wears for work. He hasn't used it since before we got married.

I shift round on the bed and carefully start unbraiding

33

the plaits on the other side of his head. We're both silent; the only sound in the room is the soft clicking of beads. As I pull out the very last one, I feel a lump in my throat. Which is ridiculous.

I mean, we couldn't stay on honeymoon for ever, could we? And I am looking forward to seeing Mum and Dad again, and Suze, and getting back to real life . . .

But still. I've spent the last ten months with Luke. We haven't spent more than a few hours out of each other's sight. And now that's all ending.

Anyway. It'll be fine. I'll be busy with my new job . . . and all my friends . . .

'Done!'

I reach for my serum, put some on Luke's hair, and carefully brush it out. It's a bit wavy – but that's OK. He just looks European.

'You see?' I say at last. 'You look brilliant!'

Luke surveys his reflection doubtfully and for an awful moment I think he's going to say he's still getting a haircut. Then he smiles.

'OK. Reprieved. But it will have to come off sooner or later.'

'I know,' I say, feeling suddenly light again. 'But just not today.'

I watch as Luke gathers some papers together and puts them in his briefcase.

'So . . . what exactly are you here in Milan for?'

Luke did tell me, on the flight from Colombo – but they were serving free champagne at the time, and I'm not entirely sure I took it all in.

'We're going after a new client. The Arcodas Group.'

'That's right. Now I remember.'

Luke's company is called Brandon Communications, and it's a PR agency for financial institutions, like banks and building societies and investment houses. That's kind of how we met, actually, back when I was a financial journalist.

'We want to broaden out of finance.' Luke snaps his briefcase shut. 'This is a very large corporation with lots of different interests. They own property developments . . . leisure centres . . . shopping malls . . .'

'Shopping malls?' I look up. 'Do you get a discount?'

'If we get the account. Maybe.'

God, this is cool. Maybe Luke's company will move into fashion PR! Maybe he'll start representing Dolce & Gabbana instead of boring old banks!

'So do they have any shopping malls in Milan?' I say in helpful tones. 'Because I could go and visit one. For research.'

'They haven't got any in Milan. They're only over here for a retail conference.' Luke puts down his briefcase and gives me a long look.

'What?' I say.

'Becky . . . I know this is Milan. But please, don't go crazy today.'

'Go crazy?' I say, a little offended. 'What do you mean?'

'I know you're going to go shopping . . .'

How does he know that? Honestly, Luke has such a nerve. How does he know I'm not going to go and see some famous statues or something?

'I'm not going to go shopping!' I say haughtily. 'I simply mentioned the shopping malls to show an interest in your work.'

'I see.' Luke gives me a quizzical look, which niggles me.

'I'm actually here for the culture.' I lift my chin. 'And because Milan is a city I've never seen.'

'Uh-huh.' Luke nods. 'So you weren't planning to visit any designer shops today.'

'Luke,' I say kindly, 'I am a professional personal shopper. Do you really think I'm going to get excited by a few designer shops?'

'Frankly, yes,' says Luke.

35

I feel a swell of indignation. Didn't we make vows to each other? Didn't he promise to respect me and not ever doubt my word?

'You think I came here just to go shopping? Well, take this!' I reach for my bag, take out my purse and thrust it at him.

'Becky, don't be silly—'

'Take it! I'll just have a simple walk around the city!'

'OK then.' Luke shrugs, and pockets my purse.

Damn. I didn't think he'd actually take it.

Anyway, it doesn't matter, because I have another credit card hidden in my bag, which Luke doesn't know about.

'Fine,' I say, folding my arms. 'Keep my money. I don't care!'

'I'm sure you'll survive,' says Luke. 'You can always use the credit card you keep hidden in your bag.'

What?

How does he know about that? Has he been *spying* on me?

This has to be grounds for divorce, surely.

'Have it!' I say furiously, reaching into my bag. 'Have everything! Take the shirt off my back!' I throw my credit card at him. 'You may think you know me, Luke. But you don't. All I want is to soak up a little culture, and maybe invest in the odd souvenir or local artefact.'

'Local artefact?' echoes Luke. 'By "local artefact", do you mean "Versace shoes"?'

'No!' I say after a short pause.

Which is true.

True-ish.

I was thinking more of Miu Miu. Apparently it's really cheap over here!

'Look, Becky, just don't go overboard, OK?' says Luke. 'We're up to our luggage limits as it is.' He glances at our open cases. 'What with the South

American ritual mask and the voodoo stick . . . oh, and let's not forget the ceremonial dancing swords . . .'

How many times is Luke going to give me grief about the ceremonial dancing swords? Just because they ripped his stupid shirt.

'For the millionth time, they're presents!' I say. 'We couldn't have shipped them. We have to have them with us *as we arrive,* otherwise we won't look like proper travellers!'

'That's fine. All I'm saying is, we don't have room for South American masks *and* six extra pairs of boots.'

Oh, he thinks he's so funny.

'Luke, I'm not like that any more, OK?' I say, a little crushingly. 'I've grown up a little. I would have thought you might have noticed.'

'If you say so.' Luke picks up my credit card, scrutinizes it, then gives it back to me. 'You've only got a couple of hundred pounds left on this one, anyway.'

What?

'How do you know that?' I say in outrage. 'That's my private credit card!'

'Then don't hide the statement under the mattress. The maid in Sri Lanka found it when she was making the bed and gave it to me.' He kisses me and picks up his briefcase. 'Enjoy the city!'

As the door closes, I feel a tad disgruntled. Little does Luke know. Little does Luke know I was actually planning to buy him a *present* today. Years ago, when I first met him, Luke had this belt which he really loved, made of gorgeous Italian leather. But he left it in the bathroom one day and it got hot leg-wax on it.

Which was not entirely my fault. Like I told him, when you're in total agony, you don't think, 'What would be the most suitable implement to scrape burning wax off my shins?' You just grab the nearest thing.

37

'Anyway. So I was planning to buy him a replacement today. A little 'end of honeymoon' gift. But maybe he doesn't deserve it if he's going to spy on me and read my private credit-card statements. I mean, what a cheek. Do I read *his* private letters?

Well, actually I do. Some of them are really interesting! But the point is . . .

Oh my God. I freeze, struck by a dreadful thought. Does that mean he saw how much I spent in Hong Kong, that day he went off to see the stock exchange?

Fuck.

And he hasn't said anything about it. OK, maybe he does deserve a present, after all.

I take a sip of cappuccino. Anyway, I'm the one laughing, not Luke. He thinks he's so clever, but what he doesn't know is, I've got a secret genius plan.

Half an hour later I arrive down at reception, wearing tight black trousers (not quite capri but close enough), a stripy T-shirt and a scarf knotted round my neck, European-style. I head straight for the foreign exchange desk and beam at the woman behind it.

'Ciao!' I say brightly. 'Il . . .'

I trail off into silence.

This is a bit annoying. I almost thought if I started confidently enough, with hand gestures, Italian would just pour naturally out of my mouth.

'I'd like to change some money into Euros, please,' I say, switching into English.

'Of course.' She smiles. 'Which currency?

'Curren*cies*.' I reach into my bag and triumphantly pull out a bundle of creased-up notes. 'Rupees, dirhams, ringgits . . . ' I dump the notes on the counter and reach for some more. 'Kenyan dollars . . .' I peer at a strange pink note I don't recognize. 'Whatever that one is . . .'

It is incredible how much money I was carrying around with me, without even noticing! Like, I had

loads of rupees in my bath bag, and a whole bunch of
Ethiopian birrs inside a paperback book. Plus there
were loads of odd notes and coins floating around at
the bottom of my carry-on bag.

And the point is, this is free money! This is money
we already had.

I watch excitedly as the woman sorts it all into piles.
'You have seventeen different currencies here,' she
says at last, looking a bit dazed.

'We've been to lots of countries,' I explain. 'So, how
much is it all worth?'

As the woman starts tapping on a small computer, I
feel quite excited. Maybe the exchange rates on some
of these have moved in my favour. Maybe this is all
worth loads!

Then I feel a bit guilty. After all, it's Luke's money
too. Abruptly I decide that if it's more than a hundred
Euros, I'll give half back to him. That's only fair. But
that'll still leave me with fifty! Not bad, for doing
absolutely nothing!

'After commission . . .' The woman looks up. 'Seven
forty-five.'

'Seven hundred and forty-five Euros?' I stare at her
in amazed joy. I had no *idea* I was carrying around that
kind of money! God, it just shows! All those people
who say, 'Look after the pennies and the pounds will
look after themselves,' . . . they're right! Who would
have thought it?

I'll be able to buy a present for Luke *and* a pair of
Miu Miu shoes, and—

'Not seven hundred and forty-five.' The woman
shows me her scribbled working. 'Seven Euros, forty-
five cents.'

'What?' My happy smile slips off my face. That can't
be right.

'Seven Euros, forty-five cents,' repeats the woman
patiently. 'How would you like that?'

* * *

Seven miserable Euros? As I head out of the hotel I'm still totally affronted. How can so much genuine money be worth only seven Euros? It makes no sense. As I explained to the woman, you could buy absolutely loads in India for those rupees. You could probably buy a whole car . . . or a palace, even. But she wouldn't budge. In fact, she said she was being generous.

Hmmph. Still, I suppose seven Euros is better than nothing. Maybe Miu Miu will be having a 99.9-per-cent-off sale or something.

I start walking down the street, carefully following the map the hotel concierge gave me. He was such a helpful man! I explained to him how I wanted to take in the cultural sights of Milan, and he started talking about some painting and Leonardo da Vinci. So I politely explained I was more interested in *contemporary* Italian culture, and he started going on about some artist who does short films about death.

So then I clarified that by 'contemporary Italian culture' I was really meaning cultural icons such as Prada and Gucci – and his eyes lit up in understanding. He marked a street for me which is in an area called the Golden Quadrilateral, and is apparently 'full of culture' which he was 'sure I would appreciate'.

It's a sunny day with a light breeze, and the sunlight is glinting off windows and cars, and whizzy Vespas zipping everywhere. God, Milan is cool. Every single person I pass is wearing designer sunglasses and carrying a designer handbag – even the men!

For a moment I consider buying Luke a continental handbag instead of a belt. I try to imagine him walking into the office with a chic little number dangling from his wrist . . .

Hmmm. Maybe I'll stick to a belt.

Suddenly I notice a girl in front of me, wearing a cream trouser suit, high strappy shoes, and a pink scooter helmet with leopard-print trim.

I stare at her, gripped with desire. God, I want one of those helmets. I mean, I know I haven't got a Vespa — but I could wear the helmet anyway, couldn't I? It could be my signature look. People would call me The Girl in the Vespa Helmet. Plus, it would protect me from muggers so it would actually be a *safety* feature . . .

Maybe I'll ask where she got it.

'Excuse-moi, mademoiselle!' I call out, impressed at my own sudden fluency. 'J'adore votre chapeau!'

The girl gives me a blank look, then disappears round a corner. Which, frankly, I think is a bit unfriendly. I mean, here I am, making an effort to speak her lang—

Oh. Oh right.

OK, that's a bit embarrassing.

Well, never mind. I'm not here to buy Vespa helmets, anyway. I'm here to buy a present for Luke. That's what marriage is all about, after all. Putting your partner first. Placing his needs before your own.

Plus, what I'm thinking is, I could always fly over to Milan for the day. I mean, it wouldn't take any time from London, would it? And Suze could come too, I think in sudden delight. God, that would be fun. I have a sudden image of Suze and me, striding down the street arm in arm, swinging our bags and laughing. A girly trip to Milan! We *have* to do it!

I reach another corner and stop to consult my map. I must be getting closer. He said it wasn't that far away . . .

Just then a woman walks past me carrying a carrier bag from Versace, and I stiffen with excitement. I have to be getting close to the source! This is just like when we visited that volcano in Peru, and the guide kept pointing out signs that we were nearing the core. If I just keep my eyes peeled for more Versace bags . . .

I walk forward a little more – and there's another one! That woman in oversized shades having a cappuccino has got one, plus about six zillion carriers from Armani. She gesticulates to her friend and reaches inside one of them – and pulls out a pot of jam, with an Armani label.

I stare at it in utter disbelief. Armani jam? Armani do *jam*?

Maybe in Milan everything has a fashion label! Maybe Dolce & Gabbana do toothpaste. Maybe Prada does tomato ketchup!

I *knew* I liked this city.

I start walking on again, more and more quickly, prickling with excitement. I can sense the shops in the air. The designer bags are becoming thick on the ground. The air is becoming heavy with expensive scent. I can practically *hear* the sound of hangers on rails and zips being done up . . .

And then, suddenly, there it is.

A long, elegant boulevard stretches before me, milling with the chic-est, most designer-clad people on earth. Tanned, model-like girls in Pucci prints and heels are sauntering along with powerful-looking men in immaculate linen suits. A girl in white Versace jeans and red lipstick is pushing along a pram upholstered in Louis Vuitton monogrammed leather. A blonde woman in a brown leather miniskirt trimmed with rabbit fur is gabbling into a matching mobile phone, and dragging along her little boy, dressed head to foot in Gucci.

And . . . the shops. Shop after shop after shop. Ferragamo. Valentino. Dior. Versace. Prada.

As I venture down the street, my head swivelling from side to side, I feel giddy. It's complete culture shock. How long is it since I've seen a shop that wasn't selling ethnic crafts and wooden beads? I feel like I've been on some starvation cure, and now I'm gorging on tiramisu with double cream.

Just look at that amazing coat. Look at those *shoes*.

Where do I start? Where do I even—

I can't move. I'm paralysed in the middle of the street, like the donkey who couldn't choose between the bales of hay. They'll find me in years to come, still frozen to the spot, clutching my credit card.

Suddenly my eyes fall on a display of leather belts and wallets in the window of a nearby boutique.

Leather. Luke's belt. This is what I'm here to buy. Focus.

I totter towards the shop and push open the door, still in a daze. At once I'm hit by the overwhelming smell of expensive leather. In fact, it's so strong it actually seems to clear my head.

The shop is amazing. It's carpeted in pale taupe, with softly lit display cabinets. I can see wallets, belts, bags, jackets . . . I pause by a mannequin wearing the most amazing chocolate-brown coat, all leather and satin. I stroke it fondly, then lift the price label – and nearly faint.

But, of course, it's in lira. I smile in relief. No wonder it looks so—

Oh no. It's Euros now.

Bloody hell.

I gulp, and move away from the mannequin.

Which just proves, Dad was right all along, the single currency *was* a huge mistake. When I was thirteen I went on holiday to Rome with my parents – and the whole point about lira was, the prices looked like a lot but *they weren't really*. You could buy something for about a zillion lira – and in real life it cost about three quid! It was fantastic!

Plus, if you accidentally ended up buying a bottle of really expensive perfume, no one (i.e., your parents) could blame you, because, like Mum said, who on earth can divide numbers like that in their head?

Governments are just spoilsports.

As I start to look through a display of belts, a stocky, middle-aged man comes out of a fitting room, wearing an amazing black coat trimmed with leather, and chomping on a cigar. He's about fifty and very tanned, with grey close-cropped hair and piercing blue eyes. The only thing which doesn't look quite so good is his nose, which to be honest is a bit of a mish-mash.

'Oy, Roberto,' he says in a raspy voice.

He's English! His accent is weird, though. Kind of transatlantic meets Cockney.

A shop assistant in a black suit with angular black glasses comes hurrying out from the fitting room, holding a tape measure.

'Yes, Signore Temple?'

'How much cashmere is in this?' The stocky man smooths down the coat critically and blows out a cloud of smoke. I can see the assistant flinch as the cloud reaches his face, but he doesn't mention it.

'Signore, this is 100 per cent cashmere.'

'The best cashmere?' The stocky man lifts a warning finger. 'I don't want you palming me off, now. You know my motto. Only the best.'

The guy in black glasses gives a little wince of dismay.

'Signore, we would not, er . . . palm you off.'

The man gazes at himself silently for a few seconds – then nods.

'Fair enough. I'll take three. One to London.' He counts off on stubby fingers. 'One to Switzerland. One to New York. Got it? Now – briefcases.'

The assistant in black glasses glances over at me, and I realize it's totally obvious I'm eavesdropping.

'Oh, hi!' I say quickly. 'I'd like to buy this, please, and have it gift-wrapped.' I hold up the belt I've chosen.

'Silvia will help you.' He gestures dismissively at the till, then turns back to his customer.

I hand the belt over to Silvia and watch idly as she wraps it up in bronze shiny paper. I'm half-admiring her deft fingers and half-listening to the stocky man, who's now looking at a briefcase.

'Don't like the texture,' he states. 'Feels different. Something's wrong.'

'We have changed our supplier recently . . .' Black-glasses guy is wringing his hands. 'But it is a very fine leather, signor . . .'

He trails off as the stocky man takes his cigar from his mouth and gives him a look.

'You're palming me off, Roberto,' he says. 'I pay good money, I want quality. What you'll do is make me one up using leather from the old supplier. Got it?'

He looks over, sees me watching and winks.

'Best place for leather in the world, this. But don't take any of their crap.'

'I won't!' I beam back. 'And I love that coat, by the way!'

'Very kind of you.' He nods affably. 'You an actress? Model?'

'Er . . . no. Neither.'

'No matter.' He waves his cigar.

'How will you pay, signorina?' Silvia interrupts us.

'Oh! Er . . . here you are.'

As I hand over my Visa card I feel a glow of goodness in my heart. Buying presents for other people is so much more satisfying than buying for yourself! And this will take me up to my limit on my Visa card, so that's my shopping all finished for the day.

What shall I do next? Maybe I'll take in some culture. I could go and look at that famous painting the concierge was talking about.

I can hear a buzz of interest coming from the back of the shop, and turn idly to see what's happening. A

45

mirrored door is open to a stock room, and a woman in a black suit is coming out, surrounded by a gaggle of eager assistants. What on earth is she holding? Why is everyone so—

Then suddenly I catch a glimpse of what she's carrying. My heart stops. My skin starts to prickle.

It can't be.

But it is. She's carrying an Angel bag.

THREE

It's an Angel bag. In the flesh.

I thought they were all sold out everywhere. I thought they were totally impossible to get hold of.

The woman sets it down ceremoniously on a creamy suede pedestal, and stands back to admire it. The whole shop has fallen silent. It's like a member of the royal family has arrived. Or a movie star.

I can't breathe. I'm transfixed.

It's stunning. It's totally stunning. The calfskin looks as soft as butter. The handpainted angel is all in delicate shades of aquamarine. And underneath is the name 'Dante' written in diamante.

I swallow, trying to get control of myself, but my legs are all wobbly and my hands feel sweaty. This is better than when we saw the white tigers in Bengal. I mean, let's face it, Angel bags are probably *rarer* than white tigers.

And there's one, in front of my nose.

I could just buy it, flashes through my brain. *I could buy it!*

'Miss? Signorina? Can you hear me?' A voice pierces my thoughts, and I realize Silvia at the till is trying to get my attention.

'Oh,' I say, flustered. 'Yes.' I pick up the pen and scribble any old signature. 'So . . . is that a real Angel bag?'

'Yes it is,' she says in smug, bored tones, like a bouncer who knows the band personally and is used to dealing with besotted groupies.

'How much . . .' I swallow. 'How much is it?'

'Two thousand Euros.'

'Right.' I nod.

Two thousand Euros. For a bag.

But if I had an Angel bag I wouldn't need to buy any new clothes. Ever. Who needs a new skirt when you have the hippest bag in town?

I don't care how much it is. I have to have it.

'I'd like to buy it please,' I say in a rush.

There's a stunned silence around the shop – then all the assistants burst into peals of laughter.

'You cannot buy the bag,' says Silvia pityingly. 'There is a waiting list.'

Oh. A waiting list. Of course there would be a waiting list. I'm an idiot.

'Do you want to join the list?' She hands my card back.

OK, let's be sensible. I'm not really going to go on a waiting list in Milan. I mean, for a start, how would I pick it up? I'd have to get them to Fedex it. Or come over specially, or—

'Yes,' I hear my own voice saying. 'Yes please.'

As I write down my details, my heart is thumping. I'm going on the list. I'm going on the Angel bag list!

'Here we are.' I hand back the form.

'That's fine.' Silvia pops the form in a drawer. 'We will call you when one is available.'

'And . . . when might that be?' I say, trying not to sound too anxious.

'I cannot say.' She shrugs.

'How many people are ahead of me on the list?'

'I cannot say.'

'Right.'

I feel a tiny dart of frustration. I mean, *there it is.*

There's the bag, a few feet away from me . . . and I can't have it.

Never mind. I'm on the list. There's nothing more I can do.

I pick up the carrier bag containing Luke's belt and slowly walk away, pausing by the Angel bag. God, it's heart-stopping. The coolest, most beautiful bag in the world. As I gaze at it, I feel a tinge of resentment. I mean, it's not *my* fault I haven't put my name down before now. I've been travelling round the world! What was I supposed to do, cancel my honeymoon?

Anyway. Calm down. It doesn't matter, because the point is, I *will have one*. I will. Just as soon as—

I'm suddenly struck by a blinding insight.

'I was just wondering,' I say, hurrying back to the till. 'Do you know if everyone on the waiting list actually *wants* an Angel bag?'

'They are on the list,' says Silvia, as though I'm a total moron.

'Yes, but they might all have changed their minds,' I explain, my words tumbling out in excitement. 'Or already have bought one! And then it would be my turn! Don't you *see*? I could have this bag!'

How can she look so impassive? Doesn't she understand how important this is?

'We will be contacting the customers in turn,' says Silvia. 'We will be in touch if a bag becomes available for you.'

'I'll do it for you if you like,' I say, trying to sound helpful. 'If you give me their numbers.'

Silvia looks at me silently for a moment.

'No thank you. We will be in touch.'

'All right,' I say, deflating. 'Well, thanks.'

There's nothing more I can do. I'll just stop thinking about it and enjoy the rest of Milan. Exactly. I give a final longing glance at the Angel bag, then head out of the shop on to the sunny street.

I wonder if she's phoning up the people on the list yet.

No. Stop it. Walk away. I'm not going to obsess about this. I'm not even going to *think* about it. I'm going to focus on . . . culture. Yes. That big painting, or whatever it is—

Suddenly I stop dead in the street. I've given her the number of Luke's flat in London. But didn't he say something a while ago about putting in new phone lines?

What if I've left *the wrong number*?

Quickly I retrace my steps and burst into the shop again.

'Hi!' I say breathlessly. 'I just thought I'd give you another set of contact details, in case you can't get through.' I rummage about in my bag and pull out one of Luke's cards. 'This is my husband's office.'

'Very well,' says Silvia a little wearily.

'Only . . . come to think of it, if you speak to him, I wouldn't mention the actual *bag*.' I lower my voice a little. 'Say, "The Angel has landed."'

'The Angel has landed,' echoes Silvia, writing it down as though she makes coded phone calls all the time.

Which, now I think about it, maybe she does.

'The person to ask for is Luke Brandon,' I explain, handing over the card. 'At Brandon Communications. He's my husband.'

Across the shop, I'm aware of the stocky man looking up from a selection of leather gloves.

'Luke Brandon,' repeats Silvia. 'Very well.' She puts the card away and gives me a final nod.

'So, have you phoned anyone on the list yet?' I can't resist asking.

'No,' says Silvia evenly. 'Not yet.'

'And you will phone as *soon* as you know? Even if it's late at night? I won't mind—'

'Mrs Brandon,' snaps Silvia in exasperation. 'You are on the list! You will have to wait your turn! I cannot do any better than that!'

'Are you so sure about that?' a raspy voice cuts in and we both look up to see the stocky man approaching us across the shop.

I gape at him in astonishment. What's he doing?

'Excuse me?' says Silvia haughtily, and he winks at me.

'Don't let them palm you off, girl.' He turns to Silvia. 'If you wanted to, you could sell her this bag.' He jerks his stubby thumb at the Angel bag on the pedestal and puffs on his cigar.

'Signore—'

'I've been listening in on your conversation. If you haven't called anyone on the waiting list, they don't know this has come in. They don't even know it exists.' He pauses meaningfully. 'And you've got this young lady here, wants to buy it.'

'That is not the point, signore.' Silvia smiles tightly at him. 'There is a strict protocol . . .'

'You have discretion. Don't tell me you don't. Oy, Roberto!' he suddenly calls. From the corner, the man in the black glasses hurries over.

'Signor Temple?' he says smoothly, his eyes darting at me. 'Everything is all right?'

'If I wanted this bag for my ladyfriend, would you sell it to me?' The man blows out a cloud of smoke and raises his eyebrows at me. He looks like he's enjoying this.

Roberto glances at Silvia, who jerks her head at me and rolls her eyes. I can see Roberto taking in the situation, his brain working hard.

'Signor Temple.' He turns to the man with a charming smile. 'You are a very valued customer. It is a very different matter . . .'

'Would you?'

'Yes,' says Roberto after a pause.

'Well then.' The man looks at Roberto expectantly.

There's silence. I can't breathe. I can't move.

'Silvia,' says Roberto at last, 'wrap up the bag for the signorina.'

Oh my God. Oh my GOD!

'It's my pleasure,' says Silvia, shooting me a dirty look.

I feel giddy. I can't believe this has happened.

'I don't know how to thank you!' I stutter. 'That's the most wonderful thing anyone's ever done for me, ever!'

'My pleasure.' The man inclines his head and extends his hand. 'Nathan Temple.'

His hand is strong and pudgy, and feels surprisingly well moisturized.

'Becky Bloomwood,' I say, shaking it. 'I mean, Brandon.'

'You really wanted that bag.' He raises his eyebrows appreciatively. 'Never seen anything like it.'

'I was desperate for it!' I admit with a laugh. 'I'm so grateful to you!'

Nathan Temple waves his hand in a 'don't mention it' gesture, takes out a lighter and lights his cigar, which has gone out. When it's puffing strongly again he looks up.

'Brandon . . . as in Luke Brandon.'

'You know Luke?' I stare at him in amazement. 'What a coincidence!'

'By reputation.' He blows out a cloud of cigar smoke. 'He has quite a name, your husband.'

'Signor Temple.' Roberto comes bustling over with several carrier bags, which he hands to Nathan Temple. 'The rest will be shipped according to your orders.'

'Good man, Roberto,' says Nathan Temple, clapping him on the back. 'See you next year.'

'Please let me buy you a drink,' I say quickly. 'Or lunch! Or . . . anything!'

'Unfortunately I have to go. Nice offer, though.'

'But I want to thank you for what you did. I'm so incredibly grateful!'

Nathan Temple lifts his hands modestly.

'Who knows. Maybe one day you can do a favour for me.'

'Anything!' I exclaim eagerly, and he smiles.

'Enjoy the bag. All right, Harvey.'

Out of nowhere, a thin, blond guy in a chalk-striped suit has appeared. He takes the bags from Nathan Temple and the two walk out of the shop.

I lean against the counter, radiant with bliss. I have an Angel bag. I have an Angel bag!

'That will be two thousand Euros,' comes a surly voice behind me.

Oh right. I'd kind of forgotten about the two thousand Euros part.

I automatically reach for my purse – then stop. Of course. I don't have my purse. And I've maxed out my Visa card on Luke's belt . . . and I only have seven Euros in cash.

Silvia's eyes narrow at my hesitation.

'If you have trouble paying . . .' she begins.

'I don't have trouble paying!' I retort at once. 'I just . . . need a minute.'

Silvia folds her arms sceptically as I reach into my bag again and pull out a Bobbi Brown 'Sheer Finish' compact.

'Do you have a hammer?' I say. 'Or anything heavy?'

Silvia is looking at me as though I've gone completely crazy.

'Anything will do . . .' Suddenly I glimpse a hefty-looking stapler sitting on the counter. I pick it up and start bashing as hard as I can at the compact.

'*Oddio!*' Silvia screams.

'It's OK!' I say, panting a little. 'I just need to . . . there!'

The whole thing has splintered. Triumphantly I pull out a Mastercard which was glued to the backing. My Def Con One, Code Red Emergency card. Luke *really* doesn't know about this one. Not unless he's got X-ray vision.

I got the idea of hiding a credit card in a powder compact from this brilliant article I read on money management. Not that I have a problem with money, or anything like that. But in the past, I have had the odd little . . . crisis.

So this idea really appealed to me. What you do is, you keep your credit card somewhere really in-accessible like frozen in ice or sewn into the lining of your bag, so you'll have time to reconsider before making each purchase. Apparently this simple tactic can cut your unnecessary purchases by 90 per cent.

And I have to say, it really does work! The only flaw is, I keep having to buy new powder compacts, which is getting a bit expensive.

'Here you are!' I say, and hand it to Silvia, who is peering at me as though I'm a dangerous lunatic. She swipes it gingerly through her machine, and a minute later I'm scrawling my signature on the slip. I thrust it back at her, and she files it away in a drawer.

There's a tiny pause. I'm almost exploding with anticipation.

'So . . . can I have it?' I say.

'Here you are,' she says sulkily, and hands me the creamy carrier.

My hands close over the cord handles and I feel a surge of pure, unadulterated joy.

It's mine.

As I get back to the hotel that evening, I'm floating on air. This has been one of the best days of my entire life.

I spent the whole afternoon walking up and down the Via Montenapoleone with my new Angel bag prominently displayed on my shoulder . . . and everyone admired it. In fact, they didn't just admire it . . . they gawped at it. It was like I was a sudden celebrity!

About twenty people came and asked me where I got it, and a woman in dark glasses who *had* to be an Italian movie star got her driver to come and offer me three thousand Euros for it. And, best of all, all I kept hearing was people saying, '*La ragazza con la borsa di Angel*'! Which I worked out means The Girl with the Angel Bag! That's what they were calling me!

I drift blissfully through the revolving doors into the foyer to see Luke standing by the reception desk.

'There you are!' he says, sounding relieved. 'I was beginning to worry! Our taxi's here.' He ushers me out into a waiting taxi, and slams the door. 'Linate Airport,' he says to the driver, who immediately zooms into an oncoming stream of traffic to a chorus of beeps.

'So how was your day?' I say, trying not to flinch as we're nearly hit by another taxi. 'How was the meeting?'

'It went well! If we can get the Arcodas Group as clients it'll be seriously good news. They're expanding hugely at the moment. It's going to be an exciting time.'

'So . . . do you think you will get them?'

'We'll have to woo them. When we get back I'm going to start preparing a pitch. But I'm hopeful. I'm definitely hopeful.'

'Well done!' I beam at him. 'And was your hair OK?'

'My hair was fine.' He gives a wry smile. 'In fact . . . it was admired by all.'

'You see?' I say in delight. 'I knew it would be!'

'And how was your day?' asks Luke as we swing

round a corner at about a hundred miles an hour.

'It was fantastic!' I glow. 'Absolutely perfect. I adore Milan!'

'Really?' Luke looks intrigued. 'Even without this?' He reaches into his pocket and produces my purse.

God, I'd forgotten all about that.

'Even without my purse!' I say with a little laugh. 'Although I did manage to buy you a little something.'

I hand over the bronze-wrapped package and watch excitedly as Luke pulls out the belt.

'Becky, that's wonderful!' he says. 'Absolutely . . .' He trails off, turning it over in his hands.

'It's to replace the one I ruined,' I explain. 'With the hot wax, remember.'

'I remember.' He sounds utterly touched. 'And . . . this is really all you bought in Milan? A present for me?'

'Er . . .'

I give a kind of noncommittal shrug and clear my throat, playing for time.

OK. What do I do?

Marriages are based on honesty and trust. If I don't tell him about the Angel bag then I'm betraying that trust.

But if I *do* tell him . . . I'll have to explain about my Def Con One, Code Red Emergency credit card. Which I'm not sure is such a wild idea.

I don't want to spoil the last precious moments of our honeymoon with some stupid argument.

But we're *married*, I think in a rush of emotion. We're husband and wife! We shouldn't have secrets! OK, I'm going to tell him. Right now.

'Luke—'

'Wait.' Luke cuts me off, his voice a little gruff. 'Becky, I want to apologize.'

'What?' I gape at him.

'You said you'd changed. You said you'd grown up. And . . . you have.' He spreads his hands. 'To be

56

honest, I was expecting you to come back to the hotel having made some huge, extravagant purchase.'

Oh God.

'Er . . . Luke . . .' I venture.

'I'm ashamed of myself,' he says, frowning. 'Here you are. Your first visit to the fashion capital of the world – and all you've bought is a present for me. Becky, I'm really moved.' He exhales sharply. 'Chandra was right. You do have a beautiful spirit.'

There's silence. This is my cue to tell him the truth.

But how? How?

How can I tell him I don't have a beautiful spirit, I have a crappy old normal one?

'Well . . .' I swallow several times. 'Er . . . you know. It's just a belt!'

'It's not just a belt to me,' he says quietly. 'It's a symbol of our marriage.' He clasps my hand for a few moments, then smiles. 'I'm sorry . . . what did you want to say?'

I could still come clean.

I could still do it.

'Um . . . well . . . I was just going to tell you . . . the buckle's adjustable.' I give him a slightly sick smile, and turn away, pretending to be fascinated by the view out of the window.

OK. So I didn't tell the truth.

But in my defence, if he'd just paid attention when I'd read him *Vogue*, he would have seen for himself. I mean, I'm not hiding it or anything. Here I am with one of the most coveted status symbols in the world on my arm – and he hasn't even noticed!

And anyway, that is absolutely the last time I lie to him. From now on, no more white lies, no more grey lies, no more fibs. We will have a perfect marriage of honesty and truth. Yes. Everyone will admire our harmonious, loving ways, and people will call us The Couple Who—

'Linate Airport!' The driver's voice interrupts my thoughts. I turn to look at Luke with a sudden apprehensive thrill.

'Here we are,' he says, and meets my eyes. 'Still want to go home?'

'Absolutely!' I reply firmly, ignoring the tiny nerves in my stomach.

I get out of the taxi and stretch my legs. Passengers are milling about with trolleys, and a plane is taking off with a thunderous roar, almost right above me.

God, we're really doing it. In a few hours we'll be in London. After all these months away.

'By the way,' says Luke, 'there was a message from your mother on my mobile this afternoon. She wanted to know if we were still in Sri Lanka, or had we gone to Malaysia yet?'

He raises his eyebrows comically at me, and I feel a giggle rise. They are all going to get such a shock! They're all going to be so thrilled to see us!

And suddenly I'm full of excitement. This is it! We're on our way home!

FOUR

Oh my God. We've done it. We're back! We're actually back on English soil.

Or at least, English tarmac. We spent last night in a hotel, and now we're driving along the Surrey roads in a hired car, all ready to surprise Mum and Dad. In about two minutes, we'll arrive at their house!

I can barely keep still for excitement. In fact, I keep banging my knee on the South American tribal mask. I can just see the looks on Mum and Dad's faces when they see us! Mum's face will light up, and Dad will look astounded, then his face will break into a smile . . . and we'll be running to each other through the clouds of smoke . . .

Actually, maybe there won't be any clouds of smoke. I'm thinking of *The Railway Children*. But anyway, it'll be fantastic. The most fantastic reunion ever!

To be honest, Mum and Dad have probably found it quite hard-going without me. I'm their only daughter, and this is the longest they've ever had to go without seeing me. Ten whole months, with barely any contact.

I will so make their day, coming back home.

We're in Oxshott now, my home town, and I look out of the window as we drive through the familiar streets, past all the houses and gardens I've known since I was a child. We go by the little parade of shops, and everything looks exactly the same. The guy from the newsagent glances up as we stop at a traffic light and lifts his hand in recognition, as though it's just a normal day. He doesn't look amazed to see me or anything.

Don't you understand? I want to yell at him. I've been away for nearly a year! I've seen the world!

We swing into Mayfield Avenue and for the first time I feel just the tiniest twinge of nerves.

'Luke, should we have called?' I say.

'Too late now,' Luke calmly replies, and signals left.

We're nearly at our street. Oh God. I really am starting to feel jittery.

'What if we give them a heart attack?' I say in sudden panic. 'What if they're so shocked to see us that they have seizures?'

'I'm sure they'll be fine!' Luke laughs. 'Don't worry!'

And now we're in Elton Road, my parents' road. We're coming up to their house. We're here.

Luke pulls into the drive and stops the engine. For a moment neither of us moves.

'Ready?' he says into the silence.

'I guess so!' I say, my voice sounding unnaturally high.

Feeling self-conscious, I get out of the car and slam the door. It's a bright, sunny day and the street is quiet apart from a few birds twittering and the distant sound of a lawn-mower.

I walk up to the front door, hesitate and look at Luke. This is the big moment. With a sudden surge of excitement, I lift my hand and firmly press the bell.

Nothing happens.

I hesitate – then ring it again. But there's silence.

They're not in.

How can they not be in?

As I stare at the front door, I feel indignant. Where on earth are my parents? Don't they realize their only beloved daughter is back from her round-the-world trip?

'We could go for a coffee and come back later,' suggests Luke.

'I suppose so,' I say, trying to hide my disappointment.

This has ruined my whole plan. I was all ready for our great emotional reunion! Not going off for a cup of crappy old coffee.

Disconsolate, I walk up the path and lean on the wrought-iron gate. I fiddle with the broken catch, which Dad has been saying he's going to mend for twenty years, and look at the roses which Mum and Dad had put in last year for our wedding. God, we've nearly been married a year. That's a weird thought.

Suddenly I hear the distant sound of voices travelling along the street. I raise my head and squint along the pavement. A pair of figures has just rounded the corner. I peer harder – and feel a sudden jolt.

It's them! It's Mum and Dad! Walking along the street. Mum's in a print dress and Dad's in a pink short-sleeved shirt, and they both look tanned and healthy.

'Mum!' I shriek, my voice bouncing off the pavement. 'Dad!' I open my arms wide. '*We're back!*'

Mum and Dad look up, and both freeze to the spot. Suddenly I notice they've got someone else with them, too. Some woman. Or girl. I can't see properly in this bright sunlight.

'Mum!' I cry again. 'Dad!'

The slightly strange thing is, they aren't moving. They must be too shell-shocked by my appearance or something. Maybe they think I'm a ghost.

'I'm back!' I yell. 'It's me, Becky! Surprise!'

There's an odd pause.

Then, to my utter astonishment, Mum and Dad start retreating.

What . . . What are they doing?

I stare at them in bewilderment.

It's kind of like I always pictured our reunion – but in reverse. They were supposed to be running *towards* me.

They disappear round the corner again. The street is silent and empty. For a few moments I'm too baffled to speak.

'Luke, was that Mum and Dad?' I say at last.

'I think so.' Luke sounds equally puzzled.

'And did they really . . . back away from me?'

I can't help sounding a bit stricken. My own parents, running away from me as though I've got the plague.

'No!' says Luke quickly. 'Of course not. They probably just didn't see you. Look!' He suddenly points. 'There they are again.'

Sure enough, round the corner have appeared Mum and Dad again, this time without any girl. They walk along for a few steps, then Dad dramatically grabs Mum and points at me.

'It's Becky!' he says. 'Look!'

'Becky!' exclaims Mum in a stilted voice. 'It can't be true!'

She sounds just like she did in the amateur dramatics Agatha Christie last year, when she played the lady who discovered the body.

'Becky! Luke!' Dad calls.

And now they really are running towards us, and I feel a huge swell of emotion rising.

'Mum!' I shout. 'Dad! We're back!'

I race towards them, throwing my hands out. I land in Dad's arms, and the next moment Mum's there too, and we're all in a great big hug.

'You're home!' Dad exclaims. 'Welcome back, darling!'

'Is everything all right?' Mum peers at me anxiously. 'Are you OK?'

'We're fine! We just decided to come home! We

wanted to see you all!' I squeeze Mum tightly. 'We knew you'd be missing us!'

All three of us walk back to the house, where Dad shakes Luke's hand and Mum gives him an enormous hug.

'I can't believe it,' she says, looking from Luke to me. 'I just can't believe it. Luke, your hair! It's so *long!*'

'I know.' He grins at me. 'It'll be coming off before I go to work.'

I'm feeling too joyful to start arguing with him. *This* is how I imagined it. Everyone together and happy.

'Come in and have a cup of coffee!' says Mum, getting out her doorkeys.

'We don't want coffee!' says Dad at once. 'We want champagne! This is something to celebrate!'

'They may not want champagne!' retorts Mum. 'They may be jet-lagged! Are you jet-lagged, love? Do you want to lie down?'

'I'm fine!' Impulsively I hug Mum with my free arm. 'It's just lovely to see you.'

'It's lovely to see *you*, darling!' She hugs me back and I inhale the familiar scent of her Tweed perfume, which she's been wearing as long as I can remember.

'That's a relief to hear!' I laugh. 'Because it almost looked like you were . . .' I break off, feeling a bit awkward.

'What, love?'

'Well, it kind of *looked* as if you were . . . backing away from me!' I give another little laugh, to show what a ridiculous idea this is.

There's a pause — and I see Mum and Dad glance at each other.

'Dad dropped his spectacles!' says Mum brightly. 'Didn't you, love?'

'That's right!' Dad chimes in heartily. 'I dropped my specs.'

'We had to go back for them,' Mum explains.

Both she and Dad are watching me with alert expressions.

What's going on? Are they *hiding* something?

'Is that Becky?' A shrill voice pierces the atmosphere, and I look round to see Janice, our next-door neighbour, peering over the fence. She's wearing a pink flowery dress with matching eyeshadow, and her hair has been dyed a very strange shade of auburn. 'Becky!' She clasps her hands breathlessly to her chest. 'It *is* you!'

'Hi, Janice!' I say with a beam. 'We're back!'

'You look so well!' she exclaims. 'Don't they look well? So *brown*!'

'That's travelling for you,' I say nonchalantly.

'And Luke! You look just like Crocodile Dundee!' Janice is goggling at us both with open admiration, and I can't help feeling gratified.

'Let's go in,' says Mum, 'and you can tell us all about it!'

This is the moment I've pictured so many times. Sitting down with friends and family and telling all about our foreign adventures. Spreading out a crinkly map . . . describing sunrises over mountains . . . looking at the avid faces . . . listening to the gasps of admiration . . .

Except that now it's actually happening, it isn't going quite like I imagined.

'So where did you go?' asks Janice as soon as we sit down at the kitchen table.

'We went everywhere!' I say proudly. 'Name any country in the world!'

'Ooh! Did you go to Tenerife?'

'Er . . . no.'

'Did you go to Majorca?'

'Er . . . no,' I say, feeling a twinge of annoyance. 'We went to Africa, South America, India . . .' I spread my arms. 'Everywhere!'

'Goodness!' says Janice, wide-eyed. 'Was Africa hot?'

'Pretty hot.' I smile.

'I can't stand the heat.' Janice shakes her head. 'Never could. Even in Florida.' She suddenly brightens. 'Did you go to Disneyland?'

'Er . . . no.'

'Oh well.' Janice looks sympathetic. 'Never mind. Maybe next time!'

Next time? What, next time we spend ten months travelling round the world?

'It certainly sounds like a lovely holiday,' she adds encouragingly.

It wasn't a *holiday*! I want to exclaim. It was a *travelling experience*! Honestly. I bet when Christopher Columbus came back from America, people didn't meet him off the boat with 'Ooh, Christopher, did you go to Disneyland?'

I glance up at Mum and Dad – but they're not even listening. They're standing by the sink, and Mum's murmuring something to Dad.

I don't like this. There is definitely something going on. I glance at Luke, and he's watching Mum and Dad, too.

'We brought you presents!' I exclaim loudly, reaching for my carrier bag. 'Mum! Dad! Have a look!'

With some difficulty, I pull out the South American mask and present it to Mum. It's in the shape of a dog's face, with big teeth and huge circular eyes, and I have to say it looks pretty impressive.

'I brought it all the way back from Paraguay!' I add with a glow of pride.

I feel like such an explorer! Here I am, bringing rare artefacts of the indigenous South American culture to Oxshott. I mean, how many people in Britain have even *seen* one of these? Maybe a museum will ask to borrow it for an exhibition, or something!

'Goodness!' says Mum, turning it over a little nervously. 'What is it?'

'It's a traditional ritual mask made by Chiriguano Indians, isn't it?' says Janice brightly.

'Have you been to Paraguay, Janice?' I say, taken aback.

'Oh no, love.' She takes a sip of coffee. 'I've seen them in John Lewis.'

For a moment I can't quite speak.

'You've seen them in . . . John Lewis?' I say at last.

'In Kingston. The gift department.' She beams. 'You can buy everything in John Lewis these days!'

'Never knowingly undersold,' chimes in Mum.

I do not believe this. I've lugged this mask approximately six thousand miles around the globe. It was supposed to be a rare and exotic treasure. And all the time it's been on sale at bloody John Lewis.

Mum glimpses my face.

'But yours will be the real thing, love!' she says quickly. 'We'll put it on the mantelpiece next to Dad's golf trophy!'

'OK,' I say a bit gloomily. I glance up at Dad, and he's still staring out of the window, not listening to a word. Maybe I'll give him his present later.

'So, what's been happening here?' I ask, taking a cup of coffee from Mum. 'How's Martin? And Tom?'

'Both well, thank you!' says Janice. 'Tom's living with us for a while.'

'Ah.' I give an understanding nod.

Tom is Janice and Martin's son, and he's had a bit of a disaster with his marriage. His wife Lucy left him, basically because he wouldn't have a tattoo done to match hers.

'They've sold their house,' Janice says, looking wistful. 'Did very well out it, actually.'

'And is he OK?'

Mum and Janice exchange looks.

'He's been throwing himself into his hobbies,' says Janice at last. 'Keeping himself busy. His new thing is woodwork. He's made all sorts for us!' She looks slightly beleaguered. 'Three garden benches . . . two bird tables . . . and now he's working on a two-storey summerhouse!'

'Wow!' I say politely. 'That's great!'

The oven-timer suddenly starts pinging, and I look up in surprise. Has Mum taken to baking while we've been away?

'Are you cooking something?' I peer at the oven, which appears to be dead.

'No!' Mum gives a trill of laughter. 'That's to remind me to check eBay.'

'eBay?' I stare at her. 'What do you mean, eBay?'

How would Mum know about eBay? She doesn't know anything about computers. Two years ago, I suggested she give Luke a new mouse mat for Christmas and she went to a pet shop.

'You know, darling! Internet shopping. I'm bidding on a Ken Hom wok, a pair of candlesticks . . .' She pulls a flowery notepad out of her pocket and consults it. 'Oh yes, and a hedge-trimmer for Dad. Only used once!'

'eBay is marvellous!' chimes in Janice. 'Such fun. Have you used it, Becky?'

'Well . . . no.'

'Oh, you'd love it,' says Mum at once. 'Although I couldn't get through last night to check on my Portmeirion plates.' She clicks her tongue. 'I don't know *what* was wrong.'

'The domain servers were probably down,' says Janice knowledgeably. 'I've been having trouble with my modem all week. Biscuit, Becky?'

I cannot get my head round this. Mum? On eBay? Next she'll be saying she's up to level six on Tomb Raider.

'But you haven't even got a computer,' I say. 'You hate modern technology.'

'Not any more, love! Janice and I did a course. We've gone broadband!' She looks at me seriously. 'Let me give you a word of advice, Becky. If you're going broadband, I'd install a decent firewall.'

OK. This is all wrong. Parents are not supposed to know more about computers than their children. I nod carelessly and take a sip of coffee, trying to hide the fact that I don't have a clue what a firewall is.

'Jane, it's ten to twelve,' says Janice cautiously to Mum. 'Are you going to . . .'

'I don't think so,' she says. 'You go on.'

'What is it?' I look from face to face. 'Is something wrong?'

'Of course not!' says Mum, putting down her coffee cup. 'It's just we agreed to go to the Marshalls' drinks party today, with Janice and Martin. But don't worry. We'll send our apologies.'

'Don't be silly!' I say at once. 'You must go. We don't want to mess up your day.'

There's a pause.

'Are you sure?' says Mum.

I feel a twinge of hurt. She wasn't supposed to say that. She was supposed to say, 'How could my precious daughter mess up my day?'

'Of course!' I say, in over-bright tones. 'You go to your drinks party and we'll have a proper chat later.'

'Well, OK,' says Mum. 'If you're sure.'

'I'll pop and get ready,' says Janice. 'Lovely to see you back, Becky!'

As she disappears out of the kitchen door I look at Dad, who's still staring broodingly out of the window.

'Are you OK, Dad? You've been really quiet.'

'Sorry,' he says, turning round with a quick smile. 'I'm just a little distracted at the moment. Thinking about . . . a golf match I've got next week. Very important.' He mimes playing a putt.

'Right,' I say, trying to sound cheerful.

But inside I feel more and more uneasy. He's not really thinking about golf. Why is he so cagey?

What is going on?

Suddenly I remember the woman on the pavement. The one I saw before Mum and Dad started shuffling away.

'So . . . who was that I saw you with earlier?' I say lightly. 'That woman you were with.'

It's like I've let off a gunshot or something. Mum and Dad are both paralysed. I can see their eyes darting towards each other, then looking away again. They both look totally panic-stricken.

'Woman?' says Mum at last. 'I didn't . . .' She looks at Dad. 'Did you see a woman, Graham?'

'Maybe Becky means . . . that passer-by,' he says in stilted tones.

'That's right!' exclaims Mum in her am-dram voice again. 'There was a woman just passing by on the street. A stranger. That must have been it, love.'

'Right. Of course.'

I try to smile, but inside I feel a bit sick. Are Mum and Dad *lying* to me?

'Well . . . you go off to your drinks party!' I say. 'Have a great time!'

As the front door slams, I feel like bursting into tears. I was *so* looking forward to today. But now I almost wish we'd never come back. No one seems particularly excited to see us. My rare, exotic treasure isn't exotic *or* rare. And what's going on with Mum and Dad? Why are they being so weird?

'Do you want another cup of coffee?' says Luke.

'No thanks.' Miserably I scuff my foot on the kitchen floor.

69

'Are you OK, Becky?'

There's a pause.

'No,' I admit in a small voice. 'Not really. Coming home isn't like I thought it would be.'

'Come here.' Luke holds out his arms and I nestle into his chest. 'What were you expecting? That they would drop everything and throw a party?'

'No! Of course not!' There's silence. I look up and meet Luke's eye. 'Well . . . maybe. Kind of. We've been away all this time and it's like . . . we just popped out to the shops!'

'It was always going to be a gamble, surprising everyone,' he says reasonably. 'They weren't expecting us for another two months. It's no wonder they're a bit thrown.'

'I know. But it's not just that.' I take a deep breath. 'Luke – do you think Mum and Dad seem to be . . . hiding something?'

'Yes,' says Luke.

'*Yes?*'

I'm gobsmacked. I was expecting him to say, 'Becky, you're imagining things,' like he usually does.

'There's certainly something going on.' Luke pauses. 'And I think I know what it might be.'

'What?' I stare at him, agog.

'That woman who was with them. The one they wouldn't tell us about? I reckon she's an estate agent. I think they're considering moving house.'

'Moving house?' I echo in dismay. 'Why would they do that? This is a lovely house! It's perfect!'

'It is a bit big for them now you've gone.'

'But why on earth wouldn't they tell me?' My voice rises in distress. 'I'm their daughter! I'm their only child! They should confide in me!'

'Maybe they thought you might get upset,' suggests Luke.

'I wouldn't get upset!' I exclaim indignantly.

Abruptly I realize I *am* upset.

'Well, OK. Maybe I would. But still, I can't believe they'd keep it a secret!'

I break away from Luke's arms and walk over to the window. I can't bear the idea of Mum and Dad selling this place. My eye sweeps over the garden in sudden nostalgia. They *can't* leave this garden. They just can't. Not after all the effort Dad's made with the begonias.

Suddenly my attention is caught by the sight of Tom Webster in next-door's garden. He's dressed in jeans and a T-shirt reading 'My wife left me and all I got was this lousy T-shirt' and is struggling to carry the hugest plank of wood I've ever seen.

Blimey. He looks quite ferocious.

'It may not be that,' Luke is saying behind me. 'I may be wrong.'

'You're not wrong.' I turn round miserably. 'It has to be that. What else could it be?'

'Well . . . don't think about it. Come on. It's the christening tomorrow. You'll see Suze!'

'Yes.' I feel my spirits rise. 'That's true.'

Luke's right. Maybe today hasn't gone quite according to plan – but tomorrow will be fantastic. I'll be reunited with Suze again, my best, most closest friend in the whole entire world. I just can't *wait*.

FIVE

The twins' christening is being held at Suze's parents' house in Hampshire, because they've been living there while the East Wing of Tarquin's Scottish castle is being rebuilt. They would have used his house in Pembrokeshire, but it's being lived in by some distant cousins at the moment. And his house in Sussex is being used as a location for a Jane Austen film.

This is what Suze's family is like. Nobody has just one house. On the other hand, nobody has a power shower, either.

As we crackle down the familiar gravel drive, I'm jumping with excitement.

'Hurry up!' I say as Luke manoeuvres the car into a parking space. He hasn't even turned off the engine before I'm leaping out of the car and sprinting towards the house. Now I'm here, I just can't wait to see Suze!

The heavy front door is ajar and I cautiously push it open. Inside, the huge flagstoned hall is decorated with the most amazing arrangements of lilies. A pair of waiters are striding through with champagne glasses on a tray. And on the ancient chair by the fireplace is a discarded saddle. Nothing's changed here, then.

The waiters disappear down a corridor, and I'm left alone. As I walk cautiously over the flagstones, I suddenly feel a bit nervous. What if Suze backs away like my parents? What if she's gone all weird, too?

And then, with a jolt, I spot her through an open door, standing in the drawing room. Her blond hair is up in a chignon and she's wearing a gorgeous print wrap dress. And in her arms is a tiny baby dressed in a long christening robe. Wow. That must be one of the twins.

Tarquin is standing near by, holding a second baby which is also in a christening robe. And although he's wearing the most ancient suit in the world, he's actually looking pretty good! Not quite as ... stoaty as he used to look. Maybe Tarquin will get better-looking as he gets older, it occurs to me. When he's fifty he'll probably be a sex-god!

A blond-haired toddler is clutching his leg, and as I watch, he gently prises his fingers off.

'Ernie,' he says patiently.

Ernie? I feel an almighty shock. My godson, Ernest? But last time I saw him he was a tiny little baby.

'Wilfie looks like a girl!' Suze is saying to Tarquin, her brow crumpled in that familiar way. 'And Clementine looks like a boy!'

'My sweet, they both look exactly like babies in christening robes,' says Tarquin.

'What if they're both gay?' Suze is looking anxiously at Tarquin. 'What if their hormones got mixed up when they were in the womb?'

'They're fine!'

I feel ridiculously shy, hovering by the door. I don't want to interrupt. They look like a family. They *are* a family.

'What's the time?' Suze tries to consult her watch, but Ernie is now clinging on to her arm, trying to jump up. 'Ernie, sweetheart, I need to do my lipstick! Leave Mummy's arm alone ... Can you take him for a sec, Tarkie?'

'Let me just put Clemmie down somewhere...'

Tarquin starts looking around the room as though a cot might magically spring up out of nowhere.

'I'll take her if you like,' I say, my voice a little jumpy.

There's silence. Suze whips round.

'Bex?' As she sees me, her eyes widen to the size of dinner plates. '*Bex?*'

'We're back!' I give a tremulous laugh. 'Surprise!'

'Oh my God! Oh my *God*!'

Suze thrusts the baby at Tarquin, who manfully does a kind of juggling act with the two of them. She races towards me and throws her arms around my neck.

'Bex! Mrs Brandon!'

'Mrs Cleath-Stuart!' I return, feeling tears prick at my eyes. I knew Suze wouldn't have changed. I *knew* it.

'I can't believe you're back!' Suze's face is glowing. 'Tell me all about your honeymoon! Tell me every single thing you—' She breaks off suddenly, staring at my bag. 'Oh my God,' she breathes. 'Is that a *real* Angel bag?'

Ha! You see? People who know, know.

'Of course it is.' I swing it nonchalantly on my arm. 'Just a little souvenir from Milan. Er . . . I wouldn't mention it in front of Luke, though,' I add, lowering my voice. 'He doesn't exactly know about it.'

'Bex!' says Suze half-reprovingly, half-laughing. 'He's your husband!'

'Exactly.' I meet her eye, and we both start giggling. God, it's just like old times.

'So, how's married life?' asks Suze.

'It's perfect.' I sigh happily. 'Totally blissful. Well, you know. Like couples are on their honeymoon!'

'I was pregnant on our honeymoon.' Suze looks a bit discomfited. She reaches out and strokes the Angel bag in awe. 'I didn't even know you were going to Milan! Where else did you go?'

'We went everywhere! All over the world!'

'Did you go to the ancient shrine of Mahakala?' comes a booming voice from the door. I swivel round to see Suze's mother, Caroline, coming into the room. She's in the strangest dress I've ever seen, made out of what looks like pea-green canvas.

'Yes!' I say in delight. 'We did!'

It was Caroline who got me into the idea of travelling in the first place, when she told me her best friend in the world was a Bolivian peasant.

'The ancient Inca city of Ollantaytambo?'

'We stayed there!'

Caroline's eyes gleam, as though I've passed the test, and I feel a glow of pride. I am a genuine traveller! I won't add that we were in the five-star spa.

'Just saw the vicar,' Caroline's telling Suze. 'He was saying some rubbish about warm water for the baptism. I said absolutely not! A bit of cold water'll do these infants the power of good.'

'Mummy!' wails Suze. 'I especially *asked* for warm water! They're still so tiny!'

'Nonsense!' booms Caroline. 'At their age, you were swimming in the lake! At the age of six months you were trekking with me up the Tsodila Hills of Botswana. No warm water there!'

Suze gives me a despairing look, and I grin back sympathetically.

'I'd better go,' she says. 'Bex, I'll see you later. You will stay a couple of days, won't you?'

'We'd love to!' I say happily.

'Oh, and you *must* meet Lulu!' she adds, halfway out of the door.

'Who's Lulu?' I call back, but she doesn't hear.

Oh well. I'll soon find out. It's probably her new horse, or something.

I find Luke outside, where a tented walkway has been set up between the house and the church, just like at

Suze's wedding. As we start walking along the matting, I can't help feeling a tingle of nostalgia. It was here that we first talked about getting married, in a roundabout sort of way. And then Luke proposed.

And now here we are. Married for nearly a year!

I hear footsteps coming up behind and look round to see Tarquin hurrying along the matting, holding a baby.

'Hi, Tarkie!' I say as he joins us. 'So . . . which twin is this?'

'This one is Clementine,' Tarquin says with a beam. 'Our little Clemmie.'

I peer more closely, and try to hide my surprise. Blimey. Suze is right. She does look like a boy.

'She's beautiful!' I say quickly. 'Absolutely gorgeous!'

I'm trying to think of something to say which will emphasize her very *feminine* qualities, when there's a faint sound from up above. A kind of chopper-chopper-chopper. Now it's getting louder. I look up, and to my astonishment, a huge black helicopter is approaching. In fact . . . it's landing, in the field behind the house.

'Do you have a friend with a helicopter?' I say, amazed.

'Arm . . . actually, that's mine,' says Tarquin bashfully. 'Lent it to a friend for a spin.'

Tarquin has a *helicopter*?

OK, you'd think a man with a zillion houses and a helicopter could afford a nice new suit.

By now we've arrived at the church, which is bustling with guests. Luke and I slip into a pew near the back, and I look around at all Suze's relations. There's Tarquin's dad, wearing an aubergine-coloured smoking jacket, and there's Fenella, Tarquin's sister. She's dressed in blue and is shrieking excitedly at some girl with blond hair I don't recognize.

'Who's that, Agnes?' comes a piercing voice behind me. I glance round, and a woman with grey hair and a gigantic ruby brooch is peering at the blonde girl too, through a lorgnette.

'That's Fenella, dear!' says the woman in green sitting next to her.

'I don't mean Fenella! I mean the other girl, talking to her.'

'D'you mean Lulu? That's Lulu Hetherington.'

I feel a tweak of surprise. Lulu isn't a horse. She's a girl.

I look at her a bit more carefully. Actually, she does look quite like a horse. She's very thin and rangy, like Suze, and wearing a pink tweed suit. As I watch, she laughs at something Fenella says – and she's got one of those smiles which exposes all her teeth and gums.

'She's one of the godmothers,' Agnes is saying. '*Super* girl. She's Susan's best friend.'

What?

I look up, taken aback. That's ridiculous. *I'm* Suze's best friend. Everyone knows that.

'Lulu moved into the village six months ago and they've become quite inseparable!' Agnes is continuing. 'We see them out riding together every day. She's so like dear Susan. Just look at the two of them together!'

At the front of the church, Suze has appeared, holding Wilfrid. And I suppose there is a superficial likeness between her and Lulu. They're both tall and blonde. They've both got their hair in the same chignon. Suze is talking to Lulu, her face shining with animation, and as I watch, they both burst into peals of laughter.

'And of course they have so much in common!' Agnes's voice cuts through the air behind me. 'What with the horses and the children . . . they're *wonderful* support for each other.'

'Every girl needs a best friend,' says the other woman wisely.

She breaks off as the organ starts playing. The congregation stands up and I reach for my service sheet along with everyone else. But I can't read a word. I'm a bit jumbled up inside.

Those people have got it all wrong. That girl isn't Suze's best friend. *I* am.

After the service is over, we all head back to the house, where a string quartet is playing in the hall and waiters are circulating with drinks. Luke is immediately accosted by some friend of Tarquin's who knows him through business, and I stand for a while on my own, brooding on what I heard in the church.

'Bex!' As I hear Suze's voice behind me, I wheel round in relief.

'Suze!' I beam at her. 'That was great!'

Just seeing Suze's friendly face sweeps all my worries away. Of course we're still best friends. Of course we are!

I have to remember that I've been away for a long time. So of course Suze had to make friends with people locally or whatever. But the point is – I'm back now!

'Suze, let's go shopping tomorrow!' I say impulsively. 'We can go up to London . . . I'll help you with the babies . . .'

'Bex, I can't.' Her brow wrinkles. 'I promised Lulu I'd go riding tomorrow morning.'

For a moment I'm silenced. Couldn't she cancel riding?

'Oh, right.' I try to smile. 'Well . . . no problem. We'll do it another time!'

The baby in Suze's arms has started to wail lustily and she pulls a face.

'I've got to go and feed them now. But then I *must* introduce you to Lulu. You two will love each other!'

'I'm sure we will!' I say, trying to sound enthusiastic. 'See you later!'

I watch as Suze disappears into the library.

'Champagne, madam?' says a waiter behind me.

'Oh right. Thanks.'

I take a glass of champagne off the tray. Then, with a sudden thought, I take another. I head for the library door and am about to reach for the handle when Lulu comes out, closing the door behind her.

'Oh hello!' she says in a posh, clipped voice. 'Suze is feeding in there, actually.'

'I know.' I smile. 'I'm her friend, Becky. I've brought her some champagne.'

Lulu smiles back – but her hand doesn't move off the door handle.

'I think she'd probably like some privacy,' she says pleasantly.

For a moment I'm too astounded to reply.

Privacy? From *me*?

I was with Suze when she gave birth to Ernie! I feel like retorting. I've seen more of her than you *ever* will!

But no. I'm not going to get into scoring points when we've only just met. Come on. Make an effort.

'So you must be Lulu,' I say as warmly as I can, and hold out my hand. 'I'm Becky.'

'You're Becky. Yes, I've heard about you.'

Why does she look amused? What has Suze said?

'And you're Clementine's godmother!' I say heartily. 'That's . . . lovely!'

I'm trying as hard as I can to make a connection. But there's just something about her that makes me shrink away. Her lips are a bit too thin. Her eyes are a bit too cold.

'Cosmo!' she suddenly barks. I follow her gaze and see a toddler blundering into the string quartet. 'Come away, darling!'

'Cosmo! Great name,' I say, trying to be friendly. 'Like, after the magazine?'

'The *magazine*?' She stares at me as though I'm a

total imbecile. 'Actually, it comes from the ancient Greek word Kosmos. Meaning "perfect order".'

I feel a prickle of embarrassment, tinged with resentment. How was I supposed to know that?

Anyway, *she's* the stupid one, because how many people have heard of *Cosmo* magazine? About a million. And how many have heard of some old Greek word? About three. Exactly.

'Do you have children?' she says with polite interest.

'Er . . . no.'

'Do you keep horses?'

'Er . . . no.'

There's silence. Lulu seems to have run out of questions. I guess it's my turn.

'So . . . how many children do you have?'

'Four,' she replies. 'Cosmo, Ludo, Ivo and Clarissa. Two, three, five and eight.'

'Wow. That must keep you busy.'

'Oh, it's a different world, when you have children,' she says smugly. 'Everything changes. You can't imagine.'

'I probably can,' I say with a laugh. 'I helped out Suze when Ernie was newborn. So I know what it's like—'

'No.' She gives me a patronizing smile. 'Until you've actually been a mother you have no idea. None at all.'

'Right,' I say, feeling squashed.

How can Suze be friendly with this woman? How?

Suddenly there's a rattling at the library door and Suze appears. She's holding a baby in one arm and her mobile in the other and is a picture of consternation.

'Hi Suze!' I say quickly. 'I was just bringing you a glass of champagne!' I hold it out to her, but Suze doesn't seem to notice.

'Lulu, Wilfie's got a rash!' she says anxiously. 'Have yours ever had this?'

'Let's have a look,' says Lulu, expertly taking the

baby out of Suze's grasp. She examines him for a moment. 'I think it's heat rash.'

'Really?'

'It looks like nettle rash to me,' I say, trying to join in. 'Has he been near any nettles recently?'

No one seems interested in what I think.

'You want Sudocrem,' says Lulu. 'I'll get some for you, if you like. I'm popping to the chemist's later on.'

'Thanks, Lulu. You're an angel!' Suze takes Wilfie back gratefully, just as her mobile rings.

'Hi!' she says into it. 'At last! Where are you?' As she listens her whole face crumples in dismay. 'You're joking!'

'What's wrong?' Lulu and I both say, simultaneously.

'It's Mr Happy!' wails Suze, turning to Lulu. 'He's got a puncture! He's by Tiddlington Marsh.'

'Who's Mr Happy?' I say in bewilderment.

'The entertainer!' says Suze desperately. 'There's a whole roomful of children in there, just waiting for him!' She gestures to a pair of double doors, beyond which I can see lots of children in party dresses and smart little shirts, racing about and throwing cushions at each other.

'I'll zip along and pick him up,' says Lulu, putting down her glass. 'At least we know where he is. I'll only be ten minutes. Tell him to stay put and look out for the Range Rover.'

'Lulu, you're a total star,' says Suze, subsiding in relief. 'I don't know what I'd do without you.'

I feel a twinge of jealousy. *I* want to be the one who helps Suze. *I* want to be the total star.

'I don't mind picking him up!' I say. 'I'll go!'

'You don't know where it is,' says Lulu kindly. 'Better if I go.'

'What about the children?' Suze glances nervously at the room, where the sound of screaming kids is getting louder.

'They'll just have to wait. If there isn't an entertainer, there isn't an entertainer.'

'But—'

'I'll entertain them!' I say before I can stop myself.

'*You?*' They both turn and gape at me.

'Yes, me,' I say confidently.

Ha. I'll show them who's the most supportive friend to Suze.

'Bex . . . are you sure about this?' says Suze, looking anxious.

'No problem!' I say.

'But—'

'Suze . . .' I put a hand on her arm. 'Please. I think I can amuse a few children for ten minutes.'

Oh my God.

This is utter mayhem.

I can't hear myself think. I can't hear anything except the screaming of twenty excited children running round a room, bashing each other.

'Er . . . excuse me . . .' I begin.

The shrieks increase in volume. I'm sure someone's being murdered in here, only I can't see who because it's all a blur.

'Sit down!' I bellow over the noise. 'Sit down, everyone!'

They're not even stopping for a beat. I climb up on to a chair and put my hands round my mouth.

'Anyone who sits down . . .' I roar, 'will get a SWEETIE!'

Abruptly the screaming stops and there's a crash as twenty children bump down on to the floor.

'Hello everybody!' I say brightly. 'I'm . . . I'm Wacky Becky!' I waggle my head. 'Everybody say, "Hello Wacky Becky!"'

There's silence.

'Where's my sweetie?' pipes up a little girl.

82

'Er . . .'

I scrabble in my bag, but there's nothing except some herbal sleeping tablets I bought for getting over jet lag. Orange flavoured.

Could I . . .

No. No.

'Later!' I say. 'You have to sit still . . . and then you get a sweetie.'

'This conjuror is *rubbish*,' says a boy in a Ralph Lauren shirt.

'I'm not rubbish!' I say indignantly. 'Watch! Er . . .'

I quickly put my hands over my face, then pull them away.

'Boo!'

'We're not babies,' says the boy scornfully. 'We want tricks!'

'Why don't I sing you a nice song?' I say in soothing tones. 'Row, row, row the boat . . . la la la . . . the moat . . .'

'Do a trick!' squeals the little girl.

'We want a trick!' yells the boy.

'Do. A. Trick! Do. A. Trick!'

Oh God. They're chanting. And the boys are banging the floor with their fists. Any minute, they're going to get up and start bashing each other again. A trick. A trick. My mind scurries about frantically. Do I *know* any tricks?

'OK!' I say in desperation. 'I'll do a trick! Watch this!'

I spread my arms with a flourish, then reach behind my back with swirly, elaborate movements, spinning it all out as long as I can.

Then I unhook my bra through my shirt, trying to remember what colour it is.

Oh yes. It's my bright-pink one with the bows. Perfect.

The entire room is agog.

'What are you doing?' says a little girl with wide eyes.

'Wait and see!'

Trying to keep the air of mystery, I loop one bra-strap discreetly over my arm, then the other. The children are all staring at me avidly.

Now I've got my confidence back, I think I'm doing rather well at this. In fact, I'm a bit of a natural!

'Watch very carefully,' I say in a solemn, magician's voice, 'as I am now going to make something . . . APPEAR!'

A couple of children gasp.

I could really do with a drum roll here.

'One . . . two . . . three . . .' In a flash of pink I pull my bra out from my sleeve, and hold it aloft. 'Ta-daah!'

The whole room erupts in ecstatic cheers.

'She did magic!' a red-haired boy shouts.

'Again!' squeals the little girl. 'Do it again!'

'Do you want to see me do it again?' I say, beaming in delight.

'Yaaaaay!' they all scream.

'I don't *think* so!' comes a bright, clipped voice from the door. I turn round – and Lulu is standing there, looking at me with undisguised horror.

Oh no.

Oh God. My bra is still whirling round in my hand.

'They wanted me to do a trick,' I explain, with an attempt at a nonchalant shrug.

'I hardly think those are the sort of "tricks" that children are going to appreciate!' she says, raising her eyebrows. She turns to the room with a bright, mummy smile. 'Who wants to see Mr Happy?'

'We want Wacky Becky!' yells the boy. 'She took off her bra!'

Fuck.

'Wacky Becky's got to . . . er . . . go now!' I say brightly. 'But see you next time, children!'

84

Without quite meeting Lulu's eye I squash my bra into a tiny ball, stuff it into my bag and back out of the room. I head over to the buffet table, where Luke is helping himself to salmon.

'Are you OK?' he says in surprise. 'You're very pink.'

'I'm . . . fine.' I grab his glass and take a deep gulp of champagne. 'Everything's fine.'

But it's not really fine.

I keep waiting for Lulu to leave, so I can have a good chat with Suze – but she doesn't. She hangs around, helping to make the children's tea, and clear up. Every time I try to help, she's there before me with a damp cloth or a beaker or some piece of mummy advice. She and Suze keep up a constant dialogue about the children, and it's impossible for me to get a word in.

It's not until about ten o'clock at night that she leaves, and I finally find myself alone in the kitchen with Suze. She's sitting by the Aga, feeding one of the twins and yawning hugely every three minutes.

'So you had a lovely honeymoon?' she says wistfully.

'It was fantastic. Totally perfect. We went to this amazing place in Australia where you could scuba-dive, and—

I break off as Suze yawns again. Maybe I'll tell her tomorrow.

'How about you? How's life with three kids?'

'Oh, you know.' She gives a tired smile. 'It's fine. Exhausting. Everything's different.'

'And . . . you've been spending loads of time with Lulu,' I say casually.

'Isn't she great?' says Suze, her face lighting up.

'Er . . . great.' I pause carefully. 'She does seem a *teeny* bit bossy . . .'

'*Bossy?*' Suze looks up in shock. 'Bex, how can you

say that? She's been my total saviour out here! She's helped me so much!'

'Oh right.' I backtrack hastily. 'I didn't mean—'

'She knows exactly what I'm going through.' Suze sighs. 'I mean, she's had four! She really *understands*.'

'Right.'

And I don't understand. That's what she means.

As I stare into my glass of wine, there's a sudden heaviness about my head. None of my reunions are going quite like I thought they would.

I stand up and wander over to the Aga, where lots of family photos are always pinned up on the cork wall. There's a picture of me and Suze dressed up for a party in feather boas and glittery make-up. And one of Suze and me in hospital with a tiny Ernie.

Then, with a pang, I notice a brand-new picture of Suze and Lulu, sitting on their horses, in matching riding jackets and hairnets. They're beaming at the camera and look just like identical twins.

And as I gaze at it, I feel a sudden determination growing. I'm not losing my best friend to some bossy horse-faced riding queen. Whatever Lulu can do, I can do.

'Maybe I'll come riding with you and Lulu tomorrow,' I say casually. 'If you've got a spare horse.'

I'll even wear a hairnet, if that's what it takes.

'You'll come?' Suze looks up, staggered. 'But . . . Bex. You don't ride.'

'Yes I do,' I say airily. 'Luke and I did some riding on honeymoon, actually.'

Which is sort of true. Nearly. We were going to go on a camel ride in Dubai, except in the end we went snorkelling instead.

But anyway, it doesn't matter. It'll be fine. I mean, come on. Riding can't be that hard. You just sit on the horse and steer. Easy.

SIX

By ten o'clock the next morning I'm ready. And I don't
want to boast – but as I survey myself in the mirror, I
look utterly fab! Luke drove me to the riding shop in
the next village first thing this morning, and I totally
kitted myself out. I'm wearing snowy white jodhpurs,
a tailored black riding jacket, shiny boots and a
beautiful new velvet riding hat.

Proudly I reach for my *pièce de resistance* – a big red
rosette with shiny ribbons. There were loads of them
for sale, so I bought one in every colour! I carefully pin
it on to my collar like a corsage, smooth down my
jacket and look at the effect.

God, I look so cool. I look like I'm going to win at
Crufts.

No. I don't mean Crufts. I mean the other one. The
horse one.

Maybe I'll start riding every day in Hyde Park, I
think in a sudden burst of excitement. Maybe I'll get
really good. Then I can come down here every weekend and ride with Suze. We can go in for gymkhanas
and stuff and be a team! And she'll forget all about
stupid Lulu.

'Tally-ho!' says Luke, coming into the bedroom.
'You look very dashing.'

'I look cool, don't I?' I beam at him.

'Very sexy.' He raises his eyebrows. 'Great boots. How long are you going to be?'

'Not that long,' I say knowledgeably. 'We're just going to go for a hack through the woods.'

I got that word 'hack' at the riding shop.

'Becky . . .' Luke looks at me carefully. 'Have you ever been on a horse in your life?'

'Yes!' I say after a pause. 'Of course I have!'

Once. When I was ten. And I fell off. But I probably wasn't concentrating or something.

'Just be careful, won't you?' he says. 'I'm not quite ready to become a widower.'

Honestly. What is he worrying about?

'I'd better go!' I say, glancing at my special new 'equestrian' watch with compass built in. 'I'll be late!'

The horses are all kept some way from the house in a stable block, and as I approach, I can hear the sound of whinnying and hooves clattering on the stable yard.

'Hi!' says Lulu, appearing round the corner in a pair of ancient jodhpurs and a fleece. 'All set –' She breaks off as she sees me. 'Oh my God.' She snorts with laughter. 'Suze, come and look at Becky!'

'What is it?' Suze hurries round the corner and stops dead.

'Gosh, Bex,' she says. 'You're very . . . smart!'

I take in Suze's filthy old jodhpurs, her muddy boots and her battered riding hat.

'I wanted to make an effort!' I say, trying to sound light and matter-of-fact.

'What's that?' Lulu is looking incredulously at my rosette.

'It's a corsage. They were selling them in the riding shop,' I add pointedly.

'For the horses,' says Suze gently. 'Bex, they go on the horses.'

'Oh.'

For a moment I'm a bit discomfited. But then . . .

why shouldn't people wear them too? God, horsey people are so narrow-minded.

'Here we are!' Albert, who runs the horses at Suze's parents' place, interrupts us. He's leading an enormous brown horse along by the reins. 'We're putting you on Ginger today. He's pretty good-natured, aren't you, boy?'

I freeze in horror. This? He's expecting me to get on this monster?

Albert hands me the reins and I take them automatically, trying not to panic. The horse takes a step forward with an enormous heavy hoof, and I give a frightened jump out of the way. What if it steps on my foot?

'Aren't you going to mount?' says Lulu, swinging herself up into the saddle of a horse which is, if anything, bigger than mine.

'Of course!' I say with a nonchalant laugh.

How? How am I supposed to get up there?

'Want a leg up?' says Tarquin, who has been talking to Albert a few yards away. He comes up behind me and before I know it, he's hefted me right up on to the saddle.

Oh my God.

I'm so *high*. When I look down, I feel dizzy. Suddenly Ginger takes a step sideways, and I try not to gasp in fright.

'Shall we go?' calls Suze, who is on her old black horse Pepper, and with a clip-clop she's off through the gate, into the field. Lulu makes a clicking sound with her tongue, swings her horse round and follows.

Right. My turn. Go.

Go on, horse. *Move.*

I have no idea what to do next. Do I kick it? Experimentally I pull on one of the reins, but nothing happens.

'Gee-up,' I mutter under my breath. 'Gee-up, Ginger!'

Suddenly, as though he's noticed that his friends have gone, he starts walking forward. And it's . . . OK. It's fine. It's just a bit more . . . *bumpy* than I imagined. I look ahead at Lulu, and she's totally comfortable. In fact, she's got her reins gathered up in one hand, which I think is just showing off.

'Close the gate!' she yells to me.

Close the gate? I think in panic. How am I supposed to close the gate?

'I'll do it,' calls Tarquin. 'Have a good time!'

'OK!' I call back gaily.

Right. As long as we just keep ambling along, I'll be OK. In fact, this could almost be fun. The sun's shining, the breeze is ruffling the grass, the horses are all lovely and shiny, and we all look really picturesque.

And I'm not trying to show off, but I think I look the best. My clothes are *definitely* the best. Some people are walking along the side of the field on a footpath, and as we pass by I give them a nonchalant 'Don't I look great on my horse?' nod and twirl my riding crop. And they look really impressed! They probably think I'm a professional or something.

Maybe I've found my natural talent. Maybe Luke and I should buy some horses and a few acres of land. We could really get into it. We could do eventing and show jumping, like Suze—

Shit. What's going on? All of a sudden, Ginger has started jolting up and down.

Is this trotting?

I look at Suze and Lulu, and they're both rising up and falling in time with their horses.

How are they doing that?

I try to copy – but all that happens is I crash painfully back on to the saddle. Ouch. God, saddles are hard. Why don't they make them padded? If I was a horse-saddle designer I'd make them really soft and comfy, with furry cushions and drinks holders maybe, and—

'Shall we canter?' calls Suze over her shoulder. Before I can reply she's kicked her horse, and it's zooming away like National Velvet, closely followed by Lulu.

'We don't have to canter, Ginger,' I say quickly to the horse. 'We can just—'

Oh my Goooooood. He's taken off after the others.

Fuck. Oh fuck. I am going to fall off. I know I am. My whole body is rigid. I'm clenching on to the saddle so hard it's hurting my hands.

'Are you OK, Bex?' shouts Suze.

'Fine!' I call back in a strangled voice.

I just want this to stop. The wind is streaming past my face. I feel ill with terror.

I'm going to die. My life is over. The only plus I can think of is it'll sound really cool when they report it in the papers.

A keen horsewoman, Rebecca Brandon (née Bloomwood) died whilst out cantering with her friends.

Oh God. I think he's slowing down. At last. We're trotting . . . we're kind of jogging . . . and finally coming to a halt.

Somehow I manage to unclench my hands.

'Isn't it lovely?' says Suze, turning round on Pepper. Her blond hair is streaming out from under her hat and her cheeks are flushed pink. 'Shall we have a really good gallop?'

Gallop?

You have to be kidding. If Ginger takes one more step I'll throw up.

'Can you jump yet, Bex?' she adds. 'There's just a couple of little ones coming up. But you should be able to manage them,' she says encouragingly. 'You're really good!'

For a moment I can't speak.

'I just need to . . . er . . . adjust my stirrup,' I manage at last. 'You two go on.'

I wait until the two of them are out of sight before I slither to the ground. My legs are all shaky and I feel nauseous. I am never leaving solid ground again. Never. Why on earth would people do this for fun?

My heart pumping, I sink down on to the grass. I take off my new riding hat – which, to be honest, has been hurting my ears since I put it on – and throw it down dolefully.

Suze and Lulu are probably miles away by now. Galloping along and talking about nappies.

I sit there for a few minutes, getting my composure back and watching Ginger munch at the grass. Then at last I rouse myself and look around the empty field. Right. What am I going to do now?

'Come on,' I say to Ginger. 'Let's walk back.' I stand up and cautiously pull the reins – and to my astonishment he obediently follows.

This is more like it. This is the way to do it.

As I walk across the grass, I start to relax a bit. A horse is actually a pretty cool accessory. Who says you need to get on it? I could still go to Hyde Park every day. I could buy a really pretty horse and just lead it around like a dog. And if any passers-by asked, 'Why aren't you riding?' I'd just give them a knowing smile and say, 'We're resting today.'

We wander along for a while and at last come to an empty road. I stand for a moment, looking from left to right. In one direction, the road disappears up a hill and round a corner. In the other, I can see what seems to be quite a sweet little village. All beamed houses, and a patch of grass, and—

Ooh. Are those . . . shops?

OK. This day is looking up.

* * *

Half an hour later I feel a lot better.

I've bought some gorgeous cheese with walnuts in it, and some gooseberry preserve, and some huge radishes, which Luke will love. And best of all – I found this amazing little shop that sells hats. Right here in this village! Apparently the milliner is local and is practically the next Philip Treacy. I mean, not that I wear hats that often . . . but I'm bound to be invited to a wedding soon, or Ascot or something. And the prices were fantastic. So I bought a white one decorated with ostrich feathers and a black velvet one all covered in jewels. They're a bit cumbersome in their hat boxes, but they were *so* worth it.

Ginger whinnies as I approach the lamp-post where I tied him up, and stamps his foot on the ground.

'Don't worry!' I say. 'I haven't left you out.' I bought him a bag full of Chelsea buns and some 'extra sheen' shampoo for his mane. I reach in my bag and feed him one of the Chelsea buns, trying not to shudder as he slobbers on my hand.

The only slight problem now is . . . where am I going to put all my shopping? I can't very easily hold all these carrier bags and lead Ginger along the road. I look consideringly at him. Should I try to mount him, *carrying* my shopping? What did people do in the olden days?

Then suddenly I notice a big buckle-type thing on one of Ginger's saddle straps. I could easily hang a bag off that. I pick up one of the paper carriers and loop it over the buckle – and it hangs there perfectly! And now I look properly, there are handy buckle things all over Ginger's tack. Genius! This must be what they're meant for!

Happily I start hanging bags from every available hook, strap and buckle on Ginger's tack. This is great. I never realized a horse could hold so much shopping. Last of all I tie my two hat boxes on to the side.

They are so gorgeous, all pink and white candy stripes.

OK. We're ready.

I untie Ginger and start leading him out of the village, trying to stop the hat boxes bobbing up and down too much. A couple of people gawp as we go by, but that's OK. They're probably just not used to strangers in these parts.

We're just approaching the first bend when I hear a clattering sound ahead. The next moment, Suze and Lulu appear on their horses.

'There she is!' says Lulu, shading her eyes against the sun.

'Bex!' cries Suze. 'We were worried! Are you OK?'

'I'm fine!' I call back. 'We've been having a lovely time!'

As they near, I can see Suze and Lulu exchanging stunned glances.

'Bex . . . what have you done to Ginger?' says Suze, her eyes running over all the bags and boxes in disbelief.

'Nothing,' I say. 'He's fine. I just took him shopping. I got these two great hats!'

I wait for Suze to say 'Let's see them!' but she looks totally gobsmacked.

'She took a horse . . . shopping,' says Lulu slowly. She glances at me, then leans over and whispers something in Suze's ear.

Suddenly Suze gives a helpless snort and claps her hand to her mouth.

I feel my face flame.

She's laughing at me.

Somehow I never thought Suze would laugh at me.

'I'm just not that great at riding,' I say, trying to keep my voice steady. 'I thought I'd let you two gallop off. Anyway. Come on. We'd better get back.'

The other two swing their horses round and we

make our way slowly back to Suze's house, practically in silence.

As soon as we're back at the house, Lulu heads off home, and Suze has to rush in and feed the twins. I'm left in the stable yard with Albert, who is a total sweetie and helps me untie all my bags and packages from Ginger's tack.

I'm walking out, laden with bags, when Luke approaches, still in his Barbour and wellingtons.

'So how was it?' he says cheerfully.

'It was . . . all right,' I say, staring at the ground. I'm waiting for Luke to ask what's wrong, but he seems distracted.

'Becky, I've just had a call from Gary at the office,' he says. 'We need to get going on the Arcodas Group pitch. I'm really sorry, but I'm going to have to head back to town. But listen. Why don't you stay on here for a few days?' He smiles. 'I know how desperate you were to see Suze.'

And suddenly I feel a swell of emotion. He's right. I was desperate to see Suze and I'm bloody well going to. Who cares about stupid Lulu? I'm going to have a proper chat with my best friend, right now.

I hurry into the house, to find her feeding both the twins at once, while Ernie fights for a place on her lap.

'Suze, listen,' I say eagerly. 'It's your birthday coming up. I want to treat you to something really special. Let's go to Milan! Just the two of us!'

'*Milan?*' She looks up, her face strained. 'Ernie, stop it, sweetheart. Bex, I can't go to Milan! What about the babies?'

'They could come with us!'

'No they *couldn't*,' says Suze, sounding almost sharp. 'Bex, you just don't understand!'

I feel a smarting at her words. Why does everyone

keep telling me I don't understand? How do they know?

'OK then,' I say, trying to stay cheerful. 'Let's have a fab birthday lunch right here! I'll bring all the food, you won't have to do a thing . . .'

'I can't,' says Suze, without looking at me. 'Actually I've . . . I've already made plans for my birthday. Lulu and I are going to a spa for the day. A special mother-and-baby day. She's treating me.'

I stare at her, unable to hide my shock. Suze and I always spend our birthdays together.

'Right.' I swallow several times. 'Well . . . have fun. Enjoy it!'

There's silence in the kitchen. I don't know what to say.

I've never not known what to say to Suze.

'Bex . . . you weren't here,' says Suze suddenly, and I can hear the distress in her voice. 'You weren't here. What was I supposed to do? Have no friends?'

'Of course not!' I say brightly. 'Don't be silly!'

'I couldn't have survived without Lulu. She's been a real support to me out here.'

'Of course she has.' Tears are suddenly pricking at my eyes and I turn away, fiercely blinking them back. 'Well . . . you have fun together. I'm sure you will. Sorry I came back and got in the way.'

'Bex, don't be like that. Look . . . I'll speak to Lulu about the spa. I'm sure we could find a third place.'

I feel a sting of humiliation. She's taking pity on me. I can't bear it.

'No!' With an almighty effort I manage a laugh. 'Really, it's no big deal. I probably wouldn't have time anyway. In fact . . . I came in to tell you we have to go back to London. Luke's got work engagements.'

'Now?' Suze looks taken aback. 'But I thought you were going to stay for a few days.'

'We've got loads to do!' I lift my chin. 'Everything's

different for me too, you know. I'm a married woman now! I've got to set up the flat . . . look after Luke . . . throw some dinner parties . . .'

'Right.' Suze hesitates. 'Well, it's been lovely to see you, anyway.'

'You too! It's been fun! We must . . . do it again.'

We sound totally false. Both of us.

There's silence. My throat is tight. I'm going to cry.

No I'm not.

'So . . . I'll just go and pack,' I say at last. 'Thanks for a lovely time.'

I leave the room, pick up my shopping and walk away. And my bright smile lasts all the way to the stairs.

NETHER PLEATON GYMKHANA
Manor Stables
Pleaton
Hampshire

Mrs Rebecca Brandon
37 Maida Vale Mansions
Maida Vale
London NW6 0YF

30 April 2003

Dear Mrs Brandon

Thank you for your letter concerning the Neather Pleaton Gymkhana next month. I confirm that I have withdrawn your name from the following classes:

General Horsemanship
Open Jumping
Senior Dressage

Perhaps you could let me know if you still wish to enter for 'Best Kept Pony'.

With kind regards

Majorie Davies

(Organizer)

SEVEN

Anyway, it doesn't matter. I don't need Suze.

People get married and they move on and their friends change. That's all. It's perfectly normal. She has her life . . . and I have my life. It's fine. A week has gone by since the christening – and she's barely crossed my mind.

I take a sip of orange juice, pick up the *Financial Times* which Luke left on the breakfast counter, and start flicking briskly through the pages.

Now I'm married, I expect I'll make loads of new friends too. It's not like I'm dependent on Suze or anything. I'll start an evening class or a book group or something. And *my* new friends will be really nice ones who don't ride horses and have children with stupid names like Cosmo . . .

I'm flicking so furiously, I've already got to the end of the *Financial Times.* I look at it in slight surprise. Wow. That was quick. Maybe I've turned into a speed-reader without realizing.

I take a sip of coffee and spread some more chocolate spread on my toast. I'm sitting in the kitchen of Luke's flat in Maida Vale, having a late breakfast.

I mean . . . *our* flat in Maida Vale. I keep forgetting, it's half mine now! Luke lived here for ages before we were married, but when we went to live in New York he had it all done up and rented it out. And it is the trendiest place in the world. All minimalist, with this amazing stainless-steel kitchen, pale-beige carpets and just the odd piece of modern art here and there.

I do like it. Of course I do.

Although I suppose, if I'm *totally* honest, it's a tad bare for my taste. Luke has quite a different style from mine when it comes to decorating. His approach is basically 'no things anywhere', whereas mine is more 'lots of things everywhere'.

But it doesn't matter, because I read this article about couples in an interiors magazine, and it said fusing two different styles need not be a problem. Apparently all we have to do is meld our individual ideas and do some mood boards together and create a signature look.

And today is the perfect day to start. Because any minute now, all our honeymoon purchases are going to be delivered from the storage company! Luke's stayed behind from work especially to help.

I'm feeling really excited about it. Seeing all our souvenirs again! Arranging the little mementoes of our honeymoon around the apartment. It'll really make a difference to this place, having a few personal *objets* here and there.

'There's a letter for you,' says Luke, coming into the kitchen. He raises his eyebrows. 'Looks like it might be important.'

'Oh right!' I take the envelope with a dart of nerves.

Ever since we got back to London, I've been approaching all the big department stores for a job as a personal shopper. I've got a great reference from Barneys and everyone's been really nice to me – but so far all I'm getting told is that there are no openings right now.

Which, to be honest, has been a bit of a blow. I thought I'd be fighting off offers. I even had this little fantasy where all the head personal shoppers at Harrods and Harvey Nicks and Selfridges took me out to lunch and gave me free clothes to persuade me to join them.

My heart thumping, I pull the letter out of the envelope. This one is from a new shop called The Look, which hasn't even opened yet. I went to see them a couple of days ago, and I *thought* I did OK, but—

'Oh my God!' I look up in disbelief. 'I got it! They want me!'

'Fantastic!' Luke's face creases in a smile. 'Congratulations!' He puts an arm round me and gives me a kiss.

'Except . . . I won't be needed for three months,' I say, reading further down. 'That's when the store opens.' I put the letter down and look at him. 'Three whole months. That's quite a long time not to have a job.'

Or any money, I'm thinking silently.

'I'm sure you'll find something to do,' says Luke cheerfully. 'Some project or other. You'll have plenty to keep you busy.'

The buzzer suddenly goes in the hall and we look at each other.

'That must be the delivery people!' I say, feeling my spirits lift. 'Let's go down!'

Luke's penthouse has its own lift right to the front door, which is just so cool! When we first moved in, I spent the whole time just riding up and down. Until we got complaints from the neighbours.

'So, where shall we tell them to put everything?' he says as he presses the ground-floor button.

'I thought we could pile it all up in the corner of the sitting room,' I suggest. 'Behind the door. Then I can sort it out while you're at work.'

'Good idea.' Luke nods.

I'm silent for a few moments. I've suddenly remembered about the twenty Chinese silk dressing gowns. Maybe I'll be able to smuggle them in without Luke seeing.

'And if there was any overspill,' I add casually, 'we could always put it in the second bedroom.'

'Overspill?' Luke frowns. 'Becky, how much stuff are you expecting?'

'Not that much!' I say quickly. 'Hardly anything! I just meant if they've packed things in really huge boxes or something. That's all.'

Luke looks a bit suspicious and I turn away, pretending to be adjusting my watch strap. Now the moment's nearly here, I'm feeling just the odd tiny qualm.

I kind of wish I'd told him about the wooden giraffes now. Should I quickly confess?

No. It doesn't matter. It'll be fine. Luke's flat is huge. I mean, it's vast! He'll never notice a few extra things.

We push open the double doors of Luke's building and walk out, to see a man in jeans waiting on the side of the road by a small van.

'Mr Brandon?' he says, looking up.

I feel a small whoosh of relief. I *knew* we hadn't bought that much stuff. I knew it. I mean, just look at that van. It's tiny!

'Yes. That's me.' Luke holds out his hand with a pleasant smile.

'Any idea where we can park the lorries?' The man scratches his head. 'Only we're on a double yellow round the corner.'

'Lorries?' echoes Luke. 'What do you mean, lorries?' His smile has kind of frozen on his face.

'We've got two lorries to unload. Can we take them into the parking bay there?' The man gestures at the forecourt of the building.

'Of course!' I say quickly, as Luke doesn't seem able to speak. 'Go ahead!'

The man disappears and there's silence.

'So!' I say brightly. 'This is fun!'

'Two lorries?' says Luke in disbelieving tones.

'It must be a shared load!' I say quickly. 'With someone else. I mean, *obviously* we haven't bought two lorry-loads full of stuff.'

Which is true.

I mean, it's ridiculous! In ten months, we couldn't possibly have—

I'm *sure* we couldn't have—

Oh God.

There's a rumbling from round the corner, and a big white lorry appears, closely followed by another. They reverse into the forecourt of Luke's building, and there's a huge grinding noise as the backs are lowered. Luke and I hurry round and peer into the crowded depths.

Wow. It's an amazing sight. The whole lorry is crammed with objects and furniture. Some wrapped in plastic, some in paper, and some barely wrapped at all. As I feast my eyes on all the stuff, I start to feel quite emotional. It's like seeing a home-video of our entire honeymoon. The kilims from Istanbul. The gourds from Peru. And I'd totally forgotten about buying that papoose!

Some men in overalls start lifting things up and carrying them out. We stand aside to let them pass, but I'm still gazing around the inside of the lorry, lost in memories. I suddenly glimpse a tiny bronze statue and turn round with a smile.

'The Buddha! Do you remember when we got that? Luke?'

Luke isn't listening to a word. I follow his gaze – and feel a slight flip of apprehension. He's staring in disbelief at a man carrying a huge paper-wrapped package out of the other lorry. A wooden giraffe's leg is poking out of it.

Shit.

And now here comes another overalled man with the matching one.

'Becky . . . what are these giraffes doing here?' asks Luke evenly. 'I thought we agreed *not* to buy them.'

'I know,' I say hurriedly. 'I know we did. But we would have regretted it. So I took an executive decision. Honestly Luke, they'll look great! They'll be the focal point of the whole apartment!'

'And where did *those* come from?' Now Luke's looking at a pair of huge porcelain urns which I got in Hong Kong.

'Oh yes,' I say quickly. 'I was going to tell you about those. Guess what? They're copies of real Ming! The man said—'

'But what the fuck are they doing here?'

'I . . . bought them. They'll be perfect in the hall. They'll be a focal point! Everyone will admire them!'

'And that rug?' He points to a huge, multicoloured rolled-up sausage.

'It's called a "dhurrie", actually . . .' I tail away at his expression. 'I got it in India,' I add feebly.

'Without consulting me.'

'Er . . .'

I'm not sure I like Luke's expression.

'Ooh look!' I exclaim, trying to distract him. 'It's the spice rack you bought at that Kenyan market.'

Luke totally ignores me. He's goggling at a huge, unwieldy contraption being unloaded from the first lorry. It looks like a combination of a xylophone and a set of hanging copper saucepans, all in one.

'What the hell is *that*? Is that some kind of musical instrument?'

The gongs all start clanging loudly as the men

unload it, and a couple of passers-by nudge each other and giggle.

Even I'm having second thoughts about this one.

'Er . . . yes.' I clear my throat. 'Actually, that's an Indonesian gamelan.'

There's a short silence.

'An Indonesian gamelan?' echoes Luke, his voice a little strangled.

'They're cultural!' I say defensively. 'I thought we could learn to play it! And it'll be a great focal point—'

'Exactly how many focal points are we planning to *have*?' Luke looks beside himself. 'Becky, is *all* this stuff ours?'

'Dining table coming out!' calls a guy in overalls. 'Mind yourselves.'

Thank goodness. OK, quick. Let's redeem the situation.

'Look, darling,' I say hurriedly. 'It's our dining table from Sri Lanka. Remember? Our personalized table! Our symbol of married love.' I give him an affectionate smile, but he's shaking his head.

'Becky—'

'Don't spoil the moment!' I put an arm round him. 'It's our special honeymoon table! It's our heirloom of the future! We have to watch it being delivered!'

'OK,' says Luke at last. 'Whatever.'

The men are carefully carrying the table down the ramp and I have to say, I'm impressed. Bearing in mind how heavy it is, they seem to be managing it quite easily.

'Isn't it exciting?' I clutch Luke's arm as it comes into sight. 'Just think! There we were in Sri Lanka . . .'

I break off, a little confused.

This isn't the wooden table, after all. It's a transparent glass table, with curved steel legs. And another guy behind is carrying a pair of trendy red felt-covered chairs.

I stare at it in horror. A cold feeling is creeping over me.

Shit. Shit.

The table I bought at the Copenhagen Design Fair. I had *totally* forgotten about that.

How could I forget I bought a whole dining table? How?

'Hold on,' Luke's calling, his hand raised. 'Guys, that's the wrong table. Ours is wooden. A big carved wood table from Sri Lanka.'

'There's one of them an' all,' says the delivery guy. 'In the other lorry.'

'But we didn't buy this!' says Luke.

He gives me a questioning look and I quickly rearrange my features as though to say 'I'm as baffled as you are!'

Inside, my mind is working frantically. I'll deny I've ever seen it, we'll send it back, it'll all be fine . . .

' "Shipped by Mrs Rebecca Brandon," ' the guy reads aloud from the label. 'Table and ten chairs. From Denmark. Here's the signature.'

Fuck.

Very slowly, Luke turns towards me.

'Becky, did you buy a table and ten chairs in Denmark?' he says, almost pleasantly.

'Er . . .' I lick my lips nervously. 'Er . . . I . . . I might have.'

'I see.' Luke closes his eyes for a moment as though weighing up a maths problem. 'And then you bought another table – and ten *more* chairs – in Sri Lanka?'

'I forgot about the first one!' I say desperately. 'I totally forgot! Look, it was a very long honeymoon, I lost track of a few things . . .'

Out of the corner of my eye I can see a guy picking up the bundle of twenty Chinese silk dressing gowns. Shit.

I think I have to get Luke away from these lorries as soon as possible.

'We'll sort it all out,' I say quickly. 'I promise. But now, why don't you go upstairs and have a nice drink? You just relax! And I'll stay down here and do the supervising.'

An hour later it's all finished. The men close up the lorries, and I hand them a hefty tip. As they roar away I look up to see Luke coming out of the front door of the building.

'Hi!' I say. 'Well, that wasn't too bad, was it?'

'Do you want to come upstairs a minute?' says Luke in a strange voice.

I feel a slight quailing inside. Is he cross? Maybe he found the Chinese dressing gowns.

As we travel up in the lift I smile at Luke a couple of times, but he doesn't smile back.

'So . . . did you put all the stuff in the sitting room?' I say as we approach the front door. 'Or in the—'

My voice dies away as the door swings open.

Oh my God.

Luke's flat is totally unrecognizable.

The beige carpet has completely disappeared under a sea of parcels, trunks and pieces of furniture. The hall is crammed with boxes which I recognize from the outlet in Utah, plus the batik paintings from Bali and the two Chinese urns. I edge past them into the sitting room, and gulp as I look around. There are packages everywhere. Rolled-up kilims and dhurries are propped up in one corner. In another, the Indonesian gamelan is jostling for space with a slate coffee table turned on its side and a native American totem pole.

I'm sensing it's my turn to speak.

'Gosh!' I give a little laugh. 'There are quite a lot of . . . rugs, aren't there?'

'Seventeen,' says Luke, still in the same strange voice. 'I've counted.' He steps over a bamboo coffee table which I got in Thailand and looks at the label of a large wooden chest. 'This box apparently contains forty mugs.' He looks up. 'Forty mugs?'

'I know it sounds a lot,' I say quickly. 'But they were only about 50p each! It was a bargain! We'll never need to buy mugs ever again!'

Luke regards me for a moment.

'Becky, I never want to buy *anything* ever again.'

'Look . . .' I try to step towards him, but bump my knee on a painted wooden statue of Ganesh, god of Wisdom and Success. 'It's . . . it's not that bad! I know it *seems* a lot. But it's like . . . an optical illusion. Once it's all unpacked, and we put it all away, it'll look great!'

'We have five coffee tables,' says Luke, ignoring me. 'Were you aware of that?'

'Er . . . well.' I clear my throat. 'Not exactly. So we might have to . . . rationalize a bit.'

'Rationalize?' Luke looks around the room incredulously. 'Rationalize this lot? It's a mess!'

'Maybe it looks a bit of a mish-mash at the moment,' I say hurriedly. 'But I can pull it all together! I can make it work! It'll be our signature look. If we just do some mood boards—'

'Becky,' interrupts Luke, 'would you like to know what mood I'm in right now?'

'Er . . .'

I watch nervously as Luke shifts two packages from Guatemala aside and sinks down on the sofa.

'What I want to know is . . . how did you pay for all this?' he says, wrinkling his brow. 'I had a quick check through our bills, and there's no record of any Chinese urns. Or giraffes. Or tables from Copenhagen . . .' He gives me a hard look. 'What's been going on, Becky?'

I'm totally pinned. Even if I did want to run, I'd probably skewer myself on Ganesh's tusks.

'Well . . .' I can't quite meet his eye. 'I do have this . . . this credit card.'

'The one you keep hidden in your bag?' says Luke without missing a beat. 'I checked that, too.'

Oh God.

There's no way out of this.

'Actually . . . not that one.' I swallow hard. 'Another one.'

'*Another* one?' Luke is staring at me. 'You have a *second* secret credit card?'

'It's just for emergencies! Everyone has the odd emergency—'

'What, emergency dining tables? Emergency Indonesian gamelans?'

There's silence. I can't quite reply. My face is flaming red and my fingers are all twisted in knots behind my back.

'So, you've been paying it off secretly, is that it?' He looks at my agonized face and his expression changes. 'You *haven't* been paying it off?'

'The thing is . . .' My fingers twist even tighter. 'They gave me quite a big limit.'

'For God's sake, Becky!'

'It's OK! I'll pay it off! You don't need to worry about anything. I'll take care of it.'

'With what?' retorts Luke.

There's a sharp silence and I stare back at him, stung.

'When I start my job,' I say, my voice trembling a little. 'I am going to have an income, you know, Luke. I'm not some kind of *freeloader*.'

Luke looks at me for a few moments, then sighs.

'I know,' he says more gently. 'I'm sorry.' He holds out his arm. 'Come here.'

After a moment I pick my way across the crowded

floor to the sofa. I find a tiny space to sit down and he puts his arm round me. For a while we both look silently at the ocean of clutter. It's like we're two survivors on a desert island.

'Becky, we can't carry on like this,' says Luke at last. 'Do you know how much our honeymoon cost us?'

'Er . . . no.'

Suddenly it strikes me that I have absolutely no idea what anything has cost. It was me who bought the round-the-world air tickets. But apart from that, Luke's been doing all the paying, all the way along.

Has our honeymoon *ruined* us?

I dart a glance at Luke – and for the first time see how stressed he looks.

Oh God. Suddenly I feel a pang of deep fear. We've lost all our money and Luke's been trying to hide it from me. I can just tell. It's my wifely intuition.

I suddenly feel like the wife in *It's A Wonderful Life* when James Stewart comes home and snaps at the children. Even though we're on the brink of financial disgrace, it's my role to be brave and serene.

'Luke, are we *very* poor?' I say, as calmly as I can.

Luke turns his head and looks at me.

'No Becky,' he says patiently. 'We're not very poor. But we will be if you keep buying mountains of crap.'

Mountains of *crap*? I'm about to make an indignant retort when I see his expression. Instead, I close my mouth and nod humbly.

'So I think . . .' Luke pauses. 'I think we need to institute a budget.'

EIGHT

A budget.

This is OK. I can handle a budget. Easily. In fact, I'm looking forward to it. It'll be quite liberating, knowing exactly how much I can spend.

Plus everyone knows the point about budgets is that you make them work *for* you. Exactly.

'So . . . how much is my budget for today?' I say, hovering by the study door. It's about an hour later and Luke is searching for something in his desk. He looks a bit stressed.

'I'm sorry?' he says without looking up.

'I was just wondering what my budget is for today. About twenty pounds?'

'I guess so,' says Luke distractedly.

'So . . . can I have it?'

'What?'

'Can I have my twenty pounds?'

Luke stares at me for a moment as though I'm completely mad, then takes his wallet out of his pocket, gets out a twenty-pound note and hands it to me. 'OK?'

'Fine. Thanks.'

I look at the note. Twenty pounds. That's my challenge. I feel like some wartime housewife being given her ration book.

It's a very weird feeling, not having my own income.

Or a job. For three months. How am I going to survive three whole months? Should I get some other job to fill the space? Maybe this is a great opportunity, it occurs to me. I could try something completely new!

I have a sudden image of myself as a landscape gardener. I could buy some really cool wellingtons and specialize in shrubs.

Or . . . yes! I could start up some company offering a unique service that no one has ever provided, and make millions! Everyone would say, 'Becky's a genius! Why didn't *we* think of that?' And the unique service would be . . .

It would consist of . . .

OK, I'll come back to that one.

Then, as I watch Luke putting some papers in a Brandon Communications folder, I'm seized by a brilliant idea. Of course. I can help him in his work!

I mean, that's the whole point of marriage. It should be a partnership. Everyone knows the best marriages are where the husband and wife support each other in everything.

Plus I saw this TV movie last night where the couple split up, and it was because the wife didn't take any interest in the man's work, but his secretary did. So the husband left the wife and then she murdered him and went on the run and ended up shooting herself. Which just shows what can happen.

I'm filled with inspiration. This is my new project. Project: Supportive Wife. I can get totally involved in the running of his company, like Hillary Clinton, and everyone will know it's really me who has all the good ideas. I have a vision of myself standing by Luke's side in a pastel suit, beaming radiantly while ticker tape rains down on us.

'Luke, listen,' I say. 'I want to help.'

'Help?' He looks up with an absent frown.

'I want to help you out with the business. With

112

our business,' I add, a touch self-consciously.

I mean, it is sort of my company too. It's called Brandon Communications, isn't it? And I am called Rebecca Brandon now, aren't I?

'Becky, I'm not sure—'

'I really want to support you, and I'm free for three months! It's perfect! I could come in and be a consultant. You wouldn't even have to pay me very much.'

Luke looks slightly gobsmacked.

'What exactly would you consult on?'

'Well . . . I don't know yet,' I admit. 'But I could inject some new thoughts. Blue-sky thinking.'

Luke sighs.

'Sweetheart, we're really busy with this Arcodas pitch. I haven't got time to take you in. Maybe after the pitch is over—'

'It wouldn't *take* time!' I say in astonishment. 'I'd *save* you time! I'd be a help! You once offered me a job, remember?'

'I know I did. But taking on a real, full-time job is a bit different from filling in three months. If you want to change career, that's different.'

He goes back to sorting through his papers and I stare at him crossly. He's making a big mistake. Everyone knows companies have to cross-pollinate with other industries. My personal-shopping experience would probably be invaluable to him. Not to mention my background as a financial journalist. I'd probably revolutionize the whole company in a week. I'd probably make him millions!

As I'm watching, Luke tries to put a file away and bumps his shin on a wooden carton full of saris.

'Jesus Christ,' he says irritably. 'Becky, if you really want to help me . . .'

'Yes?' I say eagerly.

'You can tidy up this apartment.'

* * *

Great. Just great.

Here I am, prepared to devote myself to Luke's company. Here I am, all set to be the most supportive wife in the world. And Luke thinks I should *tidy up.*

I heft a wooden carton on to the slate coffee table, prise the lid off with a knife, and white foam peanuts cascade out everywhere like snowflakes. I dig in through the foam and pull out a bubble-wrapped parcel. For a few seconds I peer at it blankly – then suddenly I remember. These are the hand-painted eggs from Japan. Each one depicts a scene from the legend of the Dragon King. I think I bought five.

I look around the crowded room. Where am I going to put a set of fragile hand-painted display eggs? There isn't a single spare surface. Even the mantelpiece is crammed with stuff.

A helpless frustration is growing inside me. There isn't anywhere to put *anything.* I've already filled up all the cupboards, and my wardrobe, and the space under the bed.

What did I buy a load of stupid painted eggs for, anyway? What was I thinking? For a moment I consider dropping the box on the floor, accidentally on purpose. But I can't quite bring myself to do it. They'll have to go in the 'later' pile.

I put the egg back in the wooden carton, clamber over a pile of rugs and shove it behind the door, on top of six bolts of Thai silk. Then I sink down on to the floor in total exhaustion. God, this is tiring. Plus now I've got to clear up all the bloody foam peanuts.

I wipe my brow and glance at my watch. I've been at it now for a whole hour, and if I'm honest, the room doesn't look any better than before. In fact . . . it looks worse. As I survey the clutter, I feel suddenly full of gloom.

What I need is a cup of coffee. Yes.

I head out to the kitchen, already feeling lighter, and

turn the kettle on. And maybe I'll have a biscuit, too. I open one of the stainless-steel cupboards, find the tin, select a biscuit and put the tin away again. Every single movement makes a little clanging sound that echoes through the silence.

God, it's quiet in here, isn't it? We need to get a radio.

I trail my fingers over the granite worktop and find myself giving a gusty sigh.

Maybe I'll give Mum a ring and have a nice chat. Except she's still being all weird. I tried phoning home the other day and she sounded all shifty, and said she had to go because the chimney sweep was there. Like we've ever had a chimney sweep in all my life. She probably had people viewing the house or something.

I could phone Suze . . .

No. I feel a twinge of hurt. Not Suze.

Or Danny! I think in sudden inspiration. Danny was my best friend when we lived in New York. He was a struggling fashion designer then – but all of a sudden he's doing really well. I've even seen his name in *Vogue*! But I haven't spoken to him since we got back.

It's not a great time to be calling New York – but that's OK. Danny never keeps regular hours. I dial his number and wait impatiently as it rings.

'Greetings!'

'Hi!' I say. 'Danny, it's—'

'Welcome to the ever-expanding Danny Kovitz empire!'

Oh right. It's a machine.

'For Danny's fashion tips . . . press one. To receive a catalogue . . . press two. If you wish to send Danny a gift or invite him to a party, press three . . .'

I wait till the list comes to an end and a beep sounds.

'Hi!' I say. 'Danny, it's Becky! I'm back! So . . . give me a ring sometime!' I give him my number, then put down the receiver.

The kettle comes to a noisy boil and I briskly start spooning grounds into the coffee pot, thinking of who else to call. But ... there's no one. The truth is, I haven't lived in London for two years. And I've kind of lost touch with most of my old friends.

I'm lonely, pops into my head with no warning.

No I'm not. I'm fine.

I wish we'd never come home.

Don't be silly. It's all great. It's fab! I'm a married woman with my own home and ... and plenty to be getting on with.

Suddenly the buzzer rings and I look up in surprise. I'm not expecting anyone.

It's probably a package. Or maybe Luke decided to come home early! I walk out into the hall and pick up the entryphone.

'Hello?'

'Becky, love?' crackles a familiar voice. 'It's Mum.'

I gape at the receiver. Mum? Downstairs?

'Dad and I have come to see you,' she continues. 'Is it all right if we pop up?'

'Of course!' I exclaim in bemusement, and hit the buzzer. What on earth are Mum and Dad doing here?

I quickly go into the kitchen, pour the coffee and arrange some biscuits on a plate, then hurry back out to the lift.

'Hi!' I say as the doors open. 'Come on in! I've made you some coffee!'

As I hug Mum and Dad I can see them glancing at each other apprehensively.

What is going on?

'I hope we're not disturbing you, love,' says Mum as she follows me into the flat.

'No! Of course not!' I say. 'I mean, obviously I have my chores ... things to be getting on with ...'

'Oh yes,' Mum nods. 'Well, we don't want to take up

your time. It's just . . .' She breaks off. 'Shall we go and sit down?'

'Oh. Er . . .' I glance through the door of the sitting room. The sofa is surrounded by boxes spilling their contents, and covered in rugs and foam peanuts. 'We haven't *quite* got the sitting room straight yet. Let's go in the kitchen.'

OK. Whoever designed our trendy kitchen bar stools obviously never had their parents come over for a cup of coffee. It takes Mum and Dad about five minutes to climb up on to them, while I watch, completely petrified they're going to topple over.

'Spindly legs, aren't they?' puffs Dad as he tries for the fifth time. Meanwhile Mum's inching slowly on to the seat, gripping the granite breakfast bar for dear life.

At last, somehow, they're both perched up safely on the steel seats, looking all self-conscious, as though they're on a TV talk show.

'Are you all right?' I ask anxiously. 'Because I could go and get some different chairs . . .'

'Nonsense!' says Dad at once. 'This is very comfy!'

He is *so* lying. I can see him clenching his hands round the edges of the slippery seat and glancing down at the slate floor below as though he's balanced on a 44th-floor ledge.

'The seats are a little hard, aren't they, love?' ventures Mum. 'You should get some nice tie-on cushions from John Lewis.'

'Er . . . maybe.'

I hand Mum and Dad their cups, pull out a bar stool for myself and nonchalantly swing myself up on to it.

Damn. That hurt.

God, they *are* a bit tricky to get on to. Stupid shiny seats. And the balance is all wrong, somehow.

OK. I'm up. I'm cool.

'So . . . are you both well?' I say, reaching for my cup of coffee.

There's a short silence.

'Becky, we came here for a reason,' says Dad. 'I have something to tell you.'

He looks so grave, I feel a stab of panic. Maybe it's not the house after all. Maybe it's something worse.

'It's to do with me,' he continues.

'You're ill,' I say before I can stop myself. 'Oh God. Oh God. I knew there was something wrong—'

'I'm not ill. It's not that. It's . . . something else.' He pauses for a few moments, massaging his temples, then looks up. 'Becky, years ago—'

'Break it to her gently, Graham!' Mum interrupts.

'I *am* breaking it to her gently!' retorts Dad, swivelling round, his bar stool teetering dangerously. 'That's exactly what I'm doing!'

'You're not!' says Mum. 'You're rushing in!'

Now I'm totally bewildered.

'Break what to me gently?' I say, looking from face to face. 'What's going on?'

'Becky, before I met your mother . . .' Dad avoids my gaze, 'there was another . . . lady in my life.'

'Right,' I say, my throat thick.

Mum and Dad are getting divorced and that's why they're selling the house. I'm going to be the product of a broken home.

'We lost touch,' Dad continues. 'But recently . . . events have occurred.'

'You're confusing her, Graham!' exclaims Mum.

'I'm not confusing her! Becky, are you confused?'

'Well . . . a bit,' I admit.

Mum leans over and takes my hand.

'Becky, love, the long and the short of it is . . . you have a sister.'

A *sister*?

I stare at her blankly. What's she talking about?

118

'A half-sister, we should say,' echoes Dad, nodding earnestly. 'Two years older than you.'

My brain is short-circuiting. This doesn't make any sense. How could I have a sister and not know about it?

'Dad has a daughter, darling,' says Mum gently. 'A daughter he knew nothing about until very recently. She got in touch with us while you were on honeymoon. We've seen each other a few times, haven't we, Graham?' She glances at Dad, who nods. 'She's . . . very nice!'

The kitchen is completely silent. I swallow a few times. I can't quite take this in.

All of a sudden it hits me. I look up.

'That girl! The day we got back.' My heart is pounding. 'The one you were with. Was that . . . ?'

Mum glances at Dad, who nods.

'That was her. Your half-sister. She was visiting us.'

'When we saw you, love . . . we didn't know what to do!' says Mum, giving an anxious laugh. 'We didn't want to give you the shock of your life!'

'We decided we'd tell you when you'd settled in a bit,' chimes in Dad. 'When you'd got a bit sorted out.'

Now I feel totally dazed. That was her. I've *seen* my half-sister.

'What's . . . what's her name?' I manage.

'Her name's Jessica,' says Dad after a pause. 'Jessica Bertram.'

Jessica. My sister Jessica.

Hi. Have you met my sister Jessica?

I look from Dad's worried face to Mum's bright, hopeful eyes – and suddenly I feel very weird. It's like a bubble is rising up inside me. Like a load of really strong emotions are pushing their way out of my body.

I'm not an only child.

I have my own sister. *I have a sister.*

I have a *SISTER*!

NINE

For the past week I haven't been able to sleep. Or concentrate on anything. In fact, it's all been a bit of a blur. I can't think about anything except the fact that I, Rebecca Brandon, née Bloomwood, have a sister. I've had a sister my whole life!

And today at last I'm going to meet her!

Just the thought makes me feel exhilarated and jumpy all at once. How will we be the same? How will we be different? What will her voice be like? What will her *clothes* be like?

'Do I look OK?' I say to Luke for the millionth time, and survey my appearance anxiously in the mirror. I'm standing in my old bedroom at my parents' house, putting the finishing touches to my 'meeting-my-long-lost-sister' outfit.

It's taken me several days to decide, but after a lot of thought I've gone for a look which is casual but still special. I'm wearing my most flattering Seven jeans, some boots with spiky heels, a T-shirt made ages ago for me by Danny, and a gorgeous pale-pink Marc Jacobs jacket.

'You look great,' says Luke patiently, looking up from his mobile phone.

'It's like ... balancing formal with informal,' I explain. 'So the jacket says, "This is a special occasion."

Whereas the jeans say, "We're sisters, we can be relaxed with each other!" And the T-shirt says . . .'

I pause. Actually I'm not sure what the T-shirt says, apart from 'I'm friends with Danny Kovitz.'

'Becky,' says Luke, 'I don't honestly think it matters what you wear.'

'What?' I wheel round in disbelief. 'Of course it matters! This is one of the most important moments of my life! I'll always remember what I was wearing the day I met my sister for the first time. I mean . . . you remember what *you* were wearing when you met me for the first time, don't you?'

There's silence. Luke looks blank.

He *doesn't* remember? How can he not remember?

'Well, *I* remember,' I say crossly. 'You were wearing a grey suit and a white shirt and a dark-green Hermès tie. And I was wearing my short black skirt and my suede boots and that awful white top which made my arms look fat.'

'If you say so.' Luke raises his eyebrows.

'Everyone knows first impressions are everything.' I smooth down my T-shirt. 'I just want to look right. Like a sister.'

'What do sisters look like?' asks Luke, looking amused.

'They look . . . fun!' I think for a moment. 'And friendly. And supportive. And like they'll tell you if your bra-strap is showing.'

'Then you do look exactly like a sister.' Luke kisses me. 'Becky, relax! It's going to be fine!'

'OK. I'll relax.'

I know I'm a bit wound-up. But I can't help it! I just can't get over the idea of me being a sister after being an only child for so long.

I mean, not that I've *minded* being on my own or anything. Mum and Dad and I have always had a great time together. But you know. Sometimes I've heard other people talking about their brothers and sisters and kind of wondered what it was like. I never thought I would actually get to find out!

What's really spooky is that all this week, I've suddenly been noticing sisters. They're everywhere! For example, the film of *Little Women* was on telly the other afternoon – and straight afterwards was a programme about the Beverley Sisters! And every time I've seen two women together in the street, instead of just noticing what they were wearing, I've thought, 'Are they sisters?'

It's like, there's a whole world of sisters out there. And finally, I'm part of it.

I feel a smarting in my eyes and blink hard. It's ridiculous, but ever since I heard about Jessica, my emotions have been all over the place. Last night I was reading this brilliant book called *Long-Lost Sisters – The Love They Never Knew They Had* and tears were just streaming down my cheeks! The stories were just amazing. One was about these three Russian sisters who were in the same concentration camp during the war but they *didn't know it*.

Then there was this woman who was told her sister had been killed but she would never believe it, and then she got cancer and there was no one to look after her three children, but they found the sister alive, just in time for them to say goodbye . . .

Oh God, I'm going to cry, just thinking about it.

I take a deep breath and wander over to the table where I've put my present for Jessica. It's a big basket full of Origins bath stuff, plus some chocolates, plus a little photo album of pictures of me when I was little.

I've also got her a silver-bean necklace from Tiffany which exactly matches mine, but Luke said it might be a bit much, presenting her with jewellery on our first meeting. Which I didn't really understand. I mean, I'd love it if someone gave me a Tiffany necklace! I wouldn't be 'overwhelmed' or whatever he said.

But he was really insistent, so I said I'd keep it for later.

I run my eyes over the basket in slight dissatisfaction. Should I maybe—

'The present is fine,' says Luke, just as I open my mouth. 'You don't need to add any more.'

How did he know what I was going to say?

'OK,' I say reluctantly. I look at my watch and feel a swoop of excitement. 'Not long now! She'll be here soon!'

The plan is, Jessica's going to phone when her train gets into Oxshott station, then Dad will go and pick her up. It's pure coincidence that she's going to be in London this week. She lives in Cumbria, which is miles away – but apparently she was coming down anyway, for an academic conference. So she's come down a day early, especially to meet me!

'Shall we go down?' I say, looking at my watch again. 'She might be early!'

'Wait.' Luke snaps his phone shut. 'Becky, before all the excitement starts ... I wanted to have a quick word. On the subject of our honeymoon purchases.'

'Oh right.'

I feel a twinge of resentment. Why does he have to bring this up *now*? This is a special day! There should be a general reprieve from all arguments, like in the war when they played football on Christmas Day.

Not that we're at war or anything. But we did have a bit of a row yesterday when Luke found the twenty Chinese dressing gowns under the bed. And he keeps asking when I'm going to sort out the apartment. So I keep telling him I'm working on it.

Which is true. I have been working on it. Sort of.

But it's so *exhausting*. And there's nowhere to put anything. Plus I've had the news of my long-lost sister to deal with! It's no wonder I've been a tad distracted.

'I just wanted to let you know that I've spoken to the furniture merchants,' says Luke. 'They'll be coming by on Monday to take away the Danish table.'

'Oh right,' I say sheepishly. 'Thanks. So, are they giving us a full refund?'

'Almost.'

'Oh well! So we didn't do too badly in the end!'

'No, we didn't,' agrees Luke. 'Unless you count the storage costs, the delivery costs, the expense of packaging it all up again—'

'Right,' I say hurriedly. 'Of course. Well anyway . . . all's well that ends well!'

I try a conciliatory smile, but Luke's not even looking. He's opening up his briefcase and pulling out a wad of – Oh God.

Credit-card bills. My secret Code Red Emergency bills, to be exact. Luke asked for them the other day and I had no choice but to get them out of their hiding place.

I was kind of hoping he wouldn't read them, though.

'Right!' I say, my voice slipping up two notches higher. 'So . . . you've seen those, then!'

'I've paid them all off,' says Luke shortly. 'Have you cut up the card?'

'Er . . . yes.'

Luke turns and gives me a hard look.

'Have you really?'

'Yes!' I say, nettled. 'I threw the pieces in the bin!'

'OK.' Luke turns back to the bills. 'And there isn't anything else to come? Anything you've paid for recently?'

I feel a tiny clenching in my stomach.

'Er . . . no,' I say. 'That's all.'

I can't tell him about the Angel bag. I just can't. He still thinks all I bought in Milan was a present for him. That's about my only redeeming feature right now.

And anyway, I can pay it off myself, no problem. I mean, in three months I'll have a job and my own income! It'll be easy!

To my slight relief my mobile phone starts ringing. I scrabble in my bag and pull it out – and Suze's number is flashing on the display.

Suze.

At once I feel a gigantic leap of nerves. I gaze at her name, a familiar hurt starting to rise inside me.

I haven't spoken once to Suze since I left her house. She hasn't called . . . and neither have I. If she's all busy and happy with a fab new life, then so am I. She doesn't even know I've got a sister.

Not yet.

I press Green and take a deep breath.

'Hi, Suze!' I exclaim in airy tones. 'How are you? How's the family?'

'I'm fine,' says Suze. 'We're all fine. You know . . . same old . . .'

'And how's Lulu?' I say lightly. 'I expect you two have been busy doing lots of fun things together?'

'She's . . . fine.' Suze sounds awkward. 'Listen, Bex . . . about that. I wanted to—'

'Actually, I've got a bit of exciting news of my own.' I cut her off. 'Guess what? It turns out I've got a long-lost sister!'

There's a shocked silence.

'What?' says Suze at last.

'It's true! I've got a half-sister that I never knew about. I'm meeting her today for the first time. She's called Jessica.'

'I . . . can't believe it.' Suze sounds totally poleaxed. 'You've got a *sister*?'

'Isn't it great? I've always wanted a sister!'

'How . . . how old is she?'

'Only two years older than me. Hardly any difference! I expect we'll become really good friends,' I add carelessly. 'In fact . . . we'll be much *closer* than friends. I mean, we've got the same blood and everything. We'll have a lifelong bond.'

'Yes,' says Suze after a pause. 'I . . . suppose you will.'

'Anyway, I must go! She'll be here any moment! I can't wait!'

'Well . . . good luck. Have fun.'

'We certainly will!' I say brightly. 'Oh, and do give my love to Lulu. Have a lovely birthday with her, won't you?'

'I will,' says Suze, sounding defeated. 'Bye, Bex. And . . . congratulations.'

As I switch off the phone I'm a bit hot about the face. Suze and I have never been like this with each other before.

But it's not my fault.

She's the one who went out and got a new best friend. Not me.

I thrust my mobile phone back into my bag and look up to see Luke regarding me with a raised eyebrow.

'Suze all right?'

'She's fine,' I say a little defiantly. 'Come on. Let's go down.'

As I come down the stairs, I start prickling with excitement. I'm almost more keyed-up than when I got married. This is one of the biggest days of my life ever!

'All set?' says Mum, as we go into the kitchen. She's wearing a smart blue dress and is wearing her Special Occasion make-up where she uses lots of shiny highlighter under her eyebrows to 'open up the eyes'. I've seen it in the make-up book Janice gave her for Christmas.

'Did I hear you say you're selling some furniture?' she adds as she turns on the kettle.

'We're returning a table,' says Luke easily. 'We seem

126

to have ordered two by mistake. But it's been taken care of.'

'Only I was going to say, you should sell it on eBay!' says Mum. 'You'd get a good price!'

eBay.

That's a thought.

'So . . . you can sell anything on eBay, can you?' I ask casually.

'Oh yes!' says Mum. 'Anything at all.'

Like, say, hand-painted eggs depicting the legend of the Dragon King. OK. This could be the answer.

'Let's all have a nice coffee,' says Mum, reaching for some mugs. 'While we're waiting.'

We all glance involuntarily at the clock. Jessica's train should arrive at Oxshott in five minutes. Five minutes!

'Yoo-hoo!' There's a knocking at the back door and we all look round to see Janice peering through the glass.

Oh my goodness. Where did she get that sparkly blue eyeshadow?

Please don't let her give any to Mum, I find myself praying.

'Come on in, Janice!' says Mum, opening the door. 'And Tom! What a nice surprise!'

Blimey, Tom's looking rough. His hair is rumpled and unwashed, his hands are all blistered and cut and there's a deep furrow in his brow.

'We just came to wish you luck,' says Janice. 'Not that you need it!' She pops her box of Canderel down on the counter, then turns to look at me. 'So Becky. A sister!'

'Congratulations,' says Tom. 'Or whatever you say.'

'I know!' I say. 'Isn't it amazing?'

Janice shakes her head and looks at Mum a little reproachfully.

'I can't believe you've been keeping this a secret from us, Jane!'

'We wanted Becky to be the first to know,' says Mum, patting me on the shoulder. 'Hazelnut whirl, Janice?'

'Lovely!' says Janice, taking a biscuit from the plate and sitting down. She nibbles thoughtfully for a few moments, then looks up. 'What I don't understand is . . . why did this girl get in touch? After all this time?'

Ha! I've been *waiting* for someone to ask that.

'There was a very good reason,' I say with an air of solemn drama. 'It's because we've got a hereditary disease.'

Janice gives a little scream.

'A disease! Jane! You never told me that!'

'It's not a *disease*,' says Mum. 'Becky, you know it's not a disease! It's a "factor".'

'A "factor"?' echoes Janice, looking even more horrified than before. 'What kind of factor?' I can see her eyeing her hazelnut whirl as though she's afraid it might contaminate her.

'It's not life-threatening!' laughs Mum. 'It just makes your blood clot. Something along those lines.'

'Don't!' Janice winces. 'I can't bear talking about blood!'

'The doctors told Jess she should warn other members of her family to get tested, and that was the spur. She'd always known she had a father somewhere, but didn't know his name.'

'So she asked her mother who her long-lost father was . . .' chimes in Janice avidly, as though she's following a Ruth Rendell mini-series on the telly.

'Her mother is dead,' explains Mum.

'Dead!' gasps Janice.

'But her aunt had the name of Jessica's father written down in an old diary,' explains Mum. 'So she got it out – and gave it to Jessica.'

'And what was the name?' breathes Janice.

There's a pause.

128

'Mum, it was Graham!' says Tom, rolling his eyes. 'Graham Bloomwood. Obviously.'

'Oh yes,' says Janice, looking almost let down. 'Of course it was. And so . . . she rang you?'

'Wrote a letter,' says Mum. 'Once she'd tracked us down. We couldn't believe it! We were in a state of shock for days. You know, that's why we didn't come to the Hawaiian quiz evening at the church,' she adds. 'Graham didn't really have a migraine.'

'I knew it!' says Janice in triumph. 'I said to Martin at the time, "Something's not right with the Bloomwoods." But I had no idea it was a long-lost family member!'

'Well,' says Mum comfortingly, 'how could you?'

Janice is silent for a moment, taking it all in. Then suddenly she stiffens and lays a hand on Mum's arm.

'Jane, just be careful. Has she laid any claim to Graham's fortune? Has he altered his will in her favour?'

OK. Janice has definitely been watching too many TV murder mysteries.

'Janice!' says Mum with a laugh. 'No! It's nothing like that. As it happens, Jess's family is . . .' she lowers her voice discreetly, 'rather *well off.*'

'Ah!' breathes Janice.

Mum lowers her voice still further. 'They're rather big in *frozen food.*'

'Oh I *see,*' says Janice. 'So she's not all alone in the world, then.'

'Oh no,' says Mum, back to normal. 'She's got a step-father and two brothers. Or is it three?'

'But no sisters,' I chime in. 'We've both had that gap in our life. That . . . unfulfilled longing.'

Everyone turns to look at me.

'Have you had an unfulfilled longing, Becky?' says Janice.

'Oh yes. Definitely.' I take a pensive sip of coffee.

'Looking back, I think I always somehow *knew* I had a sister.'

'Really, love?' says Mum in surprise. 'You never mentioned it.'

'I never said anything.' I give Janice a brave smile. 'But deep down I knew.'

'Goodness!' says Janice. 'How did you know?'

'I felt it in here,' I say, clasping my hands to my heart. 'It was as if . . . a part of me was missing.'

I make a sweeping gesture with my hand – and make the mistake of catching Luke's eye.

'Which particular part of you was missing?' he says with apparent interest. 'Not a vital organ, I hope.'

God, he has no heart. None. Last night, he kept reading out bits from my *Long-Lost Sisters* book, looking up and saying, 'You cannot be serious.'

'The soulmate part, *actually*,' I shoot back.

'Thanks.' He raises his eyebrows.

'Not *that* kind of soulmate! A sisterly soulmate!'

'What about Suzie?' says Mum, looking up in surprise. 'She's been like a sister to you, surely. She's such a dear girl.'

'Friends come and go,' I say, looking away. 'She's not like family. She doesn't understand me like a true sister would.'

'It must have been such a shock!' Janice looks at Mum sympathetically. 'Especially for you, Jane.'

'It was,' says Mum, sitting down at the table. 'I can't pretend it wasn't. Although of course, the affair happened *long* before Graham met me.'

'Of course!' says Janice hastily. 'Of course it did! I wasn't for a moment *suggesting* that . . . that he . . . you . . .'

She breaks off, flustered, and takes a gulp of coffee.

'And in some ways . . .' Mum pauses, stirring her drink with a rueful smile. 'In some ways it was to be expected. Graham was quite the Don Juan when he was younger. It's no wonder he found women throwing themselves at him.'

'That's . . . right,' says Janice doubtfully.

We all look out of the window to see Dad coming over the lawn towards the back door. His greying hair is all tousled, his face is red, and even though I've told him a million times not to, he's wearing socks with his sandals.

'Women could never resist him,' says Mum. 'That's the truth of it.' She brightens a little. 'But we're having therapy to help us through the crisis.'

'Therapy?' I echo in astonishment. 'Are you serious?'

'Absolutely!' says Dad, coming in at the back door. 'We've had three sessions already.'

'She's a very nice girl, our therapist,' says Mum. 'Although a bit *nervy*. Like all these young people.'

Wow. This is news to me. I had no idea Mum and Dad were having therapy. But there again, I suppose it makes sense. I mean, bloody hell. How would I feel if Luke suddenly announced he had a long-lost daughter?

'Therapy!' Janice is saying. 'I can hardly believe it!'

'We have to be realistic, Janice,' says Mum. 'You can't expect this kind of revelation to have no repercussions.'

'A discovery of this scale can tear a family apart,' agrees Dad, popping a hazelnut whirl into his mouth. 'It can rock the very foundations of a marriage.'

'Goodness.' Janice claps a hand over her mouth, looking from Mum to Dad and back with wide eyes. 'What . . . what sort of repercussions are you expecting?'

'There'll be anger, I expect,' says Mum knowledgeably. 'Recriminations. Coffee, Graham?'

'Yes thanks, love.' He beams at her.

'Therapy is a pile of crap,' says Tom suddenly. 'I tried it with Lucy.'

We all turn and look at him. He's holding a cup of coffee in both hands, and glowering at us over the top of it.

'The therapist was a woman,' he adds, as though that explains everything.

'I think they often are, love,' says Mum cautiously.

'She took Lucy's side. She said she could understand her frustrations.' Tom's hands clench more tightly round his cup. 'What about *my* frustrations? Lucy was supposed to be my wife! But she wasn't interested in *any* of my projects. Not the conservatory, not the ensuite bathroom . . .'

OK, I have a feeling this could go on for a while.

'I love your summerhouse, Tom!' I cut in quickly. 'It's very . . . big!'

Which is true.

In fact, it's monstrous. I nearly died when I saw it out of the window this morning. It's three storeys high, with gables and a deck.

'We're just a bit worried about the planning regulations, aren't we?' says Janice, nervously glancing at Tom. 'We're worried it might be classed as a residence.'

'Well, it's a real achievement!' I say encouragingly. 'To build something like that!'

'I enjoy working with wood,' says Tom in a gruff voice. 'Wood doesn't let you down.' He drains his cup. 'In fact, I'd better get back to it. Hope it all goes well.'

'Thanks, Tom!' I say. 'See you soon!'

As the back door closes behind him there's an awkward silence.

'He's a sweet boy,' says Mum at last. 'He'll find his way.'

'He wants to make a boat next,' says Janice, looking strained. 'A boat, on the lawn!'

'Janice, have another coffee,' says Mum soothingly. 'Shall I put a splash of sherry in it?'

For a moment Janice looks torn.

'Better not,' she says at last. 'Not before twelve.'

She rootles in her handbag and produces a little pill which she pops into her mouth. Then she zips up her bag again and smiles brightly. 'So! What does Jessica look like? Have you got any pictures?'

'We took some, but they didn't come out!' says Mum regretfully. 'But she's . . . she's nice-looking, isn't she, Graham?'

'Very nice-looking!' says Dad. 'Tall . . . slim . . .'

'Dark hair,' adds Mum. 'Quite a *reserved* girl, if you know what I mean.'

I'm listening avidly as they describe her. Although I glimpsed her in the street that day we got back, the sunlight was so bright and I was so distracted by Mum and Dad's weird behaviour, I didn't get a proper view. So all week, I've been trying to imagine what she looks like.

Mum and Dad keep saying how tall and slim she is, so I've kind of pictured her like Courteney Cox. All willowy and elegant, in a white silk trouser suit, maybe.

I keep having visions of our first meeting. We'll fling our arms round each other, and hug each other as tightly as we can. Then she'll smile at me, brushing away the tears, and I'll smile back . . . and we'll have an instant connection. Like we already know each other and understand each other better than anyone else in the world.

I mean, who knows? Maybe it'll turn out that we'll have sisterly psychic powers. Or maybe we'll be like these twins I read about in *Long-Lost Sisters,* who were separated at birth but went on to have the same jobs and marry men with the same name.

I'm gripped by this idea. Maybe it'll turn out that

Jessica is a personal shopper too and is married to a man called Luke! She'll turn up in exactly the same Marc Jacobs jacket as me, and we can go on breakfast TV and everyone will say—

Oh, except she's not a personal shopper, I suddenly remember. She's training to be a doctor. Doctor of geography.

No. Geology.

But then . . . didn't *I* once think about training to be a doctor? I mean, that *can't* just be coincidence.

'And where does she live?' Janice is asking.

'In the North,' says Mum. 'A village called Scully, in Cumbria.'

'The North!' says Janice, with as much trepidation as though Mum's said the North Pole. 'That's a long way to travel! What time does she arrive?'

'Well,' Mum looks at the clock and frowns, 'that's a point. She should have arrived by now. Graham love, what time does Jess's train get in?'

'I thought it was about now . . .' Dad's brow wrinkles. 'Maybe I should phone the station. See if there's been a problem.'

'I'll do it if you like,' says Luke, looking up from the newspaper he's been reading.

'She did say she'd phone . . .' Mum is saying, as Dad goes out to the hall telephone.

Suddenly the doorbell rings.

We all stare at each other, frozen. A few moments later, Dad's voice comes from the hall. 'I think it's her!'

Oh my God.

My heart starts thumping like a piston engine.

She's here. My new sister. My new soulmate!

'I'll slip away,' says Janice. 'Let you have your precious family moment.' She squeezes my hand, then disappears out of the back door.

'Let me just tidy my hair,' says Mum, hurrying out to the hall mirror.

'Quick!' I say. 'Where's the present?'

I can't wait any longer. I have to meet her! Now!

'Here it is,' says Luke, handing me the cellophane-wrapped gift basket. 'And Becky . . .' He puts a hand on my arm.

'What?' I say impatiently. 'What is it?'

'I know you're excited to meet Jessica,' he says. 'And so am I. But remember, you are strangers. I'd just . . . take it easy.'

'We're not strangers!' I say in astonishment. 'She's my *sister*! We've got the same blood in us!'

Honestly. Doesn't Luke know anything?

I hurry out to the hall, clutching the basket. Through the frosted-glass pane of the front door I can see an indistinct, blurry figure. That's her!

'By the way,' says Mum as we advance towards the door, 'she likes to be called Jess.'

'Ready?' says Dad with a twinkle.

This is the moment! This is it! I quickly adjust my jacket, smooth down my hair and put on my widest, most welcoming and loving smile.

Dad reaches for the handle and pulls back the front door with a flourish.

And there, standing on the doorstep, is my sister.

TEN

My first thought is that she's not *exactly* like Courteney Cox. Nor is she wearing a white silk trouser suit.

Her dark hair is cropped short, and she's wearing a plain, workmanlike brown shirt over jeans. I guess it's a kind of . . . utility chic.

And she's pretty! Pretty-ish. Even though I'd say her make-up is maybe a bit *too* natural.

'Hi,' she says in a flat, matter-of-fact voice.

'Hi!' I say tremulously. 'I'm Becky! Your long-lost sister!'

I'm about to rush forward and fling my arms around her neck when I realize that I'm holding the basket. So instead, I thrust it at her. 'This is from me!'

'It's a present, love!' adds Mum helpfully.

'Thanks,' says Jess, looking down at it. 'That's great.'

There's a short silence. I'm waiting for Jess to tear off the wrappings impatiently, or say 'Can I open it right now?' or even just exclaim 'Ooh, Origins! My favourite!' But . . . she doesn't.

But then, she's probably being polite, it occurs to me. I mean, she's never met me before. Maybe she thinks I'm all formal and correct, and she has to be too. What I must do is put her at her ease.

'I just can't believe you're here,' I say momentously.

'The sister I never knew I had.' I put a hand on her arm and look right into her eyes, which are hazel with little specks.

Oh my God. We're bonding. This is just like one of the scenes in my *Long-Lost Sisters* book!

'You knew, didn't you?' I say, smiling to conceal my rising emotion. 'Didn't you somehow know you had a sister all along?'

'No,' says Jess, looking blank. 'I had no idea.'

'Oh, right,' I say, feeling a bit discomfited.

She wasn't supposed to say that. She was supposed to say, 'I always felt you in my heart!' and burst into tears.

I'm not quite sure what to say next.

'Anyway!' says Mum cheerfully, 'come on in, Jess! You must need some coffee after your journey!'

As she ushers Jess in, I look in surprise at the brown rucksack she's carrying. It's not very big at all. And she's staying a whole week at the conference!

'Is that all your luggage?' I say.

'That's all I need.' She shrugs. 'I'm a light packer.'

A 'light packer'! Ha! I knew it!

'Did you Fedex the rest?' I say in an undertone, and give her a friendly, 'I understand' look.

'No.' She glances at Mum. 'This is all I've brought.'

'It's OK.' I smile conspiratorially. 'I won't say anything.'

I knew we'd be kindred spirits. I *knew* it.

'How lovely to see you again, Jess.' Dad steps forward. 'Welcome, my dear girl!'

As he gives Jess a hug, I suddenly feel a bit weird. It's as though it's hitting me for the first time. Dad has another daughter. Not just me. Our whole family is bigger now.

But then . . . that's what families are about, isn't it? Getting bigger. Adding new members.

'This is Luke, my husband,' I say quickly.

'How do you do?' he says pleasantly, coming forward. As he shakes her hand I feel a little glow of pride in each of them. I look at Mum, and she gives me an encouraging smile.

'Let's go through!' she says. She leads the way into the living room, where there are flowers on the table, and plates of biscuits laid out invitingly. We all sit down, and for a few moments there's silence.

This is unreal.

I'm sitting opposite my half-sister. As Mum pours out the coffee I peer at her, mapping her face on to mine, trying to see the similarities between us. And there are loads! Or at least . . . some.

So we're not exactly identical twins – but there's definitely a resemblance if you look carefully enough. Like, she's got pretty much the same eyes as mine, except a different colour and a slightly different shape. Plus her nose would be just like mine if it didn't have that pointy end. And her hair would be *exactly* the same! If she just grew it a bit and dyed it and maybe put on a deep-conditioning treatment.

She's probably scrutinizing me in exactly the same way, I suddenly realize.

'I've hardly been able to sleep!' I say, and give her a slightly bashful smile. 'It's so exciting to meet you at last!'

Jess nods, but doesn't say anything. Gosh, she *is* very reserved. I'll have to draw her out a bit.

'Am I anything like you imagined?' I give a self-conscious little laugh and smooth my hair back.

Jess surveys me for a moment, moving her eyes around my face.

'I didn't really imagine what you'd be like,' she says at last.

'Oh right.'

'I don't imagine things much,' she adds. 'I just take them as they come.'

'Have a biscuit, Jess,' says Mum pleasantly. 'These are pecan and maple.'

'Thanks,' says Jess, taking one. 'I love pecan nuts.'

'Me too!' I look up in astonishment. 'I love them too!'

God, it just shows. Genes will out. We were brought up miles away from each other in different families . . . but we still have the same taste!

'Jess, why didn't you call from the station?' Dad says, taking a cup of coffee from Mum. 'I would have picked you up. You didn't need to take a cab!'

'I didn't get a cab,' says Jess. 'I walked.'

'You walked?' says Dad in surprise. 'From Oxshott station?'

'From Kingston. I took the coach down.' She gulps her coffee. 'It was far cheaper. I saved twenty-five pounds.'

'You walked all the way from Kingston?' Mum looks appalled.

'It was no distance,' says Jess.

'Jess is a very keen walker, Becky,' explains Mum. She smiles at Jess. 'It's your main hobby, isn't it, love?'

This is too much. We should be on a documentary or something!

'Me too!' I exclaim. 'It's my hobby, too! Isn't that amazing?'

There's silence. I look around the bewildered faces of my family. Honestly. What's wrong with them?

'Is walking your hobby, love?' says Mum uncertainly.

'Of course it is! I walk round London all the time! Don't I, Luke?'

Luke gives me a quizzical look.

'Certain streets of London have been pounded down by your feet, yes,' he agrees.

'Do you do power walking, then?' says Jess, looking interested.

'Well . . .' I think for a few moments. 'It's more like

'. . . I combine it with other activities. For variety.'

'Like cross-training?'

'Er . . . kind of.' I nod, and take a bite of biscuit.

There's another little silence. It's like everyone's waiting for everyone else to speak. God, why are we all so awkward? We should be *natural*. We're all family, after all!

'Do you like films?' I ask at last.

'Some,' replies Jess, frowning thoughtfully. 'I like films that say something. That have some sort of message.'

'Me too,' I agree fervently. 'Every film should definitely have a message.'

Which is true. I mean, take *Grease*. That's got loads of messages. Like, 'Don't worry if you're not the cool one at school because you can always perm your hair.'

'More coffee, anyone?' says Mum, looking round. 'There's another pot ready in the kitchen.'

'I'll go,' I chip in, leaping up from the sofa. 'And Luke, why don't you come and . . . er . . . help me? In case I . . . can't find it.'

I know I don't sound very convincing, but I don't care. I'm just dying to talk to Luke.

As soon as we're in the kitchen I shut the door and look at him eagerly. 'So? What do you think of my sister?'

'She seems very nice.'

'Isn't she great? And there are so many similarities between us! Don't you think?'

'I'm sorry?' Luke stares at me.

'Jess and me! We're so alike!'

'*Alike?*' Luke looks flabbergasted.

'Yes!' I say, a tad impatiently. 'Weren't you listening? She likes pecan nuts, I like pecan nuts . . . she likes walking, I like walking . . . we both like films . . .' I make a whirling motion with my hands. 'It's like there's already this amazing understanding between us!'

140

'If you say so.' Luke raises his eyebrows and I feel a small twinge of hurt.

'Don't you like her or something?'

'Of course I like her! But I've hardly spoken two words to her. And nor have you.'

'Well . . . I know,' I admit. 'But that's because we're all so *stilted* in there. We can't chat properly. So I thought I'd suggest the two of us go out together somewhere. Really have a chance to bond.'

'Like where?'

'I don't know. For a walk. Or . . . a little shopping trip, maybe!'

'Aha,' he nods. 'A little shopping trip. Good idea. I'm assuming this would be on your daily budget of twenty pounds.'

What?

I cannot *believe* he's bringing up the budget at a time like this. I mean, how many times do you go shopping with your long-lost sister for the very first time?

'This is a one-off, extraordinary event,' I explain. 'Clearly I need an extra budget.'

'I thought we agreed, no one-offs,' says Luke. 'No "unique opportunities". Don't you remember?'

I feel a surge of outrage.

'Fine!' I say, folding my arms. 'I won't bond with my sister.'

There's silence in the kitchen. I give a huge sigh and glance surreptitiously at Luke, but he seems totally unmoved.

'Becky!' Mum's voice interrupts us. 'Where's the coffee? We're all waiting!' She comes into the kitchen and looks from Luke to me in alarm. 'There isn't a problem, is there? You're not arguing?'

I turn to Mum.

'I want to take Jess out shopping, but Luke says I've got to stick to my budget!'

'Luke!' exclaims Mum reproachfully. 'I think that's a

lovely idea, Becky! You two girls should spend some time together. Why not pop to Kingston? You could have lunch, too.'

'Exactly!' I dart a resentful look at Luke. 'But I haven't got any money except twenty quid.'

'And as I say, we're on a budget,' says Luke in implacable tones. 'I'm sure you'd agree that successful budgeting is the first rule of a happy marriage, Jane?'

'Yes, yes, of course . . .' says Mum, looking distracted. Suddenly her face brightens. 'The Greenlows!'

The who?

'Your cousins in Australia! They sent a cheque for your wedding present! I've been meaning to give it to you. It's in Australian dollars – but even so, it's quite a lot . . .' She roots around in a drawer and pulls it out. 'Here we are! Five hundred Australian dollars!'

'Wow!' I take the cheque from her and examine it. 'Fantastic!'

'So now you can go and treat yourself and Jess to something nice!' Mum squeezes my arm with a smile.

'You see?' I shoot Luke a triumphant look, and he rolls his eyes.

'OK. You win. This time.'

Feeling suddenly excited, I hurry into the living room.

'Hi, Jess!' I say. 'D'you want to go out somewhere? Like to the shops?'

'Oh.' Jess looks taken aback. 'Well . . .'

'Go on, love!' says Mum, coming in behind me. 'Have a little spree!'

'We can go and have lunch somewhere . . . really get to know each other . . . what do you think?'

'Well . . . OK,' she says at last.

'Excellent!'

I feel a zing of anticipation. My first-ever shopping trip with my sister! This is so thrilling!

'I'll just go and get ready.'

'Wait,' says Jess. 'Just before you go. I brought you something too. It's not much, but . . .'

She goes over to her rucksack, opens it, and takes out a parcel wrapped up in paper printed all over with the words 'Happy New Year 1999'.

That is so cool!

'I *love* kitsch wrapping paper!' I say, admiring it. 'Where did you find it?'

'It was free from the bank,' says Jess.

'Oh,' I say in surprise. 'Er . . . excellent!'

I rip off the wrapping and find a plastic box, divided into three compartments.

'*Wow!*' I exclaim at once. 'That's fantastic! Thank you so much! It's just what I wanted!' I fling an arm round Jess's neck and give her a kiss.

'What is it, love?' says Mum, looking at it with interest.

To be honest, I'm not actually quite sure.

'It's a food saver,' explains Jess. 'You can keep leftovers in it, and they all stay separate. Rice . . . casserole . . . whatever. I couldn't live without mine.'

'That's brilliant! It'll be *so* useful.' I look at the three compartments thoughtfully. 'I think I'll keep all my lip balms in it.'

'Lip balms?' says Jess, looking taken aback.

'I'm *always* losing them! Aren't you?' I put the lid back on and admire it for a few more moments. Then I pick up the wrapping paper and scrumple it into a ball.

Jess winces as though someone just trod on her foot.

'You could have folded that up,' she says, and I look at her, puzzled.

Why on earth would I *fold* used wrapping paper?

But then, maybe this is one of her pet habits that I'll have to get used to. We all have little quirks.

'Oh right!' I say. 'Of course. Silly me!'

143

I uncrease the crumpled paper, smooth it out and fold it carefully into quarters.

'There we are.' I beam at her and drop it in the waste-paper bin. 'Let's go!'

ELEVEN

It only takes fifteen minutes by car to get to Kingston, which is the nearest big shopping centre to Mum and Dad. I find a meter, and after about twenty attempts, manage to park the car vaguely in a straight line.

God, parking is a stress. Everyone just hoots at you the whole time. And it's very difficult to back into a space with lots of people watching, making you feel self-conscious. People should realize that, instead of nudging their friends and pointing.

Anyway, never mind. The point is, we're here! It's a fantastic day, sunny but not too warm, with tiny clouds scudding across the blue sky. As I get out, I look around the sunlit street, feeling all buzzy with anticipation. My first shopping trip with my sister! What shall we do first?

As I start to feed the parking meter, I go through all the options in my head. We should definitely go and get a free makeover. And check out that new underwear shop Mum was talking about . . .

'How long exactly are we planning to stay here?' asks Jess as I shove in my sixth pound coin.

'Er . . .' I squint at the meter. 'This should take us up to six o'clock . . . and after that parking's free!'

'Six o'clock?' She looks a bit stunned.

'Don't worry!' I say reassuringly. 'The shops don't close at six. They'll be open till at least eight.'

And we *have* to go into a department store and try on lots of evening dresses. One of my best times ever was when I spent a whole afternoon trying on posh dresses in Harrods with Suze. We kept putting on more and more outrageous million-pound frocks, and swooshing around, and all the snooty assistants got really annoyed and kept asking had we made our choice yet?

At last Suze said she *thought* she had . . . but she wanted to see it with a Cartier diamond tiara just to make sure, and could Jewellery possibly send one up?

I think that's when they asked us to leave.

A giggle rises at the memory, and I feel a sudden wistful pang in my chest. God, Suze and I used to have fun together. She is just the best person in the world for saying 'Go on! Buy it!' Even when I was stony broke, she'd say 'Buy it! I'll pay! You can always pay me back.' And then she'd buy one too, and we'd go and have a cappuccino.

But anyway. There's no point getting all nostalgic.

'So!' I turn to Jess. 'What do you feel like doing first? There are loads of shops here. Two department stores . . .'

'I hate department stores,' says Jess. 'They make me feel ill.'

'Oh right.' I pause.

That's fair enough. Loads of people hate department stores.

'Well, there are loads of boutiques too,' I say with an encouraging smile. 'In fact, I've just thought of the perfect place!'

I lead her down a cobbled side-road, admiring my reflection in a shop-window as we go. That Angel bag was worth every single penny. I look like a movie star!

I'm slightly surprised Jess hasn't said anything

about it, actually. If my new long-lost sister had an Angel bag, it would be the *first* thing I'd mention. But then, maybe she's trying to be all cool and blasé. I can understand that.

'So . . . where do you normally shop?' I say conversationally.

'Wherever's cheapest,' replies Jess.

'Me too!' I say eagerly. 'I got the most fab Ralph Lauren top at this designer outlet in Utah. Ninety per cent off!'

'I tend to do a lot of bulk-buying,' says Jess with a little frown. 'If you buy large enough quantities, you can make pretty good savings.'

Oh my God. We are totally on the same wavelength. I *knew* we would be!

'You are so right!' I exclaim in delight. 'That's what I keep trying to explain to Luke! But he just can't see the logic.'

'So, do you belong to a warehouse club?' Jess looks at me with interest. 'Or a food co-op?'

I look at her blankly.

'Er . . . no. But on honeymoon, I did loads of excellent bulk-buying! I bought forty mugs and twenty silk dressing gowns!'

'Silk dressing gowns?' echoes Jess, looking taken aback.

'They were such an investment! I *told* Luke it made financial sense, but he just wouldn't listen . . . OK! Here we are! This is it.'

We've arrived at the glass doors of Georgina's. It's a big, light boutique selling clothes, jewellery and the most gorgeous bags. I've been coming here since I was about twelve, and it's one of my favourite shops in the world.

'You are going to *love* this shop,' I say to Jess happily, and push the door open. Sandra, one of the assistants, is arranging a collection of beaded purses on a pedestal, and she looks up as the door pings. Immediately her face lights up.

'Becky! Long time no see! Where've you been?'

'I've been on my honeymoon!'

'Of course you have. So, how's married life treating you?' She grins. 'Had your first big bust-up yet?'

'Ha ha,' I say, grinning back. I'm about to introduce Jess, when Sandra gives a sudden shriek.

'Oh my God! Is that an Angel bag? Is it *real*?'

'Yes.' I glow blissfully. 'Like it?'

'I don't believe it. She's got an Angel bag!' she calls out to the other assistants, and I hear a couple of gasps. 'Where did you *get* it? Can I touch it?'

'Milan.'

'Only Becky Bloomwood.' She's shaking her head. 'Only Becky Bloomwood would walk in here with an Angel bag. So how much did that cost you?'

'Er . . . enough!'

'Wow.' She strokes it gingerly. 'It's absolutely *amazing*.'

'What's so special?' says Jess blankly. 'I mean, it's just a bag.'

There's a pause, then we all burst out laughing. God, Jess is quite witty!

'Sandra, I want to introduce you to someone,' I say, and pull Jess forward. 'This is my sister!'

'Your *sister*?' Sandra looks at Jess in shock. 'I didn't know you had a sister.'

'Neither did I! We're long-lost sisters, aren't we Jess?' I put an arm round her.

'Half-sisters,' corrects Jess, a little stiffly.

'Georgina!' Sandra is calling to the back of the shop. 'Georgina, you have to come out here! You won't believe it! Becky Bloomwood's here – and she's got a sister! There are *two* of them!'

There's a moment's pause – then a curtain swishes back and Georgina, the owner of the shop, comes out.

She's in her fifties, with slate-grey hair and the most amazing turquoise eyes. She's wearing a velvet tunic top and holding a fountain pen, and as she sees me and Jess her eyes sparkle.

'Two Bloomwood sisters,' she says softly. 'Well, what a wonderful thing.'

I can see her exchanging looks with the assistants.

'We'll reserve two fitting rooms,' says Sandra promptly.

'If there aren't enough, we can always share a fitting room, can't we, Jess!' I say.

'I'm sorry?' Jess looks startled.

'We're sisters!' I give her an affectionate squeeze. 'We shouldn't be shy with each other!'

'It's OK,' says Sandra, glancing at Jess's face. 'There are plenty of fitting rooms. Take your time walking round . . . and enjoy!'

'I told you this was a nice place!' I say happily to Jess. 'So . . . let's start here!'

I head over to a rack full of delicious-looking tops and start leafing through the hangers. 'Isn't this gorgeous?' I pull out a pink T-shirt with a little butterfly motif. 'And this one with the daisy would really suit you!'

'Do you want to try them?' says Sandra. 'I can pop them in the fitting rooms for you.'

'Yes please!' I hand them over and beam at Jess.

But she doesn't smile back. In fact she hasn't moved from the spot. She's just standing there, with her hands in her pockets.

I suppose it can be a bit weird, shopping for the first time with someone new. Sometimes it just clicks straight away, like when I went shopping for the first time with Suze – and we both reached for the same Lulu Guinness make-up bag *simultaneously*.

But sometimes it can be a bit awkward. You don't know what each other's tastes are yet . . . and you keep trying different things and saying, 'Do you like this? Or this?'

I think Jess might need a bit of encouragement.

'These skirts are fabulous!' I say, going over to another rack filled with evening wear. 'This black one with the netting would look amazing on you!' I take it down and hold it up against Jess. She reaches for the price tag, looks at it and goes pale.

'I can't believe these prices,' she murmurs.

'They're pretty reasonable, aren't they?' I murmur back.

'And the skirt?' says Sandra, popping up behind us.

'Yes please! And I'll try it in the grey . . . ooh, and the pink!' I add, suddenly noticing a rose-coloured skirt hiding at the back.

Twenty minutes later we've been round the whole shop and two piles of clothes are waiting for us in the fitting rooms at the back. Jess hasn't said an awful lot. In fact, she's pretty much been silent. But I've made up for it, picking out all the stuff I think would look great on her, and adding it to the pile.

'OK!' I say, feeling a leap of exhilaration. 'Let's go and try on! I bet you look fantastic in that skirt! You should put it with the off-the-shoulder top, and maybe—'

'I'm not going to try anything on,' says Jess. She shoves her hands in her pockets and leans against a patch of empty wall.

I look at her, bemused.

'What did you say?'

'I'm not going to try anything on.' She nods towards the fitting rooms. 'But you go ahead. I'll wait here.'

There's a stunned silence in the shop.

'But . . . why aren't you going to try anything on?' I say.

'I don't need any new clothes,' replies Jess.

I stare at her, baffled. Across the shop, I'm aware of the assistants exchanging bewildered glances.

'You must need *something*!' I say. 'A T-shirt . . . a pair of trousers . . .'

'No. I'm fine.'

'Don't you even want to try on one of those gorgeous tops?' I hold one up encouragingly. 'Just to see what they look like on?'

'I'm not going to buy them.' Jess shrugs. 'So what's the point?'

'It's on me!' I say, suddenly realizing. 'You do know this is all my treat?'

'I don't want to waste your money. Don't let me stop you though,' she adds. 'You go on.'

I don't quite know what to do. I never imagined Jess wouldn't try anything on.

'The stuff's all in there for you, Becky,' puts in Sandra.

'Go on.' Jess nods.

'Well . . . OK,' I say at last. 'I won't be long.'

I head into the fitting room and struggle into most of the clothes. But my excitement's evaporated. It's not the same on my own. I wanted us to try things on *together*. I wanted it to be *fun*. I had visions of us dancing in and out of the fitting rooms, twirling around, swapping things over . . .

I just don't understand it. How can she not try anything on?

She must totally hate my taste, I realize with a plunge of despair. And she hasn't said anything because she wants to be polite.

'Any good?' asks Georgina as I finally emerge.

'Er . . . yes!' I say, trying to sound upbeat. 'I'll take two of the tops and the pink skirt. It's really gorgeous on!'

I glance at Jess, but she's staring into space. Suddenly she comes to, as if she's just noticed me.

'Ready?' she says.

'Er . . . yes. I'll just go and pay.'

We head over to the front desk, and Sandra starts scanning in my purchases. Meanwhile, Georgina is surveying Jess curiously.

'If you're not in the mood for clothes,' she says suddenly, 'what about jewellery?' She pulls out a tray from under the cash desk. 'We've got some lovely bracelets in. Only ten pounds. This might suit you.' She lifts up a beautiful bracelet made of plain silver ovals linked together. I hold my breath.

'It's nice,' says Jess with a nod, and I feel a huge pang of relief.

'For Becky's sister . . .' says Georgina, and I can see her eyes narrowing in calculation, 'three pounds.'

'Wow!' I beam at her. 'That's fantastic! Thank you so much, Georgina!'

'No thanks,' says Jess. 'I don't need a bracelet.'

What?

My head swivels in shock. Did she not understand?

'But . . . it's only three pounds,' I say. 'It's a total bargain!'

'I don't need it.' Jess shrugs.

'But . . .'

I'm lost for words. How can you not buy a bracelet for three pounds? How?

I mean, it's against the laws of physics or something.

'There you are, Becky!' says Sandra, handing over the rope cords of my carrier bags. There are two of them – all pale pink and glossy and scrumptious – but as my hands close round the handles I don't feel my customary rush of delight. In fact, I barely feel anything. I'm too confused.

'Well . . . bye then!' I say. 'And thanks! See you soon!'

'Bye, Becky darling!' says Georgina. 'And Jess,' she adds, a little less warmly. 'See you again, I hope.'

'Becky!' says Sandra. 'Before you go, just let me give you the leaflet about our sale.'

She hurries over, hands me a glossy leaflet, and leans forward.

'I'm not being funny or anything,' she says into my ear. 'But . . . are you *sure* she's your sister?'

As we emerge into the street, I'm a bit dazed. That didn't go exactly like I was expecting.

'So!' I say uncertainly. 'That was fun!' I glance at Jess, but she's got that composed, matter-of-fact expression and I can't tell what she's thinking. I wish just *once* she'd smile. Or say 'Yes, it was fab!'

'It's a shame you didn't find anything in Georgina's,' I venture. 'Did you . . . like the clothes?'

Jess shrugs, but doesn't say anything, and I feel a rush of despair. I knew it. She hates my taste. All that pretending she 'doesn't need any clothes' was just to be polite.

I mean, who doesn't need a T-shirt? Exactly. No one.

Well, never mind, we'll just have to find different shops. Shops that Jess likes. As we head down the sunny street, I'm thinking hard. Not skirts . . . not bracelets . . . Jeans! Everyone likes jeans. Perfect.

'I really need a new pair of jeans,' I say casually.

'Why?' Jess frowns. 'What's wrong with the jeans you're wearing?'

'Well . . . nothing. But I need some more!' I say with a laugh. 'I want some a bit longer than these, not *too* low-slung, maybe in a really dark inky blue . . .'

I look at Jess expectantly, waiting for her to join in with what kind of jeans *she* wants. But she's silent.

'So . . . do you need any jeans?' I say, feeling like I'm pushing a heavy weight uphill.

'No,' says Jess. 'But you go ahead.'

I feel a flicker of disappointment.

'Maybe another time.' I force a smile. 'It doesn't matter.'

By now we've reached the corner — and yes! L K Bennett is having a sale!

'Look at these!' I exclaim in excitement, hurrying to the big window filled with colourful strappy sandals. 'Aren't they gorgeous? What kind of shoes do you like?'

Jess runs her eyes over the display.

'I don't really bother much with shoes,' she says. 'No one ever notices shoes.'

For a moment my legs feel weak with shock.

No one ever notices shoes?

But . . . of course. She's joking! I'm going to have to get used to her dry sense of humour.

'Ohhhh you!' I say, and give her a friendly push. 'Well . . . I might just pop in and try some on, if you don't mind.'

If I try on enough pairs, I'm thinking, Jess is bound to join in too.

Except she doesn't. Nor at the next shop. Nor does she try any of the perfumes or make-up at Space NK. I'm laden with bags – but Jess still doesn't have one thing. She can't be enjoying herself. She must think I'm a crap sister.

'Do you need any . . . kitchenware?' I suggest in desperation.

We could buy cool aprons, or some chrome gadgety things . . . But Jess is shaking her head.

'I get all mine from the discount warehouse. It's much cheaper than the high street.'

'Well, what about luggage!' I exclaim in sudden inspiration. 'Luggage is one of those areas you can really forget about!'

'I don't need any luggage,' says Jess. 'I've got my rucksack.'

'Right.'

I'm totally running out of ideas. What else *is* there? Lamps maybe? Or . . . rugs?

Suddenly Jess's eyes light up.

'Hang on,' she says, sounding more animated than she has all day. 'Do you mind if I go in here?'

I stop still. We're outside a tiny, quite nondescript stationery shop that I've never been into.

'Absolutely!' My words come tumbling out in a whoosh of relief. 'Go ahead! Fantastic!'

Stationery! *That's* what she likes. Of course! Why on earth didn't I think of that before? She's a student . . . she writes all the time . . . that must be her thing!

The shop is so narrow I'm not sure I'll fit in with all my carrier bags, so I wait outside on the pavement, fizzing with anticipation. What is Jess buying? Gorgeous notebooks? Or handmade cards? Or maybe some beautiful fountain pen.

I mean, all kudos to her. I'd never even noticed this shop before!

'So what did you buy?' I demand in excitement as soon as she comes out, holding two bulging carrier bags. 'Show! Show!'

Jess looks blank.

'I didn't buy anything,' she says.

'But . . . your carrier bags! What's in them?'

'Didn't you see the sign?' She gestures to a hand-written postcard in the window. 'They're giving away used padded envelopes.'

She opens up her carriers to reveal a selection of battered Jiffy bags and a bundle of squashed-up, grey-ing bubble wrap. I stare at them, my excitement evaporating.

'I must have saved at least ten pounds,' she adds with satisfaction. 'And they'll always come in useful.'

I'm speechless.

How do I enthuse about a load of old Jiffy bags and bubble wrap?

'Er . . . fab!' I manage at last. 'They're really gorgeous! I love the . . . um . . . labels. So . . . we've both done really well! Let's go and have a cappuccino!'

* * *

There's a coffee shop round the corner, and as we approach it my spirits begin to rise. So maybe the shopping hasn't gone like I imagined it. But it doesn't matter. The point is, here we are, two sisters, coming for a cappuccino and a gossip together! We'll sit at a lovely marble table and sip our coffees, and tell each other all about ourselves . . .

'I brought a flask,' comes Jess's voice behind me.

I turn round in bemusement to see Jess taking a white plastic flask out of her rucksack.

'What?' I say faintly.

'We don't want that over-priced coffee.' She jabs a thumb at the café. 'The mark-up at those places is appalling.'

'But . . .'

'We can sit on this bench. I'll just wipe it clean.'

I gaze at her in rising dismay. I cannot have my first-ever coffee with my long-lost sister sitting on some grotty old bench, swigging out of a flask.

'But I want to go into a nice coffee shop!' The words rush out before I can stop them. 'And sit at a marble table, and have a proper cappuccino!'

There's silence.

'Please?' I say plaintively.

'Oh,' says Jess. 'Well, OK.' She closes up her flask. 'But you should get into the habit of making your own. You could save hundreds of pounds a year. Just buy a second-hand flask. And you can use coffee grounds at least twice. The flavour's fine.'

'I'll . . . bear that in mind,' I say, barely listening.

'Come on!'

The coffee shop is all warm and aromatic, with a fabulous smell of coffee. There are spotlights dancing on the marble tables, and music playing, and a happy, cheerful buzz.

'You see?' I beam at Jess. 'Isn't this nice?'

'A table for me and my sister, please,' I add happily to a waiter standing by the door.

I so love saying that! *My sister*.

We sit down and I put all my shopping bags on the floor – and feel myself start to relax. This is better. We can have a nice, cosy, intimate chat and really bond. In fact, this is what we should have done first of all.

A waitress who looks about twelve and is wearing a badge saying 'It's my first day!' approaches our table.

'Hi!' I beam. 'I'd like a cappuccino . . . but I'm not sure what my sister would like.'

My sister. It gives me a warm glow every time!

'We should be having champagne, really,' I can't resist adding. 'We're long-lost sisters!'

'Wow!' says the waitress. 'Cool!'

'I'll just have some plain tap water, thanks,' says Jess, closing her menu.

'Don't you want a nice frothy coffee?' I ask in surprise.

'I don't want to pay vastly inflated prices to a global money-making corporation.' She gives the waitress a severe look. 'Do *you* think a 400 per cent profit margin is ethical?'

'Erm . . .' The waitress looks stumped. 'Did you want ice in your water?' she says at last.

'Have a coffee too,' I say quickly. 'Go on. She'll have a cappuccino.'

As the waitress scuttles away, Jess shakes her head disapprovingly.

'Do you know the real cost of making a cappuccino? It's a few pence. And we're being charged nearly two pounds.'

'But you get a free chocolate in the saucer,' I explain.

God, Jess has a bit of a thing about coffee, doesn't she? But anyway. Never mind. Change the subject.

'So!' I lean back and spread my arms. 'Tell me all about yourself.'

'What do you want to know?' says Jess.

'Everything!' I say enthusiastically. 'Like . . . what are your hobbies, apart from walking?' Jess ponders for a few moments.

'I like caving,' she says at last, as the waitress puts down two cappuccinos in front of us.

'Caving!' I echo. 'Is that where you . . . go into caves?'

Jess gives me a look over her cup.

'That's basically it, yes.'

'Wow! That's really . . .'

I'm struggling for words. What can I say about caves? Apart from they're all dark and cold and slimy.

'That's really interesting!' I say at last. 'I'd love to go in a cave!'

'And of course rocks,' Jess adds. 'That's my main interest.'

'Me too! Especially great big shiny rocks from Tiffany's!' I laugh, to show I'm joking, but Jess doesn't react.

I'm not entirely sure she got it.

'My Ph.D. is on the petrogenesis and geochemistry of fluorite-hematite deposits,' she says, showing more animation than she has all day.

I don't think I understood one bit of that.

'Er . . . great!' I say. 'So . . . how come you decided to study rocks?'

'My father got me into it,' says Jess, and her face relaxes into a little smile. 'It's his passion too.'

'Dad?' I say in amazement. 'I never knew he was into rocks!'

'Not your dad.' She gives me a scathing look. '*My* dad. My stepfather. The man who brought me up.'

Right.

Of course she didn't mean Dad. That was really stupid.

There's an awkward silence, broken only by the

158

chinking of cups. I'm slightly lost for things to say. Which is ridiculous. This is my sister! Come on!

'So, are you going on holiday this year?' I ask at last. God, I must be desperate. I sound like a hairdresser.

'I don't know yet,' says Jess. 'It all depends.'

Suddenly I'm seized by the most marvellous idea.

'We could go on holiday together!' I say in excitement. 'Wouldn't that be great? We could get a villa in Italy or something . . . really get to know each other . . .'

'Rebecca, listen,' Jess interrupts flatly. 'I'm not looking for another family.'

There's a sharp silence. My face is suddenly hot.

'I . . . I know,' I say uncertainly. 'I didn't mean—'

'I don't *need* another family,' she presses on. 'I said this to Jane and Graham in the summer. That's not why I tracked you down. It was my responsibility to contact you about the medical situation. That's all.'

'What do you mean by "that's all"?' I falter.

'I mean it's nice to meet you. And your Mum and Dad are great. But you've got your life . . .' She pauses. 'And I've got mine.'

Is she saying she doesn't want to get to know me? Her own *sister*?

'But we've only just found each other!' I say in a rush. 'After all these years! Don't you find it amazing?' I lean forward and put my hand next to hers. 'Look! We have the same blood!'

'So what?' Jess looks unmoved. 'It's just a biological fact.'

'But . . . haven't you always wanted a sister? Haven't you always wondered what it would be like?'

'Not particularly.' She sees my face. 'Don't get me wrong. It's been interesting to meet you.'

Interesting? It's been *interesting*?

I stare down at my cappuccino, pushing the froth around with my spoon.

She doesn't want to get to know me. My own sister doesn't want to get to know me. What's wrong with me?

Nothing's going the way I planned it. I thought today would be one of the best days of my life. I thought shopping with my sister would be *fun*. I thought we'd be bonded by now. I thought we'd be having coffee, surrounded by all our fab new things, giggling and teasing each other . . . planning where to go next . . .

'So, shall we go back to your Mum's?' says Jess, draining her cup.

'What, already?' I say, looking up in shock. 'But we've got hours left. You haven't even bought anything yet!'

Jess looks at me, and sighs impatiently.

'Look, Becky. I wanted to be polite, so I came along today. But the truth is, I really can't stand shopping.'

My heart sinks. I knew she wasn't having a good time. I have to salvage this.

'I know we haven't found the right shops yet.' I lean forward eagerly. 'But there are more. We can go into different ones—'

'No,' Jess interrupts. 'You don't get it. I don't like shopping. Full stop.'

'Catalogues!' I say in sudden inspiration. 'We could go home, get a load of catalogues . . . it'd be fun!'

'Can't you get this through your head?' exclaims Jess in exasperation. 'Read my lips very carefully. I. Hate. Shopping.'

I drive home in a state of total shock. My brain feels like it's short-circuited. Every time I try to think about it, everything explodes in little disbelieving sparks.

When we arrive home, Luke is in the front garden, talking to Dad. As he sees us pulling into the drive he looks stunned.

'What are you doing back so soon?' he says, hurrying over to the car. 'Is anything wrong?'

'Everything's fine!' I say dazedly. 'We were just . . . quicker than I thought.'

'Thanks for the lift,' says Jess, getting out.

'It was a pleasure.'

As Jess heads towards Dad, Luke gets into the car beside me. He closes the door and gives me a shrewd look.

'Becky, are you OK?'

'I'm . . . fine. I think.'

I can't quite get my head round the day. My mind keeps replaying the way I fantasized it would be. The two of us sauntering along, swinging our bags, laughing happily . . . trying on each other's things . . . buying each other friendship bracelets . . . calling each other by little nicknames . . .

'So? How was it?'

'It was . . . fab!' I force a bright smile. 'It was really good fun. We both had a great time.'

'What did you buy?'

'A couple of tops . . . a really nice skirt . . . some shoes . . .'

'Mm-hmm.' Luke nods. 'And what did Jess buy?'

For a moment I can't speak.

'Nothing,' I whisper at last.

'Oh Becky.' Luke sighs and puts his arm round me. 'You didn't have a great time, did you?'

'No,' I say in a tiny voice. 'Not really.'

'I did have my doubts.' He strokes my cheek. 'Listen Becky, I know you wanted to find a soulmate. I know you wanted Jess to be your new best friend. But maybe you'll have to accept you're just . . . too different.'

'We're *not* too different,' I say stubbornly. 'We're sisters.'

'Sweetheart, it's OK,' says Luke. 'You can admit it if

161

you don't get along. No one will think you've failed.'

Failed?

The word flicks me on the raw.

'We do get along!' I say. 'We do! We just need to find a bit more . . . common ground. So she doesn't like shopping.' I swallow a few times. 'But that doesn't matter! I like other things than shopping!'

Luke is shaking his head.

'Accept it. You're different people and there's no reason why you should get on.'

'But we've got the same blood! We can't be that different! We *can't* be!'

'Becky—'

'I'm not going to give up, just like that! This is my long-lost sister we're talking about, Luke! This could be my only chance to get to know her.'

'Sweetheart—'

'I know we can be friends,' I cut him off. 'I *know* we can.'

With a sudden determination I wrench open the car door and get out.

'Hey, Jess!' I call, hurrying across the lawn. 'After your conference, do you want to come and stay for the weekend? I promise we'll have a good time.'

'That's a nice idea, love!' says Dad, his face lighting up.

'I'm not sure,' says Jess. 'I really have to get back home . . .'

'Please. Just one weekend. We don't need to go shopping!' My words are tumbling out of me. 'It won't be like today. We can do whatever you like. Just have a really low-key, easy time. What do you think?'

There's silence. My fingers are twisting into knots. Jess glances at Dad's hopeful face.

'OK,' she says at last. 'That would be nice. Thanks.'

PGNI First Bank Visa
7 Camel Square
Liverpool L1 5NP

Mrs Rebecca Brandon
37 Maida Vale Mansions
Maida Vale
London NW6 0YF

12 May 2003

Dear Mrs Brandon

Thank you for your application for the High Status Golden Credit Card. We are glad to inform you that you have been successful.

In answer to your questions, the card will be delivered to your home address and will resemble a credit card. It cannot be 'disguised as a cake' as you suggest.

Nor can we provide a distraction outside as it arrives.

If you have any further questions please do not hesitate to contact me and we hope you enjoy the benefits of your new card.

Yours sincerely

Peter Johnson
Customer Accounts Executive

PGNI First Bank Visa
7 Camel Square
Liverpool L1 5NP

Ms Jessica Bertram
12 Hill Rise
Scully
Cumbria

12 May 2003

Dear Ms Bertram

Thank you for your letter.

I apologize for approaching you with the offer of a High Status Golden Credit Card. I did not mean to cause any offence.

By saying you had been personally handpicked for a twenty-thousand-pound credit limit, I was not intending to imply that you are 'debt-ridden and irresponsible' nor to defame your character.

As a gesture of goodwill I enclose a gift voucher of £25, and look forward to being of service should you change your mind on the issue of credit cards.

Yours sincerely

Peter Johnson
Customer Accounts Executive

TWELVE

I'm not giving up. No way.

So maybe my first meeting with Jess didn't go quite as I planned. Maybe we didn't exactly hit it off like I thought we would. But this weekend will be better, I just know it will be. I mean, in hindsight, the first meeting was *bound* to be a bit awkward. But this time we'll have got through that first hurdle and will be far more relaxed and easy with each other. Exactly!

Plus, I'm far more prepared than I was last time. After Jess had left last Saturday, Mum and Dad could see I was a bit down, so they made a pot of tea and we had a good old chat. And we all agreed it's impossible to get on with someone straight away if you don't know anything about them. So Mum and Dad racked their brains for all the details they knew about Jess, and wrote them all down. And I've been learning them all week.

Like, for instance: she did nine GCSEs and got As in all of them. She never eats avocados. As well as caving and walking, she does something called potholing. She likes poetry. And her favourite dog is a . . .

Fuck.

I grab the crib sheet and scan down.

Oh yes. A border collie.

It's Saturday morning, and I'm in the spare room,

making my final preparations for Jess's arrival. I bought a book this week called *The Gracious Hostess*, and it said the guest room should be 'well thought out, with little individual touches to make your guest feel welcome'.

So on the dressing table are flowers and a book of poetry, and by the bed I've put a careful selection of magazines: *Rambling News*, *Caving Enthusiast* and *Potholing Monthly*, which is a magazine you can only order from the Internet. (I had to take out a two-year subscription actually, just to get a copy. But that's all right. I can just forward the other twenty-three copies to Jess.)

And on the wall is my *pièce de resistance*, which I am so proud of. It's an enormous poster of a cave! With stalag— things.

I fluff up the pillows, feeling a beat of anticipation. Tonight will be totally different from last time. For a start, we won't go *near* any shops. I've just planned a nice, simple, relaxed evening in. We can watch a movie and eat popcorn, and do each other's nails, and really chill. And then later on I'll come and sit on her bed and we can wear matching pyjamas and eat peppermint creams, and talk long into the night.

'This all looks very nice,' says Luke, coming in behind me. 'You've done a great job.'

'Thanks,' I say with a bashful shrug.

'In fact, the whole apartment looks amazing!' He wanders out, and I follow him into the hall. It *is* looking pretty good, though I say it myself. Although there are still a few boxes here and there, the whole place looks so much clearer!

'I haven't finished yet,' I say, glancing into our bedroom, where there's still a load of stuff under the bed.

'I can see. But even so, it's a tremendous achievement!' Luke looks around admiringly.

'It just took a bit of creative vision.' I give a modest smile. 'Lateral thinking.'

We walk into the sitting room, which is utterly transformed. All the piles of rugs and boxes and crates have disappeared. There are just two sofas, two coffee tables, and the Indonesian gamelan.

'Hats off to you, Becky,' says Luke, shaking his head. 'This looks great.'

'It was nothing!'

'No.' Luke frowns. 'I feel I owe you an apology. You told me you could make it all work – and I doubted you. But somehow you've done it. I would never have guessed so much clutter could be so well organized.' He looks around the room incredulously. 'There were so many things in here! Where have they all *gone*?' He laughs, and after a moment I join in.

'I've just . . . found homes for them!' I say brightly.

'Well, I'm really impressed,' he says, running his hand over the mantelpiece, which is bare except for the five hand-painted eggs. 'You should become a storage consultant.'

'Maybe I will!'

OK, I think I want to get off this subject now. Any minute Luke's going to start looking a bit more closely and say something like, 'Where are the Chinese urns?' or 'Where are the wooden giraffes?'

'So . . . is the computer on?' I say casually.

'Yup,' says Luke, picking up one of the eggs and looking at it.

'Great!' I beam at him. ' Well, I'll check my emails and . . . why don't you make us some coffee?'

I wait until Luke's safely in the kitchen, then hurry to the computer and type in www.eBay.co.uk.

eBay has totally saved my life. Totally.

In fact, what did I ever do before eBay? It is the most brilliant, genius invention since . . . well, since whoever invented shops.

The minute I got back from Mum's last Saturday I

joined, and put up for sale the Chinese urns, the wooden giraffes and three of the rugs. And in three days they'd all been sold! Just like that! So the next day I put up five more rugs and two coffee tables. And since then, I haven't stopped.

I quickly click on 'Items I'm Selling', glancing at the door every so often. I mustn't be long or Luke'll come in and see me, but I'm desperate to see if anyone has bid on the totem pole.

A moment later the page appears ... and yes! Result! Someone's bid fifty pounds! I feel a hit of adrenalin and punch the air with a whoop (a quiet one, so Luke won't hear). It's such a power kick, selling stuff! I'm totally addicted!

And the best thing of all is, I'm killing two birds with one stone. I'm solving our clutter problems – *and* I'm making money. Quite a lot of money, actually! I don't want to boast – but every single day this week I've made a profit. I'm just like a City bond trader!

For example, I got £200 for the slate coffee table – and we certainly didn't pay more than a hundred for it. I got £100 for the Chinese urns, and £150 each for the five kilims, which only cost about £40 each in Turkey, if that. And best of all, I made a cool £2,000 on ten Tiffany clocks I don't even remember buying! The guy even paid in cash and came to pick them up! Honestly, I'm doing so well, I could make eBay trading my career!

I can hear Luke getting mugs out in the kitchen, and I click off 'Items I'm Selling'.

Then, very quickly, I log on to 'Items I'm Bidding On'.

Obviously I joined eBay very much as a *seller* rather than a bidder. But I just happened to be browsing the other day when I came across this amazing orange vintage coat from the fifties with big black buttons. It's a total one-off, and no one had made a single bid on it. So I made a tiny exception, just for that.

And also for a pair of Prada shoes which only had one bid on them, for fifty quid. I mean, Prada shoes for fifty quid!

And that fantastic Yves Saint Laurent evening dress which some other bidder got in the end. God, that was annoying. I won't make that mistake again.

I log on to the vintage coat — and I don't believe it. I bid £80 yesterday, which is the reserve price – and I've been trumped with £100. Well, I'm not losing this one. No way. I quickly type in '£120' and close down, just as Luke comes in with a tray.

'Any emails?' he says.

'Er . . . some!' I say brightly, and take a cup of coffee. 'Thanks!'

I haven't told Luke about the whole eBay thing because there's no need for him to get involved in every mundane detail of the household finances. In fact, my job is to shield him from all that.

'I found these in the kitchen.' Luke nods towards a tin of luxury Fortnum and Mason chocolate biscuits on the tray. 'Very nice.'

'Just a little treat.' I smile at him. 'And don't worry. It's all within the budget.'

Which is true! My budget is so much bigger now, I can afford to splash out!

Luke takes a sip of coffee. Then his eyes fall on a pink folder lying on his desk.

'What's this?'

I *wondered* when he was going to notice that. It's the other project I've been working on this week. Project: Supportive Wife.

'That's for you,' I say casually. 'Just a little thing I've put together to help you. My ideas for the future of the company.'

It hit me in the bath the other day. If Luke wins this great big pitch, he's going to have to expand the company. And I know all about expansion.

The reason is, when I was a personal shopper at Barneys I had this client Sheri, who owned her own business. And I heard the whole saga of how she expanded too fast and all the mistakes she made, like renting six thousand square feet of office space in TriBeCa which she never used. I mean, at the time I thought it was really boring. I actually dreaded her appointments. But now I realize it's all totally relevant to Luke!

So I decided to write down everything she used to keep going on about, like consolidating your key markets and acquiring competitors. And that's when an even better idea came to me. Luke should buy up another PR firm!

I even know which one he should buy. David Neville, who used to work for Farnham PR, set up on his own three years ago, when I was still a financial journalist. He's really talented and everyone keeps saying how well he's doing. But I know he's secretly been struggling, because I saw his wife Judy at the hairdresser's last week and she told me.

'Becky . . .' Luke's frowning. 'I haven't got time for this.'

'But it'll be useful to you!' I say quickly. 'When I was at Barneys I learned all about—'

'*Barneys?* Becky, I run a PR company. Not a fashion store.'

'But I've had these ideas—'

'Becky,' Luke interrupts impatiently, 'right now my priority is bringing in new business. Nothing else. I don't have time for your ideas, OK?' He stuffs the folder into his briefcase without opening it. 'I'll look at it sometime.'

I sit down, feeling a bit crestfallen. The doorbell rings and I look up in surprise.

'Oh! Maybe that's Jess, early!'

'No, it'll be Gary,' says Luke. 'I'll let him in.'

Gary is Luke's second-in-command. He ran the London office while we were living in New York and on honeymoon, and he and Luke get on really well. He even ended up being Luke's best man at our wedding.

Kind of.

The wedding's a bit of a long story, actually.

'What's Gary doing here?' I ask in surprise.

'I told him to meet me here,' replies Luke, heading out to the entryphone and buzzing it. 'We have some work to do on the pitch. Then the two of us will go to lunch.'

'Oh, right,' I say, trying to hide my disappointment.

I was really looking forward to spending a bit of time with Luke today, before Jess arrives. He's so busy these days. He hasn't been home once before eight all week, and last night he didn't arrive back until eleven.

I mean, I know they're working hard at the moment. I know the Arcodas pitch is important. But still. For months and months, Luke and I were together twenty-four hours a day . . . and now I hardly ever see him.

'Maybe I could help with the pitch!' I say, having a sudden brainwave. 'I could join the team!'

'I don't think so,' says Luke, without even looking up.

'There must be something I could do,' I say, leaning forward eagerly. 'Luke, I really want to help the company. I'll do anything!'

'It's all pretty much under control,' says Luke. 'But thanks.'

I feel a twinge of resentment. Why won't he let me get involved? You'd think he'd be *grateful*.

'Do you want to come out to lunch with us?' he adds kindly.

'No. It's fine.' I give a little shrug. 'Have fun. Hi, Gary,' I add, as he appears at the front door.

'Hi, Becky!' says Gary cheerfully.

'Come in,' says Luke, and ushers him into the study.

The door closes – then almost immediately it opens again and Luke looks out. 'Becky, if the phone rings, could you answer it? I don't want to be disturbed for a few minutes.'

'OK!' I say.

'Thanks.' He smiles and touches my hand. 'That's a real help.'

'No problem!' I say brightly. The door closes again, and I'm almost tempted to give it a kick.

Answering the phone is *not* what I meant by helping the company.

I wander morosely down the corridor towards the sitting room and close the door with a resentful bang. I'm an intelligent, creative person. I could help them, I know I could. I mean, we're supposed to be a partnership. We're supposed to do things *together*.

The phone rings and I jump. Maybe it's Jess. Maybe she's here! I hurry to the receiver and pick up.

'Hello?'

'Mrs Brandon?' comes a man's raspy voice.

'Yes!'

'It's Nathan Temple here.'

My mind is totally blank. Nathan? I don't know any Nathans.

'You may recall, we met in Milan a few weeks ago.'

Oh my God. It's the man from the shop! I should have recognized his voice straight away.

'Hello!' I say in delight. 'Of course I remember! How are you?'

'I'm well, thank you,' says Nathan Temple. 'And you? Enjoying your new bag?'

'I absolutely love it!' I exclaim. 'It's changed my whole life! Thank you *so* much again for what you did.'

'It was my pleasure.'

There's a short silence. I'm not entirely sure what to say next.

'Maybe I could buy you lunch,' I exclaim impulsively. 'As a proper thank you. Anywhere you like!'

'That's not necessary.' He sounds amused. 'Besides which, my doctor has put me on a diet.'

'Oh, right. That's a shame.'

'However, since you mention it –' His raspy voice cuts me off. 'As you said yourself in Milan . . . one good turn deserves another.'

'Absolutely! I really owe you one! If there's anything I can do, *anything* at all . . .'

'I was thinking of your husband, Luke. I was hoping he might do me the smallest of favours.'

'He'd love to!' I exclaim. 'I know he would!'

'Is he there? Might I have a quick word?'

My mind works quickly.

If I get Luke to the phone now I'll have to disturb him. And explain who Nathan Temple is . . . and how I met him . . . and about the Angel bag . . .

'You know what?' I say, turning back to the phone. 'He's not in right now, I'm afraid. But can I take a message?'

'The situation is this. I'm opening a five-star hotel on the island of Cyprus. It's going to be a top-of-the-range resort and I'm planning a big launch. Celebrity party, press coverage. I'd very much like your husband to be involved.'

I stare at the phone in disbelief. A celebrity party in Cyprus? A five-star hotel? Oh my God, how cool is that?

'I'm sure he'd love to!' I say, regaining my voice. 'It sounds fantastic!'

'Your husband's very talented. He has a very classy reputation. Which is what we want.'

'Well,' I glow with pride, 'he is pretty good at what he does.'

'I gather he specializes in financial institutions, though. Would a hotel launch be a problem?'

My heart starts thudding. I can't let this opportunity slip away. I have to sell Brandon Communications.

'Not at all,' I say smoothly. 'We at Brandon Communications are skilled in all areas of public relations, from finance to big business to hotels. Versatility is our motto.'

Yes! I sound so professional!

'You work for the company, then?'

'I have a . . . small consultancy role,' I say, crossing my fingers. 'Specializing in strategy. And by sheer chance, one of our current strategies is an expansion into the . . . er . . . five-star-travel arena.'

'Then it looks like we might be able to help one another out,' says Nathan Temple, sounding pleased. 'Perhaps we could set up a meeting this week? As I say, we're very anxious to have your husband Luke on board.'

'Please, Mr Temple,' I say in my most charming manner. 'You did me a favour. Now this is my chance to repay it. My husband would be delighted to help you. In fact, he'll make it a priority!' I beam at the phone. 'Let me take your number, and I'll get Luke to call you later today.'

'I look forward to your husband's call. Nice talking to you again, Mrs Brandon.'

'Please! Call me Becky!'

As I replace the receiver I'm grinning from ear to ear. I am a star.

A total and complete star.

There's Luke and Gary, slaving away over their pitch – and meanwhile I've snaffled them a fabulous new client without even trying! And not even some dreary old bank. A five-star hotel in Cyprus! A huge, prestigious job!

Just then the study door opens and Luke comes out, holding a folder. As he picks up his briefcase he glances over and gives me a distracted smile.

174

'All right, Becky? We're off to lunch. Who was that on the phone?'

'Oh, just a friend of mine,' I say carelessly. 'By the way, Luke ... maybe I will come along to lunch after all.'

'OK,' says Luke. 'Great!'

He has *so* underestimated me. He has no idea, does he? When he hears how I've been wheeling and dealing with top business magnates on his behalf, he'll be totally gobsmacked. And *then* maybe he'll see just how much of a help I can be to him. *Then* maybe he'll start to appreciate me a bit more.

Just wait till I tell them the news. Just wait!

All the way to the restaurant, I'm hugging my secret to me with glee. Honestly, Luke should hire me! I should become some kind of ambassador for the company!

I mean, I'm obviously gifted at networking. It obviously comes naturally to me. A chance meeting in Milan — and this is what results. A brand-new client for the company. And the point is, it was effortless!

It's all about instincts. You either have them or you don't.

'All right, Becky?' says Luke as we enter the restaurant.

'Fine!' I give him a mysterious smile. He is going to be so impressed when I tell him the news. He'll probably order a bottle of champagne straight away. Or even throw me a little party. That's what they do when they win a big pitch.

And this one could be huge. It could be an amazing new business opportunity for Luke! He could start a whole division devoted to five-star hotels and spas. Brandon Communications Luxury Travel. And I could be divisional director, maybe.

Or the one who tries out the spas.

'So ... still on the dinner we're hosting,' Gary is

saying to Luke as we sit down. 'You've sorted out the gifts?'

'Yup,' says Luke. 'They're at home. What about transport? Have we organized cars for them?'

'I'll get someone on to it.' Gary makes a note, then looks up at me. 'Sorry, Becky. This must be boring. You know this pitch is pretty important to us.'

'That's OK,' I say with a demure smile. 'Luke was just telling me how getting new business is your number-one priority right now?'

'Absolutely.' Gary nods.

Ha!

'I expect it's quite hard work, bringing in new clients,' I add innocently.

'Yes, it can be.' Gary smiles.

Ha-di-ha ha!

As the waiter pours mineral water for Luke and Gary, I suddenly notice three girls at a nearby table, nudging each other and pointing at my Angel bag. Trying to hide my delight, I casually adjust the bag on my chair, so that the embossed angel and 'Dante' is clearly visible.

It's just amazing. Everywhere I go, people notice this bag. Everywhere! It is the best thing I have ever bought, ever, *ever*. And now it's brought Luke new business, too. It's a lucky charm!

'Cheers!' I say, lifting my glass as the waiter retreats. 'To new clients!'

'New clients,' Luke and Gary echo in unison. Gary takes a sip of water, then turns to Luke. 'So Luke, just regarding the last proposal we're making. I spoke to Sam Church the other day—'

I can't wait a moment longer. I *have* to tell them.

'Speaking of churches!' I interrupt in bright tones.

There's a startled pause.

'Becky, we weren't talking about churches,' says Luke.

'Yes you were! Kind of.'

Luke looks bemused. OK, I could have managed this a little more smoothly. But never mind.

'So, *speaking* of churches . . .' I press on. 'And . . . er . . . religious buildings in general . . . I suppose you've heard of a man called Nathan Temple, have you?'

I look from Luke to Gary, unable to hide my elation. Both men look back at me curiously.

'Of course I've heard of Nathan Temple,' says Luke.

Ha! I knew it.

'He's a pretty big player, huh? Pretty important.' I raise my eyebrows in a cryptic manner. 'He's probably someone you'd really like to network with. Maybe even get as a new client?'

'Hardly!' Luke gives an explosive laugh and takes a sip of water.

I pause uncertainly. What's 'hardly' supposed to mean?

'Of course you would!' I persist. 'He'd be a great client!'

'No, Becky. He wouldn't.' Luke puts down his glass. 'Sorry Gary, what were you saying?'

I stare at him, discomfited.

This is not going according to plan. I had the whole conversation mapped out in my head. Luke was going to say, 'I'd adore Nathan Temple as a client, of course – but how does one *get* to him?' Then Gary was going to sigh and say, 'No one can get to Nathan Temple.' And then I was going to lean across the table with a confidential little smile . . .

'So, I've spoken to Sam Church,' resumes Gary, taking some papers out of his briefcase. 'And he gave me these. Have a look.'

'Wait!' I interrupt, trying to haul the conversation back on track. 'So Luke, why wouldn't you want

Nathan Temple as a client? I mean, he's rich . . . he's famous . . .'

'Infamous, more like,' puts in Gary with a grin.

'Becky, you do know who Nathan Temple is?' says Luke.

'Of course I do,' I say. 'He's a top businessman and . . . er . . . hotelier . . .'

Luke raises his eyebrows.

'Becky, he runs the seediest chain of motels in the land.'

My smile freezes on my face. For a few moments I can't quite speak.

'What?' I manage at last.

'Not any more,' says Gary. 'Be fair.'

'Then he used to,' says Luke. 'That's how he made his money. Value Motels. Waterbeds thrown in for free. And whatever other business went on behind closed doors.' He pulls a disdainful face and sips his water.

'You've heard the rumour he's considering buying up the *Daily World*,' says Gary.

'Yes,' says Luke with a grimace. 'Spare us. You know he has a conviction for GBH? The man's a criminal.'

My head is spinning. Nathan Temple? A criminal? But . . . he seemed so nice. He was so sweet! He got me my Angel bag!

'Apparently he's reformed.' Gary shrugs. 'Become a new person. So he says.'

'A new person?' says Luke dismissively. 'Gary, he's little better than a gangster.'

I nearly drop my glass on the floor. I owe a favour to a *gangster*?

'"Gangster"'s a little harsh,' says Gary, amused. 'That was years ago.'

'These people never change,' says Luke firmly.

'You're a hard man, Luke!' says Gary with a laugh. Then he suddenly spots my face. 'Becky, are you OK?'

'Fine!' I say shrilly, and take a gulp of wine. 'Lovely!'

I feel hot and cold all over. This is not going to plan. This is not going remotely to plan.

My first brilliant networking triumph. The first big client I woo for Brandon Communications. And he turns out to be a motel king with a criminal conviction.

But how was I supposed to know? How? He seemed so charming. He was so well dressed!

I swallow several times.

And now I've said Luke will work for him.

Kind of.

I mean . . . I didn't actually *promise* anything, did I? Oh God.

I can hear my own voice now, gaily chirping, 'My husband would be delighted to do it. In fact he'll make it a priority!'

I gaze at my menu, trying to stay calm. OK, it's obvious what I have to do. I have to tell Luke. Yes. Just confess the whole thing. Milan . . . the Angel bag . . . the phone call today . . . everything.

This is what I have to do. It's the grown-up option.

I glance at Luke's taut face as he reads through his paperwork and feel a spasm of fear clutch at my insides.

I can't.

I just can't.

'It's funny you should have mentioned Nathan Temple, Becky,' says Gary, sipping his water. 'I haven't even told you this yet, Luke, but he's been in touch with us about doing the PR for some new hotel.'

I stare at Gary's broad, amiable face and feel a huge wave of relief.

Thank God. Thank *God*.

Of course they would have made an official approach too. Of course! I've been worrying about

179

nothing! Luke will do the job and I'll be quits with Nathan Temple and everything will be fine . . .

'I take it we'll decline?' Gary adds.

Decline? My head jerks up.

'Can you think what it would do to our reputation?' says Luke with a short laugh. 'Turn down the job. But tactfully,' he adds with a frown. 'If he's buying the *Daily World* we don't want to offend him.'

'Don't decline!' I blurt out before I can stop myself.

Both men turn to me in surprise, and I force a light-hearted laugh. 'I mean . . . shouldn't you look at both sides of the argument? Before you make your decision.'

'Becky, as far as I'm concerned there *is* only one argument,' says Luke crisply. 'Nathan Temple is not the sort of character I want associated with my company.' He opens his menu. 'We should order.'

'Don't you think that's a bit judgemental?' I say desperately. '"Cast not the first clout" and all that.'

'What?' Luke sounds astonished.

'It's the Bible!'

Luke gives me a look.

'Do you mean "stone"?' he says.

'Er . . .'

Oh. Maybe he's right. But honestly. Stone . . . clout . . . what's the difference?

'The point is—' I begin.

'The point is,' Luke interrupts, 'Brandon Communications does not want to be associated with someone who has a criminal record. Let alone the rest of it.'

'But that's so . . . narrow-minded! Most people have probably got a criminal record these days!' I gesture widely with my arms. 'I mean, who sitting round this table does not have some kind of criminal record?'

There's a short silence.

'Well,' says Luke. 'I don't. Gary doesn't. You don't.'

I look at him, taken aback. I suppose he's right. I don't.

That's quite a surprise, actually. I'd always thought of myself as living on the edge.

'Even so—'

'Becky, what's brought this on, anyway?' Luke frowns. 'Why are you so obsessed with Nathan Temple?'

'I'm not *obsessed*!' I say hurriedly. 'I'm just . . . interested in your clients. And prospective clients.'

'Well, he's not my client. Nor my prospective client,' says Luke in final tones. 'And neither will he ever be.'

'Right.' I swallow. 'Well . . . that's pretty clear.'

There's silence as we all study our menus. At least, the other two are studying their menus. I'm pretending to study mine, while my mind goes skittering round and round.

So I can't persuade Luke. So I'll just have to manage the situation. This is what supportive wives do, anyway. They deal with problems discreetly and efficiently. I bet Hillary Clinton's done this kind of thing millions of times.

It'll be fine. I'll simply phone up Nathan Temple, thank him for his kind offer and say unfortunately Luke's really, really busy . . .

No. I'll say he *tried* to call but no one answered . . .

'Becky? Are you OK?'

I look up to see both men gazing at me. Abruptly I realize I'm tapping the table harder and harder with one of Gary's pencils.

'I'm great!' I say, and quickly put it down.

OK. I have a plan. What I will do is . . . I will say that Luke is ill.

Yes. Genius. No one can argue with that.

So as soon as we get home and Luke is closeted with Gary in the study, I hurry to the phone in our bedroom.

I kick the bedroom door shut and hurriedly dial the number Nathan Temple gave me. To my huge relief, it clicks straight on to voice-mail.

And now I listen properly, he sounds *exactly* like a motel king with a criminal past. Why on earth didn't I hear it before? I must be deaf or something!

The beep goes, and I jump in fright.

'Hi!' I say, trying to keep my voice light and easy. 'This is a message for Mr Temple. It's Becky Brandon here. Er . . . I told my husband all about your hotel, and he thought it sounded fab! But I'm afraid he's not very well at the moment. So he won't be able to do the launch after all. Which is a real shame! Anyway, I hope you find someone else! Bye!'

I put the phone down and sink on to the bed, my heart thumping.

There. Sorted.

'Becky?' Luke opens the door, and I start in terror.

'What? What is it?'

'It's OK,' he says, laughing. 'Nothing's wrong. I just wanted to tell you, Jess is here.'

THIRTEEN

'She's coming up in the lift,' says Luke, opening the front door. 'Who were you on the phone to, by the way?'

'Nobody,' I say quickly. 'I was just . . . er . . . phoning up the speaking clock.'

It's fine, I tell myself firmly. It's done. Everything's sorted.

I can hear the lift moving, down below. Jess is on her way!

Quickly I grab my crib sheet and skim it one last time. Border collies . . . hates avocados . . . maths teacher was called Mr Lewis . . .

'Becky, I'd put that away before she arrives,' says Luke, looking amused.

'Oh. Yes.'

I stuff it into my pocket and take a few deep breaths to prepare myself. Now she's here, I'm starting to feel just a tad nervous.

'Listen Becky,' says Luke, watching me. 'Before she arrives . . . I sincerely hope you two hit it off this time. But are you keeping a sense of proportion? You don't have all your hopes pinned on this visit, do you?'

'Honestly Luke!' I say. 'Who do you think I am?'

Of *course* I have all my hopes pinned on this visit. But that's fine, because I know it's going to work out.

Things will be different this time. For a start, we won't do anything that Jess doesn't want to do. I'm just going to follow her lead.

And the other thing I must remember is a tip which Luke gave me. He said it was great that I was so friendly towards Jess – but that she's quite reserved, and maybe great big hugs weren't her style. So he suggested I should be a bit more collected, just until we know each other better. Which is a fair point.

From the hall comes the noise of the lift, getting closer. I almost can't breathe. Why is this lift so *slow*?

And then suddenly the doors are opening to reveal Jess in jeans and a grey T-shirt, holding her rucksack.

'Hi!' I cry, running forward. 'Welcome! We can do whatever you want this weekend! Anything! Just name it! You're the boss!'

Jess doesn't move. In fact, she seems frozen to the spot.

'Hi Jess,' says Luke more calmly. 'Welcome to London.'

'Come on in!' I spread my arms. 'Make yourself at home! No avocados here!'

Jess stares at me as though bemused – then glances at the buttons of the lift, almost as if she wants to go back down again.

'Let me take your bag,' says Luke. 'How was your conference?'

He ushers Jess into the flat, and at last she walks in, looking around warily.

'It was good, thanks,' she says. 'Hi, Becky.'

'Hi! It's so great you're here! I'll show you your room.'

I open the door of the guest room proudly, waiting for her to comment on the cave picture, or *Potholing Monthly*. But she says nothing, just 'Thanks,' as Luke puts down her bag.

'Look,' I point out. 'It's a cave!'

'Er . . . yes,' says Jess, looking slightly bewildered.

There's a pause – and I feel a tiny spasm of alarm. Don't say the atmosphere's going to be awkward.

'Let's all have a drink!' I exclaim. 'Let's open a bottle of champagne!'

'Becky . . . it's only four o'clock,' says Luke. 'Maybe a cup of tea would be more appropriate?'

'I'd love a cup of tea,' says Jess.

'Tea then!' I say. 'Excellent idea!'

I lead the way into the kitchen, and Jess follows, peering all around the flat.

'Nice place,' she says.

'Becky's done a great job on it,' says Luke pleasantly. 'You should have seen it this time last week. We'd had a load of purchases delivered from honeymoon . . . and you could not *move* for stuff.' He shakes his head. 'I still don't know how you did it, Becky.'

'Oh, you know.' I give a modest smile. 'Just a question of organization.'

I'm just switching on the kettle as Gary comes into the kitchen.

'This is my associate, Gary,' says Luke. 'This is Becky's half-sister, Jess. She comes from Cumbria.'

'Ah!' says Gary as he shakes Jess's hand. 'I know Cumbria! Beautiful part of the country. Whereabouts do you live?'

'A village called Scully,' replies Jess. 'It's pretty rural. Very different from this.'

'I've been to Scully!' says Gary. 'Years ago. Isn't there a famous walk near by?'

'You probably mean Scully Pike.'

'That's it! We tried to climb it – but the weather took a turn. Nearly fell off the bloody thing.'

'It can be dangerous,' says Jess. 'You have to know what you're doing. Idiots come up from the south and get in all sorts of trouble.'

'That's me,' says Gary cheerfully. 'But it's worth it

for the scenery. Those dry-stone walls are spectacular,' he adds to Luke. 'Like works of art. Miles and miles of them, strung out across the countryside.'

I'm listening to the conversation in total fascination. I'd love to get to know rural England a bit better. I'd love to see some dry-stone walls. I mean, all I know is London and Surrey, which is practically London anyway.

'We should buy a cottage in Cumbria!' I say enthusiastically as I hand round cups of tea. 'In Jess's village! Then we could see you all the time,' I add to Jess. 'Wouldn't that be great?'

There's quite a long silence.

'Yes,' says Jess at last. 'Great.'

'I don't think we'll be buying any cottages in the near future,' says Luke, raising his eyebrows at me. 'We're on a budget, remember?'

'Yes, I know,' I retort, raising my eyebrows back. 'And I'm sticking to it, aren't I?'

'Well, yes,' says Luke. 'Incredibly, you are.' He looks at the tin of Fortnum biscuits on the counter. 'Although, quite frankly, I have no idea how you're managing it.' He opens the fridge. 'Look at all this. Stuffed olives . . . smoked lobster . . . and this is on a *budget*.'

I can't help feeling a little glow of pride. All that food is courtesy of selling those Tiffany clocks! I was so delighted, I went straight out and bought a big hamper, full of all Luke's favourite things.

'Just a question of good household management,' I say nonchalantly and offer him the plate. 'Have a luxury chocolate biscuit.'

'Hmm.' Luke gives me a suspicious look, then turns to Gary. 'We must get on.'

The two men head out of the kitchen – and I'm left alone with Jess. I pour her another cup of tea and perch on a bar stool opposite her.

'So!' I say. 'What would you like to do?'

'I'm easy,' says Jess with a shrug.

'It's up to you! Totally!'

'I don't really mind.' Jess sips her tea.

There's silence, apart from the tap dripping slowly into the sink.

Which is fine. It's just one of those relaxed, companionable silences you can have with members of your family. In fact, it *shows* we're easy with each other. It's not remotely awkward or anything . . .

Oh God, *speak*. Please.

'I'd like to do some weight-training,' says Jess suddenly. 'I normally work out every day. But I haven't been able to this week.'

'Right!' I say in delight. 'That's a brilliant idea! I'll do it too!'

'Really?' Jess looks taken aback.

'Of course!' I take a final sip of tea, then put my cup down. 'I'll just go and get ready!'

What a fab idea. Doing exercise together is totally bonding. We can go to Taylor's Health Club round the corner, where I'm a Gold Member, do a bit of a work-out, and then head to the juice bar. I know the juice bar will be open, because I've been loads of times before at about this hour of the day.

And I should think the gym bit will be open too, downstairs.

Or is it upstairs?

Anyway. Wherever it is.

I yank open my wardrobe doors and pull out my drawer full of gym kit. I could wear my Juicy tracksuit, except I might get too hot . . . or that really cool pink top, except I've seen a girl in the juice bar wearing the same exact one . . .

At last I select some black leggings with retro piping up the sides, plus a white T-shirt and my fab hi-tech trainers that I got in the States. They cost quite a lot, but then they *are* biomechanically balanced with a dual-density midsole. Plus their advanced engineering means you can take them seamlessly from the marathon track to the outdoor terrain of the trail hike.

I quickly put on the whole outfit, tie my hair up in a ponytail, and add my cool Adidas sports watch. (Which just shows how wrong Luke is. I *knew* I would need a sports watch one day.) I hurry to the guest room and knock on the door.

'Hi!'

'Come in,' Jess's voice sounds muffled and kind of weird. Cautiously I push open the door. She's changed into old grey shorts and a T-shirt and, to my surprise, is lying on the floor.

Doing sit-ups, I suddenly realize as her entire torso rises off the ground. Blimey. She's quite good at them.

And now she's doing those twisty ones I've never been able to manage.

'So . . . shall we go?' I say.

'Go where?' replies Jess, without missing a beat.

'To the gym! I thought you wanted to . . .' I trail off as she starts raising her legs off the ground, too.

OK, now that's just showing off.

'I don't need to go anywhere. I can work out here.'

Here? Is she serious? But there aren't any mirrors. There isn't any MTV. There isn't a juice bar.

My gaze falls on a snake-like scar at the top of Jess's shin. I'm about to ask how she did it when she catches me looking and flushes red. Maybe she's sensitive. I'd better not mention it.

'Don't you need weights?'

'I've got them.' She reaches in her rucksack and pulls out two old waterbottles filled with sand.

Those are her weights?

'I wouldn't go near a gym,' she says, starting to raise the bottles above her head. 'Waste of money. Half the people who join gyms never go, anyway. They buy expensive outfits and never even wear them. What's the point in that?'

'Oh, absolutely!' I say quickly. 'I totally agree.'

Jess stops, and adjusts her grip on one of the weights. Then her eye falls on the back of my leggings.

'What's that?' she says.

'Er . . .' I reach round with my hand.

Damn. It's the price tag hanging out.

'Er . . . nothing!' I say, hastily tucking it in. 'I'll just go and get some . . . weights of my own.'

As I return from the kitchen with two bottles of Evian, I can't help feeling a bit disconcerted. This isn't exactly what I had in mind. I'd pictured the two of us running effortlessly along on adjacent machines, with some upbeat song playing and the spotlights making our hair look all shiny.

Anyway. Never mind.

'So . . . I'll follow you, shall I?' I say, joining Jess on the carpet.

'I'm going on to some bicep work,' says Jess. 'It's pretty straightforward.' She starts raising her arms up and down, and I copy what she's doing. God, she exercises quite fast, doesn't she?

'Shall I put on some music?' I say after a few moments.

'I don't need music,' says Jess.

'No. Neither do I,' I say quickly.

My arms are starting to ache. This can't be good for them, surely. I glance at Jess – but she's steadfastly pumping away. Casually I lean down, pretending to adjust my shoelace. Then suddenly I have a thought.

'I won't be a moment,' I say, and hurry out to the kitchen again. A few moments later I'm back, holding two slim silver bottles.

'Here's a health drink,' I say, proudly handing one to Jess. 'So you can rebalance.'

'So I can what?' Jess puts down her weights with a frown.

'It says it on the bottle – look,' I explain. 'It has a unique blend of life-enhancing vitamins and herbs.'

Jess is scanning the label.

'It's just sugar and water. Look. Water . . . glucose syrup . . .' She puts it down. 'No thanks.'

'But it's got special properties!' I say in surprise. 'It rebalances, revitalizes and moisturizes your skin from the inside.'

'How does it do that?'

'I . . . don't know.'

'How much is it?' Jess picks the bottle up again and looks at the price label. '£2.95?' She seems totally scandalized. 'Three pounds for some sugar and water? You could buy a twenty-kilo sack of potatoes for that!'

'But . . . I don't want a twenty-kilo sack of potatoes,' I say, bemused.

'Then you should!' says Jess. 'Potatoes are one of the most nutritious, cost-effective foods available.' She eyes me reprovingly. 'People underestimate them. But did you know a potato skin has more vitamin C than an orange?'

'Er . . . no,' I say nervously. 'No, I didn't.'

'You could live off potatoes and milk.' She starts hefting her weights again. 'You'd get practically every nutrient the body needs, just from those two.'

'Right!' I say. 'That's . . . really good! Er, I'll just go and have a shower.'

As I close the door of the bedroom, I feel totally bewildered. What was all that about potatoes? I'm not even sure how we got on to the subject.

I head down the corridor, and see Luke through the door of the study, getting something down from a shelf.

'You look very sportif,' he says, glancing up. 'Going to the gym?'

'Jess and I have been working out together,' I reply, flicking my hair back.

'Excellent. So you're getting along?'

'We're getting along brilliantly!' I say, and carry on along the corridor.

Which . . . I think is true.

Although, to be honest, it's a bit hard to tell, with Jess. She doesn't exactly *overwhelm* you.

But anyway, so far, so good. And now we've done our workout, we can reward ourselves! What we need is a few drinks, and a bit of a party atmosphere and some music. Then we'll really loosen up.

As I shower, I start to feel excited. You cannot beat a good girls' night in. Suze and I had so many great evenings when we were living together. There was the time Suze had been dumped by her awful boyfriend and we spent the whole evening sending off forms in his name to receive impotence cures. There was the time we made mint juleps and both nearly got alcohol poisoning. There was the time we decided to become red-heads – and then had to find a 24-hour hairdresser.

And then there were lots of evenings where nothing special happened . . . we just watched movies and ate pizza and talked and laughed, and had a good time.

I pause, halfway through towelling my hair. It's weird, not speaking to Suze any more. She hasn't called once since I told her about having a sister. And nor have I called her.

But anyway. My chin stiffens. That's what happens in life. People find new friends and new sisters. It's called natural selection.

And Jess and I will have a fab time tonight. *Better* than I ever had with Suze.

With a fizz of anticipation, I put on some jeans and a T-shirt with 'Sisterhood' emblazoned in silver. I turn on my dressing-table light bulbs and get out every single item of make-up I own. I rummage in a box under the bed and retrieve my three wigs, four hairpieces, false eyelashes, spray glitter and tattoos. Then I open up my special cupboard where all my shoes are stored.

I love my shoe cupboard.

I mean, I *love* my shoe cupboard. It is the best thing in the entire world! All my shoes are arranged in gorgeous rows, and there's even a built-in light so you can see them properly. I look adoringly along the rows for a few moments, then get out all the most fun, spangly high-heeled ones and toss them on to the bed.

Ready for the makeovers!

Next, I prepare the sitting room. I get out all my favourite videos and spread them in a fan on the floor, add piles of magazines and light some candles. Back in the kitchen I empty crisps, popcorn and sweets into bowls, light some more candles and get out the champagne. As I look around the kitchen all the granite is gleaming, and the stainless steel is softly lit by candle flames. It looks so pretty!

I glance at my watch, and it's nearly six o'clock. Jess must have finished working out by now. I head to the guest room and tap on the door.

'Jess?' I say tentatively.

There's no answer. She must be in the shower or something. Oh well, there's no hurry.

But as I head to the kitchen, I suddenly hear her voice coming from the study. That's weird. I approach the door and gently push it open – and there's Jess, sitting at the computer with Luke and Gary either side of her, peering at the screen, where I can see Luke's head, talking against a green background.

'You can superimpose the graphics like this,' she's saying, tapping at the keyboard. 'And synchronize with the soundtrack. I can do it for you, if you like.'

'What's going on?' I say in surprise.

'It's our new corporate CD-rom,' says Luke. 'The guys who did it had no bloody idea. The whole thing needs re-editing.'

'Your sister is a real whiz at this software!' says Gary.

'I just know it backwards,' says Jess, clicking rapidly. 'The whole university went over to it a year ago. And I'm a bit of a techie. I like this kind of stuff.'

'That's fantastic!' I say. I hover at the door for a few moments, as Jess taps at the keyboard some more. 'So . . . do you want to come and have a drink? I've got everything ready for our girls' night in.'

'I'm sorry,' says Luke, looking at me in sudden realization. 'I'm keeping you, Jess. We'll be OK from here. But thanks!'

'Thanks!' echoes Gary.

They're both looking at her with such admiration, I can't help feeling a tiny tweak of jealousy.

'Come on!' I say brightly. 'There's champagne waiting.'

'Thanks again, Jess,' says Luke. 'You're a star!'

'No problem.' Jess gets up and follows me out of the room.

'Men!' I say as soon as I'm out of earshot. 'All they think about is computers!'

'I like computers,' says Jess with a shrug.

'Er . . . me too,' I backtrack hastily. 'Absolutely!'

Which is kind of true.

I mean, I love eBay.

As I lead Jess into the kitchen I feel a rush of excitement. Here it comes. The moment I've been waiting for! I reach for the CD remote control and zap it – and a moment later, Sister Sledge belts through the kitchen speakers at top volume. I bought the album especially for this!

'*We are family!*' I sing along, beaming delightedly at

Jess. I take the champagne bottle out of its ice bucket and pop the cork. 'Have some champagne!'

'I'd prefer something soft if you've got it,' she says, putting her hands in her pockets. 'Champagne gives me a headache.'

'Oh,' I say, halted. 'Well . . . OK!'

I pour her out a glass of Aqua Libra and quickly put the bottle away before she can look at the price and start talking about potatoes again.

'I thought tonight we could just relax,' I say over the music. 'Just enjoy ourselves . . . talk . . . have fun . . .'

'Sounds good,' says Jess, nodding.

'So my idea was, we could do makeovers!'

'Makeovers?' Jess looks blank.

'Come with me!' I pull her along the corridor and into the bedroom. 'We can do each other's make-up . . . try on all different clothes . . . I could blow-dry your hair if you like . . .'

'I don't know.' Jess's shoulders are hunched uncomfortably.

'It'll be fun! Look, sit down in front of the mirror. Try on one of my wigs!' I pop the blonde Marilyn one on to my own head. 'Isn't that fab?'

Jess flinches.

'I hate mirrors,' she says. 'And I never wear make-up.'

I stare at her, a bit nonplussed. How can anyone hate mirrors?

'Besides, I'm happy with the way I look,' she adds, a bit defensively.

'Of course you are!' I say in astonishment. 'That's not the point! It's just supposed to be . . . you know. Fun.'

There's silence.

'But anyway!' I say, trying to hide my deflation. 'It was just an idea. We don't have to do it.'

I take off the Marilyn wig and switch off the dressing-table light bulbs. The room is immediately plunged into semi-gloom, which is kind of how I feel. I was really looking forward to doing Jess up. I had all these great ideas for her eyes.

But never mind. Come on. We can still have a good time!

'So! Shall we . . . watch a movie?' I suggest.

'Sure.' Jess nods.

And anyway, in many ways a movie is *better*. Everyone likes movies, plus we can chat in all the boring bits. I lead the way into the sitting room and gesture enthusiastically at the fanned-out videos on the floor. 'Take your pick. They're all here!'

'Right.' Jess starts looking through the videos.

'Are you a *Four Weddings* girl . . .' I prompt her. 'Or *Sleepless in Seattle* . . . *When Harry Met Sally* . . .'

'I don't mind,' says Jess at last, looking up. 'You choose.'

'You must have a favourite!'

'These aren't really my kind of thing,' says Jess, with a little grimace. 'I prefer something a bit more heavy-weight.'

'Oh,' I say, discomfited. 'Oh right. Well . . . I can go and get a different video from the rental shop if you like! It won't take me five minutes. Tell me what you'd like to watch—'

'It's OK, I don't want to put you out.' She shrugs. 'Let's just watch one of these.'

'Don't be silly!' I say with a laugh. 'Not if you don't like any of them! We can do . . . something else! No problem!'

I smile at Jess, but inside I'm a bit disquieted. I don't quite know what else to suggest. My back-up plan was the Dancing Queen karaoke tape — but something tells me she won't want to do that either. Plus we're not wearing the wigs.

Why is everything so *awkward*? I thought we'd be laughing hysterically together by now. I thought we'd be having fun.

Oh God. We can't just sit here in silence all night. I'm going to come clean.

'Look, Jess,' I say, leaning forward, 'I want to do whatever *you* want to do. But you'll have to guide me. So . . . be honest. Suppose I hadn't invited you here for the weekend. What would you be doing right now?'

'Well . . .' Jess thinks for a moment. 'I was supposed to be at an environmental meeting this evening. I'm an activist for a local group. We raise awareness, organize pickets and protest marches . . . that kind of thing.'

'Well, let's do that!' I say eagerly. 'Let's organize a picket! It'd be fun! I could make some banners . . .'

Jess looks nonplussed.

'A picket of what?'

'Er . . . I don't mind! Anything. You're the guest – you choose!'

Jess is just staring at me in disbelief.

'You don't just *organize pickets*. You have to start with the issues. With the environmental concerns. They're not supposed to be *fun*.'

'OK,' I say hastily. 'Let's forget the picket. How about if you *hadn't* been at the meeting? What would you be doing now? And whatever it is . . . we'll do it. Together!'

Jess frowns in thought, and I watch her face in hope. And sudden curiosity. For the first time, I feel like I'm actually going to learn something about my sister.

'I'd probably be doing my accounts,' she says at last. 'In fact, I brought them with me, in case I had time.'

Her accounts. On a Friday night. Her accounts.

'Right!' I manage at last. 'Fab! Well then . . . let's do our accounts!'

OK. This is fine. This is good.

We're both sitting in the kitchen, doing our accounts. At least, Jess is doing her accounts. I'm not quite sure what I'm doing.

I've written 'Accounts' at the top of a sheet of paper and underlined it twice.

Every so often Jess glances up, and I quickly scribble something down, just to look like I'm into it. So far my page reads:

'20 pounds . . . budget . . . 200 million pounds . . . hello my name is Becky . . .'

Jess is frowning over a pile of what look like bank statements, leafing backwards and forwards.

'Is something wrong?' I ask sympathetically.

'I'm just tracking down a bit of lost money,' she says. 'Maybe it's in one of my other cashbooks.' She gets up. 'I'll be back in a moment.'

As she leaves the kitchen, I take a sip of champagne and glance towards the pile of bank statements.

Obviously I'm not going to look at them or anything. They're Jess's private property and I respect that. And anyway, it's none of my business. None at all.

The only thing is, my leg is feeling itchy. It genuinely is. I lean over to scratch it . . . then casually lean a bit further . . . and a bit more . . . until I can glimpse the bottom figure on the top statement.

£30,002.

I feel a plunge in the depths of my stomach and hastily sit up again, nearly knocking over my champagne glass. My heart is thudding in shock. Thirty thousand pounds? *Thirty thousand pounds?*

That's a bigger overdraft than I've ever had. Ever. *Ever!*

Now it's all starting to make sense. It's falling into place. No wonder she makes her own weights. No wonder she takes her coffee flask everywhere. She's probably on an economy drive, just like I went on once. She's probably read *Controlling Your Cash* by David E. Barton!

God, who would have thought it?

As Jess comes back into the room, I can't help

looking at her with new eyes. She picks up one of her bank statements and sighs heavily – and I feel a sudden wave of affection for her. How many times have *I* picked up a bank statement and sighed? We're kindred spirits!

She's perusing the figures, still looking hassled. Well, no wonder, with a whopping great overdraft like that!

'Hi,' I say, with an understanding smile. 'Still trying to track down that bit of money?'

'It must be here somewhere.' She frowns, and turns to another statement.

God, maybe the bank's about to foreclose on her or something. I should give her a few tips.

I lean forward confidingly.

'Banks are a nightmare, aren't they?'

'They're useless,' she says.

'You know, sometimes the trick is to write a nice letter. Say you've broken your leg or something. Or your dog has died.'

'I'm sorry?' Jess raises her head. 'Why would I say that?'

God, she has no idea. No wonder she's in so much trouble!

'You know! To get a bit of sympathy. Then they might waive your overdraft charges. Or even extend it!'

'I don't have an overdraft,' she says, looking puzzled. 'But—'

I stop as her words hit my brain. She doesn't have an overdraft. Which means—

I feel a bit faint.

That thirty thousand pounds is actual . . .

It's actual *money*?

'Becky, are you OK?' Jess gives me an odd look.

'I'm . . . fine!' I say in a strangled voice and take several gulps of my champagne, trying to regain my cool. 'So . . . you're not overdrawn. That's good! That's great!'

'I've never been overdrawn in my life,' says Jess firmly. 'I just don't think it's necessary. Anyone can stay within their means if they really want to. People who get into debt just lack self-control. There's no excuse.' She straightens her papers, then stops. 'But you used to be a financial journalist, didn't you? Your mum showed me some of your articles. So you must know all this.'

Her hazel eyes meet mine expectantly and I feel a ridiculous tweak of fear. I'm suddenly not sure I want her to know the truth about my finances. Not the *exact* truth.

'I . . . er . . . absolutely!' I say. 'Of course I do. It's all a question of . . . of planning ahead and careful management.'

'Exactly!' says Jess, regarding me with approval. 'When any money comes in, the first thing I do is put half aside to save.'

She does what?

'Excellent!' I manage. 'It's the only sensible option.'

I'm in a state of shock. When I was a financial journalist, I used to write articles telling people to save a proportion of their money all the time. But I never thought anyone actually *did* it.

Jess is looking at me with fresh interest.

'So – you do the same, do you, Becky?'

For a few seconds I can't quite find a reply.

'Er . . . well!' I say at last, and clear my throat. 'Maybe not exactly half *every* month . . .'

'I'm just the same.' Her face relaxes into a smile. 'Sometimes I only manage twenty per cent.'

'Twenty per cent!' I echo feebly. 'Well . . . never mind. You shouldn't feel bad.'

'But I do,' says Jess, leaning forward across the table. 'You must understand that.'

199

I've never seen her face look so open.

Oh my God. We're bonding.

'Twenty per cent of what?' comes Luke's voice as he and Gary enter the kitchen, both looking in good spirits.

I feel a prickle of alarm.

'Er . . . nothing,' I say.

'We're just talking about finances,' says Jess to Luke. 'We've both been doing our accounts.'

'Your *accounts*?' says Luke, giving a small shout of laughter. 'What accounts would those be, Becky?'

'You know!' I say brightly. 'My financial affairs and so forth.'

'Ah.' Luke nods, getting a bottle of wine out of the fridge. 'So . . . have you called out the SWAT teams yet? And the Red Cross?'

'What do you mean?' says Jess, puzzled.

'They're traditionally summoned to disaster areas, aren't they?' He grins at me.

Ha-di-bloody-ha.

'But . . . Becky's a former financial journalist!' says Jess, sounding rather shocked.

'Financial journalist?' Luke looks highly amused. 'You want to hear a story about your sister's days as a financial journalist?'

'No,' I say quickly. 'She doesn't.'

'The cashpoint card,' says Gary reminiscently.

'The cashpoint card!' Luke slaps the table in delight. 'This was during Becky's illustrious career as a TV finance expert,' he says to Jess. 'She was filming an item on the perils of cashpoint use. She put in her own cashpoint card to demonstrate . . .' He starts laughing again. 'And it got swallowed on camera.'

'They showed it the other night on a TV clips show,' says Gary to me. 'The bit where you start bashing the machine with your shoe is a classic!'

I shoot him a look of fury.

'But why did it get swallowed?' says Jess, looking perplexed. 'Were you . . . *overdrawn*?'

'Was Becky overdrawn?' says Luke cheerfully, getting out some glasses. 'Is the Pope Catholic?'

Jess looks confused.

'But Becky, you said you saved half your salary every month.'

Shit.

'I'm sorry?' Luke slowly turns round. 'Becky said she did *what*?'

'That's . . . that's not exactly what I said,' I say, flustered. 'I said it's a *good idea* to save half your salary. In principle. And it is! It's a very good idea!'

'How about not running up huge credit-card bills which you keep secret from your husband?' says Luke, raising his eyebrows. 'Is that a good idea in principle?'

'Credit-card bills?' says Jess, looking at me in horror. 'So . . . you're in debt?'

God, why does she have to say it like that? *Debt*. Like it's some kind of plague. Like I'm about to go to the workhouse. I mean, get real. This is the twenty-first century. *Everyone*'s in debt.

'You know how doctors make the worst patients?' I say with a little laugh. 'Well, financial journalists make the worst . . . er . . .'

I wait for her to laugh too, or at least give a sympathetic smile. But she just looks totally appalled.

I feel a sudden rankling inside. OK, so I may have had the odd debt in my time. But she doesn't have to look quite so *disapproving*.

'By the way, Jess,' says Gary. 'We've run into a tiny glitch with that program.'

'Really?' Jess looks up. 'I'll come and have a look if you like.'

'Are you sure?' Gary glances at me. 'We don't want to interrupt your evening . . .'

'It's fine,' I say, waving my hand. 'Go ahead!'

* * *

When they've all disappeared into the study, I wander along the corridor and into the sitting room. I slump down on the sofa and stare miserably at the blank television.

Jess and I haven't bonded one little bit.

We don't get on. That's the truth.

I feel suddenly weary with disappointment. I've been trying so hard ever since she arrived. I've been making every effort. I bought the picture of the cave . . . and I prepared all those yummy snacks . . . and I tried to plan the best evening I could. And she hasn't even *tried* to join in. OK, so maybe she didn't like any of my films. But she could have pretended, couldn't she? If it was me, I would have pretended.

Why does she have to be such a *misery*? Why can't she just have *fun*?

As I gulp my champagne, tiny needles of resentment are starting to prick at me.

How can she hate shopping? How? She's got thirty grand, for God's sake! She should *adore* shopping!

And another thing. Why is she so obsessed with potatoes? What's so great about bloody potatoes?

I just don't understand her. She's my sister, but I don't understand one single thing about her. Luke was right all along. It *is* all nurture. Nature doesn't come into it.

I give a huge sigh, then dolefully start leafing through the videos. Maybe I'll watch one of them on my own. And have some popcorn. And some of those yummy Thorntons chocolates.

Jess probably doesn't even eat chocolate. Unless it's chocolate she's made herself, out of potatoes.

Well, good for her. *I'm* going to stuff my face and watch a nice movie.

I'm just reaching for *Pretty Woman* when the phone rings.

'Hello?' I say, picking up.

'Hello, Bex?' comes a familiar high-pitched voice. 'It's me.'

'Suze!' I feel a huge rush of joy. 'Oh my God! Hi! How are you?'

'Oh, I'm fine! Are you OK?'

'I'm fine! I'm fine!'

Suddenly with all my heart I wish Suze was here. Like the old days in Fulham. I miss her so much. *So* much.

But everything's different now.

'So, how was the spa with Lulu?' I ask, trying to sound casual.

'It was . . . fine,' she says after a pause. 'You know. Kind of . . . a bit different . . . but fun!'

'Good!'

There's an awkward silence.

'And . . . and I was wondering how it's all going with your new sister,' says Suze hesitantly. 'Are you . . . are you really good friends?'

I feel a raw smarting inside.

I can't admit the truth to Suze. I just can't admit the whole thing's been a failure. That she goes on spa trips with her new friend, but I can't even manage one evening with my own sister.

'It's great!' I say. 'Couldn't be better! We're getting on so well!'

'Really?' says Suze, sounding a bit crushed.

'Absolutely! In fact, we're having a girls' night in together right now! Watching movies . . . having a laugh . . . just hanging out. You know!'

'What are you watching?' says Suze at once.

'Er . . .' I look at the blank TV screen. '*Pretty Woman*.'

'I love *Pretty Woman*,' says Suze longingly. 'The scene in the shop!'

'I know! That is just the best scene ever!'

'And the end, when Richard Gere climbs up!' Her voice is tumbling out with enthusiasm. 'Oh God, I want to watch it right now!'

'Me too!' I say without thinking. 'I mean . . . I want to watch the . . . er . . . rest of it.'

'Oh,' says Suze in a different voice. 'I must be interrupting you. Sorry.'

'No!' I say quickly. 'I mean, it doesn't matter—'

'I'll go. You must want to get back to your sister. It sounds like you're having an amazing time.' Her voice is wistful. 'You two must have so much to talk about.'

'Yes,' I say, looking round the empty room. 'Yes, we . . . we certainly do!'

'Well . . . I'll see you sometime,' she says. 'Bye, Bex.'

'Bye!' I say, my throat suddenly thick.

Wait! I suddenly want to cry out. Don't go!

But instead I put down the receiver and stare into space. At the other end of the flat I can hear Luke, Gary and Jess all laughing about something. They've bonded with her great. It's just me who hasn't.

And all of a sudden I'm overcome with depression.

I had such huge hopes. I was so excited about having a sister. But there's no point trying any more, is there? I've done everything I can think of – and it's all failed. Jess and I are never going to be friends. Not in a million years.

I get up from the sofa, morosely shove the *Pretty Woman* video into the machine, and zap it on with the remote. All I can do is be polite for the rest of the weekend. Polite and pleasant, like a gracious hostess. I should be able to manage that.

WEST CUMBRIA BANK

45 STERNDALE STREET
COGGENTHWAITE
CUMBRIA

Ms Jessica Bertram
12 Hill Rise
Scully
Cumbria

16 May 2003

Dear Ms Bertram

Thank you for your letter.

Having gone through your accounts in great detail I can only concur that there is a discrepancy of 73 pence.

I am deeply sorry for this error by the bank and have credited your savings account by this amount, back-dated three months. I have also, as you request, added the missing interest.

May I take this opportunity to commend you yet again on your meticulous and thoughtful approach to your finances.

On a personal note, I look forward to seeing you at the upcoming Prudent Savers' Group cheese and wine evening, at which our head of personal accounts will be giving the keynote address 'Re-tightening the Purse-strings'.

Yours sincerely

Howard Shawcross

Customer Account Manager

FOURTEEN

I wake up the next morning with a splitting headache. Which could have something to do with the fact that I polished off an entire bottle of champagne myself last night, plus one and a half trays of chocolates.

Meanwhile, Jess, Luke and Gary spent hours on the computer. Even when I took them in some pizza, they barely looked up. So I just watched the whole of *Pretty Woman* and then half of *Four Weddings*, before going to bed on my own.

As I blearily put on a dressing gown, Luke is already showered and dressed in the 'casual weekend' clothes he wears when he's actually going to spend the whole time in the office.

'What time did you finish last night?' I say, my voice all hoarse and croaky.

'Not till late.' Luke shakes his head. 'I really wanted to get that CD-rom right. Fuck knows what we would have done without Jess.'

'Right.' I feel a tiny spike of resentment.

'You know, I take it back about her,' he adds, tying up his shoelaces. 'Your sister's got a lot going for her. She couldn't have been more helpful last night. In fact, she was our saviour. She certainly knows her way around a computer!'

'Really?' I say lightly.

'Oh yes. She's great!' He stands up and gives me a kiss. 'You were right. I'm very glad you invited her for the weekend.'

'Me too!' I say, forcing a bright smile. 'We're all having so much fun!'

I shuffle into the kitchen, where Jess is sitting at the counter in her jeans and a T-shirt, with a glass of water.

Cleverclogs.

I expect she'll split the atom this morning. In between sit-ups.

'Morning,' she says.

'Morning!' I say in my most pleasant, good-hostess manner.

I was re-reading *The Gracious Hostess* last night, and it says that even if your guest is annoying you, you must behave with charm and decorum.

Well, fine. I can be charming. I can be decorative.

'Did you sleep well? Let me get you some breakfast!'

I open the fridge and get out the freshly squeezed orange, grapefruit and cranberry juices. I reach into the bread bin and pull out some seeded granary bread, croissants and muffins. Then I start rooting around in the cupboards for jams. Three kinds of luxury marmalade, strawberry jam with champagne, wild blossom honey . . . and Belgian chocolate spread. Finally I get down a range of luxury coffees and teas to choose from. There. No one's going to say I don't give my guests a good breakfast.

I'm aware of Jess watching my every move, and as I turn round she's got a strange expression on her face.

'What?' I say. 'What's wrong?'

'Nothing,' she says awkwardly. She takes a sip of water – then looks up again. 'Luke told me last night. About your . . . problem.'

'My what?'

'Your spending.'

I stare at her in shock. He did, did he?

'I don't have a problem,' I say, flashing her a smile. 'He was exaggerating.'

'He said you're on a budget.' Jess looks concerned. 'It sounds like money's a bit tight at the moment.'

'That's right,' I say pleasantly.

Not that it's any of your bloody business, I add in my head. I can't *believe* Luke's been blabbing everything to her.

'So . . . how come you can afford luxury coffee and strawberry jam with champagne?' She gestures at all the food laid out on the counter.

'Thrifty management,' I say smoothly. 'Prioritizing. If you save on some items you can splash out on others. That's the first rule of financial management. As I learned at financial-journalism school,' I add in pointed tones.

OK, that's a slight lie. I didn't go to financial-journalism school. But honestly. Who does she think she is, quizzing me?

'So — which items are you saving on?' says Jess, her brow creased. 'I can't see anything in this kitchen that doesn't come from Fortnums or Harrods.'

I'm about to make an indignant rejoinder when I realize she might possibly be right. I got into a bit of a Harrods Food Hall habit after I started making all this money out of eBay. But so what? Harrods is a perfectly legitimate food shop.

'My husband appreciates a good standard of living,' I say crisply with an off-putting smile. 'My aim is to provide that for him.'

'But you could do it on less.' Jess leans forward, looking animated. 'You could make savings everywhere! I could give you some tips.'

Tips? Tips from Jess?

Suddenly the oven timer goes off with a ping and I look up in excitement. It's time!

'Are you cooking something?' says Jess, looking puzzled.

'Er . . . not exactly. Just help yourself . . . I'll be back in a minute . . .'

I hurry into the study and switch on the computer. Bidding on the orange vintage coat ends in five minutes and I am bloody well going to get it. I tap my fingernails impatiently, and as soon as the screen clears I bring up the saved eBay page.

I knew it. 'kittybee111' has bid again. £200.

She thinks she's so clever. Well, take *this*, 'kittybee111'.

I get out Luke's stopwatch from the desk and set it for three minutes. As the time gets near I poise my hands over the keyboard like an athlete on the starting blocks.

OK. One minute before the bidding ends. Go.

As quickly as I can, I type in *@00.50.

Shit. What have I typed? Delete. Retype. £200.50.

I jab 'Send' and the next screen comes up. User ID . . . password . . . I'm typing as fast as I can.

'*You are the current high bidder.*'

Ten seconds to go. My heart is thumping. What if someone else is bidding *right now*?

Frantically I click on 'Refresh'.

'What are you doing, Becky?' comes Jess's voice at the door.

Shit.

'Nothing!' I say. 'Why don't you make yourself some nice toast, while I just—'

The page is coming back up again. I can't breathe. Did I . . . did I . . . ?

'*Congratulations! You won the item!*'

'Yeeess!' I cry out, unable to stop myself, and punch the air. 'Yes! I got it!'

'Got what?' Jess has advanced across the room and is peering over my shoulder at the screen. 'Is that *you*?'

she says in shock. 'You're on a tight budget and you're buying a coat for two hundred pounds?'

'It's not like that!' I say, rattled at her expression. I get up, close the door of the study and turn to face her.

'Look,' I say in a low voice. 'It's OK. I've got all this money which Luke doesn't know about. I've been selling off all the stuff we bought on honeymoon – and I've made loads! I sold ten Tiffany clocks the other day and made two thousand quid!' I lift my chin proudly. 'So I can *easily* afford this.'

Jess's disapproving expression doesn't waver.

'You could have put that money into a high-interest savings account,' she says. 'Or used it to clear an outstanding bill.'

I quell a sudden urge to snap at her.

'Yeah well, I didn't,' I say, forcing a pleasant tone. 'I bought a coat.'

'And Luke has no idea?' Jess fixes me with an accusing gaze.

'He doesn't *need* to have any idea! Jess, my husband is a very busy man,' I explain. 'My role is to keep the household running smoothly. Not waste his time with day-to-day minutiae.'

'So you lie to him.'

I feel a rub of irritation at her tone.

'Every marriage needs an air of mystery. It's a well-known fact!'

Jess shakes her head.

'And is this how you can afford all the Fortnums jam, too?' She gestures to the computer. 'Shouldn't you just be honest?'

Oh, for God's sake. Doesn't she understand anything?

'Jess . . . let me explain,' I say kindly. 'Our marriage is a complicated, living organism which only the two of us can really understand. I naturally know what to tell Luke and what not to bother him with. Call it instinct . . . call it discretion . . . call it emotional intelligence, if you will.'

Jess regards me silently for a few moments.

'Well I think you need help,' she says at last.

'I do not need *help*!' I retort.

I shut down the computer, push back my chair and stalk past her into the kitchen, where Luke is making a pot of coffee.

'Enjoying your breakfast, darling?' I say in loud tones.

'Fantastic!' says Luke admiringly. '*Where* did you get these quails' eggs?'

'Oh . . . you know . . .' I give him an affectionate smile. 'I know you like them, so I tracked some down.' I shoot a triumphant look at Jess, who rolls her eyes.

'We're out of bacon, though,' says Luke. 'And a couple of other things. I've written them down.'

'OK,' I say, having a sudden idea. 'In fact . . . I'll go out and get them this morning. Jess, you don't mind if I do some household chores, do you? I don't expect *you* to come, of course,' I add sweetly. 'I know how much you hate and despise shopping.'

Thank God. Escape.

'It's OK,' says Jess, filling a glass of water at the tap. 'I'd like to come.'

My smile freezes on my face.

'To Harr— to the supermarket?' I say in my most warm and charming voice. 'But it'll be very boring. Please don't feel you have to.'

'I'd like to.' She looks at me. 'If you don't mind.'

'Mind?' I say, still with a fixed smile. 'Why would I mind? I'll just go and get ready.'

As I head into the hall, I'm hot with indignation. Who does she think she is, saying I need help?

She needs help, more like it. Help in how to crank her miserable mouth into a smile.

And what a bloody nerve, giving me advice on my

marriage. What does she know about it? Luke and I have a brilliant marriage! We've hardly ever even had a row!

The entryphone buzzes, and I pick up the receiver, still distracted.

'Hello?'

'Hello,' comes a man's voice. 'I have a delivery of flowers for Brandon.'

I press the button in delight. Someone's sent me flowers?

Oh my God. I clap my hand over my mouth. Luke must have sent me flowers. He's so romantic! This is probably some really cute anniversary that I'd forgotten all about, like the first time we had dinner together, or slept together or something.

Actually . . . that would be the same anniversary, now I think about it.

But anyway. The point is, this just proves it. This just proves what a fantastic relationship we have and how Jess is totally wrong. About everything.

I throw open the apartment door and stand expectantly by the lift. This'll show her! I'll take my flowers straight into the kitchen and give Luke a huge passionate kiss, and she'll say something really humble like, 'I had no idea what a perfect relationship you two had.' And I'll smile kindly and say, 'You know, Jess . . .'

My thoughts are interrupted as the lift doors start opening. And oh . . . my God. Luke must have spent an absolute *fortune*!

Two uniformed delivery men are carrying the most enormous bouquet of roses – plus a huge fruit basket full of oranges, papayas and pineapples, all wrapped up in trendy raffia.

'Wow!' I say in delight. 'Those are absolutely fantastic!' I beam at the man offering me a clipboard and scribble my signature.

212

'And you'll pass them on to Mr Brandon,' says the man as he gets back into the lift.

'Of course!' I say gaily.

A moment later his words register on my brain.

Hang on a minute. These are for *Luke*? Who on earth is sending flowers to Luke?

I spot a card nestling amongst the flowers, and pull it out with a pleasant thrill of curiosity. Then, as I scan the words, I freeze.

Dear Mr Brandon

I was extremely sorry to hear of your illness. Please let me know if I can be of any help. And be assured, we can delay the hotel launch as long as is necessary to enable your full recovery.

All best wishes

Nathan Temple.

I stare at it, paralysed with horror. This wasn't supposed to happen.

Nathan Temple wasn't supposed to send flowers. He wasn't supposed to delay the hotel launch. He was supposed to go *away*.

'What's that?' comes Luke's voice. I start in panic and look up to see him coming out of the kitchen towards me.

In one seamless movement I crumple Nathan Temple's card and stuff it into the pocket of my dressing gown.

'Hi!' I say, my voice a little high-pitched. 'Aren't these great?'

'Are those for me?' says Luke incredulously, spotting the delivery label. 'Who are they from?'

Quick. Think.

'They're . . . um . . . from me!' I say brightly.

'From *you*?' Luke stares at me.

'Yes! I thought I'd like to send you some flowers. And . . . er . . . fruit. Here you are, darling! Happy Saturday!'

Somehow I manhandle the enormous bouquet and basket into Luke's arms, then kiss him lightly on the cheek. Luke is looking bewildered.

'Becky, I'm very touched,' he says. 'Really. But why did you send me all this? Why did you send me a fruit basket?'

For a few moments I can't quite think of an answer.

'Do I have to have a *reason* to send my husband a fruit basket?' I say at last, managing to sound a little hurt. 'I just thought they could be a token of our marriage. You know, we're coming up to our very first anniversary!'

'Right,' says Luke after a pause. 'Well . . . thank you. That's lovely.' He peers more closely at the bouquet. 'What's this?'

As I follow his gaze, my stomach gives an almighty flip. Nestling amongst the flowers is a set of gold plastic lettering, spelling out 'Get Well Soon'.

Shit.

'"Get Well Soon"?' Luke looks up, taken aback.

My mind races frantically.

'That . . . that . . . doesn't *mean* "Get Well Soon",' I say, with a laugh. 'It's . . . in code!'

'In *code*?'

'Yes! Every marriage needs a secret code between husband and wife! You know, for little loving secret messages. So I thought I'd introduce one!'

Luke stares at me for a long while.

'So what does "Get Well Soon" mean?' he says at last. 'In our secret code.'

'It's actually . . . er . . . very easy.' I clear my throat self-consciously. '"Get" means . . . "I". And

"Well" means . . . "Love". And "Soon" means . . .'

' "You"?' offers Luke.

'Yes!' I say. 'You're getting the idea! Isn't it cunning?'

There's silence. My hands are clenched by my sides. Luke is regarding me quizzically.

'And you wouldn't − say − have ordered the wrong package from the florist's by mistake?' he suggests.

Oh.

Now, that's a *much* better explanation. Why didn't I think of that?

'You've rumbled me!' I exclaim. 'Drat! How did you guess? You just know me too well. Now, er . . . go and have some nice breakfast and I'll go and get ready for the supermarket.'

As I put on my make-up my heart is thumping.

What am I going to do about this?

What if Nathan Temple phones up to see how Luke is? What if he sends more flowers?

What if he wants to come and visit Luke's sick-bed? I feel a swoosh of panic and blob a bit of mascara on my eyelid. In exasperation I thrust the mascara wand down.

OK, just . . . stay calm. Let's go through all the options I have.

Option 1: Tell Luke everything.

No. No way. Just the thought of it makes my stomach churn. He's so busy with this Arcodas pitch. It'll just get him all hassled and angry. Plus, as his supportive wife I should be shielding him from this kind of irritation.

Option 2. Tell Luke something.

Like the edited highlights. Maybe tweaked in a way that makes me look good and possibly leaves out the name Nathan Temple . . .

Oh God. Impossible.

Option 3. Manage situation in discreet Hillary-style manner.

But I tried that already. And it didn't work.

Anyway, I bet Hillary had help. What I need is a team. Like in *The West Wing*. Then it would all be so easy! I'd just go up to Alison Janney and say quietly, 'We have a problem – but don't let the President know.' And she'd murmur, 'Don't worry, we'll contain it.' Then we'd exchange warm but tense smiles, and walk into the Oval Office, where Luke would be promising a group of underprivileged kids that their playground would be saved. And his eyes would meet mine with a flicker . . . and we'd flashback to the two of us waltzing in the White House corridors the night before, watched only by an impassive security guard . . .

The grinding of a dustbin truck outside brings me back to reality with a bump. Luke isn't President. I'm not in *The West Wing*. And I still don't know what to do.

Option 4. Do nothing.

This has a lot of obvious advantages. And the point is . . . do I actually *need* to do anything?

I reach for my lipliner and start applying it thought-fully. I mean, let's stand back for a moment. Let's get this whole thing in a bit of proportion. All that has actually happened is that someone has sent Luke some flowers. That's all.

Plus he wants Luke to work for him. And reckons he's owed a favour.

And is a gangster.

No. Stop it. He's not a gangster. He's a . . . a businessman with a former criminal conviction. It's totally different.

And anyway. *Anyway*. He was probably just being polite in that note, wasn't he? I mean, get real. Like he's really going to hold up an entire hotel launch so Luke can do it. It's a ridiculous idea!

216

The more I think along these lines, the more re-
assured I feel. Nathan Temple can't seriously be
expecting Luke to work for him. He'll have found
some other PR company already. The whole thing will
be under way and he'll have forgotten all about
Brandon Communications. Exactly. So I don't have to
do anything! It's all fine.

Even so, I might write a short letter of thanks. And
kind of mention that Luke's unfortunately taken a turn
for the worse.

So before we head off to the supermarket I scribble a
polite card to Nathan Temple and drop it in the pillar
box outside. As I stride away I actually feel rather
satisfied. I have this whole situation under control,
and Luke doesn't know a thing. I am super-wife!

My spirits rise even further as we walk into the
supermarket. God, supermarkets are great places.
They're all light and bright and music is playing, and
they're always giving away free samples of cheese or
something. Plus you can buy loads of CDs and make-
up, and it all goes on the credit-card bill as Tesco.

The first thing that catches my eye as I walk in is a
display of speciality teas, with a free flower-shaped tea
infuser if you buy three.

'Bargain!' I say in delight, grabbing three boxes at
random.

'It's not really a bargain,' intones Jess's disapproving
voice beside me, and I feel an immediate rise in
tension.

Why did she have to come along?

Anyway, never mind. I'll just stay polite and
courteous.

'It *is* a bargain,' I explain. 'They're giving away a free
gift.'

'Do you ever drink jasmine tea?' she retorts, looking
at the box in my hand.

'Er . . .'

Jasmine tea. That's the one that tastes like old compost heaps, isn't it?

But so what? I want the tea infuser.

'You can always find a use for jasmine tea,' I say airily, and plonk it in my trolley. 'Right! What next?'

I push the trolley towards the vegetable section, pausing to pick up a copy of *InStyle* as I go.

Ooh. And the new *Elle* is out, too. With a free T-shirt!

'What are you doing?' comes Jess's sepulchral voice in my ear.

Is she going to quiz me all the way round the bloody shop?

'I'm shopping!' I say brightly, and sling a new paperback book into the trolley.

'You could get that out of the library for nothing!' says Jess, looking horrified.

The *library*? I look at her in equal horror. I don't want some thumbed copy in a horrible plastic jacket which I have to remember to take back.

'It's a modern classic, actually,' I say. 'Everyone should have their own copy.'

'Why?' she persists. 'Why can't you get it out of the library?'

I feel a prickle of annoyance.

Because I just want my own nice shiny copy! And piss off and leave me alone!

'Because . . . I might want to make notes in the margin,' I say loftily. 'I have quite an interest in literary criticism, you know.'

I push my trolley on, but she comes hurrying after me.

'Becky, look. I want to help you. You have to gain control of your spending. You have to learn to be more frugal. Luke and I were talking about it—'

'Oh really?' I say, stung. 'How nice for you!'

'I can give you some tips . . . show you how to be thrifty—'

'I don't need your help!' I retort in indignation. 'I'm thrifty! I'm as thrifty as they come.'

Jess looks incredulous.

'You think it's thrifty to buy expensive magazines you could read for nothing in a public library?'

For a moment I can't quite think of a reply. Then my glance falls on *Elle*. Yes!

'If I didn't *buy* them, I wouldn't get the free gifts, would I?' I retort in triumph, and wheel my trolley round the corner.

Ha. So there, Miss Smarty-pants.

I head to the fruit section and start loading bags into my trolley.

How thrifty is this? Nice healthy apples. I look up – and Jess is wincing.

'What?' I say. 'What is it now?'

'You should buy those loose.' She gestures to the other side of the aisle, where a woman is laboriously picking her way through a mound of apples and filling a bag. 'The unit cost is far lower! You'd save . . . twenty pence?'

Well, whoopee doo. Twenty whole pence!

'Time is money,' I reply coolly. 'Frankly, Jess, it's not worth my while to be sorting through apples.'

'Why not?' she says. 'After all, you're unemployed.'

I gasp in affront.

Unemployed? *Unemployed?*

I am not unemployed! I'm a skilled personal shopper! I have a job lined up!

In fact . . . I'm not even going to dignify that with a response. I turn on my heel and stalk over to the salad counter. I fill two huge cartons full of luxury marinated olives, take them back to the trolley – and stop in astonishment.

Who put that huge sack of potatoes in my trolley?

Did I say I wanted a big sack of potatoes? Did I say I wanted *any* potatoes?

What if I'm on the Atkins diet?

I look around furiously, but Jess is nowhere to be seen. And the bloody thing's too heavy to lift on my own. It's OK for her, Miss Body Builder of the Year. Where's she got to, anyway?

Suddenly, to my astonishment, I spot her coming out of a side door, holding a big cardboard box and talking to a store employee. What's she doing now?

'I've been speaking with the produce manager,' she says, approaching me. 'We can have all these bruised bananas for nothing.'

She's been doing . . . *what*?

I look in the box – and it's full of the most revolting, manky bananas I've ever seen.

'They're perfectly good, if you cut away the black bits,' says Jess.

'But I don't want to cut away the black bits!' My voice is shriller than I intended. 'I want to have nice yellow bananas! And I don't want this stupid great sack of potatoes, either!'

'You can make three weeks' worth of meals from that one sack,' says Jess, looking offended. 'They're the most economical, nutritious food you can buy. One potato alone—'

Oh God, please. Not another potato lecture.

'Where am I supposed to put them?' I interrupt. 'I haven't got a cupboard big enough.'

'There's a cupboard in the hall,' says Jess. 'You could use that. If you joined a warehouse club you could use it to store flour and oats, too.'

I stare at her, baffled.

Oats? What do I want oats for? And anyway, clearly she hasn't looked *inside* that cupboard.

'That's my handbag cupboard,' I point out. 'And it's totally full.'

Jess shrugs.

'You could get rid of some of your handbags.'

For a moment I'm too staggered to reply. Is she seriously suggesting I should get rid of some of my handbags . . . for *potatoes*?

'Let's carry on,' I say at last, and push the trolley forward as calmly as I can.

Stay polite. Stay gracious. She'll be gone in twenty-four hours.

But as we progress round the store I am really starting to lose my cool. Jess's voice is constantly droning in my ear like a bumble-bee, on and on until I want to turn round and swat her.

You could make your own pizzas for half the price . . . have you considered buying a second-hand slow-cooker? . . . Store-brand washing powder is 40p cheaper . . . You can use vinegar instead of fabric softener . . .

'I don't want to use vinegar!' I almost snap. 'I want to use fabric softener, OK?' I put a bottle of it into the trolley and stalk off towards the juice section, Jess following behind.

'Any comments?' I say as I load two cartons into the trolley. 'Anything wrong with lovely healthy orange juice?'

'No,' says Jess, shrugging. 'Except you could get the same health benefits from a glass of tap water and a cheap bottle of vitamin C tablets.'

OK. Now I seriously want to slap her.

Defiantly I dump another two cartons in my trolley, yank it round and head to the bread section. There's a delicious smell of baking in the air, and as I get near I see a woman at a counter, demonstrating something to a small crowd of people.

Ooh, I love this kind of thing.

She's got a shiny chrome gadget plugged into the

wall, and as she opens it up, it's full of heart-shaped waffles, all golden brown and yummy looking.

'The waffle-maker is quick and easy to use!' she's saying. 'Wake up every morning to the smell of fresh waffles baking.'

God, wouldn't that be great? I have a sudden vision of me and Luke in bed, eating heart-shaped waffles and maple syrup, with big frothy cappuccinos.

'The waffle-maker normally costs £49.99,' the woman is saying. 'But today we are selling it at a special reduced price of ... twenty-five pounds. That's fifty per cent off.'

I feel an electric jolt. Fifty per cent off?

OK, I have to have one of these.

'Yes please!' I say, and push my trolley forward.

'What are you doing?' says Jess in horror.

'I'm buying a waffle-maker, obviously.' I roll my eyes. 'Can you get out of my way?'

'No!' says Jess, planting herself firmly in front of the trolley. 'I'm not going to let you waste twenty-five pounds on a gadget you don't need.'

I stare at her in outrage. How does she know what I do or don't need?

'I *do* need a waffle-maker!' I retort. 'It's on my list of things I need. In fact, Luke said only the other day, "What this house really needs is a waffle-maker."'

Which, OK, is a lie. But he might have done. How does she know?

'Plus I'm *saving* money, in case you hadn't noticed,' I add, determinedly pushing the trolley round her. 'It's a bargain!'

'It's not a bargain if you don't need one!' She grabs the trolley and tries to haul it back.

'Get your hands off my trolley!' I say indignantly. 'I need a waffle-maker! And I can easily afford it! Easily! I'll take one,' I add to the woman, and take a box off the table.

'No she won't,' says Jess, grabbing it out of my arms. What? *What?*

'I'm only doing it for your own good, Becky! You're addicted to spending! You have to learn how to say no!'

'I can say no!' I practically spit in fury. 'I can say no whenever I like! I'm just not choosing to say it right now! I *will* take one,' I say to the confused-looking woman. 'In fact, I'll take two. I can give one to Mum for Christmas.'

I snatch two boxes and defiantly put them in my trolley.

So there.

'So you're just going to waste fifty pounds, are you?' says Jess contemptuously. 'Just throw away money you don't have.'

'I'm not throwing it away.'

'Yes you are!'

'I'm bloody not!' I retort. 'And I *do* have the money. I have plenty of money.'

'You're living in a total fantasyland!' Jess suddenly shouts. 'You have money until you run out of stuff to sell. But what happens then? And what happens when Luke finds out what you've been doing? You're just storing up trouble!'

'I'm not storing up trouble!' I lash back angrily.

'Yes you are!'

'No I'm no—'

'*Will you two sisters just stop fighting for once!*' interrupts an exasperated woman's voice, and we both jump.

I look around in bewilderment. Mum isn't here, is she?

Then suddenly I spot the woman who spoke. She isn't even looking at us. She's addressing a pair of toddlers in a trolley seat.

Oh.

I push the hair back off my hot face, suddenly

223

feeling a bit shamefaced. I glance over at Jess – and she's looking rather shamefaced too.

'Let's go and pay,' I say in dignified tones, and push the trolley on.

We drive home in total silence. But underneath my calm exterior I'm seething.

Who does she think she is, lecturing me? Who does she think she is, telling me I have a problem?

We get home and unload the shopping with minimal communication. We're barely even looking each other in the eye.

'Would you like a cup of tea?' I ask with exaggerated formality as I put the last packet away.

'No thanks,' she replies, equally formally.

'I'll just busy myself in the kitchen, if you can amuse yourself for a while.'

'Fine.'

She disappears into her room and the next moment comes out again holding a book called *Petrography of British Igneous Rocks.*

Boy, she really knows how to have fun.

As she sits down on a bar stool, I flick on the kettle and get down a couple of mugs. A few moments later Luke wanders in, looking harassed.

'Hi darling!' I say, injecting even more warmth into my voice than normal. 'I got us a lovely waffle-maker! We can have waffles every morning!'

'Excellent!' he says distractedly, and I shoot a glance of vindication at Jess.

'Would you like a cup of tea?'

'Er . . . yes. Thanks.' He rubs his brow and peers behind the kitchen door. Then he looks on top of the fridge.

'Are you OK?' I say. 'Is anything wrong?'

'I've lost something.' He frowns. 'It's ridiculous. Things can't just *vanish.*'

'What is it?' I say sympathetically. 'I'll help you look.'

'Don't worry.' Luke shakes his head. 'It's just a work thing. It'll turn up. It can't have disappeared.'

'But I want to help!' I run an affectionate hand along his shoulders. 'I've already told you that, darling. Tell me what you're looking for, and we'll search as a team. Is it a file . . . or a book . . . some papers . . . ?'

'That's kind of you.' He kisses me. 'Actually, it's nothing like that. It's a box of clocks. From Tiffany. Ten of them.'

My heart stops dead.

Across the room I'm aware of Jess lifting her head out of her book.

'Did you say . . . Tiffany clocks?' I manage.

'Uhuh.' He nods. 'You know we're hosting a big dinner with the Arcodas Group tomorrow night? It's all part of the pitch. We're basically trying to butter them up. So I bought a load of clocks as corporate gifts – and now they've disappeared.' His brow furrows even further. 'I just don't know what the fuck can have happened to them. One minute they were here . . . the next, they've vanished!'

I can feel Jess's eyes on me like laser beams.

'That's a lot of clocks to go missing,' she says tonelessly.

Oh just fuck off.

I'm swallowing hard. How can I have sold Luke's corporate gifts? How can I have been so stupid? I mean, I *thought* I didn't remember buying them on honeymoon . . .

'Maybe I put them down in the garage.' Luke reaches for his keys. 'I'll go and have a look.'

Oh God. I have to confess.

'Luke . . .' I say in a tiny voice. 'Luke, please don't get angry . . .'

'What?' He swivels on his heel – and as he sees my face he's suddenly alert. 'What is it?'

'Well.' I lick my dry lips. 'I might possibly have—'

'What?' His eyes are narrowing. 'What might you have done, Becky?'

'Sold them,' I whisper.

'*Sold* them?'

'You wanted me to de-clutter the place!' I wail. 'I didn't know how to do it! We had too much stuff! So I've been selling everything on eBay. And I . . . I sold the clocks too. By mistake.'

I'm biting my lip, half-hoping Luke might smile, or even laugh. But he just looks exasperated.

'Jesus Christ, Becky. We are up to our fucking *eyes*. We really need this kind of hassle.' He reaches for his mobile, jabs in a number and listens for a few seconds. 'Hi Marie? We've got a small problem with the Arcodas Group dinner tomorrow night. Call me back.' He snaps his phone shut and there's silence.

'I didn't know!' I say desperately. 'If you'd *told* me they were corporate gifts . . . if you'd let me help . . .'

'*Help?*' Luke cuts me off. 'Becky, you have to be kidding.'

Shaking his head, he stalks out of the room.

I look over at Jess. I can see 'I told you so' in a big thought bubble above her head. A moment later, she gets up and follows him into the study.

'If I can do anything,' I hear her saying in a low voice, 'just let me know.'

'It's fine,' he replies. 'But thanks.'

Jess says something else, but now her voice is muffled. She must have closed the door.

Suddenly I *have* to know what she's saying. I walk silently to the door of the kitchen – then creep out to the hall. I edge as close as I can to the study door and press my ear against it.

'I don't know how you can live with her,' Jess is saying, and I feel a jolt of indignant shock. Then I stiffen, waiting for Luke's response.

There's silence from the room. I can't breathe. I can't move. All I'm aware of is my ear pressed against the wooden door.

'It's difficult,' comes Luke's voice at last.

Something cold plunges into my heart.

Luke finds it difficult to live with me.

There's a noise as if someone's coming towards the door, and I leap back in fright. I hurry back to the kitchen and close the door. My heart is throbbing and my eyes feel a little hot.

We've only been married eleven months. How can he find it difficult to live with me?

The kettle's come to a boil, but I don't want tea any more. I open the fridge, get out a half-open bottle of wine and slosh it into a glass. I drain the entire thing in a few gulps, and am refilling it as Jess comes back into the kitchen.

'Hi,' she says. 'It seems like Luke's sorted out the gift problem.'

'Great,' I say tightly, and take another swig of wine.

So she and Luke sort everything out now, do they? She and Luke have little conversations which I'm not invited to. As I watch her sit down and open her book again, a great tide of hurt anger starts swelling up inside me.

'I would have thought you might take my side,' I say, trying to sound calm. 'We are supposed to be sisters, after all.'

'What do you mean?' Jess frowns.

'You could have defended me!'

'*Defended* you?' Jess looks up. 'You think I'm going to defend you when you're that irresponsible?'

'Oh, so I'm irresponsible,' I say, a little savagely. 'And you're perfect, I suppose.'

'I'm not perfect! But yes! You're irresponsible!' Jess claps her book shut. 'Frankly, Becky, I think you need to get your act together. You seem to have no idea of

personal duty . . . you're obsessed by spending money
. . . you *lie* . . .'

'Well, you're a misery!' My words come out in a
roar. 'You're a skinflint miserable cow who doesn't
know how to have a good time!'

'*What?*' Jess looks utterly dumbfounded.

'I made every effort this weekend!' I cry. 'I did everything I could to make you welcome, and you wouldn't
join in with anything! OK, so you don't like *When
Harry Met Sally*. But you could have pretended!'

'So you'd rather I was insincere?' says Jess, folding
her arms. 'You'd rather I lied? That just about sums
you up, Becky.'

'It's not *lying* to pretend you like something!' I shout
in frustration. 'I just wanted us to have a good time
together! I did research, and I planned your room, and
everything . . . and you're so cold! It's like you don't
have any feelings!'

Suddenly I feel close to tears. I can't believe I'm
yelling at my sister. I break off and take a few deep
breaths. Maybe I can retrieve things. Maybe we can
still make it work.

'The thing is, Jess . . . I did it all because I wanted us
to be friends,' I say, my voice trembling a little. 'I just
wanted us to be friends.'

I look up, expecting to see her face softening. But
she looks almost more contemptuous than before.

'And you always have to get what you want,' she
says. 'Don't you, Becky?'

I feel my face flame in shock.

'Wh— what do you mean?' I falter.

'I mean you're spoilt!' Her harsh voice cuts into my
head. 'What you want, you get! Everything's handed to
you on a plate. If you get into trouble, your parents bail
you out – and if they don't, Luke does! Your whole life
makes me feel sick.' She gestures with her book. 'It's
empty! You're shallow and materialistic . . . and I've

never *met* anyone so obsessed with their own appearance and shopping . . .'

'Talk about obsessed!' I shriek. 'Talk about *obsessed*! You're obsessed by saving money! I've never met anyone so bloody miserly! You've got thirty grand in the bank and you go around like you're penniless! Getting free bubble wrap and horrible bruised bananas! Who *cares* if washing powder costs forty pence less?'

'You'd care if you'd been buying your own washing powder since the age of fourteen,' snaps back Jess. 'Maybe if you took a little more care of the forty pences here and there you wouldn't get into trouble. I heard about how you nearly ruined Luke in New York. I just don't understand you!'

'Well, I don't understand *you*!' I yell, in tears. 'I was so excited when I heard I had a sister, I thought we'd bond and be friends. I thought we could go shopping, and have fun . . . and eat peppermint creams on each other's beds . . .'

'Peppermint creams?' Jess looks at me as though I'm crazy. 'Why would we want to eat peppermint creams?'

'Because!' I flail my arms in frustration. 'Because it would be *fun*! You know, "fun"?'

'I know how to have fun,' snaps Jess.

'Reading about *rocks*?' I grab *Petrography of British Igneous Rocks*. 'How can rocks be interesting? They're just . . . rocks! They're the most boring hobby in the world! Which just about suits you!'

Jess gasps in horror.

'Rocks are . . . *not* boring!' she lashes back, grabbing her book. 'They're a lot more interesting than peppermint creams and mindless shopping and getting yourself into debt!'

'Did you have a fun-bypass operation, or something?'

'Did you have a responsibility-bypass operation?' yells Jess. 'Or were you just born a spoilt brat?'

We glare at each other, both panting slightly. The kitchen is silent apart from the whirr of the fridge-freezer.

I'm not entirely sure what the Gracious Hostess is supposed to do in this situation.

'Fine.' Jess's chin tightens. 'Well . . . I don't think there's any point me sticking around. I can catch a coach back to Cumbria if I leave now.'

'Fine.'

'I'll get my stuff.'

'You do that.'

She turns on her heel and leaves the kitchen, and I take a swig of wine. My head is still pounding with screams, and my heart is racing.

She can't be my sister. She can't be. She's a miserable, tightwad, sanctimonious cow and I never want to see her again.

Never.

THE CINDY BLAINE SHOW

Cindy Blaine TV Productions
43 Hammersmith Bridge Road
London W6 8TH

Mrs Rebecca Brandon
37 Maida Vale Mansions
Maida Vale
London NW6 0YF

22 May 2003

Dear Mrs Brandon

Thank you for your message.

We are sorry to hear you will no longer be able to appear on the Cindy Blaine show
'I Found a Sister And A Soulmate'.

May we suggest that you appear instead on our upcoming show 'My Sister Is A
Bitch!!!' Please give me a call if this idea appeals to you.

Very best wishes

Kayleigh Stuart
Assistant Producer

(mobile: 077878 3456789)

Finerman Wallstein

Attorneys at Law
Finerman House
1398 Avenue of the Americas
New York, NY 10105

Mrs Rebecca Brandon
37 Maida Vale Mansions
Maida Vale
London NW6 0YF

27 May 2003

Dear Mrs Brandon

Thank you for your message. I have altered your will according to your instructions. Clause 5, section (f) now reads:

'And nothing at all to Jess since she's so mean. And anyway she's got heaps of money.'

With kind regards

Jane Cardozo

FIFTEEN

I don't care. Who needs a sister? Not me.

I never wanted one in the first place. I never *asked* for one. I'm fine on my own.

And anyway, I'm not on my own. I've got a strong and loving marriage. I don't need some crummy sister!

'Stupid sister,' I say aloud, wrenching the lid off a pot of jam. It's nearly two weeks since Jess left. Luke's got a late meeting in town, and Mum and Dad are coming over on their way to the airport, so I'm making breakfast for everyone.

'Sorry?' says Luke, coming into the kitchen. He looks pale and tense, as he has for the last few days. The Arcodas Group are making their decision about the pitch and now all he can do is wait. And Luke's not that good at waiting.

'I was just thinking about Jess,' I say, plonking the jam pot down roughly. 'You were absolutely right about her. We were never going to get on in a million years! I've never met such a misery-guts!'

'Mmm,' says Luke absently, pouring himself some orange juice.

He could be a little more supportive.

'Next time I'll take your advice,' I say, trying to engage his attention. 'I should never even have invited her here. I can't believe we're actually supposed to be related!'

'I thought she was all right in the end,' says Luke. 'But I can see why you two wouldn't get on.'

I feel a flicker of resentment.

He wasn't supposed to say 'I thought she was all right.' He was supposed to say 'What a total bitch, I can't believe you put up with her for even a minute!'

'Becky . . . what are you doing?' Luke's gaze lands on the crumbs and plastic packaging littering the granite worktop.

'Making waffles!' I say brightly.

And that just proves another thing. Jess was totally wrong. I've used the waffle-maker practically every day. So there! I almost wish she was here to see it.

The only thing is, I'm not very good at making the mixture. So what I do is buy ready-made waffles, cut them into heart shapes and put them in the waffle-maker to heat up.

But what's wrong with that? I'm using it, aren't I? We're eating waffles, aren't we?

'Waffles . . . again?' says Luke, with the tiniest of grimaces. 'I think I'll pass, thanks.'

'Oh,' I say, discomfited. 'Well, how about some toast? Or eggs? Or . . . muffins?'

'I'm fine on coffee.'

'But you have to have something!' I say, regarding him in sudden alarm. He's definitely got thinner, worrying about this pitch. I need to feed him up.

'I'll make you some pancakes!' I say eagerly. 'Or an omelette!'

'Becky, leave it!' he snaps. 'I'm fine.' He strides out of the kitchen, snapping open his mobile phone. 'Any news?' I hear him say before the study door closes.

I look down at the broken waffle in my hand. A cold feeling is creeping over me.

I know Luke's really tense about work. And that's

probably why he's being a bit short-tempered with me at the moment. It doesn't mean there's any bigger problem or anything.

But I keep remembering what I overheard him say to Jess that night. That he finds it difficult to live with me.

I feel a familiar little stab in my heart and sit down, my head swirling. I've been thinking about it all week, trying to make sense of it.

How can I be difficult to live with? I mean . . . what do I do wrong?

Abruptly I reach for a pencil and paper. OK. Let's look deep down inside myself and be really really honest. What do I do that could be difficult to live with? I write down a heading and underline it firmly.

Becky Bloomwood: Difficulties of Living With
1.

My mind is blank. I cannot think of a single thing.

Come on. Think. Be truthful and unsparing. There must be something. What are the fundamental problems between us? What are the real issues?

Suddenly it hits me. I'm always leaving the lid off my shampoo and Luke complains that he steps on it in the shower.

Becky Bloomwood: Difficulties of Living With
1. Leaves shampoo lid off

Yes. And I'm scatty. I'm always forgetting the number for the burglar alarm. There was the time I had to phone the police and ask them, and they got the wrong message and sent two squad cars round.

Becky Bloomwood: Difficulties of Living With
1. Leaves shampoo lid off

2. Forgets alarm number

I gaze at the list uncertainly. It doesn't seem quite enough somehow. There must be more to it. There must be something really significant and profound.

All of a sudden I gasp and clap my hand to my mouth.

The CDs. Luke's always complaining that I take them out and don't put them back in their cases.

Which I know doesn't sound *that* profound – but maybe it was the last straw in the haystack. And besides, they always say it's the little niggling things which count in a relationship.

OK. I'm going to put this right.

I hurry to the sitting room and head straight for the jumbled pile of CDs by the music system. As I sort them out I feel a kind of lightness. A liberation. This will be the turning point in our marriage.

I stack them neatly and wait till Luke walks past the door on his way to the bedroom.

'Look!' I call out, with a note of pride in my voice. 'I've organized the CDs! They're all back in their proper boxes!'

Luke glances into the room.

'Great,' he says with an absent nod, and carries on walking.

I stare after him reproachfully.

Is that all he can say?

Here I am, mending our troubled marriage, and he hasn't even *noticed*.

Suddenly the buzzer goes in the hall, and I leap to my feet. This must be Mum and Dad. I'll have to get back to our marriage later.

OK. So I knew that Mum and Dad had really got into all their counselling and stuff. But somehow I wasn't expecting them to turn up with slogans on their sweatshirts. Mum's reads 'I am Woman, I am Goddess' and Dad's says 'Don't Let the Passive-Aggressive Bastards Get You Down.'

'Wow!' I say, trying to hide my surprise. 'Those are great!'

'We got them at the centre,' says Mum with a beam. 'Aren't they fun?'

'So you must be really enjoying your therapy.'

'It's marvellous!' exclaims Mum. '*So* much more interesting than bridge. And so sociable! We did a group session the other day and who do you think should have turned up? Marjorie Davis, who used to live across the road!'

'Really?' I say in surprise. 'Did she get married, then?'

'Oh no!' Mum lowers her voice tactfully. 'She has *boundary issues*, poor thing.'

I can't quite get my head round all this. What on earth are boundary issues?

'So . . . er . . . do *you* have issues?' I say as we go into the kitchen. 'Has it all been really hard going?'

'Oh, we've been to the abyss and back,' says Mum, nodding. 'Haven't we, Graham?'

'Right to the edge,' says Dad agreeably.

'But the rage and guilt are behind us now. We're both empowered to live and love.' She beams at me and roots around in her holdall. 'I brought a nice Swiss roll. Shall we put the kettle on?'

'Mum's found her inner goddess,' says Dad proudly. 'She walked on hot coals, you know!'

I gape at her.

'You walked on hot coals? Oh my God! I did that in Sri Lanka! Did it hurt?'

'Not at all! It was painless!' says Mum. 'I kept my gardening shoes on, of course,' she adds as an afterthought.

'Wow!' I say. 'That's . . . er . . . brilliant.'

'We still have a lot to learn though,' says Mum, briskly slicing the Swiss roll. 'That's why we're going on this cruise.'

'Right,' I say after a pause. 'Yes. The . . . therapy cruise.' The first time Mum told me about this I thought she had to be joking. 'So the idea is you sail round the Med and everyone has therapy sessions.'

'It's not *just* therapy!' says Mum. 'There are sight-seeing expeditions, too.'

'And entertainment,' puts in Dad. 'Apparently they have some very good shows. And a black-tie dinner dance.'

'All our chums from the centre are going,' adds Mum. 'We've already organized a little cocktail party for the first night! Plus . . .' She hesitates. 'One of the guest speakers specializes in reunions with long-lost family members. Which should be particularly interesting for us.'

I feel an uncomfortable twinge. I don't want to think about long-lost family members.

There's silence, and I can see Mum and Dad exchanging looks.

'So . . . you didn't really hit it off with Jess,' ventures Dad at last.

Oh God. I can tell he's disappointed.

'Not really,' I say, looking away. 'We're just . . . not very similar people.'

'And why should you be?' says Mum, putting a supportive hand on my arm. 'You've grown up totally separately. Why should you have anything more in common with Jess than with . . . say . . .' She thinks for a moment. 'Kylie Minogue.'

'Becky's got far more in common with Jess than Kylie Minogue!' exclaims Dad at once. 'Kylie Minogue's Australian, for a start.'

'That doesn't prove anything,' says Mum. 'We're all in the Commonwealth, aren't we? Becky would probably get on very well with Kylie Minogue. Wouldn't you, darling?'

'Er . . .'

'They'd have nothing to say to each other,' says Dad, shaking his head. 'I'm telling you.'

'Of course they would!' retorts Mum. 'They'd have a lovely conversation! I expect they'd become great friends!'

'Now Cher,' says Dad. '*That's* an interesting woman.'

'Becky doesn't want to be friends with Cher!' says Mum indignantly. 'Madonna, maybe . . .'

'Yes well, the day I meet Kylie Minogue, Cher *or* Madonna, I'll let you know, OK?' I say, a little more snappily than I mean to.

There's silence, and both Mum and Dad turn to survey me. Then Mum glances at Dad.

'Graham, go and give Luke his coffee.' She hands a mug to Dad and, as soon as he's gone, gives me a searching look.

'Becky, love!' she says. 'Are you all right? You seem a bit tense.'

Oh God. There's something about Mum's sympathetic face which makes my composure crumble. Suddenly all the worries I've been trying so hard to bury start rising to the surface.

'Don't worry about Jess,' she says kindly. 'It doesn't matter in the least if you two girls don't get on. Nobody will mind!'

I swallow a few times, trying to keep control of myself.

'It's not Jess,' I say. 'At least, it's not just Jess. It's . . . Luke.'

'Luke?' says Mum in astonishment.

'Things aren't going too well at the moment. In fact . . .' My voice starts to wobble. 'In fact . . . I think our marriage is in trouble.'

Oh God. Now I've said it aloud it sounds totally

true and convincing. *Our marriage is in trouble.*

'Are you sure, love?' Mum looks perplexed. 'You both seem very happy to me!'

'Well we're not! We've just had this horrible huge row!'

Mum stares at me for a few moments, then bursts into laughter. I feel indignation rise inside me.

'Don't laugh! It was awful!'

'Of course it was, love!' she says. 'You're coming up to your first anniversary, aren't you?'

'Er . . . yes.'

'Well then. That's the time for your First Big Row! You knew that, didn't you, Becky?'

'What?' I say blankly.

'Your First Big Row!' She tuts at my expression. 'Dear me! What do the women's magazines teach you girls nowadays!'

'Er . . . how to put on acrylic nails?'

'Well! They should be teaching you about happy marriages! All couples have a First Big Row at around a year. A big argument, then the air is cleared, and everything's back to normal.'

'God, I never knew that,' I say slowly. 'So . . . our marriage isn't in trouble after all?'

This all makes sense. In fact it makes a lot of sense. A First Big Row — and then everything's calm and happy again. Like a thunderstorm. Clear air and renewal. Or one of those forest fires that seem awful but in fact are *good* because all the little plants can grow again. Exactly.

And the real point is — yes! This means none of it was my fault! We were going to have a row anyway, whatever I did! I'm really starting to cheer up again. Everything's going to be lovely again. I beam at Mum and take a huge bite of Swiss roll.

'So . . . Luke and I won't have any more rows,' I say, just to be on the safe side.

'Oh no!' says Mum reassuringly. 'Not until your Second Big Row, which won't be until—'

She's interrupted by the kitchen door banging open and Luke appearing in the kitchen. He's holding the phone, his face is all lit up and he's got the hugest grin I've ever seen on his face.

'We got it. We've got the Arcodas Group!'

I knew everything was going to be all right! I *knew* it. It's all lovely! In fact, it's been like Christmas all day long!

Luke cancelled his meeting and went straight into the office to celebrate – and after seeing Mum and Dad off in a taxi, I joined him there. God, I love the Brandon Communications office. It's all funky with blond wood and spotlights everywhere, and it's such a happy place. Everyone just mills around, beaming and swigging champagne all day!

Or at least, they do when they've just won an enormous pitch. All day long, there's been the sound of laughter and excited voices everywhere, and someone's programmed all the computers to sing 'Congratulations' every ten minutes.

Luke and his senior people held a quick celebration/strategy meeting which I sat in on. At first they were all saying things like 'The work starts here' and 'We need to recruit' and 'There are huge challenges ahead.' But then Luke suddenly exclaimed, 'Fuck it. Let's party. We'll think about the challenges tomorrow.'

So he got his assistant on the phone to some caterers, and at five o'clock loads of guys in black aprons appeared in the offices with more champagne, and canapés arranged on cool perspex boxes. All the employees piled into the biggest conference room, and there was music on the sound system, and Luke made a little speech in which he said it was a great day for Brandon C and well done, and everyone cheered.

And now a few of us are going out to dinner for *another* celebration! I'm in Luke's office redoing my make-up, and he's changing into a fresh shirt.

'Congratulations,' I say for the millionth time. 'It's fantastic.'

'It's a good day. ' Luke grins at me, doing up his cuffs. 'I've been wanting a big mainstream client like this for years. This could pave the way for so much.'

'I'm so proud of you.'

'Ditto.' Luke's face suddenly softens. He comes over and wraps his arms round me. 'I know I've been distracted lately. And I'm sorry.'

'It's OK,' I say, looking down. 'And I'm . . . I'm sorry I sold the clocks.'

'That doesn't matter!' Luke strokes my hair. 'I know things haven't been easy for you. What with coming home . . . your sister . . .'

'Yes, well,' I say at once. 'Let's not think about her. Let's think about *us*. The future.' I pull his head down and kiss him. 'It's all going to be great.'

For a while we're both silent. But in a good way. It's just us, in each other's arms, relaxed and content and together, like we used to be on honeymoon. I feel a sudden swell of relief. Mum was so right! That First Big Row totally cleared the air! We're closer than ever!

'I love you,' I murmur.

'I love *you*.' Luke kisses my nose. 'We should get going.'

'OK.' I beam at him. 'I'll go down and see if the car's here yet.'

I head along the corridor, floating on a cloud of joy. Everything's perfect. Everything! As I pass the caterers' trays, I pick up a glass of champagne and take a few sips. Maybe we'll go dancing tonight. After dinner. When everyone else has gone home, Luke and

242

I will go on to a club and celebrate properly, just the two of us.

I trip happily down the stairs, still holding my glass, and open the door into reception. Then I stop, puzzled. A few yards away, a thin-faced guy in a chalk-striped suit is talking to Janet, the receptionist. He seems kind of familiar, somehow – but I can't quite place him . . .

Then all of a sudden my stomach does a back-flip.

Yes I can.

It's that guy from Milan. The one who carried Nathan Temple's bags out of the shop. What's he doing here?

Cautiously I take a few steps forward so I can hear their conversation.

'So Mr Brandon's *not* ill?' he's saying.

Shit.

I retreat behind the door and slam it shut, my heart thumping. What do I do now?

I take a gulp of champagne to calm my nerves – and then another. A couple of guys from IT saunter past and give me an odd look, and I smile gaily back.

OK. I can't cower behind this door for ever. I inch my head above the glass panel in the door until I can see into reception – and thank God. Chalk-stripe guy has gone. With a whoosh of relief I push the door open and stride nonchalantly into the reception area.

'Hi!' I say casually to Janet, who's typing busily on her computer. 'Who was that just now? That man talking to you.'

'Oh, him! He works for a man called . . . Nathan Temple?'

'Right. And . . . what did he want?'

'It was weird!' she says, pulling a face. 'He kept asking if Luke was "better".'

'And what did you say?' I'm trying not to sound too urgent.

'Well, I said he's fine, of course! Never better!' She laughs gaily – then as she sees my face she suddenly stops typing. 'Oh my God. He isn't fine, is he?'

'What?'

'That was a doctor, wasn't it?' She leans forward, looking stricken. 'You can tell me, Becky. Did Luke catch some tropical disease while you were away?'

'No! Of course not!'

'Is it his heart then? His kidneys?' Her eyes are watering. 'You know . . . I lost my aunt this year. It really hasn't been easy for me . . .'

'I'm sorry,' I say, flustered. 'But honestly, don't worry! Luke's fine! Everything's fine, it's all fine . . .'

I glance up – and the words wither on my lips.

Please no.

This can't be happening.

Nathan Temple himself is walking into the building.

He's bigger and more barrel-chested than I remember, and is wearing the same leather-trimmed coat he was trying on in Milan. He exudes power and money and a smell of cigars. And his sharp blue eyes are looking right at me.

'Well, hello,' he says in his Cockney rasp. 'Mrs Brandon. We meet again.'

'Hell– hello!' I say. 'Gosh! What a . . . lovely surprise!'

'Still enjoying the bag?' He gives me the glimmer of a smile.

'Er . . . yes! It's fab!'

I have to get him out of here is running through my brain. *I have to get him out of here.*

'I've come to talk about my hotel with your husband,' he says pleasantly. 'Will that be possible?'

'Right!' I swallow. 'Of course. Great! The only thing is, Luke's a bit tied up, unfortunately. But would you like a drink? We could go to a bar . . . have a really nice chat . . . you could tell me all about it . . .'

Yes. Genius. I'll hustle him out . . . buy him a few drinks . . . Luke will never know . . .

'I don't mind waiting,' he says, easing his huge frame down into a leather chair. 'If you let him know I'm here.' His eyes meet mine with a little glint. 'I gather he's recovered from his illness?'

My heart gives a swoop.

'Yes!' I say brightly. 'He's . . . he's a lot better! Thanks for the flowers!'

I glance at Janet, who's been following this exchange in slight bewilderment.

'Shall I ring up and tell Luke?' she says, reaching for the phone.

'No! I mean . . . don't worry! I'll pop up myself,' I say, my voice a little shrill.

I start walking towards the lifts, my heart hammering with nerves.

OK. I can still deal with this. I get Luke out of the building the back way by telling him somebody's spilt water on the foyer floor and it's really slippery. Yes. And we get in the car . . . then I pretend I've forgotten something, and I go *back* to Nathan Temple, and I say—

'Becky?'

I leap about ten feet and look up to see Luke coming down the stairs, two steps at a time. His face is glowing and he's putting on his coat.

'So is the car here yet?' He peers at my frozen expression in surprise. 'Sweetheart . . . are you all right?'

Or I could tell Luke everything.

I stare at him dumbly for a few seconds, my stomach churning.

'Er . . . Luke?' I manage at last.

'Yes?'

'There's . . . there's something I have to tell you.' I swallow hard. 'I should have told you ages ago, but

245

'. . . I didn't . . . and I was dealing with it, but . . .'

Suddenly I realize that Luke isn't listening to a word. His eyes are darkening in shock as they focus beyond me, on Nathan Temple.

'Is that—' He shakes his head in disbelief. 'What's *he* doing here? I thought Gary was getting rid of him.'

'Luke—'

'Hold on, Becky. This is important.' He pulls out his phone and taps in a number. 'Gary,' he says in low tones. 'What's Nathan Temple doing in our foyer? You were supposed to be dealing with it.'

'Luke—' I try again.

'Sweetheart, wait a minute.' He turns back to the phone. 'Well, he's here. Larger than life.'

'Luke, please, listen.' I tug his arm urgently.

'Becky, whatever it is, can't it wait till later?' says Luke with a touch of impatience. 'I have a problem here that I have to sort out . . .'

'But that's what I'm trying to tell you!' I say in desperation. 'It's about your problem! It's about Nathan Temple!'

Luke stares at me as though I'm making no sense.

'How can it be to do with Nathan Temple? Becky, you don't even *know* Nathan Temple!'

'Er . . . well . . . actually . . . yes I do.' I bite my lip. 'Kind of.'

There's silence. Slowly Luke closes up his phone.

'You "kind of" know Nathan Temple?'

'Here's Mr Brandon!' rings out a voice and we both look up to see that Janet at the reception desk has spotted us. 'Luke, you've got a visitor!'

'Just coming, Janet,' calls back Luke with a professional smile. He turns to me, still smiling. 'Becky, what the fuck has been going on?'

'It's . . . it's a bit of a long story,' I say, hot-faced.

'Were you planning to share this story with me at

any stage?' Luke's smile is fixed in place, but there's a definite edge to his voice.

'Yes! Of course! I was just . . . waiting for the right moment.'

'Do you think possibly *this* might be a good moment? Bearing in mind he's a few fucking yards away?'

'Er . . . yes! Absolutely.' I swallow nervously. 'Well. It all began . . . er . . . in a shop, as it happens . . .'

'Too late,' interrupts Luke in an undertone. 'He's coming.'

I follow Luke's gaze and feel a flip of apprehension. Nathan Temple has got out of his chair and is advancing towards us.

'So here he is.' His hoarse voice greets us. 'The elusive Luke Brandon. You've been keeping your husband from me, young lady, haven't you?' He wags a mock-accusing finger at me.

'Of course not!' I laugh shrilly. 'Er . . . Luke, do you know Nathan Temple? We met in Milan, um . . . remember, darling?' I give a bright, fake smile as if I'm a dinner-party hostess and this is all perfectly normal.

'Good evening, Mr Temple,' says Luke calmly. 'How nice to meet you properly.'

'It's a pleasure.' Nathan Temple claps Luke on the back. 'So, you're feeling better, I hope.'

Luke's eyes flicker towards me, and I shoot back an agonized expression.

'I'm feeling quite well,' he replies. 'May I ask what this . . . unexpected visit is regarding?'

'Well,' says Nathan Temple, reaching in his coat pocket for a monogrammed silver cigar case, 'seems you won't take calls from my office.'

'I've been very busy this week,' replies Luke without flinching. 'I do apologize if my secretaries have failed to pass on your messages. Was there something in particular you wanted to discuss?'

247

'My hotel project,' says Nathan, offering Luke a cigar. '*Our* hotel project, I should say.'

Luke starts to reply — but Nathan Temple lifts a hand to stop him. He carefully lights his cigar and puffs on it a few times. 'Forgive me for turning up here out of the blue,' he says at last. 'But when I want something, I don't hang around. I go and get it. Much like your good wife here.' His eyes twinkle. 'I'm sure she told you the story.'

'I think she was probably saving up the best part,' says Luke with a tight smile.

'I like your wife,' Nathan Temple says affably. He blows out a cloud of smoke and runs appraising eyes over me. 'You want to come to work for me any time, sweetheart, you just give me a ring.'

'Gosh!' I say, a bit thrown. 'Er . . . thanks!'

I glance apprehensively at Luke. A vein is throbbing in his forehead.

'Becky,' he says in polite, measured tones, 'might we have a little word? Do excuse us for a moment,' he adds.

'No problem.' Nathan Temple waves his cigar. 'I'll finish this up. Then we can talk.'

Luke marches me into a little meeting room and closes the door. Then he turns to face me, his face all tight and businesslike. I've seen him like this when he bawls out employees.

Oh God. Suddenly I'm scared.

'OK, Becky, start from the beginning. No—' he interrupts himself. 'Cut to the middle. How do you know Nathan Temple?'

'I met him when we were in Milan.' I falter. 'I was in this shop and he . . . he did me this favour.'

'He did you a *favour*?' Luke looks taken aback. 'What kind of favour? Were you taken ill? Did you get lost?'

There's a long, agonized silence.

'There was this . . . handbag,' I say at last.

'A handbag?' Luke looks bewildered. 'He bought you a handbag?'

'No! I bought it. But he got me to the top of the list. He was really sweet! And I was really grateful . . .' I'm twisting my hands into knots. 'So then when we were back in England he phoned up and said he wanted you to be involved with his hotel . . .'

'And what did you say?' says Luke, his voice dangerously quiet.

'The thing is . . .' I swallow. 'I thought you'd love to do a hotel launch.'

The door suddenly bursts open and Gary comes into the room.

'What's going on?' he says, wide-eyed. 'What's Nathan Temple doing here?'

'Ask Becky.' Luke gestures towards me. 'It seems she's been having quite a correspondence with him.'

'I didn't know who he was!' I say defensively. 'I had no idea! He was just this lovely Cockney man who got me my bag . . .'

'Bag?' says Gary, his head swivelling alertly from me to Luke. 'What bag?'

'Becky appears to have offered my services to Nathan Temple in return for a handbag,' says Luke curtly.

'A *handbag*?' Gary looks stunned.

'It wasn't just any old handbag!' I exclaim, rattled. 'It was a limited-edition Angel bag! There's only a few of them in the whole world! It was on the cover of *Vogue*! All the movie stars want one and everything!'

Both men stare at me in silence. Neither seems that impressed.

'And anyway,' I say, my face burning, 'I thought doing a hotel launch would be fab! It's five-star and everything! You'd get to meet celebrities!'

'*Celebrities?*' echoes Luke, suddenly losing it.

'Becky, I don't *need* to meet those kind of celebrities! I don't need to be launching some tacky criminal's hotel! I need to be here, with my team, focusing on my new client's needs.'

'I didn't realize!' I say desperately. 'I thought it was a brilliant networking coup!'

'Calm down, boss,' says Gary to Luke soothingly. 'We haven't promised him anything—'

'She has.' Luke gestures towards me and Gary swivels round in shock.

'I didn't . . . promise, exactly.' My voice shakes a little. 'I just said . . . you'd be delighted.'

'You realize how much harder this makes it for me?' Luke is holding his head in his hands. 'Becky, why didn't you *tell* me? Why didn't you tell me about it in Milan?'

There's silence.

'Because the Angel bag cost two thousand Euros,' I say at last in a tiny voice. 'I thought you'd be cross.'

'Jesus Christ.' Luke sounds at the end of his tether.

'And then I didn't want to bother you! You were so busy with the Arcodas pitch . . . I thought I'd deal with it myself. And I *was* dealing with it.'

'Dealing with it,' echoes Luke incredulously. 'How were you dealing with it?'

'I told Nathan Temple you were ill,' I gulp.

Very slowly Luke's expression changes.

'The bunch of flowers,' he says in even tones. 'Was that from Nathan Temple?'

Oh God.

'Yes,' I whisper.

'He sent you flowers?' says Gary in disbelief.

'And a fruit basket,' says Luke shortly.

Gary gives a sudden snort of laughter.

'It's not funny,' says Luke, his voice like whiplash. 'We've just won the biggest pitch of our lives. We should be out celebrating. Not having to deal with bloody Nathan Temple sitting in our foyer.' He sinks down into a chair.

'We don't want to make an enemy of him, Luke,' says Gary, pulling a small face. 'Not if he's going to buy the *Daily World*.'

There's silence in the little room, apart from the ticking of a clock.

I don't dare say a word.

Then Luke abruptly stands up. 'We can't sit here all day. I'll go and see him. If I have to do the job I have to do the job.' He gives me a look. 'I just hope the handbag was worth it, Becky. I really hope it was worth it.'

I feel a sudden stab of pain.

'Luke, I'm sorry,' I say desperately. 'I'm really sorry. I never meant . . . I never realized . . .'

'Yeah, Becky,' he interrupts in weary tones. 'Whatever.'

He leaves the room, followed by Gary. And I just sit there in silence. Suddenly I feel a tear rolling down my cheek. Everything was so perfect. And now it's all ruined.

SIXTEEN

Things aren't good.

In fact, this has been the worst week of our entire marriage.

I've barely seen Luke, he's been so tied up with work. He's had meetings every day with the Arcodas Group, plus there's been a huge crisis with one of his banking clients, and one of his main account managers was rushed to hospital with meningitis. It's all been total mayhem.

And today, instead of having a chance to relax and regroup, he's got to fly out to Cyprus to visit Nathan Temple's hotel and start planning the launch. A launch which he doesn't want to do.

And it's all my fault.

'Can I do anything?' I say nervously as I watch him put shirts into a suitcase.

'No,' he says shortly. 'Thanks.'

This is how he's been all week. All quiet and scary and barely looking me in the eye. And when he does look me in the eye, he looks so fed up that my stomach flips over and I feel a bit sick.

I'm trying really hard to keep positive and look on the bright side. I mean, it's probably totally normal for couples to have blips like this. Just like Mum said. This is the Second Big Row of our marriage, and the air will clear again and everything will be fine . . .

Except I'm not sure the Second Big Row should come two days after the First Big Row.

And I'm not sure it should last a whole week.

I tried emailing Mum on her cruise ship to ask her advice, but I got a message back saying that the Mind Body Spirit cruise was a retreat from the outside world, and no passengers were contactable.

Luke zips up his suit carrier and disappears into the bathroom without even looking at me, and I feel a stab of pain. He'll be gone in a few minutes. We can't leave each other like this. We just can't.

He comes out again and dumps his sponge bag in his suitcase.

'It's our first anniversary soon, you know,' I say in a scratchy voice. 'We should . . . plan something.'

'I'm not even sure if I'll be back,' says Luke.

He sounds like he doesn't care, either. Our first anniversary and he's not even interested. Suddenly my head is hot and I can feel tears pushing at my eyes. The whole week has been awful and now Luke's leaving and he won't even smile at me.

'You don't have to be so unfriendly, Luke,' I say in a rush. 'I know I fucked up. But I didn't mean to. I've said I'm sorry about a zillion times.'

'I know,' says Luke in the same weary tones he's been using all week.

'What do you expect me to do?'

'What do you expect *me* to do, Becky?' he retorts in sudden exasperation. 'Say it doesn't matter? Say I don't mind that just when I should be putting all my efforts into the Arcodas Group, I find myself flying off to some God-forsaken island?' He clicks his case shut with sharp gestures. 'You want me to say I'm *happy* to be associated with some hideous, tacky hotel?'

'It won't be tacky!' I exclaim in dismay. 'I'm sure it won't! Nathan Temple said it was going to be of the highest quality! You should have seen him in that shop in Milan, Luke. He would only accept the best! The best leather . . . the best cashmere . . .'

'And I'm sure he'll have the best waterbeds,' says Luke with a sarcastic edge to his voice. 'Becky, don't you understand? I have a few principles.'

'So do I!' I say in shock. 'I have principles! But that doesn't make me a *snob*!'

'I am not a snob,' retorts Luke tightly. 'I simply have standards.'

'You are a snob!' My voice rushes out before I can stop it. 'Just because he used to run motels! I've been looking up Nathan Temple on the internet. He does loads for charity, he helps people—'

'He also dislocated a man's jaw,' cuts in Luke. 'Did you read about that?'

For a few moments I'm halted.

'That was . . . years ago,' I say at last. 'He's made amends . . . he's reformed . . .'

'Whatever, Becky.' Luke sighs and picks up his briefcase. 'Can we just leave it?'

He heads out of the room and after a moment I follow him.

'No. We can't leave it. We have to talk, Luke. You've barely looked at me all week.'

'I've been busy.' He reaches into his briefcase, takes out a foil strip of Ibuprofen and pops out a couple of tablets.

'No you haven't.' I bite my lip. 'You've been punishing me.'

'Can you *blame* me?' Luke thrusts his hands through his hair. 'This has been a hell of a week.'

'Then let me help!' I say eagerly. I follow him into the kitchen where he's running water into a glass. 'There must be something I could do. I could be your assistant . . . or do research . . .'

'Please!' Luke interrupts, and swigs down his

Ibuprofen. 'No more help. All your "help" does is waste my bloody time. OK?'

I stare at him, my face burning. He must have looked at my ideas in the pink folder. He must have thought they were total crap.

'Right,' I say at last. 'Well . . . I won't bother any more.'

'Please don't.' He walks off into the study, and I can hear him opening desk drawers.

As I'm standing there, the blood thumping round my head, I hear the sound of the letterbox. I go into the hall, where a package is lying on the doormat. It's a slim Jiffy bag for Luke, with a smudged postmark. I pick it up and stare at the handwriting, written in black marker pen. It kind of looks familiar – except it's not.

'You've got a parcel,' I say.

Luke comes out of the study holding a pile of files, and dumps them in his briefcase. He takes the package from me, rips it open and pulls out a computer disc, together with a letter.

'Ah!' he exclaims, sounding more pleased than he has all week. 'Excellent.'

'Who's it from?'

'Your sister,' says Luke.

I feel like he's hit me in the solar plexus.

My sister? *Jess?* My eyes drop down to the package in disbelief. That's Jess's handwriting?

'Why . . .' I'm trying to keep my voice calm. 'Why is Jess writing to you?'

'She's edited that CD-rom for us.' He scans to the bottom of the page. 'She really is a total star. She's better than our own IT guys. I *must* send her some flowers.'

His voice is all warm and appreciative, and his eyes are glowing. As I watch him, suddenly there's a huge lump in my throat.

He thinks Jess is fab, doesn't he? Jess is fab . . . and I'm crap.

'So Jess has been a help to you, has she?' I say, my voice trembling.

'Yes. To be honest, she has.'

'I suppose you'd rather she was here than me. I suppose you'd rather we swapped places.'

'Don't be ridiculous.' Luke folds up the letter and pops it back in the Jiffy bag.

'If you think Jess is so great, why don't you just go and live with her?' I hear my voice coming out in a rush of distress. 'Why don't you just go and . . . and talk about computers together?'

'Becky, calm down,' says Luke in amazement.

But I can't calm down. I can't stop.

'It's OK! You can be honest with me, Luke! If you prefer a miserable skinflint with zero dress sense and zero sense of humour to me . . . just say so! Maybe you should marry her if she's so great! She's such a bundle of fun! I'm *sure* you'd have a wonderful time with her . . .'

'Becky!' Luke cuts me off with a look which chills me to the marrow. 'Just stop right there.'

He's silent for a few moments, folding up the Jiffy bag. I don't dare move a muscle.

'I know you didn't get along with Jess,' he says at last, looking up. 'But you should know this. Your sister is a good person. She's honest, reliable and hard-working. She spent hours on this for us.' He taps the disc. 'She volunteered to do it herself, and she didn't ask for any pay or any thanks. I would say she's a truly selfless person.' He takes a few steps towards me, his face unrelenting. 'You could learn a lot from your sister.'

My face is hot and cold with shock. I open my mouth to speak – but nothing will come out.

'I have to go.' Luke looks at his watch. 'I'll get my stuff.'

He strides out of the kitchen. But I can't move from the spot.

'I'm off.' Luke reappears at the kitchen door holding his case. 'I'm not sure when I'll be back.'

'Luke . . . I'm sorry.' At last I've found my voice, even if it is all shaky. 'I'm sorry I've been such a disappointment to you.' I raise my head, trying to keep a grip on myself. 'But if you really want to know . . . you've been a disappointment to me, too. You've changed. You were fun on honeymoon. You were fun and you were laid-back and you were kind . . .'

Suddenly I have a memory of Luke as he was. Sitting on his yoga mat with his bleached plaits and his earring. Smiling at me in the Sri Lankan sunshine. Reaching over to take my hand.

I feel a stab of unbearable yearning. That easy, happy guy bears no resemblance to the taut-faced man standing in front of me.

'You're different.' The words come out in a sob and I can feel a tear trickling down my cheek. 'You've gone back to the way you used to be before. The way you promised you'd never be again.' I wipe away the tear roughly. 'This isn't what I thought married life would be like, Luke.'

There's silence in the kitchen.

'Me neither,' says Luke. There's a familiar wryness to his voice, but he isn't smiling. 'I have to go. Bye, Becky.'

He turns to leave, and a few moments later I hear the front door slam.

I swallow hard a few times, trying to keep control of myself. But tears are already coursing down my cheeks and my legs are wobbling. I sink down on to the floor and bury my face in my knees. He's gone. And he didn't even kiss me goodbye.

For a while I don't move. I just sit there in the hall, hugging my knees, occasionally wiping my eyes with my sleeve. Eventually my tears dry up and I take a few deep breaths, feeling calmer. But the sick, hollow feeling in my stomach is still there.

Our marriage is in tatters. And it hasn't even been a year.

At last I rouse myself and get stiffly to my feet. I feel numb and spaced-out. Slowly I walk into the silent, empty dining room, where our carved wooden table from Sri Lanka is standing proudly in the middle of the room.

The sight of it makes me want to cry all over again. I had such dreams for that table. I had such dreams of what our married life was going to be like. All the visions are piling back into my head: the glow of candlelight, me ladling out hearty stew, Luke smiling at me lovingly, all our friends gathered round the table . . .

Suddenly I feel an overwhelming, almost physical longing. I have to talk to Suze. I have to hear her sympathetic voice. She'll know what to do. She always does.

I hurry, almost running, to the phone and jab in the number.

'Hello?' It's answered by a high-pitched girl's voice – but it's not Suze.

'Hi!' I say, taken aback. 'It's Becky here. Is that—'

'It's Lulu speaking! Hi, Becky! How are you?'

Her bright, abrasive voice is like sandpaper on my raw senses.

'I'm fine,' I say. 'Is Suze there, by any chance?'

'She's just putting the twins into their car seats, actually! We're off for a picnic, to Marsham House. Do you know it?'

'Er . . .' I rub my dry face. 'No. I don't.'

'Oh, you should definitely visit it! Cosmo, sweetie! Not on your dungarees! It's a super National Trust house. And wonderful for the children, too. There's a butterfly farm!'

'Right,' I manage. 'Great.'

'I'll get her to call back in two secs, OK?'

'Thanks.' I say in relief. 'That would be great. Just tell her . . . I really need to talk to her.'

I wander over to the window, press my face against the glass and stare down at the passing traffic below. The traffic lights at the corner turn red and all the cars come to a halt. The lights turn green again and the cars all zoom off in a tearing hurry. Then they turn red again – and a new set of cars comes to a stop.

Suze hasn't called. It's been more than two secs.

She isn't going to call. She lives in a different world now. A world of dungarees and picnics and butterfly farms. There's no room for me and my stupid problems.

My head feels thick and heavy with disappointment. I know that Suze and I haven't been getting on that well recently. But I thought . . . I honestly thought . . .

I swallow hard.

Maybe I could call Danny. Except . . . I've left about six messages for him and he's never returned any of them.

Anyway. Never mind. It doesn't matter. I'll just have to pull myself together on my own.

I walk with as much determination as I can muster to the kitchen. What I will do is . . . I will make myself a cup of tea. Yes. And take it from there. I flick on the kettle, drop a tea bag in a mug and open the fridge.

No milk.

For an instant I feel like falling sobbing to the floor again.

But instead I take a deep breath and lift my chin. Fine. I'll go and buy some milk. And stock up generally. It'll be good to get some fresh air and take my mind off things.

I get my bag, slick on some lip gloss and head out of

the apartment. I walk briskly through the gates and down the street, past the weird shop with all the gold furniture and into the delicatessen on the corner.

The moment I get inside I start to feel a bit more steady. It's so warm and soothing in here, with the most delicious smell of coffee and cheese and whichever soup they're cooking that day. All the assistants wear long striped ticking aprons, and look like they're genuine French cheese-makers.

I pick up a wicker basket, head to the milk counter and load in a couple of pints of organic semi-skimmed. Then my eye falls on a pot of luxury Greek yoghurt. Maybe I'll buy a few little treats to cheer myself up. I put the yoghurt into my basket, along with some individual chocolate mousses. Then I reach for a gorgeous hand-blown glass jar of gourmet brandied cherries.

That's a waste of money, a voice intones in my head. *You don't even like brandied cherries.*

It sounds a bit like Jess's. Weird. And anyway, I *do* like brandied cherries. Kind of.

I shake my head irritably and thrust the jar into my basket, then move along to the next display and reach for a mini olive and anchovy focaccia pizza.

Overpriced rubbish, comes the voice in my head. *You could make it yourself at home for 20p.*

Shut up, I retort mentally. No I couldn't. Go away.

I dump the pizza in my basket, then move along the displays more swiftly, putting in punnets of white peaches and miniature pears, several cheeses, dark-chocolate truffles, a French strawberry gateau . . .

But Jess's voice is constantly in my head, like a burr.

You're throwing money away. What happened to the budget? You think indulging yourself like this will bring Luke back?

'Stop it!' I say aloud, feeling rattled. God, I'm going crazy. Defiantly I shove three tins of Russian caviar into my overflowing basket, and stagger to the checkout. I drop the basket down on the counter and reach inside my bag for my credit card.

As the girl behind the till starts unloading all my stuff, she smiles at me.

'The gateau's delicious,' she says, carefully packing it into a box. 'And so are the white peaches. And caviar!' She looks impressed. 'Are you having a dinner party?'

'No!' I say, taken aback. 'I'm not having a dinner party. I'm just . . . I'm . . .'

But all of a sudden I can't continue.

All of a sudden I feel like a fool. I look at my piles of stupid, overpriced, luxury food bleeping through the register and feel my face flame. What am I doing? What am I buying all this stuff for? I don't need it. Jess is right.

Jess is right.

The very thought makes me wince and turn away. I don't want to think about Jess.

But I can't help it. I can't escape the thoughts wheeling round in my head like big black crows. Out of nowhere I hear Luke's stern voice. *She's a good person . . . She's honest, reliable and hardworking . . . You could learn a lot from your sister . . .*

You could learn a lot from your sister.

And suddenly it hits me like a bolt of lightning. I'm rooted to the spot, my head buzzing, my heart pounding.

Oh my God. This is it.

This is the answer.

'That'll be a hundred and thirty pounds, seventy-three pence,' says the girl behind the checkout with a smile. I stare back at her in a total daze.

'I . . . I have to go,' I say. 'Now.'

'But your food!' says the girl.

'I don't need any of it.'

261

I turn and stumble out of the shop, still clutching my credit card in my hand. I get on to the pavement and take long deep breaths, as though I've been winded.

It's all fallen into place. I have to go and learn from Jess.

Like Yoda.

I'll be her apprentice and she'll teach me all her frugal ways. She'll show me how to become a good person, the kind of person that Luke wants. And I'll learn how to save my marriage.

I start walking along the street more and more quickly, until I'm breaking into a run. People are staring at me but I don't care. I have to go to Cumbria. Right this minute.

I sprint all the way home, and up about three flights of stairs before I realize my lungs are nearly exploding and I'm never going to make it all the way up to the penthouse. I sit down and puff like a steam engine for a few minutes, then take the lift up the rest of the way. I burst into the apartment and run to the bedroom, where I haul a bright-red suitcase out from under the bed and start throwing things randomly into it, like they do on the telly. A T-shirt . . . some underwear . . . a pair of turquoise kitten heels with diamanté straps . . . I mean, it doesn't matter what I take, does it? I just have to get up there and build bridges with Jess.

At last I snap the case shut and heft it off the bed. I grab a jacket, wheel the case down the hall and out on to the landing, then turn and double lock the front door. I take one last look at it – then step into the lift, feeling strong with a new resolve. Everything's going to change from this moment on. My new life starts here. Off I go, to learn what's really important in—

Oh. I forgot my hair straighteners.

Instinctively I jab at the 'HALT' button. The lift,

which was about to descend, gives a kind of grumpy little bump but stays put.

I can't possibly go without my hair straighteners. And some hairspray.

And my Kiehl's lip balm. I cannot *live* without that.

OK, I might have to rethink the whole it-doesn't-matter-what-you-take strategy.

I hurry out of the lift, unlock the front door and head back into the bedroom. I haul another case out from under the bed, this one bright lime-green, and start tossing things into that, too.

Now I think about it, I should probably take extra moisturizer. And maybe one of my new hats, just in case there are any weddings. I throw in a whole load more clothes and a set of travel backgammon in case I'm bored on the train (and meet anyone who can teach me how to play).

Finally I pick up my Angel bag. And as I glimpse my reflection in the mirror, with no warning, Luke's voice resounds through my head:

I just hope the handbag was worth it, Becky.

I stop still. For a few moments I feel a bit sick.

I almost feel like leaving it behind.

Which would be just ridiculous. How can I leave behind my most prized possession?

I heft it over my shoulder and stare at myself, trying to recapture the desire and excitement I felt when I first saw it. It's an *Angel bag*, I remind myself defiantly. I have the most coveted item in existence. People are fighting over these. There are waiting lists all over the world.

I shift uncomfortably. Somehow it feels heavier on my shoulder than before. Which is very weird. A bag can't just get heavier, can it?

Oh right. I put my mobile-phone charger in there. That's why.

OK. Enough of this. I'm going. And I'm taking the bag.

I descend to the ground floor and wheel the cases out of the gates. A lit-up taxi comes barrelling along, and I stick out my hand. I load in my cases, feeling suddenly rather stirred up by what I'm planning to do.

'Euston station, please,' I say to the driver with a break in my voice. 'I'm going to reconcile with my long-lost-found-then-estranged sister.'

The driver eyes me, unmoved.

'Is that the back entrance you want, love?'

Honestly. You'd think taxi drivers would have some sense of drama. You'd think they'd learn it at taxi school.

The roads are clear, and we arrive at Euston in about ten minutes. As I totter towards the ticket booth, dragging my cases behind me, I feel as though I'm in some old black-and-white movie. There should be clouds of steam everywhere, and the shriek and whistle of trains, and I should be wearing a well-cut tweed suit and fur stole, with Marcel-waved hair.

'A ticket to Cumbria, please,' I say with a throb of emotion, and plonk a fifty-pound note on the counter.

This is where a lantern-jawed man should notice me and offer me a cocktail, or get grit out of my eye. Instead, a woman in an orange nylon uniform is regarding me as though I'm a moron.

'Cumbria?' she says. 'Where in Cumbria?'

Oh. That's a point. Does Jess's village even have a station?

Suddenly I have a blinding flash of memory. When I first met Jess, she talked about coming down from . . .

'North Coggenthwaite. A return, please. But I don't know when I'm coming back.' I give her a brave smile. 'I'm going to reconcile with my long-lost-found—'

The woman cuts me off unsympathetically.

'That'll be a hundred and seventy-seven pounds.'

What? *How* much? I could fly to Paris for that.

'Er . . . here you are,' I say, handing over some of my wad of Tiffany clock cash.

'Platform nine. Train leaves in five minutes.'

'Right. Thanks.'

I turn and start walking briskly over the concourse to platform nine. But as the huge Intercity train comes into view, my confident pace slows a little. People are streaming round me, hugging friends, hefting luggage and banging carriage doors.

I've come to a standstill. My heart is thudding and my hands feel sweaty round the suitcase handles. This has all kind of felt like a game up until now. But it's not a game. It's real. I can't quite believe I'm really going to do it.

Am I really going to travel hundreds of miles to a strange place – to see a sister who hates my guts?

SEVENTEEN

Oh my God. I'm here.

It's five hours later and I'm actually here, in Cumbria, in Jess's village. I'm in the North!

I'm walking along the main road of Scully – and it's so scenic! It's just like Gary described, with the dry-stone walls and everything. On either side of me are old stone houses with slate roofs. Beyond the houses are steep craggy hills with rocks jutting out and sheep grazing on the grass. And looming high above all the others is one huge hill which is practically a mountain.

As I pass a gorgeous little stone cottage I notice a curtain twitching and someone peering out at me. I suppose I do look a teeny bit conspicuous, with my red and lime-green suitcases. My wheels are trundling noisily on the road, plus my hat box is banging up and down with every step I take. As I walk past a bench, two old ladies in print dresses and cardigans eye me suspiciously and I can see one pointing to my pink suede shoes. I give them a friendly smile, and am about to say 'I got them at Barneys!' when they get up and shuffle off together, still glancing back at me. I take a few more strides along the street, then stop, panting slightly.

It's quite hilly, isn't it? Not that there's anything wrong with hills. This isn't a problem for me at all.

But even so, I might just take a few moments to admire the countryside and get my breath back. The taxi driver offered to take me to the door, but I told him I'd rather walk the last bit, just to steady my nerves. And also secretly take a little swig from a vodka miniature I bought on the train. I'm starting to feel a bit jittery about seeing Jess again, which is ridiculous because I had hours on the train to prepare.

I even ended up getting some expert help! I'd popped into the train bar and ordered a Bloody Mary – just for a bit of Dutch courage – and there was a whole group of Shakespearean actors in there, swigging wine and smoking, on their way to do a tour of *Henry V*. We got chatting and I ended up telling them the whole story and how I was off to try and reconcile with Jess. And they all went crazy! They said it was just like *Lear*, and ordered Bloody Marys all round, and insisted on coaching me in my speech.

I'm not sure I'll do every *single* thing they suggested. Like the tearing of the hair, or impaling myself on the fake dagger. But a lot of their tips were really helpful! Like, for example, never upstage your fellow actor, which means never stand so they have to turn away from the audience. They all agreed this was the worst possible thing I could do to my sister, and if I did, there would be zero chance of a reconciliation and frankly they wouldn't blame her. I pointed out there wouldn't be an audience, but they said nonsense, a crowd would gather.

The wind is blowing my hair all over the place, and I can feel my lips getting chapped by the strong Northern air, so I get out my lipsalve and put some on. Then, with a twinge, I reach for my mobile phone for the millionth time to see if Luke has called and I've somehow missed it. But there's no signal at all. We must be out of range. I stare for a minute at the blank little display, my heart beating with stupid hope. If there's no signal, maybe he's tried to call! Maybe he's phoning right this minute and he just can't get through . . .

But deep down inside I know it's not true. Six hours have gone by since he left. If he wanted to call, he would have called before now.

I feel hollow inside as it all comes flooding back again. Luke's harsh tone. The way he looked at me just before he left, so disappointed and kind of weary. All the things he said. Our row has been echoing angrily round my brain all day, until my head feels hot and achy.

To my horror, tears suddenly start pricking at my eyes. I furiously blink them back and sniff hard. I'm not going to cry. It's all going to be OK. I'm going to make amends and turn into a new person and Luke won't even recognize me.

Determinedly I start wheeling my cases up the hill again, until I reach the corner of Hill Rise. I stop and look along the grey stone terrace of cottages, my spine tingling with apprehension. This is it. This is Jess's road. She lives in one of these houses!

I'm reaching in my pocket to check the exact number when suddenly I notice a movement in an upstairs window a few houses along. I look up – and it's Jess! She's standing at the window, staring down at me in utter astonishment.

Despite everything that's happened between us, I feel a swell of emotion at the sight of her familiar face. This is my sister, after all. I start running up the street, my cases trundling behind me, my hat box bouncing up and down. I reach the door, breathless, and am about to lift the knocker when the door opens. Jess is standing in front of me in pale-brown cords and a sweatshirt, looking aghast.

'Becky . . . what the hell are you doing here?'

'Jess, I want to learn from you,' I say in a wobbly

voice, and lift my hands in supplication like the Shakespearean actors told me. 'I've come to be your apprentice.'

'What?' She takes a step backwards in horror. 'Becky, have you been *drinking*?'

'No! I mean, yes. A few Bloody Marys, maybe . . . but I'm not drunk, I promise! Jess, I want to be a good person.' The words come tumbling out of me in a rush. 'I want to learn from you. And get to know you. I know I've made mistakes in life . . . but I want to learn from them. Jess, I want to be like you.'

There's an ominous silence. Jess is just looking at me steadily.

'You want to be like me?' she says. 'I thought I was a "skinflint miserable cow", Becky.'

Damn. I was hoping she might have forgotten about that.

'Er . . . I'm really sorry I said that,' I mutter, abashed. 'I didn't mean it.'

Jess isn't looking that convinced. Quickly I cast my mind back to the coaching session on the train. 'Time has healed the wounds between us . . .' I begin, reaching out for her hand.

'No it hasn't!' says Jess, pulling away. 'And you've got a bloody nerve coming here.'

'But I'm asking you to help me as my sister!' I say desperately. 'I want to learn from you! You're Yoda, and I'm—'

'*Yoda?*' Jess's eyes widen in disbelief.

'You don't *look* like Yoda,' I add hastily. 'Nothing like! I just meant—'

'Yeah well, I'm not interested, Becky,' Jess interrupts. 'In you, or your latest stupid idea. Just go away.'

She slams the front door shut and I stare at it in shock. Jess has shut the door on me? Me, her own sister?

269

'But I've come all the way here from London!' I call through the door.

There's no reply.

I can't give up. Not just like that.

'Jess!' I start hammering on the door. 'You have to let me in! Please! I know we've had our differences—'

'Leave me alone!' The door is wrenched open and Jess is standing there again. But this time she doesn't just look hostile. She looks positively livid. 'Becky, we haven't just had our differences! We *are* different. I have no time for you. Frankly, I wish I'd never met you. And I have no idea what you're doing here.'

'You don't understand,' I say quickly, before she can slam the door again. 'Everything's gone wrong. Luke and I have argued. I . . . I did something stupid.'

'Well, there's a surprise.' Jess folds her arms.

'I know I've brought it on myself.' My voice starts to tremble. 'I know it's my own fault. But I think our marriage is in real trouble. I really do.'

As I say the words, I can feel tears threatening again. I blink hard, trying to hold them off.

'Jess . . . please help me. You're the only person I can think of. If I could learn from you, maybe Luke would come round. He likes you.' I feel a tightening in my throat, but force myself to look right at her. 'He likes you better than he likes me.'

Jess shakes her head, but I can't tell whether it's because she doesn't believe me or she doesn't care.

'Who is it, Jess?' comes a voice behind her, and another girl appears at the door. She's got mousy straight hair and specs and is holding a pad of foolscap paper. 'Is it another Jehovah's witness?'

'I'm not a Jehovah's witness!' I say. 'I'm Jess's sister!'

'Jess's *sister*?' The girl stares at me in astonishment, her eyes running over my outfit, my shoes and my two suitcases.

'I see what you mean,' she says to Jess, and lowers her voice a little. 'She does look a bit touched.'

Touched?

'I'm not touched!' I retort to the girl. 'And it's nothing to do with you. Jess—'

'Becky, go home,' Jess says flatly.

'But—'

'Don't you understand English? Go home!' She lifts her hand as though she's shooing away a dog.

'But . . . I'm your family!' My voice is starting to shake. 'Family help each other! Family watch out for one another. Jess, I'm your *sister*!'

'Well that's not my fault,' says Jess curtly. 'I never asked to be your sister. Bye, Becky.'

She slams the door shut again, so hard that I flinch. I lift my hand to knock again – then drop it again. There's no point, is there?

For a few moments I just stand there, staring at the brown-painted door. Then, slowly, I turn round and start trundling my suitcases back along the street.

I've come all this way for nothing.

What do I do now?

The thought of going straight home again is unbearable. All those hours on the train – to what? An empty flat.

An empty flat and no husband.

And at the thought of Luke, suddenly I can't keep control of myself any longer. Tears start pouring down my cheeks and I give a huge sob, followed by another. As I reach the corner, a couple of women with prams look at me curiously, but I barely notice. I'm crying too hard. My make-up must have smeared everywhere . . . and I haven't got a free hand to get a hanky, so I'm having to sniff . . . I need to stop. I need to sort myself out.

There's a kind of village green to my left, with a wooden bench in the middle. I head for it. I drop my cases and sink down, my head in my hands, and give way to a stream of fresh tears.

Here I am, hundreds of miles away from home, all on my own, and no one wants to know me. And it's all my own fault. I've ruined everything.

And Luke will never love me again.

My shoulders are shaking and I'm half-gasping when I dimly hear a man's voice above my head.

'Now, now. What's all this?'

I look up blearily to see a middle-aged man in cords and a green jumper looking down at me, half-disapproving, half-concerned.

'Is it the end of the world?' he says in abrupt tones. 'You've old people trying to take naps around here.' He gestures at the cottages around the green. 'You're making so much noise, you're scaring the sheep.'

He gestures up at the hill, where, sure enough, a couple of sheep are looking curiously down at me.

'I'm very sorry I'm disturbing the peace,' I gulp. 'But things aren't going that brilliantly for me at the moment.'

'A tiff with the boyfriend,' he states as though it's a foregone conclusion.

'No, I'm married actually. But my marriage is in trouble. In fact I think it might be over. And I've come all this way to see my sister, but she won't even speak to me . . .' I can feel tears spilling over on to my cheeks again. 'My mum and dad are away on a therapy cruise, and my husband's gone to Cyprus with Nathan Temple and my best friend likes someone else more than me, and I haven't got anyone to talk to. And I just don't know where to go! I mean, literally, I don't know where to go after I get up from this bench . . .'

I give an enormous hiccup, reach for a tissue and wipe my streaming eyes. Then I look up.

The man is staring at me as though stunned.

'Tell you what, love,' he says a bit more kindly. 'How does a cup of tea sound?'

'A cup of tea sounds wonderful,' I falter. 'Thank you very much.'

The man heads across the green, carrying both my suitcases as though they weigh nothing, and I totter behind with my hat box.

'I'm Jim, by the way,' he says over his shoulder.

'I'm Becky.' I blow my nose. 'This is really kind of you. I was going to have a cup of tea in London, but I'd run out of milk. In fact . . . that's kind of how I ended up here.'

'Long way for a cup of tea,' he observes dryly.

That was only this morning, I suddenly realize. It seems a million years ago now.

'We're not about to run out of milk, any road,' he adds, turning into a cottage with Scully Stores in black lettering above the doorway. A bell starts tinkling as we walk in, and from somewhere at the back I can hear a dog barking.

'Oh.' I look around with fresh interest. 'This is a shop!'

'This is *the* shop,' he corrects me. He puts down my cases and gently moves me off the mat, at which the bell stops tinkling. 'Been in the family for fifty-five years.'

'Wow.' I look around the cosy store. There are racks of fresh bread, shelves with tins and packets lined up neatly, old-fashioned jars of sweets and a display of postcards and gift items. 'This is lovely! So . . . are you Mr Scully?'

Jim gives me a slightly odd look.

'Scully is the name of the village we're in, love.'

'Oh yes.' I blush. 'I forgot.'

'My name's Smith. And I think you need that cup of tea. Kelly?' He raises his voice and a few moments later a girl appears through a door at the back. She's about thirteen, skinny with fine hair pulled into a ponytail and carefully made-up eyes, and is holding *Heat* magazine.

'I was minding the shop, honest, Dad,' she says at once. 'I just went upstairs for a magazine.'

'It's OK, love. I'd like you to make a nice cup of tea for this lady. She's been through a bit of . . . distress.'

'Oh right.' Kelly stares at me with naked curiosity before disappearing through the back door again, and it suddenly occurs to me that I must look an absolute fright.

'Would you like to sit down?' Jim adds to me, and pulls out a chair.

'Thanks,' I say gratefully. I put down my hat box and fish in my Angel bag for my make-up case. I snap open my mirror and peer at myself – and oh God, I have never looked worse in my life. My nose is all red, my eyes are bloodshot, my eyeliner is smudged like a panda and a streak of turquoise '24-hour eye dazzle' has somehow ended up on my cheek.

I quickly take out a cleansing wipe and get rid of the whole lot until my face is bare and pink, staring sadly at me out of the mirror. Half of me feels like leaving it at that. Why should I put on any make-up? What's the point if my marriage is over?

'Here you are.' A steaming cup of tea appears in front of me on the counter, and I look up to see Kelly watching me avidly.

'Thank you so much,' I say, my voice still a little unsteady. 'You're really sweet.'

'It's no trouble,' says Kelly, as I take the first delicious sip. God, a cup of tea is the answer to everything.

'Is that . . .' I look up to see Kelly gawping at my bag with eyes like dinnerplates. 'Is that . . . a real Angel bag?'

I feel a huge inward twinge, which I manage to hide with a weak smile.

'Yes. It's a real Angel bag.'

'Dad, she's got an Angel bag!' exclaims Kelly to Jim, who's unloading bags of sugar from a box. 'I showed you about them in *Glamour* magazine!' Her eyes are shining with excitement. 'All the film stars have got them! They've sold out at Harrods! Where did you get yours?'

'In . . . Milan,' I say after a pause.

'Milan!' breathes Kelly. 'That's so cool!' Now her eyes have fallen on the contents of my make-up bag. 'Is that Stila lip gloss?'

'Er . . . yes.'

'Emily Masters has got Stila lip gloss,' she says wistfully. 'She thinks she's all that.'

I look at her lit-up eyes and flushed cheeks, and suddenly, with a huge pang, I want to be thirteen again. Going to the shops on Saturday to spend my allowance. With nothing to worry about except biology homework and whether James Fullerton fancied me.

'Look . . . have this,' I say, scrabbling in my make-up bag for a brand-new Stila lip gloss in Grapefruit. 'I'm never going to use it.'

'Really?' Kelly gasps. 'Are you sure?'

'And do you want this cream blusher?' I hand over the box. 'Not that you need blusher . . .'

'Wow!'

'Now, wait just a moment,' comes Jim's voice from across the shop. 'Kelly, you can't take this lady's make-up off her.' He shakes his head slightly at her. 'Give them back, love.'

'She offered, Dad!' says Kelly, her translucent skin staining pink. 'I didn't ask for them or anything—'

'Honestly, Jim. Kelly can have them. I'm never going to use them.' I give a shaky laugh. 'I only bought them in the first place because you got a free perfume if you spent over eighty quid . . .'

Suddenly tears spring up in my eyes again. God, Jess is right. I'm a total flake.

'Are you OK?' says Kelly in alarm. 'Have them back—'

'No, I'm fine.' I force a smile. 'I just need to . . . think about something else.'

I dab my eyes with a tissue, get to my feet and wander over to the gift display. I might as well get some souvenirs while I'm here. I pick up a pipe rack for Dad and a painted wooden tray which Mum will like. I'm just looking at a glass model of Lake Windermere and wondering whether to get it for Janice, when I notice two women standing outside the window. As I watch, they're joined by a third.

'What are they waiting for?' I say in puzzlement.

'This,' says Jim. He looks at his watch, then puts out a sign reading 'Today's bread half price'.

Immediately the women all come bustling into the shop.

'I'll take two bloomers please, Jim,' says one with metal-grey hair and a beige mac. 'Have you any reduced croissants?'

'Not today,' says Jim. 'All full price.'

'Oh.' She thinks for a moment. 'No, I won't bother.'

'I'll take three large wholemeal,' chimes in another woman in a green headscarf. Who's this?' She jerks her thumb at me. 'We saw you crying on the green. Are you a tourist?'

'They always get themselves lost,' says the first woman. 'Which hotel are you at, love? Does she speak English? *Speke Inglese?*'

'She looks Danish,' says the third woman knowledgeably. 'Who speaks Danish?'

'I'm English,' I say. 'And I'm not lost. I was upset because . . .' I swallow hard. 'Because my marriage is in trouble. And I came up here to ask my sister for help, but she wouldn't give it to me.'

'Your sister?' says the woman in the headscarf suspiciously. 'Who's your sister?'

'She lives in this village.' I take a sip of tea. 'She's called Jessica Bertram.'

There's a staggered silence. The women look like I've hit them over the head with a hammer. I look around in confusion to see Jim's jaw has dropped by about a foot.

'*You're* Jess's sister?' he says.

'Well . . . yes, I am. Her half-sister.'

I look around the silent shop – but no one's moved. Everyone is still gaping at me as if I'm an alien.

'I know we're a bit different to look at . . .' I begin.

'She said you were mad,' says Kelly bluntly.

'Kelly!' says Jim.

'What?' I look from face to face. 'She said *what*?'

'Nothing!' says Jim, darting a warning look at Kelly.

'We all knew she was going to see her long-lost sister,' says Kelly, ignoring him. 'And when she came back, she said you were crazy. I'm sorry Dad, but it's true!'

I can feel my cheeks growing bright red.

'I'm not *crazy*!' I say. 'I'm normal! I'm just . . . a bit different from Jess. We like different things. She likes rocks. I like . . . shops.'

Everyone in the shop is looking at me curiously.

'Are you not interested in rocks, then?' says the woman with the green headscarf.

'Not really,' I admit. 'In fact . . . that was a bit of an issue between us.'

'What happened?' says Kelly, agog.

'Well . . .' I scuff my foot awkwardly on the floor. 'I told Jess I'd never heard of a more boring hobby than rocks in my life, and it suited her.'

There's a general gasp of horror.

'You don't want to be rude about rocks to Jess,' says the beige-mac woman, shaking her head. 'She loves those rocks of hers, bless her.'

'Jess is a good girl,' chips in the grey-haired woman, giving me a stern look. 'Sturdy. Reliable. She'd make a fine sister.'

'Couldn't hope for better,' agrees the green-headscarf woman with a nod.

I feel defensive at their looks.

'It's not my fault! I want to reconcile with her! But she isn't interested in being my sister! I just don't know how it all went wrong. I so wanted to be friends. I arranged this whole weekend for her, but she didn't like any of it. And she was so *disapproving*. We ended up having a huge row . . . and I called her all sorts of things . . .'

'What things?' says Kelly avidly.

'Well . . .' I rub my nose. 'I said she was a misery. I said she was really boring . . .'

There's another huge gasp. Kelly looks almost over-come with horror and raises a hand as though to stop me. But I don't want to stop. This is cathartic. Now I've started, I want to confess everything.

'. . . and the most skinflint person I'd ever met in my life,' I continue, goaded by their appalled faces. 'With zero dress sense, who must have had a fun-bypass operation . . .'

I break off, but this time there's no gasp. Everyone seems to have frozen.

Suddenly I become aware of a tinkling sound in the air. A tinkling sound which, now I think about it, has been going on for a few seconds. Very slowly I turn round.

And I feel a coldness down my back.

Jess is standing in the doorway, her face very pale.

'Jess!' I stammer. 'God, Jess! I wasn't . . . I didn't *mean* any of . . . I was just explaining . . .'

'I heard you were in here,' she says, speaking with an obvious struggle. 'I came to see if you were OK. To see if you wanted a bed for the night. But . . . I think I've changed my mind.' She looks directly at me. 'I knew you were shallow and spoilt, Becky. I didn't realize you were a two-faced bitch as well.'

She turns and strides out, closing the door behind her with a bang.

Kelly is bright red, Jim's face is contorted in a wince. The whole atmosphere is prickling with awkwardness.

Then the woman in the green headscarf folds her arms.

'Well,' she says. 'You buggered that one up, didn't you love?'

I'm in a state of total shock.

I came up here to reconcile with Jess – and all I've done is made things worse.

'Here you are love,' says Jim, placing a fresh mug of tea in front of me. 'Three sugars.'

The three women are all drinking cups of tea, too, and Jim's even produced a cake. I get the feeling they're waiting for me to do something else entertaining.

'I'm not a two-faced bitch,' I say in despair, and take a sip. 'Honestly! I'm nice! I came here to build bridges! I mean, I know Jess and I don't get along. But I wanted to learn from her. I thought she could help me save my marriage . . .'

There's a sharp intake of breath around the shop.

'Is her marriage in trouble as well?' says the woman in the green headscarf to Jim, and clicks her tongue. 'Dear, oh dear.'

'It never rains but it pours,' booms the metal-hair woman lugubriously. 'Run off with a fancy woman, has he?'

Jim glances at me, then leans towards the women, lowering his voice.

'Apparently he's gone to Cyprus with a man called Nathan.'

'Oh.' Metal-hair woman's eyes open very wide. 'Oh, I *see*.'

'What are you going to do, Becky?' says Kelly, biting her lip.

Go home, flashes through my mind. *Give up.*

But I keep seeing Jess's pale face in my mind, and feeling a little stab in my heart. I know just what it's like to be bitched about. I've known enough horrible bitches in my time. An image comes to me of Alicia Bitch Long-legs, the meanest, snidest girl I ever knew.

I can't bear it if my own sister thinks I'm like her.

'I have to apologize to Jess,' I say, looking up. 'I know we'll never be friends. But I can't go home with her thinking the worst of me.' I take a sip of scalding tea, then look up. 'Is there anywhere I can stay around here?'

'Edie runs a bed and breakfast,' says Jim, gesturing at the headscarf woman. 'Got any rooms free, Edie?'

Edie reaches into her huge brown bag, brings out a notebook and consults it.

'You're in luck,' she says, looking up. 'I've one deluxe single left.'

'Edie'll take good care of you,' says Jim, so kindly that I feel ridiculous tears welling up again.

'Could I take it for tonight, please?' I say, wiping my eyes. 'Thank you very much.' I take another sip of tea, then notice my mug. It's blue pottery with 'Scully' handpainted on it in white. 'This is nice,' I gulp. 'Do you sell them?'

'On the rack at the back,' says Jim, looking at me in amusement.

'Could I have two? I mean, four?' I reach for a tissue and blow my nose. 'And I just want to say . . . thank you. You're all being so nice.'

The bed and breakfast is a large white house directly across the green. Jim carries my suitcases and I carry my hat box and my carrier bag full of souvenirs, and Edie follows behind me, giving me a list of rules I have to keep.

'No visitors after eleven . . . no parties of more than three people in the room . . . no abuse of solvents or aerosol cans . . . payment in advance, cash or cheque accepted, much obliged,' she concludes as we reach the lit-up door.

'All right from here, Becky?' says Jim, putting my cases down.

'I'll be fine. And thank you so much,' I say, feeling so grateful I half-want to give him a kiss. But I don't quite dare to – so I just watch as he walks off across the grass again.

'Much obliged,' repeats Edie meaningfully.

'Oh!' I say, realizing she means she wants to be paid. 'Absolutely!'

I scrabble inside my bag for my purse – and my fingers brush against my mobile phone. From force of habit I pull it out and peer at the display. But there's still no signal.

'You can use the payphone in the hall if there's anyone you want to call,' says Edie. 'We have a pull-down privacy hood.'

Is there anyone I want to call?

With a twinge I think of Luke in Cyprus, still furious with me. Mum and Dad engrossed in a therapy workshop on their cruise. Suze picnicking on some picturesque sun-dappled lawn with Lulu and all their children in dungarees.

'No. It's OK,' I say, trying to smile. 'I haven't got anyone to call. To be honest . . . no one will even have noticed I've gone.'

5 jun 03 16.54
to Becky
from Suze

Bex. Sorry I missed u. Why aren't u answering the phone? Had disastrous day at picnic. We all got stung by wasps. I miss u. Am coming to London to visit. Call me.

Suzexxxx

6 jun 03 11.02
to Becky
from Suze

Bex. Where R U?????????????????

Suzexxxx

EIGHTEEN

I don't sleep well.

In fact, I'm not sure I sleep at all. I seem to have spent the whole night staring at the Artexed ceiling of Edie's B&B, my mind going round and round in circles.

Except I must have slept for a bit, because when I wake up in the morning my head is full of a terrible dream where I turned into Alicia Bitch Long-legs. I was wearing a pink suit and laughing with a horrible sneer and Jess was looking all pale and crushed. In fact, now I think about it, Jess looked a bit like me.

Just the thought of it makes me feel queasy. I have to do something about this.

I'm not hungry, but Edie has cooked a full English breakfast and doesn't seem impressed when I say I normally just have a piece of toast. So I nibble at some bacon and eggs and pretend to have a go at the black pudding – then I take a final sip of coffee and leave to find Jess.

As I head up the hill to her house, the morning sun is in my eyes, and a cool wind blows through my hair. It *feels* like a day for reconciliations. Fresh starts and clean slates.

I approach the front door, ring the bell and wait, my heart thumping.

There's no reply.

OK, I am really tired of people not being in when I want to have emotional reunions with them. I squint up at the windows, wondering whether she might be hiding. Maybe I should throw some stones up at the window panes.

Except what if I broke one? Then she'd *really* hate me.

I ring the bell a few more times, then walk back down the path. I might as well wait. It's not like I've got anything else to do. I sit down on the wall and settle myself comfortably. This is fine. I'll just wait and when she arrives back home I'll spring up with a speech about how sorry I am.

The wall isn't quite as comfortable as I first thought, and I shift a few times, trying to find a good position. I look at my watch, check it's still ticking, then look at an old lady and her little dog walking slowly along the pavement on the other side of the road.

Then I look at my watch again. Five minutes have gone by.

God, this is dull.

How on earth do stalkers do it? Don't they get bored out of their minds?

I get up to stretch my legs and walk up to Jess's house. I ring the bell, just to be on the safe side, then meander back to the wall again. As I do so, I see a policeman coming up the street towards me. What's a policeman doing here, out on the street? I thought they were all tied to their desks by paperwork or zooming around inner cities in squad cars.

I feel a beat of apprehension as I see that he's looking directly at me. But I'm not doing anything wrong, am I? I mean, it's not like stalking is against the law.

Oh. Well, OK, maybe stalking *is* against the law. But I've only been doing it for five minutes. Surely that doesn't count. And anyway, how does he know I'm

284

stalking anyone? I might just be sitting here for pleasure.

'All right?' he says as he approaches.

'Fine, thanks!'

There's a pause, and he looks at me expectantly.

'Is there a problem?' I say politely.

'Could you move along, miss? This isn't a public seat.'

I feel a dart of resentment.

'Why should I?' I say boldly. 'That's what is wrong with this country! Anyone who doesn't conform is persecuted! Why shouldn't you be able to sit on a wall without being harassed?'

'That's my wall,' he says, and gestures to the front door. 'This is my house.'

'Oh right.' I flush red and leap to my feet. 'I was just . . . er . . . going. Thanks! Really nice wall!'

OK. Forget the stalking plan. I'll have to come back later.

I trail down the hill to the village green, and find myself turning towards the shop. As I enter, Kelly is sitting behind the till with a copy of *Elle* and Jim is arranging apples on the display rack.

'I went to see Jess,' I say morosely. 'But she wasn't there. I'll have to wait till she comes back.'

'Shall I read out your horoscope?' says Kelly. 'See if it says anything about sisters?'

'Now, young lady,' says Jim reprovingly, 'you're supposed to be revising for your exams. If you're not working, you can go and wait at the tea shop.'

'No!' says Kelly hastily. 'I'm revising!' She pulls a face at me, then puts *Elle* down and reaches for a book called *Elementary Algebra*.

God, algebra. I'd totally forgotten that existed. Maybe I'm quite glad I'm not thirteen any more.

I need a sugar rush, so I head towards the biscuit section and grab some chocolate digestives and

Orange Clubs. Then I drift over to the stationery shelf. I adore stationery, and you can never have too much of it. I pick up a packet of drawing pins in the shape of sheep, which will always come in useful. And I might as well get the matching stapler and folders.

'All right there?' says Jim, eyeing my full arms.

'Yes, thanks!'

I take my goodies over to the till, where Kelly rings them up.

'D'you want a cup of tea?' she says.

'Oh, no thanks,' I say politely. 'I couldn't intrude. I'd get in the way.'

'Get in the way of what?' she retorts. 'Nobody'll be in until four, when the bread comes down. And you can test me on my French vocab.'

'Oh well.' I brighten. 'If I'd be *useful* . . .'

Three hours later I'm still there. I've had three cups of tea, about half a packet of chocolate digestives and an apple, and I've stocked up on a few more presents for people at home, like a set of Toby jugs and some place mats, which will always come in handy.

Plus I've been helping Kelly with her work. Except now we've progressed from algebra and French vocab revision to Kelly's outfit for the school disco. We've got every single magazine open, and I've made her up with each eye different, just to show her what the possibilities are. One side is really dramatic, all smoky shadow and a spare false eyelash I found in my make-up bag; the other is all silvery and sixties, with white space-age mascara.

'Don't let your mother see you like that,' is all Jim keeps saying as he walks by.

'If only I had my hair pieces,' I say, studying Kelly's face critically. 'I could give you the most fantastic ponytail.'

'I look amazing!' Kelly's goggling at herself in the mirror.

'You've got wonderful cheekbones,' I tell her, and dust shimmery powder on to them.

'This is so much fun!' Kelly looks at me, her eyes shining. 'God, I wish you lived here, Becky! We could do this every day!'

She looks so excited, I feel ridiculously touched.

'Well . . . you know,' I say. 'Maybe I'll visit again. If I patch things up with Jess.'

But even at the thought of Jess, all my insides kind of crumble. The more time goes by, the more nervous I'm getting at seeing her again.

'I wanted to do makeovers like this with Jess,' I add, a bit wistfully. 'But she wasn't interested.'

'Well then, she's dumb,' says Kelly.

'She's not. She's . . . she likes different things.'

'She's a prickly character,' puts in Jim, walking by with some bottles of cherryade. 'It's hard to credit you two are sisters.' He dumps the bottles down and wipes his brow. 'Maybe it's in the upbringing. Jess had it pretty hard going.'

'Do you know her family, then?' I say, looking up in interest.

'Aye.' He nods. 'Not well, but I know them. I've had dealings with Jess's dad. He owns Bertram Foods. Lives over in Nailbury. Five miles away.'

Suddenly I'm burning all over with curiosity. Jess hasn't told me a word about her family. Mum and Dad didn't seem to know much, either.

'So . . . what are they like?' I ask, as casually as I can. 'Her family.'

'Like I say, she's had a pretty hard time. Her mum died when she was fifteen. That's a difficult age for a girl.'

'I never knew that!' Kelly's eyes widen.

'And her dad . . .' Jim leans pensively on the

counter. 'He's a good man. A fair man. Very successful. He built up Bertram Foods from nothing, through hard graft. But he's not what you'd call . . . warm. He was always as tough on Jess as he was on her brothers. Expected them to fend for themselves. I remember Jess when she started big school. She got into the high school over in Carlisle. Very academic.'

'I tried for that school,' says Kelly to me, pulling a face. 'But I didn't get in.'

'She's a clever girl, that Jess.' Jim shakes his head admiringly. 'But she had to catch three buses every morning to get there. I used to drive past on my way here – and I'll remember the sight till I die. The early-morning mist, no one else about and Jess standing at the bus stop with her big school bag. She wasn't the big strong lass she is now. She was a skinny little thing.'

He pauses, but I can't quite find a reply. I'm thinking about how Mum and Dad used to take me to school by car every day. Even though it wasn't that far away.

'They must be rich,' says Kelly, rooting around in my make-up bag. 'If they own Bertram Foods. We get all our frozen pies from them,' she adds to me. 'And ice-cream. They've a huge catalogue!'

'Oh, they're well off,' says Jim. 'But they've always been close with their money.' He rips open a cardboard box of CupaSoups and starts stacking them on a shelf. 'Bill Bertram used to boast about it. How all his kids worked for their pocket money.' He pauses, clutching a bundle of Chicken and Mushroom sachets. 'And if they couldn't afford a school trip or whatever . . . they didn't go. Simple as that.'

'School trips?' I gawp at him. 'But everyone knows parents pay for school trips!'

'Not the Bertrams. He wanted to teach them the value of money. There was a story going around one year that one of the Bertram boys was the only kid in school not to go to the pantomime. He didn't have the money and his dad wouldn't bail him out.' Jim resumes stacking the soups. 'I don't know if that was true. But it wouldn't surprise me.' He gives Kelly a mock-severe look. 'You don't know you're born, young lady. You've got the easy life!'

'I do chores!' retorts Kelly at once. 'Look! I'm helping out here, aren't I?'

She reaches for some chewing gum from the sweet counter and unwraps it, then turns to me. 'Now I'll do you, Becky!' She riffles in my make-up bag. 'Have you got any bronzer?'

'Er . . . yes,' I say, distracted. 'Somewhere.'

I'm still thinking about Jess standing at the bus stop, all pale and skinny.

Jim is squashing the empty CupaSoup box down flat. He turns, and gives me an appraising look.

'Don't worry, love. You'll make up with Jess.'

'Maybe.' I try to smile.

'You're sisters. You're family. Family always pull through for each other.' He glances out of the window. 'Ay-up. They're gathering early today.'

I follow his gaze, and see two old ladies hovering outside the shop. One of them squints at the bread display, then turns and shakes her head at the other.

'Does *nobody* buy bread full price?' I say.

'Not in this village,' says Jim. 'Except the tourists. But we don't get so many of those. It's mostly climbers who want to have a go at Scully Pike – and they don't have much call for bread. Only emergency services.'

'How d'you mean?' I say, puzzled.

'When the stupid buggers get stuck.' Jim shrugs, and reaches for the half-price sign. 'No matter. I've got to thinking of bread as a loss-leader, like.'

'But it's so yummy when it's all fresh and new!' I say, looking along the rows of plump loaves. Suddenly I feel really sorry for them, like they haven't been asked to dance. '*I'll* buy some. Full price,' I add firmly.

'I'm about to reduce it,' points out Jim.

'I don't care. I'll have two big white ones and a brown one.' I march over to the bread display and pluck the loaves off the shelf.

'What are you going to do with all that bread?' says Kelly.

'Dunno. Make toast.' I hand Kelly some pound coins and she pops the three loaves into a bag, giggling.

'Jess is right, you are mad,' she says. 'Shall I do your eyes now? What look do you want?'

'Customers'll be coming in,' warns Jim. 'I'm about to put the sign up.'

'I'll just do one eye,' says Kelly, quickly reaching for a palette of eyeshadows. 'Then when they've all gone, I'll do the other one. Close your eyes, Becky.'

She starts to brush eyeshadow on to my eyelid, and I close my eyes, enjoying the brushing, tickling sensation. I've always adored having my make-up done.

'OK,' she says. 'Now I'm doing some eyeliner. Keep still . . .'

'Sign's going up now,' comes Jim's voice. There's a pause – then I hear the familiar tinkling sound, and the bustle of people coming in.

'Er . . . don't open your eyes yet, Becky.' Kelly sounds a bit alarmed. 'I'm not sure if this has gone right . . .'

'Let me see!'

I open my eyes and grab my make-up mirror. One of my eyes is a wash of bright-pink eyeshadow, with shaky red eyeliner across the top lid. I look like I have some hideous eye disease.

'Kelly!'

'It said in *Elle*!' she says defensively, gesturing to a picture of a catwalk model. 'Pink and red is in!'

'I look like a monster!' I can't help bursting into

giggles at my lopsided face. I have never looked so terrible in my life. I glance up to see if any of the customers have noticed, and my laughter dies away.

Jess is coming into the shop.

As her eyes meet mine I feel my stomach clench in apprehension. She looks so cold and hostile, nothing like a skinny ten-year-old. For a few moments we look at each other silently. Jess's gaze runs dismissively over the magazines, the open make-up case and all my make-up scattered over the counter. Then she turns away without speaking, and begins to root through the basket of reduced cans.

The bustle of the shop has dwindled to silence. I get the feeling everyone knows exactly what's been going on.

I have to speak. Even though my heart is thudding in fear.

I glance at Jim, who gives me an encouraging nod.

'Er . . . Jess,' I begin. 'I came to see you this morning. I wanted to explain—'

'Nothing to explain.' She turns over the cans roughly, not even looking at me. 'I don't know what you're still doing here.'

'She's doing makeovers with me,' says Kelly loyally. 'Aren't you, Becky?'

I dart a grateful smile at her. But my attention is still fixed on Jess.

'I stayed because I want to talk to you. To . . . to apologize. Could I take you out to supper tonight?'

'I wouldn't have thought I was well dressed enough to have supper with you, Becky,' says Jess tonelessly. Her face is still and set – but I can see the hurt underneath.

'Jess—'

'And anyway. I'm busy.' Jess plonks three battered cans on the counter, together with one that has lost its

291

paper covering altogether and is marked at 10p. 'Do you know what this is, Jim?'

'Fruit cocktail, I think.' He frowns. 'But it could be carrots . . .'

'OK. I'll take it.' She plonks some coins on the counter and fishes a crumpled plastic carrier out of her pocket. 'I don't need a bag. Thanks.'

'Another night, then!' I say desperately. 'Or lunch . . .'

'Becky, leave me alone.'

She strides out of the shop and I just sit there, my face tingling as though I've been slapped. Gradually the hush turns into whispers, which grow into full-blown chatter. I'm aware of people looking at me curiously as they come up to the counter to pay, but I'm almost oblivious of them.

'Are you OK, Becky?' says Kelly, touching my arm tentatively.

'I've blown it.' I raise my arms in a hopeless gesture. 'You saw her.'

'She always was a stubborn little cuss.' Jim shakes his head. 'Even when she was a kid. She's her own worst enemy, that Jess. Hard on herself and hard on the rest of the world, too.' He pauses, cleaning some dirt off his Stanley knife. 'She could do with a sister like you, Becky.'

'Well, too bad,' says Kelly robustly. 'You don't need her! Just forget she's your sister. Pretend she doesn't exist!'

'Not as simple as that though, is it?' says Jim, looking up with a wry expression. 'Not with family. You can't walk away so easy.'

'I don't know.' I give a dispirited shrug. 'Maybe we can. I mean, we've gone twenty-seven years without knowing each other . . .'

'And you want to make it another twenty-seven?' Jim looks at me, suddenly stern. 'Here's the two of you.

Neither of you has a sister. You could be good friends to one another.'

'It's not my fault . . .' I begin defensively, then tail off as I remember my little speech last night. 'Well, it's not *all* my fault . . .'

'Didn't say it was,' says Jim. He serves another two customers, then turns to me. 'I've an idea. I know what Jess is doing tonight. In fact, I'll be there too.'

'Really?'

'Aye. Local environmental protest meeting. Every-one'll be there.' His eyes suddenly give a little twinkle. 'Why not come along?'

FAX MESSAGE

TO   LUKE BRANDON
           APHRODITE TEMPLE HOTEL
           CYPRUS

FROM   SUSAN CLEATH-STUART

6 JUNE 2003

<u>URGENT – EMERGENCY</u>

Luke

Becky *isn't* at the flat. No one has seen her anywhere. I still can't get through on her phone.

I'm really getting worried.

Suze

NINETEEN

OK. This is my chance to impress Jess. This is my chance to show her I'm not shallow and spoilt. I must *not* fuck this one up.

And the first crucial thing is my outfit. With a frown I survey all my clothes, which I've strewn over the bed in the B&B room. What *is* the perfect environmental-protest-group-meeting outfit? Not the leather trousers . . . not the glittery top . . . My eyes suddenly alight on a pair of combats, and I pluck them from the pile.

Excellent. They're pink, but I can't help that. And . . . yes. I'll team them with a T-shirt with a slogan. Genius!

I haul out a T-shirt that has the word 'HOT' on it and goes really well with the combats. It's not very protest-y though, is it? I think for a minute, then get a red pen out of my bag and carefully add the word 'BAN'.

'BAN HOT' doesn't exactly make sense . . . but it's the thought that counts, surely. Plus I won't wear any make-up, except a bit of eyeliner and some mascara and a translucent lip gloss.

I put it all on, and tie my hair into plaits, then admire myself in the mirror. I actually look pretty militant! Experimentally, I raise my hand in a power salute, and shake my fist at the mirror.

'Up the workers,' I say in a deep voice. 'Brothers unite.'

God, yes. I think I could be really good at this. OK. Let's go.

The protest meeting is being held in the village hall, and as I arrive I see posters up everywhere, with slogans like 'Don't Spoil Our Countryside'. People are milling around the hall, and I head to a table with cups and biscuits on it.

'Cup of coffee, love?' says an elderly man in a Barbour.

'Thanks,' I say. 'Er, I mean, thanks brother. Right on.' I give him the power salute. 'Up the strike!'

The man looks a bit confused, and I suddenly remember they're not striking. I keep getting mixed up with *Billy Elliot*.

But I mean, it's the same thing, isn't it? It's all about solidarity and fighting together for a good cause. I wander into the centre of the hall, holding my cup, and catch the eye of a youngish guy with spiky red hair and a denim jacket covered in badges.

'Welcome!' he says, breaking away from the group he's in and extending his hand. 'I'm Robin. I haven't seen you at the group before.'

'I'm Becky. Actually, I'm just a visitor. But Jim said it would be OK to come . . .'

'Of course!' says Robin, shaking my hand enthusiastically. 'Everyone's welcome. It doesn't matter whether you're a resident or a visitor . . . the issues are the same. Awareness is as important as anything else.'

'Absolutely!' I take a sip of coffee and notice the bundle of leaflets he's holding. 'I could take some of those back to London with me and give them out, if you like. Spread the word.'

'That would be great!' Robin's face creases into a smile. 'That's the kind of proactive attitude we need more of! What kind of environmental issues are you into particularly?'

Shit. Think. Environmental issues.

'Um . . .' I take a sip of coffee, playing for time. 'All sorts really! Trees . . . and er . . . hedgehogs . . .'

'Hedgehogs?' Robin looks puzzled.

Damn. That only came out because I was thinking that his hair looks just like a hedgehog.

'When they get squashed by cars,' I improvise. 'It's a real danger in today's society.'

'I'm sure you're right.' Robin frowns thoughtfully. 'So, are you in an action group specifically looking at the plight of hedgehogs?'

Shut up now, Becky. Change the subject.

'Yes,' I hear myself saying. 'I am. It's called . . . Prickle.'

'Prickle!' He smiles. 'Great name!'

'Yes,' I say confidently. 'It stands for Protect . . . Really . . . Innocent . . . er . . .'

OK. Maybe I should have chosen a word with an 'H' in it.

'Creatures . . .' I'm floundering. '. . . of all Kinds . . . including hedgehogs . . .'

I break off in relief as I see Jim approaching, together with a thin, wiry woman dressed in jeans and a plaid shirt. This must be Jim's wife!

'Greetings, Jim,' says Robin with a friendly smile. 'Glad you could make it.'

'Hi, Jim!' I say, and turn to the woman with him. 'You must be Elizabeth.'

'And you must be the famous Becky!' She clasps my hand. 'Our Kelly can't talk about anything but you.'

'Kelly's really sweet!' I beam at her. 'We had such fun today doing makeovers . . .' I suddenly catch Jim's frown. 'And er . . . revision for her exams,' I hastily add. 'Lots of algebra and French vocab.'

'Is Jess here? asks Jim, looking around the room.

'I don't know,' I say, feeling a slight apprehension. 'I haven't spotted her yet.'

'It's a shame.' Elizabeth clicks her tongue. 'Jim's told me all about it. Two sisters, not speaking to each other. And you're so young! You've got your whole lives ahead to be friends, you know. A sister is a blessing!'

'They'll make up,' says Jim easily. 'Ah. Here she is!'

I swivel round and, sure enough, there's Jess, striding towards us, looking totally gobsmacked to see me.

'What's *she* doing here?' she says to Jim.

'This is a new member of our group, Jess,' says Robin, coming forward. 'Meet Becky.'

'Hi, Jess!' I say with a nervous smile. 'I thought I'd get into the environment!'

'Becky's special interest is hedgehogs,' adds Robin.

'*What?*' Jess stares at Robin for a few seconds, then starts to shake her head. 'No. No. She's not a member of the group. And she's not coming to the meeting. She has to go. Now!'

'Do you two know each other?' says Robin in bewilderment, and Jess looks away.

'We're sisters,' I explain.

'They don't get on,' puts in Jim, in a stage whisper.

'Now, Jess,' says Robin earnestly, 'you know our group ethos. We put our personal differences aside at the door. Everyone's welcome. Everyone's a friend!' He smiles at me. 'Becky's already volunteered for some outreach work!'

'No!' Jess clasps her head. 'You don't understand what she's like—'

'Come on, Becky,' says Robin, ignoring her. 'I'll find you a chair.'

Gradually the chatter dies down and everyone sits on chairs arranged in a horseshoe shape. As I look around the row of faces I spot Edie, and the woman with metal-grey hair, who seems to be called Lorna, and several more people I recognize as customers from Jim's shop.

'Welcome, everyone,' says Robin, taking up a position in the centre of the horseshoe. 'Before we start, I have a few announcements. Tomorrow, as you know, is the sponsored endurance hike up Scully Pike. Can we have numbers, please?'

About half the people there put up their hands, including Jess. I'm half-tempted to put mine up too, only there's something about the word 'endurance' that puts me off. And 'hike', for that matter.

'Great!' Robin looks around, pleased. 'Those of you attempting it, please remember all your gear. I'm afraid the weather forecast is not good. Mist, and possibly rain.'

There's a unified rueful groan, mixed with laughs.

'But be assured, a welcoming party will be waiting at the end with hot drinks,' he adds. 'And good luck to all participants. Now –' He smiles around the room. 'I'd like to introduce a new member to the group. Becky comes to us with a specialist knowledge of hedgehogs and . . .' He looks over at me. 'Is it other small endangered creatures, or just hedgehogs?'

'Er . . .' I clear my throat, aware of Jess's eyes on me like daggers. 'Er . . . mainly just the hedgehogs.'

'So a warm welcome to Becky from all of us. OK. The serious business.' He reaches for a leather satchel and pulls out a sheaf of papers. 'The proposed Piper's Hill Shopping Centre.'

He pauses as though for effect, and there's a kind of frisson around the room.

'The council is still playing ignorant. However –' He flips through the sheaf with a flourish. 'By hook or by crook, I have managed to get hold of a copy of the plans.' Robin hands the papers to a man on the end of the row, who starts passing them along. 'Obviously we

299

have a lot of major objections. If you could all study the material for a few minutes . . .'

Silence descends upon the room. I obediently read the plans, and look at all the drawings. As I glance around, people are shaking their heads in anger and disappointment, which, frankly, doesn't surprise me.

'Right.' Robin looks around and his eyes alight on me. 'Becky, maybe we could hear from you first. As an outsider, what's your initial reaction?'

Everyone turns to look at me, and I feel my cheeks grow hot.

'Er . . . well, I can see the problems straight away,' I say tentatively.

'Exactly,' Robin says with satisfaction. 'This proves our point. The problems are obvious at first glance, to someone who doesn't even know the area. Carry on, Becky.'

'Well.' I study the plans for a second, then look up. 'For a start, the opening hours are quite restricted. I'd have it open till ten every night. I mean, people have to work during the day! They don't want to have to rush their shopping!'

I look around at the speechless faces. Everyone seems a bit stunned. They probably weren't expecting me to hit the nail on the head like that. Encouraged, I tap the list of shops. 'And these are rubbish shops. You should have Space NK . . . Joseph . . . And definitely an L K Bennett!'

There's utter silence around the room.

Jess has buried her head in her hands.

Robin appears dumbstruck, but makes a valiant attempt to smile.

'Becky . . . slight confusion here. We're not protesting about any of the features of the shopping centre. We're protesting about its very existence.'

'I'm sorry?' I peer at him uncomprehendingly.

'We don't want them to build it,' says Jess in

extra-slow, sarcastic tones. 'They're planning to ruin an area of natural beauty. That's what the protest is about.'

'Oh.' My cheeks flame. 'Oh, I see. Absolutely. The natural beauty. I was . . . actually . . . er . . . just about to mention that.' Flustered, I start riffling through the plans again, trying to think of a way to redeem myself quickly. 'It'll probably be quite a danger to hedgehogs, too,' I say at last. 'I've noticed several hedgehog hazard points. Or HHPs, as we call them.'

I can see Jess rolling her eyes. Maybe I'd better shut up now.

'Good point,' says Robin, his smile a little strained. 'So – Becky has shared some valuable hedgehog safety concerns. Any other views?'

As a white-haired man starts to speak about the desecration of the countryside, I sink back down into my chair, my heart thumping. OK. No more talking.

I'm kind of glad now I didn't mention my other major concern about the shopping centre. Which was that it isn't big enough.

'My worry is the local economy,' a smartly dressed woman is declaiming. 'Out-of-town shopping centres ruin rural life. If they build this, it'll put the village shop out of business.'

'It's a crime,' booms Lorna with the metal-grey hair. 'Village shops are the hub of the community. They need to be supported.'

More and more voices are joining in now. I can see all the customers of Jim's shop nodding at each other.

'How can Jim compete with Asda?'

'We need to keep these small shops alive!'

'The government's to blame . . .'

I know I wasn't planning to say anything more. But I just can't keep quiet.

'Excuse me?' I venture, raising my hand. 'If you all

301

want the village shop to stay alive, why don't you buy
bread at full price?'

I look around the room, to see Jess glaring at me.

'That is just *typical*,' she says. 'Everything comes
down to spending money, doesn't it?'

'But it's a shop!' I say, bewildered. 'That's the whole
point! You spend money! If you all spent a bit more
money, the shop would start booming!'

'Not everyone in the world is addicted to shopping,
OK, Becky?' snaps Jess.

'Wish they were,' puts in Jim with a wry smile. 'My
revenue's trebled since Becky came to town.'

Jess stares at him, her mouth tight. Oh God. She
looks really pissed off. I'm ruffling her feathers.

'It was just . . . an idea,' I say quickly. 'It doesn't
matter.' I shrink down in my seat again, trying to look
unobtrusive.

The discussion starts up again, but I keep my head
down, and leaf through the shopping-centre plans
again. And I have to say, I was right in the first place.
The shops *are* rubbish. Not a single good place for
handbags . . . not a single place you can get your nails
done . . . I mean, I can really see their point. What is
the point of ruining some lovely field with a crappy
shopping centre full of shops no one wants to visit?

'. . . so we on the committee have decided on immediate, pre-emptive action,' Robin is saying as I raise
my head again. 'We're holding a rally, to be held in a
week's time. We need as much support as possible.
And obviously as much publicity as possible.'

'It's difficult,' says a woman with a sigh. 'No one's
interested.'

'Edgar is writing an article for his parish magazine,'
says Robin, consulting a piece of paper. 'And I
know some of you have already drafted letters to the
council . . .'

I'm itching to speak.

I open my mouth – catch Jess's eyes on me like daggers – and close it again.

But oh God. I can't keep quiet. I just can't.

'We're producing a very informative leaflet—'

'You should do something bigger!' My voice cuts across Robin's, and everyone turns to stare at me.

'Becky, shut up,' says Jess furiously. 'We're trying to discuss this sensibly!'

'So am I!' I'm hot under all these eyes, but I press on. 'I think you should have a huge marketing campaign.'

'Wouldn't that be expensive?' says the white-haired man with a frown.

'In business, if you want to make money, you have to spend money. And it's the same here. If you want to have a result, you have to make the investment!'

'Money again!' exclaims Jess in exasperation. 'Spending again! You're obsessed!'

'You could get a sponsorship deal!' I retort. 'There must be local businesses who don't want the shopping centre either. You should get a local radio station involved . . . put together a press pack . . .'

'Excuse me, love,' a guy sitting near to Jess interrupts sarcastically. 'You're very good at talking. But what do you actually *know* about this?'

'Well, nothing,' I admit. 'Except I used to work as a journalist. So I know about press releases and marketing campaigns.' I look around the silent room. 'And for two years I worked at Barneys, the department store in New York. We used to run loads of events, like parties, and special sale weekends, and promotional evenings . . . in fact, that's an idea!' I turn to Jim in sudden inspiration. 'If you want to boost the village shop, you should celebrate it! Do something positive! You should have a shopping festival. Or a party! It would be such fun! You could have special offers, and free gifts . . . tie it into the protest . . .'

'*Shut up!*' A voice comes hurtling across the room

303

and I stop in shock, to see Jess on her feet, white with anger. 'Just shut up for once, Becky! Why does everything have to be a party? Why do you have to trivialize everything? Shopkeepers like Jim aren't interested in parties! They're interested in solid, well-thought-out action.'

'I might be interested in a party,' says Jim mildly, but Jess doesn't seem to hear him.

'You don't know anything about the environment! You don't know about bloody hedgehogs! You're making it up as you go along! Just butt out and leave us alone.'

'Now, that's a little aggressive, Jess,' says Robin. 'Becky's only trying to help.'

'We don't need her help!'

'Jess,' says Jim in soothing tones. 'This is your sister. Come on, love. Be a bit more welcoming.'

'Are these two sisters?' says the white-haired man in surprise. An interested murmuring grows around the room.

'She's not my sister.' Jess has folded her arms tight. She's refusing even to look at me, and suddenly I feel a swell of angry hurt.

'I know you don't want me to be your sister, Jess,' I say, standing up to face her. 'But I am! And there's nothing you can do about that! We have the same blood! We have the same genes! We have the same—'

'Yeah, well, I don't believe we do, OK?' Jess's voice rockets back across the room.

There's a shocked silence.

'What?' I stare at her uncertainly.

'I don't believe we share the same blood,' she says in calmer tones.

'But . . . but we know we do!' I say in confusion. 'What are you talking about?'

Jess sighs and rubs her face. When she looks up, there's only a trace of animosity left.

'Look at us, Becky,' she says, almost kindly. She gestures to me and then to herself. 'We have nothing in common. Not one thing. We can't be from the same family.'

'But . . . but my dad's your father!'

'Oh God,' says Jess, almost to herself. 'Look, Becky, I wasn't going to bring this up till later.'

'Bring up what?' I stare at her, my heart beating a little more quickly. 'Bring up what?'

'OK. Here's the thing.' Jess exhales sharply and rubs her face. 'Originally I was given the name of your dad as my father. But . . . it just doesn't seem to be making sense. So last night I had a long talk about it with my Aunty Florence. She admitted my mum was a bit . . . wild. There might have been other men.' Jess hesitates. 'She thought there probably *had* been other men, although she didn't have any names.'

'But . . . you had a test!' I say, bewildered. 'A DNA test! So that proves . . .' I trail off as Jess shakes her head.

'No. We never did. We were going to. But I had your dad's name, the dates made sense, and . . . we all just assumed.' She looks down at the ground. 'I think we assumed wrong.'

My head is spinning. They never did a DNA test? They just *assumed*?

The entire room is silent. I don't think anyone is breathing. I catch sight of Jim's anxious, kindly face, and quickly look away.

'So . . . this has all been a big mistake,' I say at last. And all of a sudden there's a huge lump in my throat.

'I think it was a mistake,' agrees Jess. She looks up and sees my stricken face. 'Come on, Becky. If you looked at us as an outsider . . . would you say we were sisters?'

'I . . . I suppose not,' I manage.

I'm reeling with shock and disappointment. But at the

same time, deep down, a tiny voice is telling me that this makes sense. I feel like for the last few weeks I've been trying to force my foot into a wrong-sized shoe. I've been ramming and ramming, chafing the skin . . . and at last I'm admitting it doesn't fit.

She's not my sister. She's not my flesh and blood. She's just . . . a girl.

I'm standing here staring at a girl I barely know, who doesn't even like me.

And all of a sudden I really don't want to be here any more.

'Right,' I say, trying to compose myself. 'Well . . . I think I'll go.' I look around the silenced room. 'Bye everybody. Good luck with the protest.'

Nobody says anything. Everyone looks too shell-shocked. With trembling hands I pick up my bag, and push back my chair. As I make my way past everyone to the door I catch the odd sympathetic look. I pause when I reach Jim, who looks almost as disappointed as I feel.

'Thanks for everything, Jim,' I say, trying to smile.

'Goodbye, love.' He clasps my hand warmly. 'It was good to know you.'

'You too. Say goodbye to Kelly for me.'

I reach the door and turn to face Jess.

'Bye, then.' I swallow hard. 'Have a nice life and everything.'

'Bye, Becky,' she says, and for the first time there's a flicker of something like compassion in her eyes. 'I hope you patch it up with Luke.'

'Thanks.' I nod, not quite sure what else to say. Then I turn and walk out into the night.

TWENTY

I feel numb. I don't have a sister. After all that.

I've been sitting on the bed in my room at the bed and breakfast for about an hour, just staring out of the window at the distant hills. It's all over. My stupid dream of having a sisterly soulmate to chat and giggle with and go shopping with and eat peppermint creams with . . . is over for good.

Not that Jess would ever have gone shopping or eaten peppermint creams with me. Or giggled, come to that.

But she might have chatted. We might have got to know each other better. We might have told each other secrets and asked each other's advice.

I give a heavy sigh and hug my knees tight to my chest. This never happened in *Long-Lost Sisters – The Love They Never Knew They Had*.

Actually, it happened once. With these two sisters who were going to have a kidney transplant and then they did the DNA test and realized they weren't sisters after all. But the point was, it turned out they were a good enough match, so they went ahead with the kidney transplant anyway. And afterwards they said they would always be sisters in the heart. (And in the kidneys, I suppose.)

The point was, they *liked* each other.

I feel a single tear roll down my cheek and brush it away crossly. There's no point getting upset. I've been an only child all my life . . . and now I am again. I only had a sister for a few weeks. It's not like I got used to it. It's not like we got attached or anything.

In fact . . . in fact, I'm *glad* this has happened. Who would want Jess for a sister? Not me. No way. I mean, she's right. We have absolutely nothing in common. We don't understand one thing about each other. We should have realized it was a mistake right from the word go.

Abruptly I get to my feet, open my suitcase and start throwing clothes into it. I'll spend the night here, then head back to London first thing in the morning. I can't waste any more time. I've got a life to get back to. I've got a husband.

At least . . . I think I've got a husband.

As my mind flashes back to the last time I saw Luke, I feel a hollow dread in my stomach. He's probably still furious with me. He's probably having a terrible time in Cyprus and cursing me every moment. I hesitate, halfway through folding up a jumper. Just the thought of going back and facing him makes me feel a bit sick.

But then my chin stiffens and I throw the jumper into the case. So what if things with Luke are shaky? I don't need some crummy sister to help me save my marriage. I'll sort it out myself. Maybe I'll buy a book. There must be one called *How To Save Your Year-Old Marriage*.

I cram in all the souvenirs I bought at Jim's shop, sit on the lid of my lime-green case and snap it shut. That's it. The end.

There's a knock on the door and I raise my head. 'Hello?'

Edie puts her head round the door.

'You've got a visitor,' she says. 'Downstairs.'

I feel a sudden flicker of hope.

'Really?' I scramble to my feet. 'I'm just coming!'

'I'd like to take this opportunity to remind you of the rules.' Edie's booming voice follows me as I run down the stairs. 'No visitors after eleven o'clock. If there's any carousing I'll have to call the authorities.'

I jump down the last few steps and hurry into the little sitting room.

'Hi!' I stop dead in my tracks. It's not Jess.

It's Robin. And Jim. And a couple of other people from the meeting. They all turn to look at me, and I can see a few glances flying about.

'Hi Becky,' says Robin, taking a step towards me. 'Are you OK?'

'Er . . . yes. I'm fine, thanks.'

Oh God. This is a pity visit. Maybe they're worried I'm going to slash my wrists or something. As Robin takes a breath to speak again, I cut in.

'Really, everybody. You don't need to worry about me. It's very sweet of you to be concerned. But I'll be all right. I'm just going to go to bed, and catch the train home tomorrow, and . . . just take it from there.'

There's silence.

'Er . . . that's not why we're here,' says Robin, and ruffles his hair awkwardly. 'We wanted to ask you something.'

'Oh,' I say, taken aback. 'Right.'

'We wondered . . . all of us . . . if you'd help us with the protest.' He looks about as though for support, and everyone nods.

'*Help* you?' I stare back, bewildered. 'But . . . I don't know anything about it. Jess was right.' I feel a stab of pain at the memory. 'I was making it all up. I don't even know about hedgehogs.'

'Doesn't matter,' says Robin. 'You've got loads of ideas, and that's what we need. You're right. We *should* think big. And Jim likes the idea of the party. Don't you, Jim?'

'If it gets folk into the shop before four o'clock, it can't be bad,' says Jim with a twinkle.

'You've got experience with these kinds of events,' chips in the white-haired man. 'You know how to go about it. We don't.'

'When you left the meeting we had a quick straw poll,' says Robin. 'And it was practically unanimous. We'd like to invite you on to the action committee. Everyone's waiting back at the hall, to hear.'

All their faces are so warm and friendly, I feel tears pricking at my eyes.

'I can't.' I look away. 'I'm sorry, but I can't. There's no need for me to be in Scully any more. I've got to get back to London.'

'Why's that, then?' says Jim.

'I have . . . things to do,' I say. 'Commitments. You know.'

'What commitments would they be?' says Jim mildly. 'You don't have a job. Your husband's abroad. Your flat's empty.'

OK, this is why you shouldn't pour out your entire sob story to people you've just met. For a few moments I'm silent, gazing at Edie's pink and purple swirly carpet, trying to get my thoughts straight. Then I look up.

'What does Jess think about all this?'

I look around the group – but no one replies. Robin won't quite meet my eyes. The white-haired man is gazing at the ceiling. Jim just has that same sad expression he had at the village hall.

'I bet she's the only one who voted against me, isn't she?' I try to smile, but my voice is wobbling.

'Jess has . . . certain opinions,' begins Robin. 'But she doesn't have to come into it—'

'She *does*! Of course she does! She's the whole

reason I'm here!' I break off, trying to stay calm. 'Look, I'm sorry. But I can't come on your committee. I hope your protest goes really well . . . but I can't stay.'

I can see Robin drawing breath to speak again.

'I can't.' I look directly at Jim. 'You have to understand. I can't.'

And I can see it in his eyes. He does understand.

'Fair enough,' he says at last. 'It was worth a try.' He nods at the others as though to say, 'It's over.'

They awkwardly murmur goodbyes and good lucks and file out of the little room. The front door bangs shut and I'm left alone, feeling flatter than ever.

When I wake up the next morning the sky is dark and swollen with grey clouds. Edie serves me a full English breakfast complete with black pudding, but I only manage a cup of tea. I pay her with the rest of my cash, then head upstairs to get ready to leave. Out of the window I can just see the hills in the distance, stretching into the mist.

I'll probably never see those hills again. I'll probably never come back here again.

Which is fine by me, I think defiantly. I hate the country. I never wanted to be here in the first place.

I put the last of my things in my red case, then decide to change into my turquoise kitten heels with diamanté straps. As I step into them I feel something small and nubby under my toes and reach down, puzzled. I pull out a small wrapped object and look at it in sudden realization.

It's the bean. It's the silver Tiffany bean necklace that I was going to give Jess, still in its little blue bag.

God, that seems a lifetime ago.

I stare at it for a few moments, then shove it my pocket, pick up my cases and stripy hat box and head downstairs, passing the payphone in the hall.

Maybe I should call Luke.

But then, what's the point? And anyway, I don't have a number for him.

Edie's nowhere to be seen, so I just pull the door of the bed and breakfast closed behind me, and trundle my cases across the green to the shop. I want to say goodbye to Jim before I leave.

As I push open the door with its familiar tinkle, Jim looks up from pricing cans of beans. He looks at my suitcases and raises his eyebrows.

'So you're off.'

'Yes. I'm off.'

'Don't go!' says Kelly mournfully from behind the counter, where *Julius Caesar* is propped up behind *100 Hot Hair Styles*.

'I have to.' I give a little laugh and put my cases down. 'But I've got some more Stila stuff for you. A goodbye present.'

As I hand her a selection of lip glosses and eye glazes, her face shines.

'I've got a present for you too, Becky,' she says abruptly. She pulls a friendship bracelet off her wrist and hands it to me. 'So you won't forget me.'

As I stare at the simple plaited band in my hand, I'm unable to speak. It's just like the bracelets Luke and I were given in the Masai Mara ceremony. Luke took his off when he went back to corporate life.

I've still got mine on.

'That's . . . fab.' I rouse myself, and smile. 'I'll always wear it.' I slip it on to my wrist, next to mine, and give Kelly a tight hug.

'I wish you weren't going.' Kelly's bottom lip sticks out. 'Will you ever come back to Scully?'

'I don't know,' I say after a pause. 'I don't think so. But listen, if you ever come to London, give me a call. OK?'

'OK.' Kelly brightens. 'Can we go to Topshop?'

'Of course!'

'Should I start saving now?' says Jim ruefully, and we both start giggling.

A tinkle at the door interrupts us and we all look up to see Edie walking into the shop in her green head-scarf, together with Lorna and the well-dressed lady from the night before. They're all looking exceedingly self-conscious.

'Edie!' says Jim, glancing at his watch in surprise. 'What can I do for you?'

'Morning, Jim,' says Edie, avoiding his eye. 'I'd like some bread, please. A wholemeal and a bloomer.'

'Bread?' says Jim, looking dumbfounded. 'But Edie . . . It's ten o'clock in the morning.'

'I know the time, thank you,' she retorts stiffly.

'But . . . it's full price.'

'I'd like some bread,' she snaps. 'Is that too much to ask?'

'Of . . . course not!' says Jim, still looking dazed. He gets down the loaves and wraps them in paper. 'That'll be one pound ninety-six.'

There's a pause, and I can hear Edie breathe in sharply. Then she rummages in her bag for her purse and unclips it.

'Two pounds,' she says, handing over the coins. 'Much obliged.'

I do not believe it. Kelly and I just sit there, goggling in silence, as the other two women buy three loaves of bread and a bag of sandwich baps between them. Lorna even throws in a couple of Chelsea buns at the last moment.

As the door closes behind them, Jim sinks down on to his stool.

'Well, who would have thought it?' He shakes his head in slow wonderment, then looks up. 'That's you, Becky.'

'It's not *me*,' I say, flushing a little. 'They probably just needed bread.'

'It was you!' says Kelly. 'It was what you said! Mum told me all about the meeting,' she adds. 'She said you seemed a nice girl, even if you were a bit—'

'Kelly,' Jim puts in quickly, 'why don't you make Becky a cup of tea?'

'No, it's OK. I'm going.' I hesitate, then reach into my pocket and pull out the little Tiffany bag. 'Jim, I wanted to ask you a favour. Could you give this to Jess? It's something I bought for her a while ago. I know everything's different now . . . but still.'

'I'm heading up to her house just now, to take a delivery,' says Jim. 'Why not leave it there yourself?'

'Oh.' I shrink back. 'No. I . . . I don't want to see her.'

'She won't be there. They've all gone off for the endurance hike. I've got a key to her house.'

'Oh, right.' I hesitate.

'I could do with the company,' adds Jim with a shrug.

'Well . . .' I look at the Tiffany bag for a few moments, then put it back in my pocket. 'OK. I'll come.'

We walk along the empty streets towards Jess's house in silence, Jim carrying a sack of potatoes on his shoulder. The clouds are growing thicker and I can feel spots of rain on my face. I'm aware of Jim shooting me the odd concerned glance.

'You'll be all right, back in London?' he says eventually.

'I guess.'

'Have you spoken to your husband?'

'No.' I bite my lip. 'I haven't.'

Jim pauses, and transfers his potatoes to the other shoulder.

'So,' he says easily, 'how did a nice girl like you end up with a marriage in trouble?'

'It's my own fault. I did some . . . stupid things. And

314

my husband got really angry. He said . . .' I swallow hard. 'He said he wished I was more like Jess.'

'Did he?' Jim looks a bit taken aback. 'I mean, Jess is a fine lass,' he hastily amends. 'But I wouldn't have . . . Any road. That's not here or there.' He coughs awkwardly and rubs his nose.

'That's why I came up here. To learn from her.' I give a gusty sigh. 'But it was a stupid idea.'

We've reached the end of Jess's street and Jim pauses for a rest before climbing the steep incline. The grey stone houses are glistening in the drizzle, stark against the distant misty hills. I can just see a flock of sheep grazing high up, like dots of cotton wool on the green.

'Too bad about you and Jess,' says Jim, and he sounds genuinely sorry. 'It's a shame, that is.'

'It's just one of those things.' I try to keep the disappointment out of my voice. 'I should have known all along. We're so different.'

'You're different, all right.' His face crinkles in amusement.

'She just seems so . . . *cold.*' I hunch my shoulders, feeling a familiar resentment rising. 'You know, I made every effort. I really did. But she never showed any pleasure . . . or feelings, even. She doesn't seem to care about anything! She doesn't seem to have any passions!'

Jim raises his eyebrows.

'Oh, Jess has got passions,' he says. 'She's got passions, all right. When we get to the house, I'll show you something.'

He picks up the sack of potatoes and we start walking up the hill. And as we get nearer Jess's house, I start to feel tiny prickles of curiosity. Not that she's anything to do with me any more. But still, I'm quite intrigued to see what her house is like.

As we reach the door, Jim roots in his pocket for a large key ring, selects a Yale key and unlocks it. I walk into the hall and look around curiously. But the place doesn't give much away. It's a bit like Jess herself. Two tidy sofas in the sitting room. A plain white kitchen. A couple of well-tended pot plants.

I head upstairs and cautiously push open the door to her bedroom. It's immaculate. Plain cotton duvet cover, plain cotton curtains, a couple of boring pictures.

'Here.' Jim is behind me. 'You want to see Jess's real passion? Take a look at this.'

He heads over to a door set into the wall of the landing, turns the key and beckons me over with a wink.

'Here are the famous rocks,' he says, swinging the door open. 'She had this cupboard made three years ago, especially to house them. Designed it herself down to the last detail, lights and all. Makes an impressive sight, don't you think?' He trails off in surprise at my face. 'Becky? Are you OK, love?'

I can't speak. I can't move.

It's my shoe cupboard.

It's my shoe cupboard, exactly. The same doors. The same shelves. The same lights. Except, instead of shoes displayed on the shelves, there are rocks. Rows and rows of carefully labelled rocks.

And ... they're beautiful. Some are grey, some crystal, some smooth, some iridescent and sparkling. There are fossils ... amethysts ... chunks of jet, all shiny under the lights.

'I had no idea ...' I swallow hard. 'They're stunning.'

'You're talking about passion?' Jim laughs. 'This is a true passion. An obsession, you might say.' He picks up a speckled grey rock and turns it over in his fingers. 'You know how she got that leg injury of hers? Clambering after some blasted rock on a mountain somewhere. She was that determined to get it, she'd risk her own safety.' Jim grins at my expression. 'Then there was the time she was arrested at Customs, for smuggling some precious crystal in under her jumper.'

I gape at him.

'Jess? *Arrested?*'

'They let her off.' He waves a hand. 'But I know she'd do it again. If there's a particular kind of rock that girl wants, she has to have it.' He shakes his head in amusement. 'She gets a compulsion. It's like a mania! Nothing'll stop her!'

My head is spinning. I'm staring at a row of rocks, all different shades of red. Just like my row of red shoes.

'She keeps all this pretty quiet.' Jim puts down the speckled rock. 'I guess she thinks people wouldn't understand—'

'I understand.' I cut him off in a shaky voice. 'Completely.'

I'm trembling all over. She's my sister.

Jess is my sister. I know it more certainly than I've ever known anything.

I have to find her. I have to tell her. Now.

'Jim . . .' I take a deep breath. 'I need to find Jess. Right away.'

'She's doing the sponsored endurance hike,' Jim reminds me. 'Starts in half an hour.'

'Then I have to go,' I say in agitation. 'I have to see her. How do I get there? Can I walk?'

'It's a fair way away,' says Jim, and cocks his head quizzically. 'Do you want a lift?'

TWENTY-ONE

I knew we were sisters. I knew it. I *knew* it.

And we're not just sisters – we're kindred spirits! After all those false starts. After all those misunderstandings. After I thought I would never have one single thing in common with her, ever.

She's the same as me. I understand her.

I understand Jess!

Everything Jim said struck a chord. Everything! How many times have I smuggled pairs of shoes in from America? How many times have I risked my own safety at the sales? I even got a leg injury, just like her! It was when I saw someone heading for the last reduced Orla Kiely purse in Selfridges and leapt off the escalator from about eight steps up.

God, if I'd just seen her rock cupboard earlier. If I'd *known*. Everything would have been different! Why didn't she tell me? Why didn't she explain?

I have a sudden memory of Jess talking about rocks on our first-ever meeting . . . and again at the flat. And a warm shame creeps over me. She did try. I just didn't listen, did I? I didn't believe her when she said they were interesting. I said rocks were . . . stupid.

And boring. Just like her.

My stomach twinges.

'Can we go any faster?' I say to Jim. We're rattling

along in his ancient Land Rover, past grassy slopes and dry-stone walls, heading higher and higher into the hills.

'Going as fast as we can,' he says. 'We'll be in time, easy.'

Sheep are scattering off the road as we thunder along, and small stones are hitting the windscreen. I glance out of the window – and quickly look away. Not that I'm afraid of heights or anything, but we seem to be approximately three inches away from a steep drop.

'All right,' says Jim, pulling into a small parking area with a crunch of gravel. 'This is where they're starting. And that's where they're climbing.' He points to the steep mountain looming above us. 'The famous Scully Pike.' His phone rings, and he reaches for it. 'Excuse me.'

'Don't worry! Thanks!' I say, and wrench open the door. I get out and look around – and just for a moment I'm floored by the scenery.

Craggy rocks and peaks are all around, interspersed with patches of grass and crevasses, and over-shadowed by the mountain – a stark, jagged outline against the grey sky. As I peer across the valley, I feel a sudden swooping, a bit like vertigo, I suppose. I honestly hadn't realized quite how high up we are. There's a little cluster of houses visible far below, which I guess is Scully – but apart from that, we could be in the middle of nowhere.

Well, come to think of it, we *are* in the middle of nowhere.

I hurry across the gravel to a small level patch where a table has been set up, with a banner reading 'Scully Environmental Group Endurance Hike, Registration'. Behind the table, two yellow flags mark the foot of a path leading up the mountain. A man whom I don't recognize is sitting at the table in an anorak and flat cap. But apart from that, the place is empty.

Where *is* everybody? God, no wonder they don't have any money if no one turns up for the sponsored walks.

'Hi,' I say to the man in the anorak. 'Do you know where Jess Bertram is? She's one of the walkers. I really need to speak to her.'

I'm totally wound up with anticipation. I cannot wait to tell her! I cannot wait to see her face!

'Too late, I'm afraid,' says the man, and gestures up the mountain. 'She's gone. They've all gone.'

'Already?' I stare at him. 'But . . . the hike starts at eleven. It's only five to!'

'It started at half past ten,' corrects the man. 'We brought it forward because of the poor weather. You'll have to wait. It'll only be a few hours.'

'Oh.' I subside in disappointment and turn away. 'All right. Thanks.'

It'll be OK. I can wait. I can be patient.

It's not that long, really, a few hours.

Yes it is. A few hours is *ages*. I want to tell her *now*. I gaze up at the mountain, my whole body throbbing in frustration. Suddenly I glimpse a couple in matching red anoraks, a few hundred yards up. They've got bibs with Scully Environmental Group on them. They're part of the hike. And look, a little beyond them, there's a guy in blue.

My mind is working quickly. They haven't got that far. Which means Jess hasn't got that far either. Which means . . . I could catch up with her. Yes!

This kind of news can't wait a few hours. I mean, we're sisters. We're real, genuine sisters! I have to tell her right now.

I hoist my Angel bag firmly on my shoulder, hurry to the start of the steep mountain path and look up at it. I can climb this. Easy. There are rocks to hold on to and everything.

I take a few tentative steps – and it's OK! Not hard at all.

'Excuse me?' The man in the anorak is standing up, regarding me in horror. 'What are you doing?'

'I'm joining the hike. Don't worry, I'll sponsor myself.'

'You can't join the hike! What about your shoes!' He points at my turquoise kitten heels in horror. 'Do you have a cagoule?'

'A *cagoule*?' I pull a face. 'Do I look like someone who would have a cagoule?'

'What about a stick?'

'I don't need a stick,' I explain. 'I'm not *old*.'

Honestly. It's only walking up a hill. What's the fuss?

Just to prove it to him, I start clambering up the path in earnest. The ground is a bit slimy with drizzle, but I stick my kitten heels into the mud as hard as I can, and grab on to the rocks lining the path – and in about two minutes I'm already past the first bend.

I'm panting a bit, and my calves are hurting, but apart from that, I'm doing great! God, it just shows, climbing really isn't that hard. I reach another bend, and look back in satisfaction. I'm practically halfway up the mountain already!

This is so easy. I always knew people who went hiking were showing off about nothing.

Down below, I can faintly hear Jim's voice yelling, 'Becky! Come back!' But I close my ears and resolutely keep on, one foot after the other. I need to hurry if I'm going to catch up with Jess.

Except she must be a pretty speedy walker. Because after about an hour of steady climbing, I still haven't caught up with her.

In fact, I haven't caught up with any of them. I kept the red couple in sight for a while, but somehow they seem to have disappeared. The guy in blue has vanished, too. And I haven't even clapped eyes on Jess.

Which is probably because she's *run* the whole way up, I think a bit disconsolately. She's probably doing twenty one-handed press-ups at the top, because climbing a mountain isn't strenuous enough. God, it isn't fair. You'd think I might have got some of the super-fit genes too.

I take a few more steps forward and stop for a breather, wincing at the sight of my mud-spattered legs. My face is hot and I'm panting hard, so I get out my Evian facial spray and spritz myself again. It's getting fairly steep up here.

Not that it's *hard* or anything. In fact, I'm really enjoying myself. Apart from the blister on my right foot, which is getting a bit painful. Maybe that guy had a point – these aren't the best shoes in the world for climbing. Although, on the plus side, the heels are really good for slippery bits.

I look around the empty, rugged mountainside. About three feet away is a rocky ledge and beyond that a sheer drop down into a valley.

Which I'm not going to look at. Or think about.

Stop it, Becky. I am *not* about to run forward and pitch myself over the edge, no matter what my brain is telling me.

I put the Evian spritzer away and look around a bit uncertainly. I have no idea how much further there is to go. I'd kind of counted on catching up with the other walkers and finding out from them. I squint ahead, trying to spot a brightly coloured anorak, but the air is getting hazy with mist.

Oh God. Maybe it's going to rain. And I don't even have a cardigan.

Suddenly I feel a bit stupid. Maybe I shouldn't have rushed up here. Maybe I should go back down. Cautiously I take a step downwards . . . but the ground is more slippery than I expected, and I'm suddenly slithering downwards towards the rocky ledge.

'Shiiit!' I grab on to a sharp rock to stop myself, and somehow haul myself back up, wrenching an arm muscle as I do so.

OK, forget that plan. I'm not going back down now. Anyway, it's probably *further* to go back down than carry on. I'll keep on following the path. It'll be fine. If I just speed up a bit I'm bound to reach Jess.

And it'll be worth it just to see her face.

She won't believe her eyes. Then I'll tell her – and she won't believe her ears! She'll be totally, utterly gobsmacked! I hug the thought to myself happily for a few moments – then, with a fresh surge of energy, keep on climbing.

I'm knackered. I can't keep going any longer.

My knees ache, my hands are sore and my feet are covered in blisters. I've been trudging for what seems like hours, but this bloody mountain goes on for ever. Every time I think I must have got to the top, I see another peak rising up in front of me.

Where's Jess? Where *is* everybody? They can't *all* be quicker than me.

I stop for a few moments, panting a little, holding on to a large boulder for balance. The view over the valley is as stunning as ever, with purple and grey clouds rolling across the sky, and a single bird soaring high above me. Maybe it's an eagle or something. To be honest, I don't care. I just want to sit down with a cup of tea. That's all I want in the world.

But I can't. I have to continue. Come on. This is what they mean by endurance.

With a huge effort I let go of the boulder and start climbing again. Left, right. Left, right. Maybe I'll try singing, like the Von Trapps. Yes. That'll cheer me on.

'*High on a hill . . .*'

No. Forget the singing.

* * *

Oh God. I can't climb any more. I just can't do it.

I must have been walking for hours and I feel sick and dizzy. My hands are numb and exhausted, and I've gashed my knee on a rock, and torn my skirt, and I don't know where I'm supposed to go next.

I stumble over a cluster of rocks and grab on to a bush for support, wincing as it pricks my hand. OK. I've got to stop for a rest. I sit down on a flat stone, fumble for the Evian facial mister and spray it into my mouth.

I'm desperate for a drink. My face is sweaty, my lungs are burning. My legs are covered in mud, with blood dripping down in rivulets from my left knee. My shoes are unidentifiable.

I spray the very last drops of Evian into my mouth. I wipe my face with a tissue from my bag and look around the empty mountainside. There is no one in sight. *No one.*

What am I going to do?

I feel a deep-down spasm of fear, which I ignore. It'll be fine. The important thing is to think positive. I'll just keep climbing. I can do it!

No I can't, comes a small voice inside.

Stop it. Think positive. I can do anything I set my mind to.

Not climb a mountain. It was a stupid idea.

Come on. Yes I can. Girlpower. Climb ev'ry mountain.

Anyway, I can't just sit on this stone for ever. I have to keep going, otherwise I'll get snow sickness and fall asleep and die. Or mountain sickness. Whatever it is.

My legs are all shaky, but somehow I force myself to my feet, wincing in pain as my shoes dig into my blisters again. Right. Just keep going. I'll get to the top – and maybe that's where the welcoming party is. And those hot drinks they were talking about. Yes. It'll be fine—

Suddenly there's a rumble of distant thunder.

Oh God. Please no.

I look up, and the sky has darkened to a menacing grey. There aren't any birds.

A raindrop hits me in the eye. Then another one.

I swallow, trying to stay calm. But inside I'm a mush of panic. What do I do now? Do I keep going up? Do I go down?

'Hi!' I call out. 'Is anyone there?' My voice echoes round the rocks, but there's no reply.

Another three raindrops land on my head.

I don't have anything waterproof. I look around the stark landscape, hollow with fear. What if I can't get down? What if I'm stuck up here in a storm?

I was so desperate to tell Jess we were sisters. Now I just feel like a fool. I should have waited. Luke's right. Why can't I wait for anything in life? It's all my own fault.

There's another distant rumble of thunder and I flinch in fright. What if I get struck by lightning? I don't even know what the rules are for being outside in a storm. It's something like stand under a tree. Or maybe *don't* stand under a tree. But which? What if I get it wrong?

Suddenly, through my agitation, I'm aware of a noise. A kind of chirping noise. Is it . . . an animal?

Oh my God.

Oh my God. It's my mobile. There's a signal up here! There's a bloody signal!

With trembling fingers I unzip my Angel bag and grab my flashing mobile. With a whoosh of disbelief I see the word 'Luke' on the little display. I jab frantically at the green button, weak with relief.

'Luke!' I say. 'It's Becky!'

'Becky? Is anyone there?' The line is crackling, and he sounds all fuzzy and distant.

'Yes!' I shout, as raindrops start falling harder on my head. 'Luke, it's me! I'm lost! I need help!'

'Hello?' comes his puzzled voice again. 'Can anyone hear me?'

I stare at my mobile in dismay.

'Yes! I can hear you! I'm here!' With no warning, tears start streaming down my face. 'I'm stuck on this awful mountain and I don't know what to do. Luke, I'm so sorry—'

'The line's not working,' I can hear him saying to someone else. 'I can't hear a bloody thing.'

'Luke!' I yell. 'Luke, I'm here! I'm right here! Don't go!'

I bang the phone frantically, and the words 'Battery low' flash at me.

'Hello?' comes Luke's voice again. 'Becky?'

'Luke, please hear me!' I cry in desperation. 'Please hear me! *Please . . .*'

But the light in the little screen is already fading. And a moment later the phone goes dead.

He's gone.

I look around the desolate, silent mountainside. I have never felt more alone in my life.

After a while, a gust of wind blows a flurry of rain into my face and I flinch. I can't just stand here. I have to find some kind of shelter.

About six feet above me is a kind of sticking-out ledge, with a cluster of rocks on top. One of them has an overhanging bit which maybe I can crouch under. The mud is all wet and slithery, but I dig in my heels and grab on to anything I can find, and somehow scrabble up there, grazing my other knee as I do so.

God, it's quite high up. I feel a bit precarious. But never mind. If I don't look down I'll be fine. Firmly I take hold of the overhanging bit of rock, and am trying to edge underneath without slipping over . . . when suddenly I glimpse a flash of yellow.

Bright yellow.

Human-waterproof-climbing-gear yellow.

Oh my God. There's someone else on the mountain. There's someone else! I'm saved!

'Hi!' I yell. 'Halloo! Over here!' But my voice is carried the wrong way by the wind and the rain.

I can't see whoever it is properly, because the overhanging rock is in the way. Very slowly and cautiously, I manoeuvre myself around the lip of the ledge until I have a better view.

And my heart stops.

It's Jess.

She's on the slope below, wearing a yellow cagoule and a backpack. Some kind of rope thing is attaching her to the mountainside, and she's digging carefully at a rock with a metal knife.

'Jess!' I shout, but my voice sounds hardly bigger than a squeak above the wind. 'Jess! JESS!'

At last her head turns – and her whole face contracts in shock.

'Jesus Christ! Becky! What the hell are you doing up here?'

'I came to tell you we're sisters!' I shout back, but I'm not sure if she can hear me through the buffeting rain. '*Sisters!*' I yell again, taking a step forward, cupping my mouth. 'We're SISTERS!'

'Stop!' shouts Jess in horror. 'That ledge is dangerous!'

'I'm fine!'

'Get back!'

'I'm OK, honestly,' I call. But she looks so alarmed, I obediently take a step back, away from the edge.

And that's when my shoe slips on the wet mud.

I can't regain my balance.

I scrabble frantically at the rocks, trying to hold on to anything, trying to save myself. But everything's too slippery. My fingers close round the roots of a shrub, but it's wet with the rain. I can't get a proper grip.

'Becky!' I hear Jess's scream as the shrub slips out of my desperate fingers. 'BECKY!'

Then I'm falling in a rush of terror, and all I can hear is screaming, and I have a glimpse of sky and then something is thwacking my head, hard.

And then everything goes black.

FEARS FOR MISSING GIRL

Fears were growing last night for the safety of Maida Vale resident Rebecca Brandon, 27. Mrs Brandon (née Bloomwood) disappeared on Thursday from the luxury flat she shares with husband Luke Brandon and has not been seen or heard from since. The alarm was raised by Mrs Brandon's friend Susan Cleath-Stuart, who arrived in London for a surprise visit.

SHOPPING

CCTV footage shows Mrs Brandon in local shop Anna's Delicatessen, shortly before her disappearance, apparently agitated. 'She just dropped her shopping and left,' said shop assistant Marie Fuller. 'She didn't buy anything.'

A distressed Ms Cleath-Stuart commented, 'That proves something's wrong! Bex would never leave her shopping behind! Never!'

CHAOS

There were scenes of chaos aboard the Mind Body Spirit cruise ship currently touring the Mediterranean as Mrs Brandon's parents, Graham and Jane Bloomwood, insisted the boat be turned around. 'You can stuff bloody tranquillity!' a hysterical Mrs Bloomwood was reported as shouting. 'My daughter's missing!'

STORMS

Meanwhile storms have prevented Mrs Brandon's husband Luke from leaving Cyprus where he has been working. He was said yesterday to be 'desperately worried' and in close contact with police. His business associate Nathan Temple has issued a reward for information leading to the recovery of Mrs Brandon. He commented yesterday, 'If anyone harms a hair of that young lady's head I will personally break all their bones. Twice.' Mr Temple was convicted in 1984 for grievous bodily harm.

TWENTY-TWO

Ow.

Ouuuch.

God, my head is agony. Oww. And my ankle's throbbing, and I feel like I might be sick any moment and something sharp is pressing into my shoulder . . .

Where am I, anyway? Why do I feel so weird?

With a huge struggle I manage to open my eyes, and get a flash of blue before they close again.

Hmm. Blue. Makes no sense. Maybe I'll go to sleep.

'Becky? Beckeee!' A voice is calling to me from a huge distance. 'Wake up!'

I force my eyes open again and find myself looking at a face. A blurred face against a blue background.

Jess.

Blimey, it's Jess. And she's all pale and anxious-looking. Maybe she lost something. A rock. That must be it.

'Can you see me?' she says urgently. 'Can you count my fingers?'

She thrusts her hand in front of me and I peer at it woozily. Boy, that girl needs a manicure.

'How many fingers?' she keeps saying. 'Can you see? Can you hear me?'

Oh right, yes.

'Er . . . three?'

Jess stares at me for a moment, then sinks back on her knees and buries her head in her hands. 'Thank God. Thank God.'

She's shaking. Why on earth is she shaking?

And then, like a tidal wave, it all comes back to me.

Oh my God. The walk. The storm. Falling. Oh God, falling. Crashing down the mountainside.

Quickly I try to block it out of my mind, but to my astonishment, tears start to seep out of the sides of my eyes and drip down into my ears.

OK. Stop it. I'm safe now. I'm on the ground. I . . . think. To be honest, I can't quite work out where I am. I peer at the bright-blue background, but it still makes zero sense. I'd say heaven – except Jess didn't fall too, did she?

'Where am I?' I manage, and Jess raises her head. She still looks white and shaken.

'My tent,' she says. 'I always carry a tent in my back-pack. I didn't dare move you – so I put it up around you.'

A tent! Now that is just so clever. Why don't I take a tent everywhere? I'll start tomorrow. Yes. A little tiny tent that I could keep in my handbag.

The only thing is, it's a bit uncomfortable here on the ground. Maybe I'll get up and stretch my legs.

I try to rise, and everything goes black and swirly.

'Oh God,' I say feebly, and sink back down again.

'Don't try to get up!' says Jess in alarm. 'You had a terrible fall. I thought . . .' She breaks off and exhales sharply. 'Anyway. Don't get up.'

Gradually I'm becoming aware of the rest of my body. My hands are all raw and scraped. With a huge effort I raise my head, and glimpse my legs, all bloody with cuts. I can feel a bruise on my cheek and I lift my hand to it.

'Ow! Is my face bleeding?'

'You're a mess,' says Jess bluntly. 'Does anything hurt really badly?'

'My ankle. The left one. It's agony.'

Jess starts prodding it and I bite my lip, trying not to cry out.

'I think it's sprained,' she says at last. 'I'll strap you up.' She switches on a torch and fastens it to a steel pole, then reaches into a tiny tin. She produces a length of bandage-type stuff and starts winding it expertly round my ankle. 'Becky, what the hell were you doing up there, anyway?'

'I – I came to find you.' Bits of the jigsaw are re-appearing in my brain. 'I was doing the sponsored endurance hike.'

Jess stares at me.

'But that wasn't the hike route! I went off the trail. The hike route was much lower. Didn't you follow the markers?'

'Markers?' I look at her blankly.

'God, you have no bloody idea about hiking, do you?' she says in agitation. 'You shouldn't have been up there! It's dangerous!'

'So why were you there?' I retort, wincing as she bandages me more and more tightly. 'What you were doing looked pretty dangerous to me.'

Jess's face closes up.

'Last time I climbed the Pike I saw some ammonite specimens,' she says eventually. 'I wanted to collect one. It's a bit foolhardy, but I don't expect you to understand—'

'No! I *do* understand!' I interrupt, and struggle on to my elbows. Oh my God. It's all coming back in a rush. I have to tell her. 'Jess, I understand. I've seen your rocks. They're fantastic. They're beautiful.'

'Lie down,' says Jess, looking worried. 'Take it easy.'

'I don't want to take it easy! Jess, listen. We're

sisters. We're honestly and truly sisters. That's why I came up the mountain. I had to tell you.'

Jess stares at me. 'Becky, you've had a bump on the head . . . you've probably got concussion . . .'

'It's not that!' The louder my voice rises, the more my head throbs, but I can't stop myself. 'I know we have the same blood. I know it! I went to your house.'

'You *what*?' Jess looks shocked. 'Who let you in?'

'I saw your rock cupboard. It's identical to my shoe cupboard in London. *Identical*. The lights . . . the shelves . . . everything!'

For the first time ever, I see Jess's composure slip a little.

'So what?' she says in brusque tones.

'So! We're the same!' I sit up eagerly, ignoring the swirling in front of my eyes. 'Jess, you know the way you feel about a really amazing rock? That's the way I feel about a great pair of shoes! Or a dress. I *have* to have it. Nothing else matters. And I know you feel the same way about your rock collection.'

'I don't,' says Jess, turning away.

'You do! I know you do!' I clutch her arm. 'You're just as obsessed as me! You just hide it better! Oh God, my head. Ow.'

I collapse back down, my head pounding.

'I'll get you a painkiller,' says Jess distractedly – but she doesn't move. She's just sitting there, the bandage loose in her hand.

I can see I've got to her.

There's silence except for the drumming of rain on the tent above us. I don't dare speak. I don't dare move.

Actually, I'm not sure I *can* move.

'You came up a mountain in a storm just to tell me this?' says Jess at last.

'Yes! Of course!'

She turns her head to look at me. Her face is paler

than ever and kind of bewildered, as though some-one's trying to trick her.

'Why? Why would you do that?'

'Because . . . because it's important! It matters to me!'

'No one's ever done anything like that for me before,' she says, and immediately looks away, fiddling in the tin again. 'Those cuts need antiseptic on them.'

She starts dabbing my legs with a cottonwool pad, and I try not to flinch as the antiseptic stings my raw flesh.

'So . . . do you believe me?' I say. 'Do you believe we're sisters?'

For a few moments Jess just stares at her feet, encased in thick socks and brown hiking boots. She raises her head and surveys my turquoise diamanté kitten heels, all scraped and covered in mud. My Marc Jacobs skirt. My ruined glittery T-shirt. Then she lifts her eyes to my bruised, battered face, and we just look at each other.

'Yes,' she says at last. 'I believe you.'

Three extra-strong painkillers later, and I'm really feeling quite a lot better. In fact, I can't stop gabbling.

'I knew we were sisters,' I'm saying, as Jess puts a plaster on my gashed knee. 'I knew it! I think I'm a bit psychic, actually. I *felt* your presence on the mountain.'

'Mm,' says Jess, rolling her eyes.

'And the other thing is, I'm getting quite similar to you. Like, I was thinking I might crop my hair short. It would really suit me. And I've started taking a real interest in rocks—'

'Becky,' interrupts Jess. 'We don't have to be the same.'

'What?' I look at her, taken aback. 'What do you mean?'

'Maybe we're sisters.' She sits back on her heels. 'But that doesn't mean we both have to have cropped hair. Or like rocks.' She reaches for another plaster and rips it open.

'Or potatoes,' I add before I can stop myself.

'Or potatoes,' agrees Jess. She pauses. 'Or . . . over-priced designer lipsticks that go out of fashion in three weeks.'

There's a little glint in her eyes as she looks at me, and I gape in astonishment. Jess is *teasing* me?

'I suppose you're right,' I say, trying to stay non-chalant. 'Just because we're biologically related, it doesn't mean we both have to like boring workouts with water bottles instead of cool weights.'

'Exactly. Or . . . mindless magazines full of ridiculous ads.'

'Or drinking coffee out of a horrible old flask.'

Jess's mouth is twitching.

'Or stupid rip-off cappuccinos.'

There's a clap of thunder, and we both jump in fright. Rain is beating on the tent like drumsticks. Jess puts a final plaster on my legs and shuts the little tin.

'I don't suppose you brought anything to eat?' she says.

'Er . . . no.'

'I've got some, but it isn't much.' Her brow wrinkles. 'Not if we're stuck here for hours. We won't be able to move, even when the storm's died down.'

'Can't you forage on the mountainside for roots and berries?' I say hopefully.

Jess gives me a look.

'Becky, I'm not Tarzan.' She hunches her shoulders and wraps her arms round her legs. 'We'll just have to sit it out.'

'So . . . you don't take a mobile when you go climb-ing?' I venture.

'I don't have one. I don't usually need one.'

'I suppose you don't usually have a stupid injured sister with you.'

'Not normally, no.' She shifts on the groundsheet and reaches behind her. 'I picked up some of your stuff, by the way. It all got scattered when you fell.'

'Thank you,' I say, taking the handful of things from her. A mini hairspray. My manicure set. A compact.

'I couldn't find your bag, I'm afraid,' adds Jess. 'God knows where it went.'

My heart stops.

My Angel bag.

My two-thousand-Euro movie-star bag. The bag that everyone in the world is clamouring for.

After all that – it's gone. Lost on a mountain in the middle of nowhere.

'It . . . it doesn't matter.' Somehow I force myself to smile. 'These things happen.'

With sore, stiff fingers, I open my compact – and amazingly, the mirror's still intact. Cautiously I take a look at myself and flinch in horror. I look like a beaten-up scarecrow. My hair is everywhere, and both my cheeks are grazed and there's a huge lump on my forehead.

'What are we going to do?' I close the compact and look up.

'We'll have to stay here until the storm dies down,' says Jess.

'Yes, but I mean . . . what shall we *do*? While we wait in the tent.'

Jess looks at me expressionlessly for a moment.

'I thought we could watch *When Harry Met Sally* and eat popcorn,' she says.

I can't help giggling. Jess does actually have a sense of humour. Underneath it all.

'Shall I do your nails?' I suggest. 'I've got my stuff here.'

'Do my *nails*?' echoes Jess. 'Becky . . . you realize we're on a mountain.'

'Yes!' I say eagerly. 'That's the whole point! It's extra-tough lacquer that lasts whatever you do. Look at this!' I show her the bottle of nail polish. 'The model's actually *climbing a mountain* in the picture.'

'Unbelievable,' says Jess, taking the bottle from me and peering at it. 'And people fall for this?'

'Come on! What else are we going to do?' I pause innocently. 'I mean, it's not like we've got anything *fun* to do, like our accounts . . .'

Jess's eyes flash at me.

'OK,' she says. 'You win. Do my nails.'

While the storm rages around us, we paint each other's nails a bright sparkly pink.

'That's great!' I say in admiration as Jess finishes my left hand. 'You could be a manicurist!'

'Thanks,' she says dryly. 'You've made my day.'

I wave my fingers in the torchlight, then get out my compact to admire my reflection.

'You need to learn to put one finger thoughtfully to your mouth,' I explain, demonstrating. 'It's the same when you get a new ring or bracelet. Just to let people see.' I offer her the mirror, but she turns away, her face closing up.

'No thanks.'

I put away the compact, thinking hard. I want to ask her why she hates mirrors. But I have to put it tactfully.

'Jess . . .' I say at last.

'Yes?'

'Why do you hate mirrors?'

There's silence, except for the whistling of the wind. At last Jess looks up.

'I dunno,' she says. 'I suppose because every time I looked into a mirror when I was young, my dad told me not to be vain.'

337

'*Vain?*' I look at her, wide-eyed. 'What, every time?'

'Most of the time.' She shrugs, then sees my face. 'Why? What did yours say?'

'My parents used to say . . .' Now I'm a bit embarrassed. 'They used to say I was the most beautiful little angel who had ever fallen down from heaven.'

'Well.' Jess hunches her shoulders as though to say 'go figure'.

I stare at my nails for a few moments.

'God, you're right,' I say suddenly. 'I've been spoilt. My parents have always given me everything. I've never had to stand on my own two feet. Ever. I've always had people there for me. Mum and Dad . . . then Suze . . . then Luke.'

'I had to stand on my feet right from the word go,' says Jess. Her face is in the torchlight shadow, and I can't make out her expression.

'He sounds quite . . . tough, your dad,' I say tentatively.

Jess doesn't answer for a few moments.

'Dad never really expressed emotion,' she says at last. 'Never really told you when he was proud. He felt it,' she adds vehemently. 'But in our family we don't go blabbing about everything the way you do.'

A sudden gust of wind loosens up a corner of the tent, blowing in a flurry of rain. Jess grabs the flap, and reaches for a metal pin.

'I'm the same,' she says, banging the metal pin back into the ground with a rock. 'Just because I don't say things doesn't mean I don't feel them.' She looks round and meets my eyes with a visible effort. 'Becky, when I came to visit your flat, I didn't mean to be unfriendly. Or . . . cold.'

'I should never have called you that,' I say in a flood of remorse. 'I'm really sorry—'

'No,' Jess interrupts. '*I'm* sorry. I could have made more effort. I could have joined in.' She puts the rock down on the ground and gazes at it for a few seconds. 'To be honest, I was a bit . . . unnerved by you.'

'Luke said you might find me overwhelming,' I say ruefully.

'I thought you were mad,' says Jess, and I give a little smile.

'No,' she says. 'Seriously. I thought you were mad. I thought your parents had sprung you from some kind of secure facility.'

'Oh,' I say, a bit discomfited. I rub my head, which has started to throb again.

'You should sleep,' says Jess, watching me. 'It's the best healer. And the best painkiller. Here's a blanket.' She gives me a sheet of something that looks like tin foil.

'Well . . . OK,' I say doubtfully. 'I'll try.'

I put my head down in the least uncomfortable place I can find, and close my eyes.

But I can't sleep. Our conversation is going round and round in my mind, with the lashing rain and flapping of the tent as a soundtrack.

I'm spoilt.

I'm a spoilt brat.

No wonder Luke got pissed off. No wonder our marriage is a catastrophe. It's all my fault.

Oh God. Suddenly tears are rising in my eyes, making my head throb even more. And my neck's all cricked . . . and there's a stone in my back . . .

'Becky, are you OK?' says Jess.

'Not really,' I admit, my voice all thick and wobbly. 'I can't get to sleep.'

There's silence, and I think Jess can't have heard, or doesn't have anything to say. But a moment later I feel something next to me. I turn round — and she's offering me a small white slab.

'It's not peppermint creams,' she says flatly.

'What is it?' I falter.

'Kendal Mint Cake. Traditional climbing food.'

'Thank you,' I whisper, and take a bite. It has a weird sweet taste, and I'm not that keen, but I take a second bite, to show willing. Then, to my horror, I feel tears starting up again.

Jess sighs, and takes a bite of Kendal Mint Cake.

'What's wrong?'

'Luke will never love me again.' I give a tiny sob.

'I doubt that,' she says.

'It's true!' My nose is running and I wipe it with my hand. 'Ever since we got back from our trip, it's been a disaster. And it's all my fault, I've ruined every-thing . . .'

'It's not all your fault,' interrupts Jess.

'What?' I gape at her.

'I wouldn't say it was all your fault,' she says calmly. 'It takes two.' She folds up the Kendal Mint Cake wrapper, unzips her backpack and slips it in. 'I mean, talk about obsessed. Luke's totally obsessed by work!'

'I know he is. But I thought he'd changed. On honeymoon he was totally laid-back. Everything was perfect. I was so happy.'

With a stab of pain I have a sudden memory of Luke and me, all brown and carefree. Holding hands. Doing yoga together. Sitting on the terrace in Sri Lanka, planning our surprise return.

I had such high hopes. And nothing worked out the way I thought it would.

'You can't be on honeymoon for ever,' points out Jess. 'It was bound to be a bit of a crash.'

'But I was so looking forward to being married,' I gulp. 'I had this image. We were all going to be sitting round the big wooden table in candlelight. Me, Luke, Suze . . . Tarquin . . . everyone happy and laughing . . .'

'And what happened?' Jess gives me a shrewd look. 'What happened to Suze? Your mum told me she was your best friend.'

340

'She was. But while I was away she . . . found some-one else.' I stare at the blue, flapping canvas, feeling a lump in my throat. 'Everyone's got new friends and new jobs and they're not interested any more. I . . . haven't got any friends.'

Jess zips up her backpack and pulls the drawstring tight. Then she looks up.

'You've got me.'

'You don't even like me,' I say dolefully.

'Well, I'm your sister,' says Jess. 'I've got to put up with you, haven't I?'

I raise my head, and there's a glimmer of humour in her eyes. And warmth. A warmth I don't think I've ever seen before.

'You know, Luke wants me to be just like you,' I say after a pause.

'Yep. Right.'

'It's true! He wants me to be thrifty and frugal.' I put the rest of my Kendal Mint Cake down behind a rock, hoping Jess won't notice. 'Will you teach me?'

'Teach *you*. To be frugal.'

'Yes! Please.'

Jess rolls her eyes.

'If you're going to be frugal, for a start you won't throw away a perfectly good piece of Kendal Mint Cake.'

'Oh. Right.' A bit shamefaced, I pick it up and take a bite. 'Er . . . yummy!'

The wind is whistling even more loudly, and the tent is flapping faster and faster. I pull Jess's tin-foil blanket around me tighter, wishing for the millionth time I'd brought a cardigan. Or even a cagoule. Then all of a sudden I remember something. I reach into the pocket of my skirt – and I don't believe it. The little lump is still there.

'Jess . . . this is for you,' I say, pulling it out. 'I came to your house to give it to you.'

341

I hand Jess the little turquoise bag. Slowly she unties it and tips the silver Tiffany bean out on to her hand.

'It's a necklace,' I explain. 'I've got the same one, look.'

'Becky.' Jess looks taken aback. 'It's . . . it's really . . .'

For an awful moment I think she's going to say 'unsuitable' or 'inappropriate'.

'Fab,' she says at last. 'It's fab. I love it. Thank you.'

She fastens the chain around her neck and I survey her in delight. It really suits her! What's a bit weird, though, is that something about her face seems different. It's kind of changed shape. Almost as if . . .

'Oh my God!' I exclaim in astonishment. 'You're *smiling*!'

'No I'm not,' says Jess at once, and I can see her trying to stop – but she can't. Her smile broadens, and she lifts a hand to finger the bean.

'Yes you are!' I can't help giggling. 'You so are! I've found your weak point. You are a Tiffany girl at heart.'

'No I'm not!'

'You are! I knew it! You know, Jess—'

But whatever I was about to say is drowned in howling wind, as with no warning, the gale whips up one side of the tent.

'Oh my God!' I shriek, as drenching rain lands in my face. 'Oh my God! The tent! Get it!'

'Shit!' Jess is hauling the flapping canvas down again, and desperately trying to anchor it, but with another huge gust it blows right out of her grasp. It billows like a sailing ship, then disappears down the mountainside.

I stare at Jess through the rain.

'What are we going to do now?' I have to shout just to be heard above the noise.

'Jesus Christ.' She rubs rain off her face. 'OK. We have to find shelter. Can you get up?'

She helps me to my feet, and I can't help crying out. My ankle is total agony.

'We'll have to make for those rocks,' says Jess, gesturing through the rain. 'Lean on me.'

The pair of us start half-limping, half-shuffling up the muddy slope, gradually getting an odd kind of rhythm. I'm gritting my teeth against the pain, willing myself not to make a fuss.

'Will anyone come to rescue us?' I manage between steps.

'Unlikely. We haven't been out long enough.' Jess pauses. 'OK. You need to get up this steep bit. Hold on to me.'

Somehow I make it up the rocky incline, aware of Jess's strong grip holding me up. God, she's in good condition. She could easily have climbed down out of the rain, it occurs to me. She could be safe and warm at home now.

'Thanks for helping me,' I say gruffly, as we start on our shuffle again. 'Thanks for staying with me.'

''s OK,' she says without missing a beat.

The rain is billowing into my face, almost choking me. My head is starting to whirl again, and my ankle is excruciating. But I have to keep going. I can't let Jess down.

Suddenly I hear a noise through the rain. But I must be imagining it. Or it was the wind. It couldn't be real.

'Hang on.' Jess stiffens. 'What's that?'

We both listen. And it is. It's real.

The real chopper-chopper sound of a helicopter.

I look up – and lights are dimly approaching through the sleeting rain.

'Help!' I scream, and wave my arms frantically. 'Here!'

'Here!' Jess yells, and thrusts her torch beam up, moving it about in the gloom. 'We're here! Help!'

The helicopter hovers above us for a few moments. Then to my dismay it moves on.

'Didn't they see us?' I gasp.

'I don't know.' Jess looks taut and anxious. 'Hard to tell. They wouldn't land here anyway. They'd land on the ridge at the top and come down by foot.'

We both stand motionless for a moment – but the helicopter doesn't return.

'OK,' says Jess at last. 'Let's keep going. At least the rocks will shelter us from the wind.'

We start moving again as before. But this time all my drive seems to have gone. I just feel exhausted. I'm drenched, and cold, and I have absolutely no reserves of energy left. We're inching up the slope with a painful slowness, heads together, arms locked around each other, both panting and gasping as rain hits us in the face.

'Wait.' I stop still. 'I can hear something.' I clutch on to Jess, craning my neck.

'What?'

'I heard something—'

I break off as a dim light flashes through the rain. It's a distant torch beam. And I can hear the sound of movement down the mountain.

Oh my God. It's people. At last.

'It's the mountain rescue!' I yell. 'They've come! Here! We need help!'

'Here!' calls Jess, and flashes her torch light in the air. 'We're here!'

The torch beam disappears briefly, then reappears.

'Help!' shouts Jess. 'We're here!'

There's no reply. Where have they gone? Have they missed us?

'Heeelp!' I scream desperately. 'Please help! Over here! Can you hear us?'

'Bex?'

A familiar high-pitched voice comes thinly over the sound of the storm. I freeze.

What?

Am I . . . hallucinating?

344

That sounded just like—

'Bex?' shouts the voice again. 'Bex, where are you?'

'*Suze?*'

As I stare upwards, a figure appears at the edge of the ridge, wearing an ancient Barbour. Her hair is plastered down on her head with the rain, and she's flashing a torch about, shielding her eyes and looking around, her brow creased in anxiety.

'Bex?' she screams. 'Bex! *Where are you?*'

I have to be hallucinating. It's like a mirage. I'm looking at a tree waving in the wind, and thinking it's Suze.

'Bex?' Her eyes have lighted on us. 'Oh my God! Bex! I've found her!' she shouts over her shoulder. 'Over here! Bex!' She starts scrambling down the ridge towards us, sending rocks flying.

'Do you know her?' says Jess, looking bewildered.

'It's Suze.' I swallow. 'It's my best friend.'

Something hard is blocking my throat. Suze came to find me. She came all this way to find me.

'Bex! Thank God!' Suze arrives in a final flurry of stones and earth, and stares at me, her face all mud-stained, her blue eyes huge with shock. 'Oh my God. You're hurt. I knew it. I knew it—'

'I'm OK,' I manage. 'Except my ankle.'

'She's here, but she's injured!' she says into her mobile, and listens for a moment. 'Tarkie's coming down with a stretcher.'

'*Tarquin?*' My head is too dazed to take this all in. 'Tarquin's here?'

'With his friend from the RAF. The stupid mountain-rescue team said it was too early. But I knew you were in trouble. I knew we had to come. I was so worried.' Suze's face suddenly crumples. 'Oh God. I was so *worried*. No one knew where you were . . . you just disappeared. We all thought. . . we didn't know what to think . . . we were trying to track your mobile signal, but there wasn't one . . . then suddenly it appeared . . . And now here you are, all . . . all beaten up.' She looks on the verge of tears. 'Bex, I'm so sorry I never called back. I'm so sorry.'

She flings her arms tightly round me. And for a few moments we just stand there, clinging on to each other, the rain lashing down on us.

'I'm fine,' I gulp at last. 'Really. I fell down the mountain. But I was with my sister. She took care of me.'

'Your sister.' Suze loosens her grip and slowly turns to Jess, who's standing, watching awkwardly, her hands stuffed in her pockets.

'This is Jess,' I say. 'Jess . . . this is Suze.'

The two look at each other through the driving rain. I can't tell what each of them is thinking.

'Hi, Becky's sister,' says Suze at last, and holds out her hand.

'Hi, Becky's best friend,' replies Jess, and takes it.

There's a crashing sound and we all look up to see Tarquin making his way towards us down the slope, in some amazingly cool-looking army gear, plus a hat with a headlamp on it.

'Tarquin,' I say. 'Hi.'

'Jeremy's coming down with the fold-up stretcher,' he says cheerfully. 'Nasty fright you gave us all, Becky. Luke?' he says into his mobile phone. 'We've found her.'

My heart stops.

Luke?

'How come . . .' My lips are suddenly trembling so much I can hardly form the words. 'How come Luke . . .'

'He's stuck in Cyprus because of bad weather,' says Suze, 'but he's been on the other end of the line the whole time. God, he's been in a state.'

'Here you are, Becky,' says Tarquin, holding out the phone to me.

346

I almost can't take it. I'm thudding all over with nerves.

'Is he still . . . angry with me?' I falter.

Suze just looks at me silently for a moment, the rain pounding down on her hair and running down her face.

'Bex, take it from me. He's not angry with you.'

I lift the phone up to my ear, wincing slightly as it presses on my bruised face.

'Luke?'

'Oh my God! Becky. Thank Christ.'

He's all distant and crackly and I can hardly make him out. But as soon as I hear his familiar voice, it's like the whole of the last few days comes to a head. Something is welling up inside me. My eyes are hot and my breath feels choked.

I want him. I want him and I want to go home.

'Thank God you're safe.' Luke sounds more overwrought than I've ever heard him. 'I was out of my mind . . .'

'I know,' I gulp. 'I'm sorry.' Tears are spilling over on to my cheeks. I can barely speak. 'Luke, I'm really sorry for everything . . .'

'Don't be sorry. *I'm* sorry. Jesus. I thought . . .' He stops, and I can hear him breathing hard. 'Just don't ever go missing again, OK?'

'I won't.' I wipe my eyes furiously with my hand. 'God, I wish you were here.'

'I'll be there. I'll be out as soon as the storm passes. Nathan's offered me his private jet. He's been absolutely great.' To my dismay, his voice is descending into a hissing crackle.

'Luke?'

'. . . hotel . . .'

He's breaking up. Nothing is making any sense.

'I love you,' I call hopelessly as the phone goes dead. I look up to see all the others watching in compassionate

347

silence. Tarquin pats my shoulder kindly with a dripping hand.

'Come on, Becky. We'd better get you into the helicopter.'

TWENTY-THREE

The hospital is all a bit of a blur. There's lots of light and noise and being asked questions and being wheeled around on a trolley – and eventually it turns out I've broken my ankle in two places and they've got to set my leg. Plus give me stitches and check I haven't got tetanus or mad-cow disease or anything.

While they're doing all that, they give me an injection of some stuff that makes me feel a bit dopey, and when everything's done I flop back on my pillows, suddenly exhausted. God, it's nice to be somewhere clean and warm and white.

In the distance I can hear someone reassuring Jess that she didn't do any damage by moving me, and then telling Suze several times that a full body scan won't be needed in this case, and no, they're not being cavalier with my health. And as it happens, he *is* the top man in the country.

'Becky?' I look up in a daze to see Tarquin advancing towards my bed, holding out a mobile phone. 'Luke again.'

'Luke?' I say into the receiver. 'Hi! Guess what? I've got a broken leg!' I look admiringly at my plaster cast, which is propped up on a support. I have *always* wanted a plaster cast.

'I heard. My poor darling. Are they looking after

you OK? Do you have everything you need?'

'Er . . . I think so. You know . . .' With no warning I give a huge yawn. 'Actually I'm pretty tired. I might go to sleep.'

'I wish I was there.' Luke's voice is low and gentle. 'Becky, just tell me one thing. Why did you go running off to the North without telling anyone?'

What? Doesn't he *realize*?

'Because I needed help, of course,' I say with a familiar wash of pain. 'Our marriage was in tatters. Jess was the only person I could turn to.'

There's silence down the phone.

'Our marriage was in what?' says Luke at last.

'Tatters!' My voice wobbles. 'You know it was! It was awful! You didn't even kiss me goodbye!'

'Darling, I was pissed off. We had a row! That doesn't mean our marriage is in tatters.'

'Oh.' I swallow. 'Well, I thought it was. I thought it was all over. I thought you wouldn't care where I was.'

'Oh Becky.' Luke's voice has gone all strange, like he's trying not to laugh. Or possibly cry. 'Do you have any idea what I've been going through?'

'No.' I bite my lip, hot with shame. 'Luke, I'm really sorry. I . . . I didn't think . . . I never realized . . .'

'Anyway.' He cuts me off. 'You're safe. That's all that matters now. You're safe.'

I'm feeling prickles of guilt all over. He's being so nice about it. But what kind of hell have I put him through? And there he is, stuck on Cyprus . . . In a rush of emotion I clutch the phone more tightly to my ear.

'Luke, come home. I know you're hating it out there. I know you're miserable. And it's all my fault. Just leave stupid Nathan Temple and his horrible hotel. Find some excuse. You can blame me.'

There's a long silence.

'Luke?' I say, puzzled.

'Yee-s,' says Luke reluctantly. 'There's something I need to say about that. I think that quite possibly . . .' He breaks off again.

'What?'

'You were right. And I was . . . wrong.'

I peer at the phone in confusion. Did I hear that properly?

'I was prejudiced,' Luke is saying. 'Now I've got to know Nathan, he's a very bright guy. Great commercial mind. We're getting on well.'

'You're getting on *well*? But . . . what about him being a convicted criminal?'

'Ah,' says Luke, sounding sheepish. 'Nathan explained about that. He was defending one of his motel staff from a drunk guest when it happened. He "went a little far", as he put it. He says it was a mistake. And I believe him.'

There's a pause. My head is throbbing. I can't quite take all this in.

'In a lot of ways he's a guy after my own heart,' Luke's saying. 'He told me the other night why he set up his motel chain. It was after he was refused entry to a smart hotel because he wasn't wearing a tie. He went straight to a pub and sketched out a business plan for Value Motels. Had twenty up and running in a year. You have to admire that drive.'

'I don't believe it,' I say, rubbing my forehead in a daze. 'You *like* him.'

'I do like him.' Luke pauses. 'And he's been tremendous over this whole affair. Couldn't have been kinder. He stayed up all night with me, listening for news.'

I wince in guilt as I imagine the two of them, taut-faced in dressing gowns, waiting by the phone. God, I am never, ever going to disappear again.

I mean, not that I was planning to. But you know.

'What about the hotel?' I say. 'Is it tacky?'

351

'The hotel is supremely tacky,' says Luke, sounding cheerful. 'But you were right. It's top-quality tack.'

I can't help giving a little giggle, which turns into an enormous yawn. God, I can feel the drugs kicking in now.

'So . . . I was right all along,' I say, my voice a little bleary. 'It was a brilliant networking coup.'

'It was a brilliant networking coup,' agrees Luke. 'Becky, I'm sorry.' He suddenly sounds more serious. 'For that and — a lot of things.' He hesitates. 'I realize you've had it hard these last few weeks. I got too obsessed by the Arcodas deal. I haven't supported you. And I didn't appreciate what a crash it was for you, coming back to Britain.'

As his words filter into my brain, they sound weirdly familiar.

Has he been talking to Jess?

Has Jess been . . . *sticking up* for me?

Suddenly I realize Luke is still talking.

'And another thing,' he's saying. 'I finally read through your pink folder on the plane. And I liked your idea. We should approach David Neville and see if he wants to sell.'

'You liked my idea?' I say in amazed delight. 'Really?'

'I loved it. Although I have no idea where you've picked up all this specialist knowledge on business expansion—'

'At Barneys! I told you!' I sink contentedly into my pillows. 'David'll want to sell, I know he will. He's really regretting having gone on his own. And they want another baby . . .' I'm stumbling over the words with sleepiness. 'And Judy says she just wants him to have a normal sara . . . salary . . .'

'Sweetheart, we'll talk about it another time. You should rest.'

'All right.' My eyelids are getting really heavy now and it's a struggle to keep them open.

'Let's start over,' says Luke softly. 'When I get back. No more tatters. OK?'

'What's that?' A horrified voice interrupts, and I see a nurse advancing towards me. 'Mobile phones are *not* allowed on the wards. And you need some sleep, young lady!'

'OK,' I say quickly down the line. 'OK.'

The nurse removes the phone from my fingers and my eyes crash shut.

When I open them again, everything is different. The room is dim. The chatter has gone. It must be night-time.

I'm absolutely parched, and my lips are painfully dry. I remember there was a jug of water on my night-stand, and I'm trying to sit up and get it when I knock something on to the floor with a clatter.

'Bex? Are you OK?' I look over to see Suze in a chair by my bed. She rubs the sleep out of her eyes and leaps up. 'D'you want something?'

'Some water,' I croak. 'If there is any.'

'Here you are.' Suze pours me out a glassful and I drink it thirstily. 'How are you feeling?'

'I'm . . . fine.' I put the glass down, feeling a lot better, then look around the dim curtained cubicle. 'Where is everyone? Where's Jess?'

'She's OK. The doctors looked her over and then Tarkie took her home. But they wanted to keep you in for observation.'

'Right.' I rub my dry face, wishing I had some moisturizer with me. Then suddenly I notice the time on Suze's wrist-watch.

'It's two o'clock!' I look up in horror. 'Suze, why are you here? You should be in bed!'

'I didn't want to go.' She bites her lip. 'I didn't want to leave you.'

353

'Sssh!' hisses a voice from the other side of my curtain. 'Keep the noise down!'

Suze and I look at each other in surprise — and suddenly I can feel giggles rising. Suze sticks out her tongue at the curtain, and I give a helpless snuffle.

'Have some more water,' says Suze in a lower voice. 'It'll keep your skin hydrated.' She pours another glassful and perches on the side of my bed. For a while neither of us speaks. I take a few more sips of water, which is lukewarm and tastes of plastic.

'This reminds me of when Ernie was born,' says Suze, watching me through the still dimness. 'Do you remember? You stayed with me all night then.'

'God yes.' I have a sudden memory of a teeny, tiny Ernie in Suze's arms, all pink and wrapped in a blanket. 'That was some night.' I meet her eyes and give a little smile.

'You know, when the twins were born . . . it didn't feel quite right, you not being there.' Suze gives a tremulous laugh. 'I know that sounds really stupid.'

'No. It's not.' I look down at my white hospital sheet, pleating it hard between my fingers. 'I've really missed you, Suze.'

'I've missed you too.' Her voice is a little husky. 'And I . . . I need to say something. I'm sorry for the way I behaved when you got back.'

'No,' I say at once. 'Don't be silly. I overreacted. You had to make other friends while I was gone. Of course you did. I was . . . stupid.'

'You weren't stupid.' She swallows hard. 'It was me. I was envious.'

'*Envious?*' I look up in shock. Suze isn't meeting my eye.

'There you were, all tanned and glamorous, with your Angel bag.' Her voice trembles a little. 'And there I was, stuck in the country with three kids. You came swanning in with all these stories about your amazing round-the-world honeymoon, and I felt really . . . drab.'

I stare at her in dismay.

'Suze, you could never be drab! Never in a million years!'

'So I was thinking –' She looks at me, her face determined. 'When you're better, let's go to Milan for the weekend. Just you and me. What do you think?'

'What about the babies?'

'They'll be fine. Tarkie'll look after them. It can be my late birthday treat.'

'What about the spa?' I say cautiously. 'Wasn't that your treat?'

For a moment Suze is silent.

'The spa was OK,' she says at last. 'But it wasn't the same as with you. No one's like you, Bex.'

'So do you hate Lulu now?' I can't help saying hopefully.

'Bex!' Suze gives a shocked giggle. 'No, I don't *hate* her. But . . .' She meets my eyes. 'I prefer you.'

I can't quite find a reply, so I reach for my water glass again – and find myself looking at a small packet on the night-stand.

'Jess left you that,' says Suze, looking a bit puzzled. 'She said we might want to eat it.'

I can't help smiling. It's Kendal Mint Cake.

'It's kind of . . . a private joke,' I say. 'I don't think she's expecting me to eat it.'

There's silence for a while, apart from the noise of a trolley being wheeled along in the distance, and the thwump of double doors opening and closing.

'So . . . you really have got a sister,' says Suze at last, and I can hear the thread of wistfulness in her voice. For a few moments I look through the dimness at her familiar, high-browed, anxious, lovely face.

'Suze . . . you'll always be my sister,' I say at last. And I hug her tight.

TWENTY-FOUR

OK. It is just amazing. In fact, it's incredible. The number of things I was convinced I didn't like . . . and now it turns out I love them!

For example:

1. Jess.
2. Black pudding. (If you put lots of tomato ketchup on it, it's actually quite yummy!)
3. Being a skinflint.

Honestly. I'm not joking. Being frugal is totally fantastic. It's so *satisfying*! How come I never realized this before?

Like, yesterday I sent Janice and Martin a postcard to thank them for their lovely flowers . . . and instead of buying one, I cut it out of a cereal box! It had 'Kelloggs' on the front! How cool is that?

Jess gave me that tip. She is teaching me so much. I've been staying with her ever since I got out of hospital — and she's been just brilliant. She gave me her bedroom because there are fewer stairs up to it than the guest room, and she helps me get in and out of the bath with my plaster cast, and she makes vegetable soup every day for lunch. She's even going to teach me how to make it too. Because if you do it with lentils and . . . and something else which I can't remember, it's a fully balanced meal in itself and it only costs 30p a portion.

And then, with the extra money you save, you can buy something really nice like one of Elizabeth's home-made fruit pies! (That was the tip I gave to Jess. You see, we're helping each other!)

I hobble over to the sink, carefully empty half the coffee grounds out of the cafetière into the bin, sprinkle on some new ones, and switch on the kettle. The rule in this house is that you re-use coffee grounds, and like Jess says, it does make total sense. The coffee only tastes a little bit crappy – and you save so much!

I have so changed. Finally, I am a frugal and sensible person. Luke will not believe it when he sees me again.

Jess is chopping an onion, and I helpfully pick up the mesh onion bag to throw away.

'Don't!' Jess looks up. 'We can use that!'

'An onion bag?' Wow. I'm learning new things all the time! 'So . . . how can you use an onion bag?'

'You can turn it into a scourer.'

'Right.' I nod intelligently, even though I'm not *entirely* sure what a scourer is.

'You know,' Jess gives me a look. 'Scouring. Like exfoliating, but for kitchens.'

'Oh *yes*!' I say, and beam at her. 'Cool!'

I get out my Thrifty Household Tips notebook and write it down. There's just so much to take in. Like, did you know you can make a garden sprinkler out of an old milk carton?

Not that I need a garden sprinkler . . . but still!

I make my way into the sitting room, one hand resting on my crutch, the other holding the cafetière.

'Hi.' Suze looks up from where she's sitting on the floor. 'What do you think?' She lifts up the banner she's been painting. It reads 'LEAVE OUR LANDSCAPE ALONE' in vibrant red and blue with an amazing leafy, grassy border.

'Wow!' I gaze at it in admiration. 'Suze, that's fantastic! You're such an amazing artist.' I look at the pile of banners draped on the sofa, which Suze has been steadily painting over the last few days. 'God, the campaign's lucky to have you.'

It's been so fantastic having Suze here. Just like old times. She's been staying in Edie's bed and breakfast for the last few days, while Tarquin has taken charge of the babies at home. Which Suze felt really guilty about – until her mother told her to brace up, and that once she left Suze behind for a whole month while she explored the foothills of Nepal, and it didn't do *her* any harm.

And it's been so great. We've just spent loads of time together, chilling, and eating, and talking about everything under the sun. Sometimes just me and Suze – and sometimes with Jess too. Like last night, the three of us made margaritas and watched *Footloose*. Which . . . I *think* Jess enjoyed. Even though she didn't know every song by heart, like we did.

Then one night, when Suze went to visit some relation of hers who lives twenty miles away, Jess and I spent the evening together. She showed me her rocks and told me all about them – and in return, I told her about my shoes and drew pictures. I think we both learned a lot.

'The campaign's lucky to have *you*,' retorts Suze, lifting her eyebrows. 'Let's face it, Bex. If it weren't for you, this protest would be three people and a dog.'

'Well. You know.' I shrug, trying to look modest. But I am secretly pretty pleased with the way things are going. I've been in charge of the protest publicity ever since I got out of hospital, and we have got so much coverage! The rally is this afternoon, and at least four local radio stations ran news stories this morning. It's been in all the local papers, and a TV crew is even talking about coming out!

It's all due to a brilliant combination of factors. First of all, it turns out the head of news at Radio Cumbria is Guy Wroxley, who I used to know in London when I was a financial journalist. He gave me the phone numbers of everyone locally who might be interested, and ran a huge feature piece yesterday afternoon on *Cumbria Watch*.

But the best thing is our fabulous human-interest story! The first thing I did when I took control was call a meeting of the environmental group. Everyone had to tell me every little thing they knew about the site, even if it didn't seem important. And it turns out that twenty years ago, Jim proposed to Elizabeth in the very field which is going to be wrecked by the shopping centre!

So we set up a photoshoot in the field, with Jim kneeling down just like he did then (except apparently he didn't kneel — but I told him to keep quiet about that), looking all mournful. The *Scully and Coggenthwaite Herald* printed it on their front page yesterday under the headline 'MASSACRE OF OUR LOVING MEMORIES', and the protest hotline (Robin's mobile) has been ringing with support ever since!

'How long have we got?' says Suze, sitting back on her heels.

'Three hours. Here you are.' I hand her a cup of coffee.

'Oh right.' Suze gives a slight grimace. 'Is this your thrifty coffee?'

'Yes!' I stare at her defensively. 'What's wrong? It's delicious!'

There's a ring at the doorbell and I hear Jess striding down the passage to answer it.

'Maybe that's another bunch of flowers,' says Suze with a giggle. 'From your admirer.'

I have been bombarded with bouquets ever since the accident, about half of them from Nathan Temple, saying things like 'In hugest gratitude' and 'In appreciation of your supportive gesture.'

Well. So he should be grateful. There was Luke, all set to fly home – and it was *me* who said he should stay in Cyprus and finish the job and I'd be fine staying with Jess for a few days. So he did – and he's on his way home today. The plane should be landing any minute.

I just know things are going to work out well between me and Luke. We've had the ups and downs . . . we've had the tempests . . . but from now on it's going to be smooth, easy waters. For a start, I'm a different person now. I've become a grown-up, prudent character. And I'm going to have a grown-up relationship with Luke. I'm going to discuss everything with him. I'm going to tell him everything. No more stupid situations where we end up at logger-heads. We're a team!

'You know, I honestly think Luke won't know me,' I say, taking a pensive sip of coffee.

'Oh, I think he will,' says Suze, studying me. 'You don't look *that* bad. I mean, the stitches are pretty awful, but that huge bruise is looking a bit better . . .'

'I don't mean in appearance!' I say. 'I mean in personality. I've totally changed.'

'Have you?' says Suze, looking puzzled.

God, don't people notice *anything*?

'Yes! Look at me! Making thrifty coffee and organizing a protest march and eating soup and . . . everything!'

I haven't even told Luke about organizing the protest. He'll be so gobsmacked when he sees his wife has become an activist. He'll be so impressed!

'Becky?' Jess's voice interrupts us and we both look up to see her standing at the door, an odd expression on her face. 'I've got something for you. Some walkers have just come back from Scully Pike. And . . . they found this.'

360

I feel a jolt of disbelief as from behind her back she produces a calfskin, hand-painted bag adorned with diamanté.

My Angel bag.

I thought I'd never ever see that again.

'Oh my God,' I hear Suze breathe.

I'm gazing at the bag, speechless. It's a bit battered and there's a tiny scratch near the handle – but apart from that it looks just the way it did. The angel is the same. The sparkling 'Dante' is the same.

'It seems fine,' Jess is saying, turning it over in her hands. 'It must have got a bit wet and thrown about, but apart from that, no harm done. Here you are.' She holds it out.

But I don't move. I can't take it from her.

'Becky?' Jess looks perplexed. 'Here!' She thrusts it towards me and I flinch.

'I don't want it.' I look away. 'This bag nearly ruined my marriage. From the moment I bought it, everything started going wrong. I think it's cursed.'

'Cursed?' says Jess, exchanging looks with Suze.

'Bex, it's not cursed,' Suze says patiently. 'It's a totally fab bag! Everyone wants an Angel bag!'

'Not me. Not any more. It's only brought me trouble.' I look from face to face, feeling suddenly rather sage. 'You know, the last few days have really taught me a lot. I've got a lot of things in perspective. And if it's a choice between my marriage or a totally fab bag . . .' I spread my arms. 'I'll take the marriage.'

'Wow,' says Suze. 'You *have* changed. Sorry,' she adds sheepishly, as she sees my face.

Honestly, what is she like? I would *always* have taken the marriage.

I'm . . . pretty sure I would.

'So what will you do with it?' asks Jess. 'Sell it?'

'You could donate it to a museum!' says Suze in

excitement. 'It could be "From the collection of Rebecca Brandon."'

'I've got a better idea,' I say. 'It can be star prize in the raffle this afternoon.' I grin at them. 'And we'll rig it so Kelly wins.'

By one o'clock the house is full of people. Everyone has gathered here for a final pep talk, and the atmosphere is just amazing. Jess and I are handing out bowls of vegetable soup, and Suze is showing all her painted banners to Robin, and everywhere there's a buzz of conversation and laughter.

God, why have I never been on a protest before? It's just the best thing ever!

'Isn't it exciting!' says Kelly, coming up with a bowl of soup in her hand. She's wearing camouflage combats and a T-shirt with 'Hands Off Our Land' written on it in marker pen.

'It's great!' I beam at her. 'So . . . have you bought a raffle ticket for later?'

'Yes, of course! I've bought ten!'

'Have this one too,' I say casually, handing her number 501. 'I've got a good feeling about it.'

'Oh right!' She tucks the ticket into her combats pocket. 'Thanks, Becky!'

I smile innocently and sip my soup. 'How's the shop looking?'

'It's fantastic!' Her eyes shine. 'We've got helium balloons everywhere, and ribbons, and sparkling wine, and loads of free gifts all ready . . .'

'It's going to be a wonderful party. Don't you think, Jess?' I add, as she walks by with a saucepan of soup. 'The party in Jim's shop.'

'Oh,' she says. 'I suppose so.' She gives a grudging, almost disapproving shrug, and ladles more soup into Kelly's bowl.

Like she's really fooling me with that act.

I mean, come on. I'm her *sister.*

'So . . . it's amazing that we got a donation to fund the party,' I remark to Kelly. 'Don't you think?'

'It's incredible!' says Kelly. 'A thousand pounds out of nowhere! We couldn't believe it!'

'Amazing,' says Jess with a small frown.

'Funny that the donor wants to stay anonymous,' I add, taking a spoonful of soup. 'Robin said they were quite firm about it.'

'Yes.' The back of Jess's neck is reddening a little. 'I heard.'

'You'd think they'd want some credit,' says Kelly, wide-eyed. 'You know, for being so generous!'

'I agree. You'd think they would.' I pause, then add casually, 'What do you think, Jess?'

'I suppose,' she replies, roughly stacking bowls on a tray. 'I wouldn't know.'

'I guess not.' I hide a smile. 'Great soup.'

'Everyone!' Jim bangs on a table and the hubbub dies down. 'Just to remind you. Our Village Shop Party begins at five, right after the protest. Everyone's welcome to come along and spend as much as they can. Even you, Edie.'

He points a finger at Edie, and the room erupts in laughter.

'Anyone who spends more than twenty pounds gets a free gift,' adds Jim. 'And everyone gets a free drink.'

'Now you're talking!' shouts the white-haired man, and there's another huge laugh.

'Bex?' comes Suze's voice in my ear. 'Phone for you. It's Luke.'

I hurry into the kitchen, a huge beam still on my face, and seize the receiver.

'Luke! Hi! Where are you? At the airport?'

'Nope, I'm already in the car.'

'That's great!' I say, my voice tumbling out. 'How

soon can you be here? There's loads going on! I'll give you directions to exactly where we'll be—'

'Becky . . . I'm afraid there's a hitch.' His voice cuts me off. 'I don't know how to tell you this . . . but I can't make it to you until much later.'

'What?' I stare at the receiver in dismay. 'But . . . why? You've been away all week! I haven't seen you!'

'I know. I'm livid. But something's come up.' He exhales sharply. 'There's a PR crisis with the Arcodas Group. Normally I'd leave it to Gary and the team, but this is a new client. It's the first problem and I'm going to have to deal with it myself.'

'Right.' My whole body is drooping in disappointment. 'I understand.'

'But I've had an idea.' He hesitates. 'Becky, come and join me.'

'What?' I gape at the phone.

'Come now. I'll send a car. I've missed you so much.'

'Me too.' I feel a pang. 'I've so missed you.'

'But it's not just that. Becky, I've spoken to Gary . . . and we're both agreed. We'd love your input on this. We could do with some bright ideas. What do you think?'

'You want me to help?' I swallow. 'Really?'

'I would love you to help.' Luke's voice is warm. 'If you're willing.'

I stare at the phone, transfixed with longing. This is exactly what I always wanted. Husband and wife helping each other. Brainstorming ideas together. A real, proper partnership.

Oh God. I want to go.

But . . . I can't let Jess down. Not now.

'Luke, I can't come.' I bite my lip. 'I really want to work with you. I really want to be part of the team. But I've got something planned for today. I promised Jess. And . . . some others. I can't just abandon them. I'm sorry.'

'Fair enough,' says Luke, sounding rueful. 'My fault for not hiring you when I had the chance. Well, I'll see you this evening.' He sighs. 'I don't know what time I'll be finished, but I'll call when I have an idea.'

'You poor thing,' I say sympathetically. 'I hope it all goes well. I'll be there in spirit. Where will you be?'

'Well, that's about the one positive thing. I'll be up in the North. Fairly near where you are, in fact.'

'Oh right,' I say, with interest. 'So what's the crisis? Another fat-cat businessman cooking the books?'

'Worse,' says Luke grimly. 'Some environmental bloody protest group which has sprung up out of nowhere.'

'An environmental group?' I say in amazement. 'You're kidding! That is such a coincidence, because—'

Abruptly I stop. My face suddenly feels hot and prickly.

It couldn't be . . .

No. Don't be ridiculous. There must be millions of protests every day, all over the country . . .

'Whoever's taken control is clearly pretty media-savvy,' Luke's saying. 'There's a rally this afternoon, they've had press coverage, TV news are interested . . .' He gives a short laugh. 'Get this, Becky. They're protesting against a shopping centre.'

The room seems to swim. I swallow hard several times, trying to stay calm.

It can't be the same thing. It can't.

We're not protesting against the Arcodas Group. I know we're not. We're protesting against Maybell Shopping Centres.

'Sweetheart, I have to go.' Luke interrupts my thoughts. 'Gary's on the other line, waiting to brief me. But I'll see you later. Oh, and have fun, doing whatever you're doing with Jess.'

'I'll . . . try,' I manage.

* * *

As I walk back into the sitting room, my heart is beating rather fast. Everyone is sitting in an attentive semi-circle watching Robin, who's holding up a big diagram of two stick figures, labelled 'Resisting Police Arrest'.

'. . . the groin area is particularly useful in this respect,' he's saying as I walk in. 'Everything OK, Becky?'

'Absolutely!' I say, my voice two notches higher than usual. 'Just one quick question. We *are* protesting against Maybell Shopping Centres?'

'That's right.'

'So this is nothing to do with the Arcodas Group.'

'Well . . . yeah.' He looks at me in surprise. 'Maybell's owned by the Arcodas Group. You knew that, didn't you?'

I open my mouth – but I can't quite reply.

I'm feeling a bit faint.

I have just orchestrated a huge media campaign against Luke's newest, most important client. Me. His wife.

'Evil bastards.' Robin looks around the room. 'Guess what I heard today. They're getting in their PR company to "deal" with us. Some bigshot firm from London. They're flying the chief guy back from holiday especially, I heard.'

Oh God. I cannot cope.

What am I going to do? What?

I have to pull out. Yes. I have to tell everyone right now that I'm pulling out and disassociate myself from the whole thing.

'They think we're small fry.' Robin's eyes are shining intensely. 'They think we have no resources. But we have our passion. We have our beliefs. And most of all . . .' He turns to me. 'We have Becky!'

'What?' I jump in panic as everyone turns towards

me and starts clapping. 'No! Please. Really. I'm . . . nothing to do with it.'

'Don't be modest!' exclaims Robin. 'You've transformed the protest! If it weren't for you, none of this would be happening!'

'Don't say that!' I gasp in horror. 'I mean . . . I just want to take a back seat. In fact . . .' I swallow hard. 'In fact there's something I need to say . . .'

Come on. Just tell them.

I catch Jim's warm gaze and look away. God, this is hard.

'Wait,' comes a trembling voice behind me, and I look round in surprise to see Jess advancing towards me. 'Before you speak, I'd like to say something.'

As she comes and stands beside me, the room falls silent in expectation. Jess lifts her chin and faces the crowd squarely.

'A lot of you heard me the other night, telling Becky that we weren't sisters. A lot of you heard me . . . disown her. Well, it turns out we are sisters.' She pauses, and a faint colour rises in her cheeks. 'But even if we weren't . . . Even if we weren't –' She looks round the room, a little fiercely. 'I would be honoured to know Becky and to count her a friend.'

'Hear, hear!' cries Jim hoarsely.

'And going on this march today . . . with all of you . . . and my sister . . .' Jess puts an arm through mine. 'It's one of the proudest moments of my life.'

The room is utterly silent.

'I'm sorry, Becky.' Jess turns to me. 'What did you want to say?'

'I . . . um . . . well,' I say weakly. 'I was just going to say . . . Let's smash 'em.'

WEST CUMBRIA BANK
45 STERNDALE STREET
COGGENTHWAITE
CUMBRIA

Ms Jessica Bertram
12 Hill Rise
Scully
Cumbria

12 June 2003

Dear Ms Bertram

I was surprised to see today that a sum of one thousand pounds has been taken from your account.

This is most unusual activity for your account and for this reason I am contacting you to ensure that a mistake has not been made.

Yours sincerely

Howard Shawcross

Customer Account Manager

TWENTY-FIVE

'Leave our land alone!' yells Robin through his loud-speaker.

'Out! Out! Out!' we all yell back, and I beam at Jess in exhilaration. If ever I had any doubts about whether I was doing the right thing, they've totally vanished.

You just have to look around. You just have to see what would be ruined. We're standing on Piper's Hill – and it's the most stunningly beautiful place I've ever been. There's a wood at the top, and wild flowers nestling in the grass, and I've already seen about six butterflies. I don't care if the Arcodas Group are Luke's clients or not. *How* could they build a shopping centre on this? Especially a crappy one with no Space NK!

'Leave our land alone!'

'Out! Out! Out!' I yell at the top of my voice. Protesting is just the coolest thing I have done, ever! I'm at the top of the hill with Robin, Jim and Jess, and the sight before us is just amazing. About three hundred people have turned up! They're marching up the lane towards the proposed site, waving placards, blowing whistles and banging drums, with two local TV crews and a bunch of journalists in tow.

I keep glancing around – but there's no sign of any-one from the Arcodas Group. Or Luke. Which I'm a tad relieved about.

I mean, not that I'm ashamed of being here. Quite the opposite. I am someone who will stand up for her beliefs and fight for the oppressed, no matter what others think.

But having said that, if Luke does turn up, I'm thinking I might put on a balaclava and quickly hide behind someone. He'll never spot me in the crowd. It'll be fine.

'Leave our land alone!'

'Out! Out! Out!'

Jess is waving her 'WILDLIFE MURDERERS' placard energetically, and blowing on her whistle. Edie and Lorna are wearing fluorescent pink wigs and holding up a huge sign which says 'KILLING OUR LAND, KILLING OUR COMMUNITY'. Suze is in a white T-shirt and army combat trousers which she pinched from Tarquin, and holding up one of her own banners. The sun is shining, and everyone's in fantastic spirits.

'Leave our land alone!'

'Out! Out! Out!'

The crowd is thickening now, and at a little nod from me, Robin puts down his placard and climbs the stepladder we've rigged up. There's a microphone in front of it, and the view of blue sky and unspoilt countryside behind him is breathtaking. The photographer I hired for the occasion kneels down and starts taking photos, and is soon joined by the TV crews and local-newspaper photographers.

The crowd gradually quietens down, and everyone turns to face Robin expectantly.

'Friends, supporters, lovers of the countryside,' he begins, his voice echoing over the quiet crowd. 'I ask you all to take a moment and look around at what we have. We have beauty. We have wildlife. We have all we need.'

He pauses for effect, just like I coached him, and looks around. The wind is ruffling his hair, and his face is flushed with animation.

'Do we need a shopping centre?'

'No! No! No!' we all yell back at the top of our voices.

'Do we need pollution?'

'No! No! No!'

'Do we need any more pointless consumerist rubbish? Does anyone need any more . . .' He casts around derisively, '*cushions*?'

'No –' I begin with everyone else – then stop myself. I could actually do with some nice cushions for our bed. In fact, I saw some really nice cashmere ones in a magazine only yesterday.

But . . . that's OK. Everyone knows activists sometimes disagree on minor technical points. And I agree with everything else Robin is saying. Just not about the cushions.

'Do we want an eyesore on our land?' shouts Robin, spreading his arms.

'No! No! No!' I yell back happily, and beam at Jess. She blows her whistle, and I look at it a bit enviously. Next time I go on a protest I'm definitely taking a whistle.

'Now let's hear from another of our activists!' yells Robin. 'Becky! Get up here!'

My head jerks up.

What? This wasn't in the plan.

'The girl who's held this campaign together!' he says. 'The girl whose ideas and spirit have made this happen! Let's hear it for Becky!'

Everyone is turning to face me, with admiring, animated faces. Robin starts applauding, and everyone gradually joins in.

'Go on, Becky,' says Jess, over the noise. 'They really want you!'

I do a quick scan around. There's no sign of Luke.

Oh, I can't resist.

I hobble through the crowd to the stepladder and

carefully climb to the top, with Robin's help. Below me is a sea of excited faces, all looking up in the sunshine.

'Hello, Piper's Hill!' I yell into the microphone, and an almighty cheer comes back from the crowd, complete with hoots and whistles and frantically beating drums.

God, this is fantastic! It's like being a popstar!

'This is our country!' I shout, gesturing at the rippling green grass around us. 'This is our land! We won't give it up!'

Another delighted cheer erupts.

'And to anyone who WANTS us to give it up . . .' I shout, waving my arms around. 'To anyone who thinks they can come and TAKE IT AWAY FROM US . . . I say this! I say GO HOME!'

There's a third uproarious cheer, and I can't help beaming. God, I've really got them going. Maybe I should be a politician!

'I say GIVE UP NOW!' I yell. 'Because we're going to FIGHT! On the BEACHES! And on the—'

There's a slight kerfuffle going on in the crowd and I break off, trying to see what's happening.

'They're coming!' I can hear people shouting.

'Boo!'

The whole crowd is hissing and jeering, and turning to look at something which I can't quite make out.

'It's them!' cries Robin, from the grass below. 'Bastards! Let 'em have it!'

And suddenly I freeze. Five men in dark suits are making their way swiftly to the front of the crowd.

One of them is Luke.

OK, I think I need to get down off this ladder. At once.

Except it's not as easy as that, when one leg is in bloody plaster. I can barely move.

'Er . . . Robin, I'd like to get down now!' I call.

'You stay there!' shouts Robin. 'Carry on with your speech! It's great!'

I frantically grasp my crutch and am trying to manoeuvre myself off the top when Luke looks up and sees me.

I have never seen him so shellshocked. He stops dead and just stares at me. I can feel my face burning, and my legs suddenly feel rather shaky.

'Don't let them intimidate you, Becky!' hisses Robin urgently from below. 'Ignore them! Keep speaking! Go *on*!'

I'm stuck. There's nothing else I can do. I clear my throat, studiously avoiding Luke's gaze.

'Um . . . We're going to fight!' I call out, my voice a little jumpy. 'I say . . . er . . . GO HOME!'

By now the five men are standing in a row, arms folded, looking up at me. Three men I don't recognize, plus Gary and Luke.

The trick is not to look at them.

'Let us keep our land!' I shout, with more confidence. 'We don't want your CONCRETE JUNGLE!'

A huge cheer breaks out, and I can't help darting a triumphant glance at Luke. I can't quite make out his expression. His brow is furrowed and he looks furious.

But there's a twitch at his mouth, too. Almost like he wants to laugh.

He meets my eye and something ripples through me. I have this awful feeling I'm about to start giggling hysterically.

'Give up!' I yell. 'Because you WON'T WIN!'

'I'll go and speak to the ringleader,' Luke says gravely to one of the men I don't recognize. 'See what I can do.'

Calmly he walks across the grass to the stepladder and climbs up three steps until he's level with me. For a moment, we just look at each other without

373

speaking. My heart is thumping inside my chest like a piston engine.

'Hello,' says Luke at last.

'Oh! Er . . . hi!' I say as nonchalantly as I can manage. 'How are you?'

'Quite a party you have here.' Luke surveys the scene. 'Is this all your doing?'

'Er . . . I had some help.' I clear my throat. 'You know how it is . . .' I catch my breath as my gaze lands on Luke's immaculate shirt cuff. Nestling beneath it, only just visible, is a tatty plaited rope bracelet.

I look away quickly, trying to stay cool. We're on opposing sides here.

'You do realize you're protesting *against* a shopping centre, Becky?'

'With crap shops,' I retort, without missing a beat.

'Don't negotiate, Becky!' Robin yells from down below.

'Spit in his face!' chimes in Edie, shaking her fist.

'You realize the Arcodas Group is my biggest client,' says Luke. 'That has crossed your mind?'

'You wanted me to be more like Jess,' I reply, a little defiantly. 'That's what you said, isn't it? "Be like your sister." Well, here you are, then.' I lean forward to the microphone and shout into it, 'Go back to London with your fancy ways! Leave us in peace!'

The crowd erupts in an approving cheer.

'Go back to London with my fancy ways?' echoes Luke in disbelief. 'What about *your* fancy ways?'

'I don't have any fancy ways,' I say haughtily. 'I've changed, if you want to know. I'm really frugal. And I care about the countryside. And evil developers coming and ruining beauty spots like this.'

Luke leans forward and whispers in my ear, 'Actually . . . they're not planning to build a shopping centre on this site.'

'What?' I look up with a frown. 'Yes they are.'

'No they're not. They changed their plans weeks ago. They're using another brownfield site.'

I stare at his face in suspicion. He doesn't look like he's lying.

'But . . . the plans,' I say. 'We've got plans!'

'Old.' He raises his eyebrows. 'Someone didn't do their research properly.' He glances down at Robin. 'Him, by any chance?'

Oh God. That actually has the ring of truth.

My mind is whirling. I can't quite take this in. They're not planning to build a shopping centre here, after all.

We're all here, shouting and yelling . . . for no reason.

'So,' Luke folds his arms, 'despite your extremely convincing publicity campaign, the Arcodas Group are not in fact villains. They have done nothing wrong.'

'Oh right.' I shift awkwardly and glance past Luke at the three scowling Arcodas Group men. 'So . . . I don't suppose they're very pleased, are they?'

'Not exactly delighted,' agrees Luke.

'Er . . . sorry about that.' I sweep my eyes over the restive crowd. 'So I suppose you want me to tell them. Is that it?'

Luke's eyes give the tiniest of flickers, the way they always do when he's got a plan.

'Well,' he says, 'as it happens, I have a better idea. Since you have helpfully gathered all this media together . . .'

He takes hold of the microphone, swivels to face the crowd and taps it for attention. There's an answering roar of boos and hisses. Even Suze is shaking her banner at him.

'Ladies and gentlemen,' Luke says in his deep, confident voice. 'Members of the press. I have an announcement to make on behalf of the Arcodas Group.'

He waits patiently until the jeers have died down, then looks around the crowd.

'We at the Arcodas Group are passionate about people. We are passionate about listening. We are the company that takes notice. I have spoken to your representative . . .' He indicates me. 'And I have taken in all her arguments.'

There's an expectant hush. Everyone is gazing up at him, agog.

'As a result of this . . . I can announce that the Arcodas Group has reconsidered the use of this site.' Luke smiles. 'There will be no shopping centre here.'

There's a moment of stunned silence – then over-joyed pandemonium breaks out. Everyone's cheering and hugging each other, whistles are blowing and drums are being beaten to death.

'We did it!' I hear Jess yelling above the clamour.

'We showed them!' shrieks Kelly.

'I would also like to draw your attention to the huge number of environmental initiatives which the Arcodas Group sponsors,' Luke says smoothly into the microphone. 'Leaflets are currently being handed out. And press packs. Enjoy.'

Hang on a minute. He's totally turning this into a positive PR event. He's hijacked it!

'You snake!' I say furiously, putting my hand over the microphone. 'You completely misled them!'

'The field is saved.' He shrugs. 'The rest is details, surely.'

'No! That's not the—'

'If your crew had done their research in the first place, we wouldn't be here and I wouldn't have to be saving the situation.' He leans down and calls to Gary, who's been handing out literature in the crowd. 'Gary, see the Arcodas folk into their car, will you? Tell them I'm staying on for some further negotiating work.'

Gary nods, and gives me a cheery wave, which I

choose to ignore. I'm still outraged with them both.

'So . . . where *is* the shopping centre being built?' I demand as I watch the rejoicing crowd. Kelly and Jess are hugging each other, Jim is clapping Robin on the back, and Edie and Lorna are waving their pink wigs in the air.

'Why?'

'Maybe I'll go and protest outside it. Maybe I should start following the Arcodas Group around and making trouble! Keep you on your toes.'

'Maybe you should,' says Luke with a wry smile. 'Becky, look, I'm sorry. But I have to do my job.'

'I know. I suppose. But . . . I thought I was making a difference. I really thought I'd achieved something.' I heave a morose sigh. 'And it was all for nothing.'

'For *nothing*?' says Luke, incredulous. 'Becky, just take a look at what you've done.' He gestures at the throng. 'Look at all these people. I've heard how you transformed the campaign. Not to mention the village . . . and this party you're throwing . . . You should be proud of yourself. Hurricane Becky, they're calling you.'

'What, I leave a trail of devastation everywhere.'

Luke looks at me, suddenly serious, his eyes warm and dark. 'You blow people away. Everyone you meet.' He picks up my hand and looks at it for a moment. 'Don't be like Jess. Be like you.'

'But you said . . .' I begin – then stop myself.

'What?'

Oh God. I was going to be all grown-up and dignified and not mention this. But I just can't help it.

'I overheard you talking to Jess,' I mumble. 'When she was staying with us. I heard you say . . . it was difficult to live with me.'

'It *is* difficult to live with you,' says Luke matter-of-factly.

I stare at him, my throat a little tight.

'It's also enriching. It's exciting. It's fun. It's the only thing I want to do. If it was easy, it would be boring.' He touches my cheek. 'Life with you is an adventure, Becky.'

'Becky!' calls Suze from below. 'The party's starting! Hi, Luke!'

'Come on,' says Luke, and kisses me. 'Let's get you off this ladder.' His strong fingers weave round mine and I squeeze them back.

'By the way, what did you mean just now when you said you were frugal?' he says as he helps me edge down the steps. 'Was it a joke?'

'No! I'm frugal! Jess taught me. Like Yoda.'

'What exactly did she teach you?' says Luke, looking a bit wary.

'How to make a water sprinkler out of a milk carton,' I say proudly. 'And gift wrap out of old plastic bags. Also, you should always write a birthday card in pencil so the person can rub out your message and use it again. It saves ninety pence!'

Luke looks at me for a long time without speaking.

'I think I need to get you back to London,' he says at last. He helps me carefully down the stepladder, holding my crutch under his arm. 'Danny called, by the way.'

'Danny called?' I say in overjoyed amazement, and miss the last step of the ladder. As I land on the grass, everything goes a little swirly.

'Ooh!' I clutch on to Luke. 'I'm all dizzy.'

'Are you OK?' says Luke in alarm. 'Is it the concussion? You shouldn't have been climbing ladders . . .'

'It's all right,' I say, a little breathless. 'I'll sit down.'

'God, I always used to get like that!' says Suze, passing by. 'When I was pregnant.'

Everything seems to empty from my mind.

I dart a startled glance at Luke. He looks equally jolted.

No. I mean . . . I couldn't . . .

I couldn't be —

All of a sudden my brain is doing frantic sums. I haven't even *thought* about . . . But the last time I . . . it must have been . . . It's been at least . . .

Oh my God.

Oh . . . my God.

'Becky?' says Luke in a strange voice.

'Um . . . Luke . . .'

I swallow hard, trying to keep cool.

OK. Don't panic. Do *not* panic . . .

WEST CUMBRIA BANK

45 STERNDALE STREET
COGGENTHWAITE
CUMBRIA

Ms Jessica Bertram
12 Hill Rise
Scully
Cumbria

22 June 2003

Dear Ms Bertram

I was shocked and grieved by the tone of your last letter.

I do 'have a life', as you put it.

Yours sincerely

Howard Shawcross

Customer Account Manager

Rebecca Brandon
37 Maida Vale Mansions
Maida Vale
London NW6 0YF

Manager
Harvey Nichols
109–125 Knightsbridge
London SW1X 7RJ

25 June 2003

Dear Sir

I am doing a piece of hypothetical research. I was wondering whether it is true that if you give birth in Harvey Nichols (accidentally, of course!) you are entitled to free clothes for life.

I would be grateful if you could let me know.

Obviously, as I have mentioned, this is a completely hypothetical enquiry.

Yours sincerely

Rebecca Brandon (née Bloomwood)

Rebecca Brandon
37 Maida Vale Mansions
Maida Vale
London NW6 0YF

Manager
Harrods Food Hall
Brompton Road
London SW1X 7XL

25 June 2003

Dear Sir

I am doing a piece of hypothetical research. I was wondering whether it is true that if you give birth in the Harrods Food Hall (accidentally, of course!) you are entitled to free food for life.

I was also wondering whether you would be entitled to anything else, such as clothes.

I would be grateful if you could let me know.

Yours sincerely

Rebecca Brandon (née Bloomwood)

Rebecca Brandon
37 Maida Vale Mansions
Maida Vale
London NW6 0YF

Signors Dolce e Gabbana
Via Spiga
Milano

25 June 2003

Chere Signores

Ciao!

Mi est British femma adoro votre fashion.

Est wondoro small questiono hypothetica: si je avais bambino in votre
shop (par mistako, naturallemento!!) est entitled a les clothes gratuite
por la viva? E por la bambino aussi?

Grazie mille beaucoup por le reply.

Con les best wishes

Rebecca Brandon (née Bloomwood)